S0-AWH-966

OUT OF TURN

Also by Tiffany Snow
No Turning Back, The Kathleen Turner Series
Turn to Me, The Kathleen Turner Series
Turning Point, The Kathleen Turner Series
Turn on a Dime - Blane's Turn
Blank Slate

OUT OF TURN

Book Four in The Kathleen Turner Series

Tiffany Snow

Montlake
Romance

The characters and events portrayed in this book are fictitious. Any similarity to real persons, living or dead, is coincidental and not intended by the author.

Text copyright © 2013 Tiffany Snow
All rights reserved.

Printed in the United States of America.

No part of this book may be reproduced, or stored in a retrieval system, or transmitted in any form or by any means, electronic, mechanical, photocopying, recording, or otherwise, without express written permission of the publisher.

Published by Montlake Romance, Seattle
All rights reserved.

www.apub.com

ISBN-13: 9781477805855
ISBN-10: 1477805850
Library of Congress Control Number: 2013911836

For Nicole.

Thank you for always asking for more. Well, demanding, actually, not asking.

(And for teaching me that sometimes, the only word that will do is the F-word.)

CHAPTER ONE

No one had shot at me in weeks, or beat me up. I hadn't been cut, punched, or slapped. No one threatened me, stalked me, or stabbed me.

It was a nice change.

And that's what I kept telling myself as I headed to my car. It was mid-afternoon, and the humid heat of late June in Indianapolis made perspiration slide down the middle of my back under the thin T-shirt I wore. The backpack I carried didn't help matters any.

The air inside my white Toyota Corolla was stifling and sliding into it felt as though I were climbing into an oven. I rolled down the windows as I drove to my apartment, waiting for the AC to kick in. The air gusting through the windows was hot but cooled my sweat-dampened skin.

I thought longingly of the huge Lexus SUV I'd had the brief privilege of driving. It had been a gift, a wonderful gift that I'd have been happy to keep, if it hadn't cost so much to drive it. Gas was too expensive for me to justify driving the luxury car—especially when I sometimes wondered how I was going to pay my rent—so I'd sold it, using the money to buy a used Toyota and what was left to help pay tuition.

I had just enough time to feed Tigger, my cat, and jump in the shower before I had to leave for work at The Drop, a bar downtown. It was Friday night and with the heat, I was sure we'd be busy.

In the summer, the owner of The Drop and my boss, Romeo, allowed the girls to wear black shorts and white T-shirts for our uniform. That would usually be a good thing, but Romeo believed sex always sells, so the shorts were nearly Daisy Dukes and the T-shirts tight, with plunging necklines. Not that I could be real choosy about it. I needed my bartending job at The Drop to pay the bills, especially since I was now taking classes during the day at the IU campus downtown rather than working for the law firm of Kirk and Trent.

"Hey, Kathleen! Can you give me a hand?"

That's me. Kathleen Turner, and sometimes I really wished I was *that* Kathleen Turner. I bet she never had to worry about paying her electric bill. Cursed with the family legacy, I had been the last to be named for a famous Turner. My dad was Ted Turner, my grandma Tina Turner, and my cousin was William Turner, though he went by his middle name, Chance. Wish I'd thought of doing that years ago.

"Yeah, sure," I replied to Tish, a waitress at The Drop who was juggling one too many plates of food. I shoved my purse under the bar and hurried to help her take the dishes to a table of five.

I was right. The bar was busy tonight and I didn't have time to even think. I was grateful for that. I didn't want to think. If I did, I'd remember.

"Another round, please."

I jerked my attention back to my job, hurrying to fill the order tossed my way. By the time closing neared, I was nearly dead on my feet. Thank God. Maybe I'd get more than three or four hours of sleep tonight.

"Have some cheese fries," Tish said, sliding onto a stool and placing a laden plate on the bar. "I'm exhausted," she sighed, picking up a dripping French fry and popping it into her mouth.

I grabbed us each a bottle of beer and leaned against the bar. The cold, bitter liquid felt good going down. My hair had come loose from its ponytail, so I redid it, pulling the long strawberry-blonde strands up and off my neck. I hated when my hair got in the way when I was working but liked it too much to have it cut short. Along with my blue eyes, I thought it was my best feature.

"Have some," Tish insisted, pushing the plate toward me.

I shook my head. "No thanks. I'm good," I said, and took another drink.

"Kathleen, you drink too much and eat too little," she said with a frown.

I snorted, my eyebrows climbing. "Yes, Mom," I teased.

Tish didn't smile back. "I'm your friend and I'm worried about you."

"I'm fine," I dismissed. To appease her, I picked up a fry and took a bite.

She hesitated. "You know, maybe you could talk to someone. I have this lady I see every once in a while—"

"No, thanks," I interrupted, taking another swig.

"But it may help . . ."

Tish stopped talking at the look I gave her, instead heaving a sigh as she ate another cheese fry.

I couldn't be mad at her, not really. She cared about me and was just trying to help. Once upon a time, I'd have probably said the same thing. Come to think of it, I actually had given the same advice in what felt like a lifetime ago. And the recipient had reacted the same way I had.

Why the fuck would I want to do that?

"It's just a breakup," I said to her, feeling bad now that she was worrying about me. "Everybody goes through them." I shrugged and finished off my beer, tossing the bottle into the trash with a loud *clunk*.

"It's just . . ." She paused and I raised my eyebrows.

"Just what?" I asked.

"You're . . . different now," she said, looking slightly abashed. "Harder, I guess. Colder. And I just really hate to see you that way."

Her words stung. I couldn't disagree with her, but it wasn't something I could fix right now. I needed an emotional distance from everyone, including myself.

"I'm sorry," I said quietly. "I don't mean to be. I just can't—"

"I know," she said, reaching out to rest a hand on my arm. "I know you need to be in this place for now—just don't let yourself stay there, okay? I miss the old Kathleen."

I gave Tish a weak smile, but I wondered whether the old Kathleen was gone for good.

"Rough night, eh, ladies?"

I turned to see that Scott, the other bartender for tonight, had grabbed his own beer and leaned against the bar behind me.

"Good tips, though," I said, stepping away from Tish.

Scott turned the volume up on the television, sipping his beer while he watched. A familiar name froze me in my tracks.

"Gubernatorial candidate Blane Kirk is back in Indy tonight attending a fund-raiser downtown after ten days on campaign stops throughout the state."

I felt as though someone had sucker punched me. My hands turned to ice. I couldn't take a deep breath. Even so, I couldn't stop myself from turning to look up at the television.

Blane.

I'd avoided all newspapers and the television for three months. This was the first time I'd seen his face since that awful day in March. The day he'd accused me of sleeping with his brother and had broken our engagement.

If I'd thought the passage of time would ease the blow of seeing his face again, I was very, very wrong.

I drank in the news footage, which showed Blane shaking hands with people in a crowd, the sunlight making his dark blond hair shine like gold. He had on a loosely knotted tie and a white shirt with the cuffs rolled back. His smile was gleaming white, dimpled, and perfect. A politician at his best. I noticed his smile still didn't reach his eyes, but then again, it rarely did.

The scene changed, showing Blane now in a tuxedo and entering the Crowne Plaza downtown. A woman was with him, his hand on her lower back. I watched, unable to tear my eyes away, as she turned and the camera caught her face.

Charlotte Page.

Dressed in a long gown of deep bronze, she exuded elegance and sensuality. Her hair was long and nearly black, her skin a warm olive. I'd once likened her to Penélope Cruz and could see the description was still apt. She was a fellow lawyer in Blane's firm, and together they made a stunning pair.

I couldn't breathe.

"I-I've . . . uh—I've got to go," I stammered, making a frantic grab for my purse under the bar.

"Yeah, sure. I'll close up," Tish hurriedly added. She frowned at Scott, but he didn't notice since he was still watching TV. I couldn't blame him. I'd told only Tish the sordid details of my breakup with Blane.

"Thanks." I managed a grateful smile before beating a hasty retreat outside. I heard Scott calling a belated goodbye to me as the door swung closed.

~

Once I reached my car, I leaned against it, my arms cushioning my head.

Just breathe.

I drove on autopilot, replaying the images of Blane in my head. It made my chest hurt and my stomach turn into knots. I regretted even the small bite of French fry I'd eaten as nausea clawed my throat.

I thought by now it would have been easier to see him with someone else.

It wasn't.

Tigger met me at the door. My two-story apartment building was in a section of Indy where police sirens were a nightly occurrence, but I hadn't had any problems as long as I'd lived there. At least, no problems that were because of the neighborhood.

I changed into shorts and a tank, opening the windows to give my AC, and my electric bill, a break. Light filtered in from the streetlamps, so I didn't bother turning on any lights in the apartment. After pouring myself a vodka tonic, I curled up on the couch, absently petting Tigger as I stared into space.

It was late, but I knew that if I went to bed I wouldn't sleep. And even if I did, nightmares plagued me more often than not. The ordeal I'd endured a few months ago at the hands of human traffickers had left mental scars, though physically I was fine. So I didn't sleep a whole lot.

My stomach churned and I resolutely took another drink. I did not want to puke, I hated throwing up, but I needed the numbness the vodka was so adept at providing. I needed not to feel anymore.

I thought about what Tish had said and wondered when, if ever, I'd feel like myself again. Normal. When I'd look forward to waking up every morning rather than dreading each new day as something to get through. When the ice inside me would melt.

I was angry with Blane, that much was true. He had believed his uncle's lies instead of me, his fiancée. He hadn't trusted me.

But I was devastated, too. Blane had devastated me, and part of me hated him for that, even as I ached to see him, talk to him. The newscast tonight had been bittersweet to watch.

I finished my drink in one long gulp, pushing Tigger aside as I got on the floor and started doing sit-ups. When the liquor didn't work to quiet my brain, I exercised, trying to get as exhausted as I possibly could. Sit-ups and push-ups when it was dark outside, running for miles when it wasn't.

I was in great shape. I wish I cared.

Running always made me think of Kade. Kade Dennon. Ex-FBI agent. Assassin-for-hire. Blane's half brother. I hadn't heard from him in months, not since the night he'd kissed me and told me I should be with him, not Blane.

I hadn't counted on how much I'd miss him no longer being in my life.

I glanced at my cell phone as I lay panting on the floor, my abdominal muscles screaming at me. I hadn't been able to make myself delete their numbers, so Blane and Kade were still listed in my contacts. I should get rid of them, and I would. Just not tonight.

A warm breeze flowed through the open window, bringing with it the familiar scent of a summer's night. At the moment, no sirens wailed and I could hear the occasional car pass by. I wondered what Blane was doing, and if it included Charlotte.

≈

Sunlight streaming through the window and a marmalade lump of feline woke me up Saturday morning. I'd fallen asleep on the floor and now my back ached. Tigger used my stomach as a pillow, his clawless paws kneading my flesh.

"Give it a rest," I grumbled at him as I sat up. He meowed a complaint about his loss of pillow and followed me into the kitchen, where I started the coffeemaker. I went for a run and showered before bolting down some caffeine. I had homework to do and had agreed to meet Clarice for lunch today.

A few hours later, I was winding my way behind a hostess as she led me through a local restaurant to the patio tables. I was glad about that. I'd be able to leave my sunglasses on. Lack of sleep left a toll that makeup couldn't always cover.

Clarice was waiting for me. She stood to give me a hug.

"So good to see you!" she said.

"You, too." My smile was genuine. I'd missed seeing and talking to her every day.

"You look great," she added as we sat down.

"Thanks, so do you." And she did look fantastic. Being in love agreed with her. She wore a long, flowing skirt with a sleeveless top and sandals. She'd been divorced for some years and had two kids. Right before Valentine's Day, the high-school science teacher she'd been dating had proposed.

"So how is Jack?" I asked, scooting my chair into the shade from the umbrella. I'd worn a spaghetti-strap sundress and didn't want my arms or shoulders to get burned.

"Jack's great—kids are good, too," she replied. "They're so excited for the wedding."

"Just them?" I teased.

She grinned. "Okay, me, too."

We laughed. "Two weeks," I said, "and you'll be Mrs. Jack Bryant."

"I know. I can't wait."

Clarice looked so happy, it practically radiated from her. It was wonderful to see and I was so glad she'd found someone who made her feel that way. She certainly deserved it.

The waitress came by and we paused to order. Clarice joined me, indulging in a glass of cold chardonnay.

"Your dress fitting is Thursday afternoon," she told me. "Can you make it?"

I was also one of her bridesmaids. "Sure," I said.

We chatted for a while about the wedding plans and where she and Jack were going on their honeymoon—Hawaii. It sounded wonderful. The waitress brought our salads, and it felt nice and normal to be having lunch with a girlfriend.

"So, how are you doing really?" Clarice asked after we'd exhausted the topic of her impending nuptials.

I stiffened. Clarice and I always refrained from talking about Blane or the breakup. I refused to let her. Since she was his secretary, I didn't want to put her in a bad position, and I didn't want to be tempted to quiz her about Blane. I'd told her he'd broken off the engagement and that was all.

My smile was forced. "I'm fine. Just takes some time, you know?"

"I know, but I worry about you," she said. "You've lost weight—it seems you hardly eat anymore. I mean don't get me wrong, you don't look bad, but I can tell you're unhappy. It's written all over you."

"Well, I can't say I recommend the breakup diet," I admitted. "But I'll be fine. I just . . . want to move on." I paused. "It certainly seems he has." I could hear the bitterness in my voice and knew I shouldn't have said that. I didn't want to know, didn't want to hear about Blane. But I also really did, and after seeing him on TV last night, I couldn't help hoping Clarice would tell me something, even though I knew it would hurt and I'd regret hearing it.

She hesitated, then carefully said, "I don't know about that."

My breath seemed to freeze in my lungs. "What do you mean?"

"He's not the same at all. I mean, yeah, he's dating other women, but it's like it was before. Blane's always been real professional at the office, but he was happy with you. I could see it. Now, I never see him crack a smile or a joke. He's just constantly on the move, pushing himself. He never slows down."

I swallowed and readjusted my sunglasses while I digested this. I knew what Clarice meant about it being "like it was before." Blane had been a playboy for years, always a different woman on his arm. I think the time he'd spent with me was the longest he'd been with someone in quite a while.

"Well, I'm sure he'll be fine," I said stiffly. "So he and Charlotte . . . ?" I left the question dangling.

Clarice's lips thinned. "Yeah, she's managed to weasel her way in."

I frowned. "I thought you liked her."

"I did, when she wasn't trying to be Blane's shadow."

"What do you mean?"

"She's always there, always wanting to help him or something. Like last night. His uncle insisted he take a date to that fund-raiser. Well, wouldn't you know Charlotte just happened to be available, so he didn't have to show up without one." Clarice's disdain was clear. "I mean, she couldn't be more obvious if she tried, but I think Blane is completely oblivious."

Clarice's mention of Blane's uncle had me clenching my fists in anger. I hated the man. A powerful senator from Massachusetts, Senator Robert Keaston had been reelected so many times, going to the polls was now a mere formality. He was also Blane's great-uncle.

Keaston had wanted me to break up with Blane, had tried to bribe me to do so. When that hadn't worked and Blane and I had gotten engaged, Keaston had lied to Blane about Kade and me having an affair. It made me furious not only that Blane was still listening to his uncle but also that Keaston was apparently being as meddlesome as ever and Blane was just letting him.

"What about you?" she asked. "Are you seeing anyone?"

I shook my head. "No. I don't want that right now. I'm not ready." The idea was ludicrous to me. I was still in love with Blane, no matter how much he'd hurt me. I couldn't just turn that off like a light switch.

Clarice studied the remaining wine in her glass as she asked with deliberate casualness, "Have you talked to Kade lately?" She knew that Kade and Blane were half brothers, though most people did not. It was a little-known fact that both Blane and Kade chose to keep that way.

"No. Why?"

She looked up at me. "Because neither has Blane. I mean, I know they used to talk several times a week. Kade would call the office or Blane would have me get him on the phone, but as far as I know, they haven't spoken since you and Blane broke up."

My stomach twisted into knots as guilt rose like nausea. It was my fault they weren't speaking. I had come between them. Even after Blane had accused me of sleeping with

Kade, I'd hoped Kade could talk some sense into him. If Blane didn't believe Kade's denials, I thought that at the very least he'd forgive him. They were brothers, after all, and history had proven them to be extremely loyal to each other. I was just the girlfriend, and as Blane had proven time and time again, girlfriends were replaceable. Brothers were not.

I couldn't eat another bite of my salad and just sipped my wine as Clarice changed the subject, sensing my distress, I think. I nodded and smiled but didn't hear ten percent of what she said, my thoughts in a jumble.

Should I try to call Kade? Figure out what was going on between him and Blane? My heart leapt at the thought of talking to him again, wanting it so bad it was like a physical need. God, I missed him.

But no, I shouldn't get involved. I was the cause of their estrangement. I certainly wasn't going to be the one who could fix it.

I was getting into my car after promising Clarice I'd be at the fitting on Thursday when I noticed him, a man was loitering near one of the storefronts lining the street.

He appeared to be window-shopping, but every few seconds, he'd glance my way. Before my training with Kade, I probably would never have noticed. But Kade had made me work until I reflexively took stock of my surroundings as though it was second nature to me.

Pretending I didn't see him, I got in my car and started the engine. I fiddled with my hair while I watched him in the rearview mirror as he hurried to get into a blue sedan.

I drove a circuitous route home, always keeping an eye on the sedan that stayed at least three or four cars behind me at all times. I had no idea who he was or why he was following me, and I certainly didn't want to lead him to my apartment. I mulled over what to do until an opportunity presented itself.

The stoplight ahead was green, so I slowed down. It turned yellow as I drew near, then red just as I hit the line. I gunned it, stomping on the accelerator and shooting through the intersection, barely missing colliding with traffic crossing the opposite direction. Tires squealed and I heard someone honk, then I was through. A glance in the mirror showed the sedan was stuck behind three cars at the light. I drove quickly to leave him behind, glad to have lost him.

Weird.

I spent the afternoon studying and doing homework before heading in to work. I tried not to dwell on the things Clarice had said, but it was futile. Blane with other women. Blane becoming close with Charlotte. Blane and Kade not speaking.

I was even more despondent than usual. But I didn't cry. I hadn't cried since the night Alisha had come over and I'd told her everything. Since then I'd carried on. I worked, I signed up for classes and started attending once the summer session began. I did my laundry, cleaned my apartment, and did all the things one did that said I was living my life.

And I tried to pretend it wasn't a lie.

I was nearly at The Drop when I saw the blue sedan.

He was trailing me like he had earlier, three cars behind. How the hell had he found me?

He must know where I live.

The thought sent a shiver of fear through me, which I quickly shrugged off. How dare he follow me? Try to scare me? The bastard.

I parked a couple of blocks from The Drop and grabbed my purse. Locking the car door, I started walking, taking the back way in between the buildings. It was light—the sun wouldn't set for a few hours—but the shadows were thick in the alleyways.

Pausing, I opened my purse and took out a compact. As I powdered my nose, I watched in the mirror. Sure enough, the same guy had gotten out of the sedan and was following me. I took quick measure of him. He was about five eleven, maybe 180 pounds. Not huge, but not small, either.

I snapped my compact closed and resumed walking. My hand remained inside my purse.

Turning a corner, I slipped into the shadows . . . and waited. When he stepped into view, he was only a foot from me and he had a gun pointed at his chest.

"Who are you and why are you following me?" I asked. The gun was steady in my two-handed grip.

"Whoa, take it easy," he said in surprise, putting his hands up.

"Answer the questions," I demanded.

"Listen, lady, I don't know what you're talking about—"

I racked the slide on the gun.

"All right, all right!" he said in alarm. "I'm just doing a job, all right?"

"You're supposed to scare me? Hurt me? Kill me?" I asked. It wouldn't be the first time, which probably explained my utter lack of shock.

"No, I swear! None of that!"

"Then what?"

The guy swallowed, his eyes on my gun. "This wasn't supposed to be a dangerous job," he muttered.

"Tell me!"

"Fine! I was just supposed to follow you, keep an eye on you, make sure nothing happened to you," he said, then added in an irritated undertone, "though it looks like you can take care of yourself well enough."

"Who hired you?" I asked, trying to process that he supposedly wasn't following me to hurt me, but to . . . protect me? Why?

He pressed his lips together, refusing to answer. I lowered my gun to point it at his knee.

"You like your knees?" I threatened.

Sweat broke out on his forehead and he swallowed heavily. "Fine," he said. "Blane Kirk hired me, okay? Now can you put the gun down? Please?"

I reeled, the name dropping like a load of bricks on my consciousness. Confusion and shock was followed quickly by rage.

Lowering the gun, I got in the guy's face.

"You tell your boss," I spat, "to leave me the fuck alone. If he sends someone else to follow me, he'll regret it and so will they."

I left him standing in the alley while I walked quickly to The Drop, my hands shaking uncontrollably as I put the gun back in my purse. When I reached work, I locked myself in a bathroom stall.

My heart was pounding and tears wet my lashes as I tried to hold them back. I breathed, closing my eyes and trying to get a grip.

Why would Blane have someone follow me? It didn't make any sense. Was he afraid I was going to go to the press about the relationship we'd had? Leak all the sordid details? There were plenty of women who could do that. And if the guy had been telling the truth about making sure nothing happened to me, then what was going on that would put me in danger?

I couldn't concentrate on any of this, my emotions still overruling my logic. Blane still thought of me, albeit in his usual heavy-handed, controlling way. It was pathetic how much of an impact that made on me. *I* was pathetic. How embarrassing.

God, I needed a drink.

I escaped the bathroom and clocked in. We were already busy and I had little time to do more than throw a quick hello to Scott and Tish, also working again tonight. However, I did find time to toss back a shot of bourbon, to steady myself.

A group of four college guys came in at some point during the night, setting up at a table close to the bar. They wore casual clothes that I could tell were expensive brands, which meant they had money. I told Scott I'd take the table and headed over there.

They were cute and funny and I flirted shamelessly as I delivered their drinks. Working for tips required its own kind of skill. I used to be friendly but kept my distance. Then a stripper I'd met a few months ago had given me some good advice.

You've got assets. Use them to your advantage. Men are fools for a nice set of boobs.

17

I'd taken it to heart and my tips had improved. Even though the uniform Romeo made us wear irritated me, it showed off an impressive display of cleavage. And judging by the college boys' lingering stares as they got more inebriated, it worked. If I was lucky, I'd get twenty bucks off that table tonight, maybe more if they got drunk enough.

Scott and I had a good rhythm when we worked together, and he was fun. He teased me mercilessly, making me laugh. I could almost push the whole incident with the man Blane had hired to the back of my mind.

But not completely, which was why I didn't turn them down when the college guys wanted me to do a round of shots with them. Business was slowing as one o'clock neared, so I didn't feel guilty leaving Scott behind the bar while I hung out with the table of four, though only two of the guys remained. The others were out on the dance floor with girls they'd picked up.

"So, Kathleen," one of them said. I thought his name was Bill or Brian, something with a B. "You busy after work?" He'd slung his arm around my waist as I stood next to their high-top table.

I tipped back the shot in my hand, the whiskey burning a fiery path down my throat to my belly, and tried to concentrate on what he'd said.

"Sorry," I replied. "Gotta get home tonight. Maybe some other time." I smiled to soften the rejection. Just because I wanted to relieve them of some of their cash didn't mean I wanted a date, even if he was a good-looking guy.

"We could have a real good time," he insisted. His hand drifted down to my ass.

"Just the three of us," the other guy chimed in. I wanted to say his name was Trey.

I looked at him in surprise and he laughed. "Betcha never done that before, right?"

If I'd expected Bill/Brian to object, I was disappointed. He seemed all for the idea. He'd gripped my waist and tugged me back between his thighs so I faced Trey, who'd scooted his stool closer.

"You're fuckin' hot, Kathleen," Bill/Brian said in my ear. "We'll take good care of you. Don't you worry."

I swallowed hard, trying to fight the rising panic in my chest just as Trey leaned over and kissed me. My hands automatically came up to push him away, but they were caught and held by the guy behind me.

Well, fuck. There goes my tip, I thought sourly.

I jerked my head back hard, cracking Bill/Brian in the face. He yelped and let me go. Now free, I hurriedly slipped out from between the two men.

"I'm not into that," I said calmly from a couple feet away. Bill/Brian was cupping his nose with his hand.

Trey spoke first. "Sorry there, Kathleen. We meant no harm."

I eyed him suspiciously, but he seemed sincere, for a drunk guy.

"Yeah, sorry," Bill/Brian said, his voice muffled from behind his hand. "The way you were acting . . . Well, we obviously got the wrong idea there."

I nodded and headed back to the bar. So I was such an obviously easy lay that a couple of college guys assumed I would be into a threesome one-night stand?

I poured myself a drink.

"Those guys get out of hand?" Scott asked, sidling up next to me.

I shook my head. "Nothing I can't handle."

He nodded wordlessly and moved away, Tish handing him an order to fill.

By the time I'd restocked the bar and had begun cleanup, the table of guys had gone. They left me fifty bucks, which I supposed was their way of saying sorry. Whatever. It was much more than I thought I'd get after nailing that guy in the face.

Scott and Tish left after I assured them I'd close up.

"You sure?" Tish asked as she grabbed her purse.

"No worries," I said. "See you Monday."

When I was alone, I locked the front door and turned off all the lights but the ones that shone directly down on the bar. I was keyed up, despite the drinks I'd had. The incident with the college guys bothered me and I still couldn't get Blane out of my head.

Maybe I should've gone home with Trey and Bill. Or Brian. Or whatever his name had been.

With a sigh, I eased myself onto a barstool and took a swig of the beer I'd grabbed. I rested my head in my hand, my elbow braced on the bar. My other hand toyed with the beer bottle. I wasn't in a hurry to get home.

Jeff, the cook at The Drop, had made me a hamburger earlier, and glowered at me until I'd taken a few bites. Jeff was ex-Army, bald, and had tattoos up and down his arms. Romeo was terrified of him, though Jeff had always been nice to me. He was a man of few words, content to cook and smoke his cigarettes, usually at the same time. He'd taken a particular interest in making me eat lately, which was sweet of him.

I was lucky, I told myself. I had great friends who cared about me. And I was being cruel to them by making them worry. I just needed to get over it already. People broke up, got divorced, or died all the time. I was not the first to experience heartbreak.

A prickling on the back of my neck had me looking over my shoulder at the expanse of windows lining the walls. I couldn't see out, could see only my reflection in the opaque glass as it reflected the dim light from the bar.

Dismissing the sensation, I finished off the beer and tossed the bottle. Time to go home.

The streets were quiet and empty at this hour. I walked slowly to my car. I loved summer nights, when the heat of the day had passed and the warm darkness was like a welcoming blanket. It had rained earlier, leaving the air smelling fresh and clean. The moon peeked from behind clouds that were clearing out and I paused to look at it. Bright and full, it was a good reminder that life goes on, that each day would get just a tiny bit easier until one day I'd wake up and not think about Blane at all.

My keys slipped out of my lax fingers, hitting the ground with the clink of metal against concrete. I grumbled a curse at my clumsiness and bent down to grab them.

A gunshot shattered the silence, making me cry out in alarm. The glass of the car window exploded above me and I instinctively crouched down, covering my head with my arms as the shards rained on me.

I scrabbled in my purse, adrenaline flooding my veins. But I hadn't yet taken my gun out when I heard the sound of gunfire again, except it was coming from another direction. Someone was shooting back, and it wasn't me.

Tires squealed and there were more gunshots. I stayed down, not wanting to get in the crossfire of whatever I'd managed to land in the middle of. Gangs maybe, who knew? Just my luck, though.

It was quiet again, save for the pounding of the blood in my ears. I gradually uncovered my head. A tickle on my face had me swiping my cheek, my hand coming away bloody. A piece of glass must have cut me. Great.

My knees were scraped from the concrete and I winced as I got to my feet. At least it appeared the shooters were gone. I glanced around to be sure, wondering if I should call the cops, then the breath left my lungs in a rush.

A man had stepped out of the shadows and stood mere feet from me, a gun in the hand at his side.

I swallowed hard, before saying, "So, I guess you were just in the neighborhood."

CHAPTER TWO

Blane Kirk stepped out of the shadows and my heart stuttered in my chest.

It felt like something out of a dream, to see him again, this close to me. I was nearly light-headed from the suddenness of his appearance, but my stomach felt like I'd been kicked in the gut.

"I was 'in the neighborhood' because you sent my bodyguard packing," he said. Blane's tone was flat, completely devoid of emotion, the same as his face.

The sound of his voice after three months sent a stab of bittersweet pain through me. How many nights had I stared at my phone, wanting it to ring, for it to be him on the other end? It took everything I had not to show the pain I was feeling, though I couldn't help pressing my arm against my abdomen to try and quiet my stomach. My insides churned with nausea and I absolutely refused to throw up in front of Blane. I'd choke on it first.

"I don't want or need a bodyguard," I bit out. "Especially from you."

"So you'd rather have gotten shot tonight?" he retorted, and I could hear anger now in his voice.

"I can take care of myself," I said stiffly. "What the hell do you care anyway?" The question came out more as an accusation and I couldn't help but hold my breath as I waited for his answer.

"The papers would have a field day if my ex-fiancée was killed on the streets of Indianapolis."

I choked on air, my lungs refusing to cooperate. Just when I thought Blane couldn't hurt me any more than he already had, he had to go and prove me wrong. I lashed out, unable to resist the instinct to hurt him back.

"I'm surprised you sent another bodyguard," I sneered. "Especially since I screwed the last one."

I was referring to Kade, his half brother, that Blane had forced to guard me several months ago. The same brother Blane had accused me of having an affair with. It had been a lie, of course, but Blane hadn't believed me when I'd told him the truth.

The silence between us was thick enough to drown in.

"Kade denied that you'd slept together." His voice was cold steel, slicing through the night.

"Oh well, *that's* a relief," I shot back, my sarcasm thick. "Good to know we have our stories straight." Blane still wanted to believe I'd had sex with Kade even after we'd both denied it? Fine with me. He could believe in chubby flying babies with bows and arrows, for all I cared.

My stomach was still churning, anger and pain both burning like acid in my gut. My head was telling me to go, to get as far away from Blane as I could. But my feet wouldn't obey. Rooted to the spot, I drank Blane in. Well over six feet, he towered over me when he was close, which wasn't the case right now. He wore jeans and a black T-shirt, the cotton stretched tightly over the muscles of his chest and shoulders.

The tickle on my cheek distracted me and I swiped at the blood oozing down the side of my face.

"You're hurt." He moved toward me, shoving the gun he held into the back of his jeans.

I threw up a hand to ward him off, hurriedly retreating until my back hit my car. "Don't you dare come any closer," I warned. "I don't want your help."

"You're bleeding," he said, though he'd stopped a couple of feet from me. Still too close, but at least he hadn't touched me. If he did, I was sure I'd fall apart.

"I'm fine." It was a phrase I'd said often in the past few months. I was pretty good at it. Sometimes I almost believed it myself.

Blane's lips pressed in a thin line as he looked at me, his eyes unfathomable in the darkness.

"I believe you didn't sleep with Kade," he said, the words seeming forced from his mouth.

"I don't care what you believe," I hissed, rage spiking hard in me. All the anger and bitterness I'd kept bottled up for the past few months now boiled to the surface. "Is that why you're here? Your conscience bothering you? Oh wait, I forgot—you don't have one."

"I'm here because William Gage is out of prison."

That gave me pause. William James Gage Sr. had been sent to jail months before, accessory to murder and attempted murder being among the many charges against him. The "attempted" part was when he'd tried to have me killed. If not for Blane, he'd have succeeded.

"How could he possibly have gotten out of jail?" I asked. It seemed incomprehensible to me.

"He has cancer. The doctors give him weeks to live, if that. Friends in high places pulled some strings so he could die outside of prison. He's on house arrest, though, and can't leave the premises."

"And you're telling me this why?"

Blane hesitated and I knew I wasn't going to like what he had to say. "Gage blames you for ending up in prison, the loss of his business, his reputation."

"That's insane," I snapped. "He's the criminal, not me. He just got caught."

"Yes, he is insane," Blane agreed. "And he hates you. I think he's going to try and have you killed. The shooting tonight was possibly his first attempt."

Ah. Now it made sense, the bodyguard thing. "Well, let him give it his best shot," I said. "I can take care of myself." It surprised me a bit how unalarmed I was at this news. That coldness in the center of my chest seemed to take it in stride that my days might be numbered. Again.

"A few self-defense classes does not make you an expert," Blane retorted.

"If I wanted your opinion, I'd ask for it." I turned away and jerked open my car door, surveying the shattered glass covering the interior. I spoke over my shoulder. "You've delivered the warning. Consider your obligation fulfilled. I'll try not to let my death interfere with your campaign."

The initial shock and ridiculous flare of hope at seeing Blane had faded, replaced by a numbness that I welcomed.

Getting the glass out of the seat concerned me now. The last thing I needed was to have to go to the hospital to get shards out of my ass. I dug around in the backseat. Surely I had a discarded work T-shirt back there?

"Here."

Blane's voice was right behind me and his hand brushed my back. I jumped about a foot.

I spun around in alarm, instinctively putting up my hands to push him away. Unfortunately, they met a bare chest. I jerked my hands back as though burned.

"Use this," Blane said, holding out his T-shirt. "For the glass."

Oh God. He was so close, his chest at eye level, his body inches from mine. The carved muscles seemed more defined than I remembered, the heat of the night making his skin glisten in the faint light. I couldn't retreat any farther, the car blocking me.

Blane didn't move and I jerked my eyes up to his. He was looking at the blood dripping down my cheek, frowning. His hand moved to touch me and I couldn't help but flinch. He froze, his hand in midair.

"Back off, Blane." I was glad to hear that my voice was steady even though I was quaking inside.

He obeyed, stepping back to put some space between us, and I breathed again, my eyes sliding shut in relief before I realized what I was doing.

Pull it together, I harshly told myself. I didn't want to show any sign of weakness. My pride wouldn't allow it.

"Fine," I said curtly, pulling the T-shirt out of his grip. I used it to brush the glass from the seat to the floor. God, how much was this going to cost to fix? Absurdly, the thought made me want to cry.

As if he knew exactly what I was thinking, Blane said, "I can have some guys come to your place tomorrow, replace the glass."

"I don't want a damn thing from you," I snapped. "Including your shirt." I tossed it at him and he caught it. I climbed into the car and jerked the door shut. Blane leaned down to the window.

"Well, that's too bad," he said. "I'm going to be around whether you like it or not, to keep you alive."

I smiled sweetly at him as I started the car. "Then you'd better hope Gage dies sooner rather than later, or he won't be the only one needing a tombstone."

My hands were still shaking when I got home, the aftershock of seeing Blane, talking to him, hitting me like a Mack truck.

I sat at my kitchen table, vodka tonic in my lax grip, staring into space.

I knew I should probably be concerned about Gage, but I couldn't bring myself to be. All I could think about was that I'd seen Blane again, spoken to him, touched him. And none of it had been good for my resolve to get over him and move on.

It depressed me, the power he had over me. Even though he'd hurt me so badly, not once but twice, I was still pathetically glad to see him despite the bitter anger like bile in my throat.

And now he was, what, "going to be around"? What did that mean? And more important, how was I going to keep it together if I had to see him again? I'd barely kept myself from falling apart tonight, my rage doubling as shield and weapon in my nearly empty arsenal.

So he believed I hadn't slept with Kade. So what? It didn't matter a hill of beans now. Blane should have believed me when it counted, when I'd stood in his office while he accused me of being unfaithful, of betraying him. That's when he should have believed me. It was far too late now for anything he said to matter.

I drank until my head swam and the room spun, falling into bed still in my work uniform. Tears I hadn't shed in months streamed down my cheeks and I curled into a ball on top of the blankets, too exhausted mentally and emotionally to get under the covers. Finally, when the sky began to lighten outside, only then did I fall asleep.

~

A gentle hand brushed the hair back from my face, slowly combing through the long strands. I sighed in my sleep. I loved it when my hair was played with. The slow, gentle touch relaxed me and I burrowed deeper in my pillow as the hand repeated the gesture. What a nice dream. I hadn't had a good dream in a long, long while, and I dreaded waking up, which would ruin it. Better to just stay asleep, enjoy the fantasy for a bit longer.

Something warm and soft was pressed against my cheek. It was also wet, and its gentle swiping dragged me up from the depths of slumber.

My brain was fogged from too much alcohol and too little sleep. My eyes felt swollen and glued shut from the tears I'd shed. Vague memories of last night drifted through my mind and I whimpered, the pain that was a constant companion washing over me as I remembered the current state of my life and the confrontation with Blane. God, had that just been last night? I felt like I'd aged ten years.

Another soft swipe along my cheek up to my forehead told me I wasn't dreaming. That realization had me jerking upright in bed, which I immediately regretted as the room tilted and spun, the vodka I'd consumed still in my system.

Blane was sitting next to me on the bed.

I gaped in shock, my brain trying to process him sitting there, a washcloth in his hand, staring intently at me.

"What the hell?" I managed to squeak out, scooting away from him.

"You didn't answer your door," he said, as though that explained everything.

"Yeah, there's a reason for that. I was sleeping!" I glanced down at the washcloth. Its pristine white was tinted pink. Blane had been cleaning the dried blood on my face that I had forgotten about last night, so preoccupied had I been with my shattered nerves.

"You didn't answer your door, or your phone, and I was pounding hard enough to wake the dead." His voice was flat. "Given what happened last night, I was worried."

"So you just decided to let yourself in to my apartment?" I knew I should have changed the locks.

That question didn't warrant a reply, since the answer was obvious.

"Well, I'm fine, so you can get the hell out. Leave your key." I combed my fingers self-consciously through my hair, knowing I looked a disaster. I rolled away from him and got up on the other side of the bed.

My head ached and my mouth felt like I'd slept with a wad of cotton in it. The cuts on my face burned and my stomach felt even worse. I should've eaten something last night.

Somehow, I made it to the bathroom and shut the door behind me. I leaned against it, just breathing.

Blane was here.

This couldn't be happening. Somehow this was a nightmare, and I'd wake up any minute.

When that didn't happen, I brushed my teeth. Looking in the mirror, I winced. The small cuts were an angry red against my pale skin, my eyes swollen and bloodshot. Dark circles that looked like bruises in my face didn't help and my hair was in a complete tangle. The T-shirt I'd worn to work last night was stained with dried blood and it was tucked half in, half out of my shorts. My knees were in a similar state as my face, with dried blood on the scrapes.

I'd looked better.

A long, hot shower made a world of difference and I felt almost human when I emerged. I knew it would be too much to hope for that Blane would have left, so I wasn't surprised to see him leaning against my kitchen counter. Ignoring him, I went back into the bedroom, discarding my towel for a pair of white shorts and a navy cami, the spaghetti straps the same color as my bra. The windows in my apartment were still open and it was already getting hot.

I had the passing embarrassment that my AC wasn't on. I had a couple of fans going in open windows, trying to draw in some air. Very white trash, I know, but hey, they helped. Blane had to be uncomfortable in the warm apartment. I shoved the thought aside. I was the one paying the bill. He could just leave if he was hot.

My hair was wet and hung past the middle of my back, but I did nothing more than brush it. Wet hair would help keep me cool. I didn't have the heart to look in the mirror. Why should I care what I looked like just because Blane was here? I hadn't invited him and certainly didn't want him to stay.

The smell of fresh coffee greeted me when I came out of the bedroom. It seemed Blane had made a pot. I didn't say anything as I poured myself a cup. What was I supposed to do? Thank him for breaking into my apartment to make coffee?

I could feel him watching me and I avoided his gaze. He'd changed since last night, still wearing jeans but now with a white polo that contrasted beautifully against his tanned skin. I noticed with some disgust that he wasn't even sweating.

I looked away and my eyes fell on the empty bottle of cheap vodka and glass I'd left on the kitchen table last night. Heat flooded my cheeks as I grabbed the bottle and threw it in the trash.

"Is there a reason you're still here?" I asked when I could no longer take the silence or his staring. "I'm sure Charlotte is wondering where you are." I couldn't help the bitterness in my voice as I finally forced my gaze to meet his.

"Charlotte's an employee," he said firmly. "Nothing more."

I remembered what Clarice said and thought about throwing that in his face, but decided to let it go. It didn't matter anyway and my pursuing it would just make me sound like a jealous bitch.

Which I totally wasn't.

The gray of his eyes sparked too many memories, the sight of him standing in my apartment making me remember the time we'd spent together. Now he seemed a stranger to me.

A stranger who'd once pushed me down on the counter behind him so he could bury his head between my legs.

My hand shook and coffee sloshed over the side of the mug, burning my hand. I hissed and quickly set the mug down, putting the burned skin to my mouth.

"You should eat something," Blane said, his eyes following my movements.

I arched an eyebrow. "Really?" I deadpanned. "You're concerned about my diet now?" This was turning more surreal by the moment.

Blane's gaze moved slowly down my body and back up. I stiffened when his eyes paused briefly at the gold locket I wore. Kade had given it to me for Christmas and it contained a tiny photo of my parents. I never took it off.

"You're too thin," he said roughly, thankfully not commenting on the locket. "And there's hardly any food in your refrigerator."

He'd gone through my refrigerator? My head felt like it was going to explode, I got so angry so fast.

"Who the hell do you think you are?" I seethed. "You break into my apartment, refuse to leave, and now you're snooping through my things?" My fists were clenched at my sides as I tried valiantly to keep calm, when all I really wanted to do was attack him until all the anger and pain and despair inside me went away.

I swear his face paled underneath his tan.

"I'm . . . sorry," he said, and his voice was thick. He swallowed, his eyes locked on mine.

A little of my anger leached away at this, the first sign that he felt anything at all.

"I'm sorry for . . . a lot of things," he continued. "And I'm not here expecting forgiveness. I know I don't deserve that from you." He paused. "But I can't stop . . . caring . . . about you. Thinking about you. Wondering how you are, what you're doing."

These were words I'd wanted to hear for months, and a part of me was stunned at what he was saying, not ever having really expected it of him. But the other part of me, the part still encased in ice, was left . . . unmoved.

"I don't know what you want me to say," I finally replied with a small shrug. "You're right—I can't forgive you. Not right now. You said I'd betrayed you, when really it was *you* who betrayed *me*. You didn't believe in me, in us."

Blane was absolutely still as I spoke, his arms crossed tight over his chest, his gaze intently focused on mine, and I had the passing thought that maybe I wasn't the only one barely holding myself together.

"Why are we having this conversation now?" I asked. "Because of Gage? Were you going to say these things to me without that threat?"

"I just thought . . . maybe . . . we could be friends," he said.

I gaped at him in disbelief. "You're not serious." I laughed, and the sound was slightly hysterical even to my own ears.

Blane moved until he stood right in front of me and my laughter died a quick death. He reached for a lock of my damp hair, and this time I didn't flinch.

"I drive by, all the time," he said, his voice hardly above a whisper. "Just to see if you're home. I've called so many times, only to hang up. I see you when I close my eyes at night. I smell your perfume at work and turn around, every time praying it's you . . . but it never is."

I studied his eyes and couldn't deny that I dearly wanted to lean forward, let Blane wrap his arms around me, and forget the past three months had ever happened.

I'd be an utter fool to do that.

I cleared my throat. "That sounds real sweet," I said quietly. "But we're over, Blane. You about killed me, twice, and I'm not so stupid as to *ever* trust you again."

His expression turned blank and he gave a curt nod. "I see. Then why all the booze, Kat?"

I stiffened at the nickname. He'd given up nickname privileges. "What are you talking about?"

"You never used to drink so much, at least not without cause. Why is there more vodka in your freezer than food? Why is it every time you're at work, there's a drink nearby?"

The blood left my face in a rush. "Were you spying on me?" It was hard to wrap my head around that.

"I've been around," he said evasively. "But I'm not the only one who's noticed."

"You've talked to other people about me?" Now the blood came rushing back, as did my anger. "You've sat around discussing me like I'm some sort of . . . of . . . pity case?" I tried to push past him, needing some space, but he grabbed me, his hands closing on my arm.

35

"Not other people," he said. "Clarice. She's worried about you. I am, too."

"I'm fine," I gritted out. "Get over yourself, Blane. I drink more now because it's my choice. It has nothing to do with you." That wasn't precisely true, but the truth didn't matter. I was humiliated that Clarice would talk to Blane about me. "I think it's time for you to leave."

"I'm not going away, Kat, whether you want me to or not. I'm not going to let Gage send someone to hurt you. And I'm not going to let you hurt yourself, either."

My pride took a beating at that last part and I struggled not to let it show. "Fabulous. Get out."

Blane's jaw was clenched tight, our gazes locked together, but he released me and stepped away. I didn't breathe properly until the door had shut behind him, then I sagged against the wall, letting it hold me up.

My instinct was to go next door and talk to Alisha, my friend and neighbor, but I knew she was out of the town for the weekend with her boyfriend, Lewis. My next thought was to reach for the vodka inside my freezer, but Blane's words stilled my hand. Yes, I'd been drinking more lately, but if he hadn't shown up out of the blue, I wouldn't have drunk as much as I had last night. So really, it was his fault.

I sighed, pushing a hand through my damp hair. I really, really hated to admit that Blane had a point about anything, but he probably did about the alcohol. I'd been using it too much as a crutch these past few months. Apparently, so much so that Clarice had felt the need to tell Blane.

Shame and humiliation washed over me. Clarice and I were going to have a talk. She'd broken my trust, and no matter how well intentioned, that didn't sit well with me.

And Blane had been spying on me in the bar? I remembered last night, when I'd felt as though someone was watching me. Had that been him? How long had he been outside, watching? Long enough to see me get propositioned for a threesome by those guys?

As if that event in itself hadn't made me feel sleazy, suspecting Blane had seen the whole thing sealed the deal.

I pushed the thought aside. I couldn't dwell on it or I'd wallow in self-pitying misery all day. I'd never kidded myself that Blane and I were of the same class, but I'd always had my dignity. Between Clarice insinuating to Blane that I was a drunken mess without him and the guys last night treating me like an easy hookup, my dignity lay in tatters at my feet.

I opened the refrigerator and peered inside. My stomach was tender, but I had to eat something. Unfortunately, there wasn't much to choose from. A nearly empty loaf of bread, the ends of which were moldy. A six-pack of beer with two bottles missing. A head of lettuce, its leaves limp and brown. Ketchup. Mayo. A half-empty bottle of soy sauce. Looked like a trip to the grocery store was in order.

I needed to check my tips from last night. My bank account was pretty low. Best to see what I'd made so I'd know how much I could spend at the store.

I'd dumped the crumpled pile of money on the table by my couch, not caring much at the time about what I'd made. The pile was now neatly stacked, but not very tall. I remembered the fifty bucks I'd made off the college guys. Bad propositions aside, that would certainly come in handy.

I sat cross-legged on the couch as I counted the money, being sure to sit on the thin blanket I'd spread over the cushions. Sweaty skin and leather did not mix.

When I came to the bottom of the handful of ones plus the fifty, I paused. A hundred-dollar bill was last in the stack. I frowned. I hadn't cashed in my ones last night and I certainly would have remembered a hundred-dollar tip. Where had it—

Blane.

He must've counted the money while I'd been in the shower, adding in the hundred.

I stared at it, unsure how I felt. I sure didn't like the charity, but then again I wasn't in a position to be proud. The electric bill that I was behind on could really use that hundred dollars. Plus, Blane was already gone. How was I supposed to return it?

I hadn't believed him when he'd said he wasn't going away. After the argument we'd had, I doubted I'd see him again anytime soon, a thought that was immediately quashed when I went outside a short while later to find a glass company's truck pulling out of the lot and Blane standing by my newly repaired car.

Déjà vu hit me hard as I remembered the first time Blane had fixed my car for me. It had felt so good then, for him to help me.

It felt quite different now.

"What are you doing, Blane?" I asked, walking up to my car. He turned toward me. "I told you I didn't want you fixing it."

"If Gage is behind this, then it's an expense for the firm to absorb," he said, eyeing me as though wary that I'd flip out on him again. He glanced at my clothes. I was wearing the same thing, had just slipped on a pair of flip-flops and my sunglasses. I'd pulled my hair back into a high ponytail. "Where are you going?"

"Weren't you the one griping about the food in my refrigerator?" I retorted. "I'm going to the grocery store." I stepped around him and climbed into my car. All the glass had been swept away and I couldn't pretend I wasn't glad it had been taken care of for me. I decided not to argue with him about it. It's not like there was anything I could do now anyway. I thought about the hundred dollars but didn't say anything. I didn't want to humiliate myself by arguing with him over the money, especially when I was in such need of it.

Blane slid into the passenger seat. "I'm going with you."

"You're what?" I stared at him.

"You're not going anywhere unprotected," he said, slamming the door shut.

Short of throwing a big-ass temper tantrum, I didn't see any way I was going to get him out of my car, and I wasn't one hundred percent sure he'd go even in the face of a tantrum.

"Fine." I threw the car in gear and sped out of the parking lot.

We didn't speak as I drove. I was acutely conscious of him. As it did in my apartment, Blane's presence overwhelmed my car, too, its confines made even smaller by the size of his body. His sunglasses hid his eyes from me now as he rested an elbow on the rolled-down window, the wind artfully ruffling his perfect hair.

"Shouldn't you be doing some campaign stuff rather than following me around?" I asked.

He glanced my way. "I've taken a temporary leave from the campaign."

39

I swallowed and focused on the road. Blane was putting his campaign on hold to play bodyguard for me?

"I bet your uncle isn't too happy about that," I said stiffly.

"It's not his decision."

I wondered if the senator agreed with that sentiment.

When I parked, Blane followed me inside, watching as I got a cart and walking beside me down the produce aisle. We could've been like any of the other couples doing their weekend shopping, if the tension between us wasn't as palpable as a living thing.

My nerves were on edge, Blane's silent vigil next to me making it hard to concentrate. He'd hooked his sunglasses on his shirt while I'd pushed mine on top of my head. Blane looked incredibly out of place, standing in front of the broccoli. Grocery shopping was something we'd never done together.

I shook my head. Best to hurry up and get this over with. Peaches were in season and on sale. I grabbed a few. Cucumbers were plentiful and a couple of those went in the cart. Lettuce. Tomatoes.

I lived a lot off sandwiches and ramen noodles, so I grabbed some prepackaged lunch meat. The soup aisle was next, where I got some more noodles, then to the bakery for a loaf of generic white bread. I caught Blane looking sideways at the bread and noodles.

"So is there an assassin hiding in frozen foods?" I asked snidely, my pride stung when I suspected he was looking down his upper-class nose at my food.

His gray eyes met mine. "None that I can see." His serious reply took the heat from my snit and I heaved an inward sigh.

"Let's go," I said, turning for the checkout.

"Wait, that's it?"

I glanced around. Blane was staring at my cart.

"That's pretty much what you do here, Blane," I said with exaggerated patience. "You put food in the cart, then you put it on the belt and pay for it so you can take it home."

His eyes flashed at my tone. "I meant, is that all you're getting."

I looked in my cart and did some quick math. If I was lucky, the groceries would be just under fifty dollars. I had food for sandwiches, salads, and noodles for dinner.

"Yeah, that's it," I snapped. "Some people have to live on a budget."

"I need some stuff, too," he said, inching me out of the way to take over the cart. "Might as well not make two trips."

"*You* need stuff?" I asked in bewilderment, having no choice but to trot after him as he started down an aisle. My purse was sitting in the cart. "What happened to Mona?"

Mona was his housekeeper and took care of the cooking. She and her husband, Gerard, lived in a house that adjoined Blane's property.

"She asked me to pick up some things," he said, grabbing some jarred pasta sauce off the shelf.

Whatever. "Fine, just keep it separate from my stuff." I reached in the cart and pushed all my things into a small pile in the back.

I followed Blane as he went back through the store. He wasn't consulting any list that I could see and I had a suspicion as to what he was doing. Meat went in the cart, steaks, chicken, and pork chops. Cereal, granola bars, pop, chips, pasta, frozen meals, potatoes, fresh vegetables. I really hoped Mona hadn't gone shopping recently because she was about to get a load of other stuff.

Blane was taking great care in picking out "Mona's" asparagus, so I rolled my eyes and wandered away. He knew I liked asparagus, but it was expensive, so I hardly ever bought it. I wondered with a sigh how this was going to play out when we got to the cashier. If I'd had my purse, I would've just left Blane standing there inspecting the strawberries.

Glancing next to me, I saw a man looking over the melons. Our eyes caught.

"I, uh, never know how to tell what's ripe," he said.

He seemed to be in his late twenties or early thirties, attractive with blond hair that looked like it had been kissed by the sun. Blue eyes, straight teeth, and a smile that was both shy and sexy—and that had me smiling back.

"Yeah, something about if it sounds hollow when you tap it, I guess," I replied with a shrug.

"They all sound hollow to me."

I laughed at his self-deprecating grimace and his smile was wider this time.

"I'm Luke," he said. "What's your name?"

"Kathleen."

"Nice to meet you, Kathleen." He held out his hand and I took it.

"Likewise."

"I don't usually do this—" he began.

"Kat, you ready to go?"

I turned to see Blane now standing behind me, his face like granite as he stared at Luke.

Nice.

TIFFANY SNOW

"Sure," I said easily as Luke glanced from me to Blane and back. "Luke, this is my . . . brother. You were saying?"

I didn't look to see how Blane was taking that.

"Ah, yeah." Luke focused on me again when Blane didn't speak. "I was wondering if you might like to go out sometime."

I could have done a little dance in delight. A cute, sexy guy was asking me out right in front of Blane and there wasn't a damn thing he could do about it. Maybe fate had a twisted sense of humor after all.

"I'd like that," I said. I grabbed a pen from my purse and scrawled my number on Luke's palm. "Here's my number. Call me."

He beamed at me and his gaze dropped to my chest before jerking back up to my face. "Thanks! I will."

Blane was a stiff wall of silence behind me as I walked toward the checkout. I probably wouldn't have given Luke my number if Blane hadn't been there. I don't usually get picked up in the grocery store, but it had been too good of an opportunity to resist.

"Your brother?" Blane asked, his voice hard with anger.

I stopped and turned. Blane's eyes were flashing gray fire. "Telling him you're my ex probably wouldn't have gone over real well," I said.

Blane grabbed my arm and pulled me close. "He was staring at your breasts," he hissed. "Which are barely covered in that getup."

"Can you blame him?" I retorted. "If I remember right, you always enjoyed them." I yanked my arm out of his grasp. "And can we stop pretending that you're buying all this food

43

for Mona? I know what you're doing and it's not going to happen."

"You can't live off ramen noodles and lettuce."

I was furious now, and it wasn't just about the groceries. My temper seemed to be on a hair trigger. "You can't shove your way back into my life, Blane, not after everything that's happened. And you certainly can't control me the way you used to." I snatched my purse from the cart. "I'm out of here."

"I have your keys," he said to my back.

His high-handedness had me seeing red. "Then I'll fucking walk," I ground out.

Tears stung my eyes as I hurried through the automatic doors. The sun was now high in the sky and stepping into the heat and humidity felt like hitting a brick wall. I slid my sunglasses back on and started trekking across the parking lot.

I couldn't handle this, didn't know how to act or what to say with Blane. My anger was too close to the surface, forgiveness too far away, for me to even pretend a level of normalcy with him. Our relationship had too much history, too much baggage, for us to carry on with any kind of pretend friendship.

I had to get him out of my life, and there was only one way to do that.

Getting my phone out of my purse, I dialed a number from memory, praying he'd pick up.

To my disappointment, the call went to voice mail.

"Kade, it's me. Kathleen. Listen, I know we haven't talked in a while," which was an understatement, "but I was hoping, if you're not too busy, that you might come back.

Just for a while. I . . ." My voice faltered. "I could really use some help, and I don't know who else to ask . . ." The absurdity of what I was asking suddenly struck me. Was I really going to ask Kade to actively work against his brother? "You know what," I said, suddenly changing my mind, "forget I called, okay? It's nothing. I'm fine. . . ."

Someone yelling my name distracted me and I turned to see Blane running flat out my way.

"Look out!" he yelled.

I turned in confusion and saw a car barreling toward me. I froze in horror, my mind moving in slow motion. Adrenaline turned my insides cold and made my muscles move. I dove to the side but not fast enough. The corner of the car hit me and I screamed as my body glanced off the metal before hitting the burning asphalt. My phone clattered from my hand and I was aware of a burning pain in my side. I heard gunshots, then nothing.

∼

Sirens were screaming when I pried open my eyes. I was lying on my back on the hot asphalt, the sun a blazing glare. My first thought was that I must have dropped my sunglasses. My second was that I'd broken my non-injury streak the moment Blane had set foot back in my life.

That seemed important.

Blane spoke and I realized he was kneeling at my side.

"Don't move, Kat."

Yeah, wasn't planning on it. My side hurt like hell, especially when I took a breath. I could tell I'd gotten scraped up from the concrete on my arm and elbow, though that pain paled in comparison.

"What happened?" I managed to croak.

"There was a car," Blane said. "It hit you."

Ah yes. Now I remembered. I'd been angry and left the store. In retrospect, probably not the smartest thing to do given what Blane had told me about Gage. My only defense was that I'd been so upset at Blane that I hadn't been thinking clearly.

The sirens were coming closer and I assumed they were for me. We'd attracted a small crowd, which had to back up when the EMTs got there. Blane stepped out of my line of sight as the technicians examined me. Once they had asked me a hundred questions ("Ma'am, can you wiggle your toes?") and realized I hadn't broken something vital, like my spine, they placed me on a gurney and started to put me in the ambulance.

This was the first time I'd been in an ambulance since I'd had to call one when my mother was so ill in the last stages of cancer. I'd insisted on riding in the back with her, and I still remember the sympathy on the EMT's face as he watched me hold my mom's hand. She'd wanted to die at home but had ended up passing in the back of that ambulance before we even reached the hospital.

That memory assaulted me now and irrational fear struck.

"Wait," I gasped, struggling to sit up against the safety restraints they'd placed across the gurney. "No, wait . . . let me out!"

"Ma'am, you need to lie still," one of the EMTs said, gently but firmly pushing me back down.

"No!" My voice was shrill now as they rolled me inside the ambulance. Medical equipment surrounded me, its silence foreboding. I couldn't see outside. I couldn't see Blane.

Panic hit and I started struggling in earnest despite the pain in my side, tugging fruitlessly at the belts that kept me prisoner. I couldn't breathe properly. Each breath was a stabbing pain.

The EMT grabbed my wrists. "You're going to be all right," he said. "Just calm down. We'll get you to the hospital."

"No, please, let me go," I begged, unable to twist away from him. My vision blurred. The heat inside the ambulance was suddenly too much like the stifling heat in a shack filled with women held at gunpoint.

The man forced my arms down to my sides. "Restrain her," he told the other guy. "Then sedate her."

Straps held my wrists in place and I couldn't move. I was breathing in shallow pants now, my gaze swiveling frantically from one man to the other.

"Blane!" Where was he? He said he'd come for me, protect me. "Blane!"

The men ignored me, one of them snapping on latex gloves before picking up a syringe. I couldn't look away from the needle as I watched him turn toward me and reach for my arm. Terror clogged my throat.

I screamed.

"What the hell are you doing to her?"

Both men turned and I saw Blane standing in the doorway, his face livid.

"Blane!" I gasped, tears leaking from my eyes.

"She's hysterical. I was about to sedate her," the man with the syringe said. "Can you calm her down?"

Blane didn't bother answering, his attention now focused on me as he took the man's place at my side.

"Calm down, Kat," he said gently, unfastening the bonds holding me. "Everything's okay. You're safe. I promise you."

His gray eyes held mine captive.

"Just breathe," he said. "Slow down. Take a deep breath."

Blane's hand was warm and strong around mine. I focused on him. The restraints were gone and I could breathe again. I realized I was shaking uncontrollably and my skin was clammy with a cold sweat.

As awareness of where I was and what had happened came to me, I wanted to crawl under the gurney in embarrassment. I couldn't believe I'd just freaked out so badly over a stupid ambulance.

"Oh my God." I breathed, covering my face with my hands. I wanted to cry. "What is wrong with me?"

"Is she calm?" the EMT standing outside asked.

"Yeah, he's got it," the other replied. "I think we're good to go."

The doors slammed shut and a moment later the engine started.

"Ma'am, I need to check your vitals. Can I have your arm please?"

I nodded, moving my arm so he could grasp it. I avoided looking at him. I could feel my face burning.

"I'm so sorry," I managed. "I don't know why I did that."

"That's okay," he said easily, adjusting a blood pressure cuff on me. "People get panic attacks sometimes. And you did just get hit by a car, so it's perfectly understandable."

"Is that what it was? A panic attack?" I asked, feeling slightly better.

"No."

Blane's curt reply had me glancing at him. I noticed he still held my hand, but I couldn't make myself let go. Not yet.

"You had a flashback."

~

My ribs were bruised, which was why it hurt so badly to breathe. I also had multiple contusions, a sprained wrist, and a mild concussion.

And judging by what Blane was telling me, possibly post-traumatic stress disorder.

After he explained the symptoms to me, I couldn't disagree with his conclusion, though it did make me feel . . . weak. Blane had been on a battlefield for months at a time, killing people and people trying to kill him. It seemed he had a right to the PTSD he'd experienced. I'd been taken and held against my will for just a week, most of which I couldn't remember. It seemed pathetic that I was so mentally fragile that I would have PTSD from that.

After giving me a prescription for pain medication, they let me out of the hospital.

"Where are the admittance papers?" I asked Blane as he helped me get to my feet from the hospital bed.

"I filled them out for you," he said.

I heaved a mental sigh. Another hospital bill, only no health insurance this time, plus the ambulance ride, X-rays, an MRI—the list was endless—I was sure I'd be paying on this for a long while.

Thank you, William Gage.

"He seems persistent, doesn't he?" I said, having no choice but to lean on Blane as we left the hospital. I didn't need to specify who I was talking about.

"It would seem so," Blane said, his voice flat. He flagged down a taxi and helped me inside, following me in before giving the driver my address.

"Wait, what about my car?" I asked. It was still in the grocery store parking lot.

"I called Gerard a while ago," Blane said. "He came by to get your keys while they were taking x-rays and drove it back to your apartment."

I sighed. I missed Gerard. It would have been nice to say hello to him.

We'd been at the hospital for hours and now it was mid-afternoon. My whole Sunday shot to hell, and I had class in the morning and homework to do tonight.

After taking more time than usual managing the stairs to my apartment even with Blane's help, I was glad to sink down onto my couch. Tigger immediately jumped in my lap.

"Are you hungry?" Blane asked.

I glanced up at him. "I can take care of myself. I'll be fine." I absently trailed my fingers through Tigger's fur. He purred, kneading my thigh with his clawless paws.

Anger flared in Blane's eyes, but his voice was calm and controlled when he spoke. "I'm not saying you can't, but I'm the reason for this and I want to keep you safe. Please let me."

I decided to be brutally honest, with both him and myself. "Blane, I can't do this," I said baldly. "I can't . . . be around you right now. We're not friends, and while you may be able to compartmentalize us into the friend zone, I can't."

I hated having to make myself so vulnerable in front of him, with my weakness on full display, but I had nothing left to hide behind.

Blane was a master at concealing his thoughts and emotions, but a flicker of pain crossed his face and was gone. He glanced down at the packet the hospital had given me. I'd set it on the coffee table and now he picked up a couple of papers from the stack.

"They gave you some prescriptions," he said. "I'll go get them filled and grab something for dinner. Here, you take this." He removed his gun from its holster and handed it to me. "Just in case. I'll be back shortly."

I thought about reminding Blane that I already owned a gun, but that would also remind him that Kade had been the one to buy it for me, so I kept my mouth shut and gave a quick nod. I had to look away from his penetrating eyes that saw too much. He hadn't said if he'd stay or leave when he got back, but at least I'd gotten a short reprieve. Moments later he'd gone, locking the door behind him on the way out.

Carefully getting off the couch, I grabbed fresh clothes and went to shower. The apartment was stifling and I still had grit on me from hitting the asphalt. Blane hadn't returned by the time I came out. I settled back on the couch, careful to sit on the blanket. I'd dressed casually again in a cami and knit shorts, though my bruised ribs had me skipping a bra. I was glad I'd done laundry yesterday.

A knock on the door had me sitting bolt upright, with fear slashing through my veins before I could even think. I took a deep breath. It was probably Blane. After all, it's not like a killer politely knocks on your door before shooting you, right?

Blane's gun was in my hand as I peered carefully through the peephole. Surprise and happiness flooded through me when I saw who it was, and I hurriedly threw open the door, a broad smile on my face.

Kade looked me over from head to toe, his eyes lingering on my breasts and short-shorts before his piercing blue gaze met mine.

"I fucking *love* summer."

CHAPTER THREE

I launched myself at Kade without a second thought to the pain that doing so produced in my ribcage. His arms encircled my waist and he lifted me off my feet. I hugged him tightly, my excitement and joy at seeing him felt like a dam had burst inside.

We stood there like that for a long moment, my arms wrapped around his neck as I breathed in his scent, savoring the feel of him after months of his absence. Which reminded me . . .

"Where the hell have you been?" I asked, pulling back. Kade loosened his grip as well and my bare feet touched the floor.

"Is that any way to greet me?" he retorted, following me inside my apartment. "You leave a bloodcurdling scream on my voice mail and don't answer your phone when I call you back, which meant I was worrying what kind of shit you'd gotten yourself into the whole way here." He flopped down beside me on the couch. "And you owe me for a speeding ticket," he finished. He frowned, glancing around the apartment. "It's fucking hot in here," he complained. "Your air broke?"

"My air is expensive."

"Screw that shit," Kade said, getting back up. He started closing the windows. "I don't look good in sweat stains."

I watched him close all the windows, then turn on the air-conditioning. I couldn't help smiling. God, it was so good to have him here again. If he wanted the air on, I didn't have it in me to stop him. And he probably was warm in his jeans and black T-shirt, though I doubted Kade could look bad in anything, sweat stains or not. His black hair was thick and a bit longer than when I'd last seen him, a lock falling over his brow when he returned to the seat beside me. I resisted the impulse to push the strands back. He fixed me with his gaze.

"So you want to explain the phone call now?" he asked.

My smile faded. Oh yeah. The phone call.

"And what's with the road rash?"

He was looking at the scrapes on my elbow and the underside of my arm from when I'd hit the concrete.

"I kinda got hit by a car," I said, my voice small.

Kade just looked at me. "Well, that's new. How the fuck did you get hit by a car?"

"William Gage is out of prison," I explained. "Blane thinks—"

"Blane?" Kade stiffened at the mention of Blane's name, his expression turning cold. "That didn't take long. So you and him are back together?"

I shook my head and gave a bitter laugh. "No way. Not after—" I stopped, suddenly acutely uncomfortable. Did Kade even know why Blane and I had broken up? "Just . . . no," I finished, unwilling to go into detail about how Blane had accused me of sleeping with Kade. I could feel my face get hot. "But I guess Gage is set on making me pay for helping send him to jail. He sent a shooter to the bar last night and a car today. I got lucky both times."

Kade's eyes glittered with an unnamed emotion, his lips twisting into the one-sided smirk I knew all too well. "So I see you're still a shitload of trouble."

I grinned at what might be considered an unusual term of endearment. "Why be boring?"

"So you just have the scrapes then?" he asked, sliding closer to me and inspecting my arm.

"Bruised ribs, sprained wrist," I said. "No permanent damage."

"On the outside," Kade said quietly, his eyes meeting mine. "How are you otherwise? Still pulling guns on anyone who surprises you?"

I stiffened at the reminder, my smile fading. I remembered what Blane had said about PTSD and hesitated. "I . . . have trouble sleeping," I said, looking away from him. "I had a flashback today when they had me strapped down in the ambulance. It was so strange. One second I was there and the next I was back in that shack . . ." I couldn't finish. Clearing my throat, I said, "I don't feel . . . normal anymore. It's like something inside is frozen. Like I'm waiting."

"Waiting for what?"

I lifted my eyes to his and shrugged. "I don't know."

"Have you talked to anyone about this?" he asked.

"I am now." And at the moment, I couldn't imagine having this conversation with anyone else. There was no one right now who I trusted to be this vulnerable with, who understood anything about what I was going through.

Except Kade.

A moment passed, then another. Kade slotted our fingers together, his hand closing over mine.

The door suddenly swung open and Blane walked in, carrying a paper bag. He stopped short, taking in Kade and me sitting together on the couch.

Kade was on his feet immediately, his stance protectively shielding me.

If I'd thought the heat in my apartment had made it hard to breathe, that was nothing compared to how it felt now.

"Long time no see, brother," Kade said, but his voice held no warmth, only warning.

"I didn't know you were in town," Blane replied, the hint of a question in his careful tone.

"Did my secretary forget to e-mail you my schedule? So sorry about that."

Kade's sneering flippancy made me wince. I should do something to help fix this. I was the problem between them. I got to my feet and stepped to the side of Kade so I could see Blane.

"I called him," I said bluntly, thinking fast. "Because of . . . Gage. Thought he might be able to help." No need for either of them to know I'd called Kade because I'd wanted to get rid of Blane.

"She says Gage is trying to kill her," Kade said. "Is this true?"

"I don't have any proof, but yeah," Blane said.

"And you're the one who's supposed to be protecting her?" Kade said dubiously. "Which is why she got hit by a fucking car, right?"

Blane's jaw locked tight at that and I flinched. He didn't reply.

"You know," Kade continued, taking a couple of steps toward Blane, "it seems to me that she might be safer with you not around. Seeing as how you're doing such a bang-up job and all." His thin-lipped smile would have made an alligator seem friendly by comparison.

I wanted to cry at how Kade was talking to Blane, his voice full of anger and contempt. I'd never heard him speak to Blane like that. He'd always been . . . not exactly deferential, but even his ingrained sarcasm had been tempered out of respect for Blane.

"It wasn't his fault," I interrupted, resting my hand on Kade's arm. "He told me. I ran off without thinking, which was stupid. Blane's not to blame."

Both men were looking at me now and I swallowed, shifting my weight nervously. Blane's gaze moved from mine to where I was touching Kade. I dropped my hand.

"I got your medicine," Blane said, ignoring Kade and setting a bag down on the table. "And something for you to eat. Kung pao. Your favorite."

"Thanks." I didn't know what else to say.

"Someone has to stay with you," he said. "It's not safe for you to be alone right now."

The already thick tension in the room increased tenfold at Blane's pronouncement. I couldn't imagine Blane staying here with me. I couldn't handle that.

"You're not staying," I said firmly. "I understand that you want to help, but that's just not going to happen."

"Kat, this is serious. He's already tried twice in as many days. God knows who he hired. He knows more criminals than any defense lawyer in town, and that's saying something."

"She said no." Kade's voice was silk-covered steel.

Blane's attention turned to Kade. "You're going to stay? Watch out for her?"

Kade gave a careless shrug. "If she wants me to. I don't treat her like a misbehaving toddler, unlike some people. It's her decision as to whether she wants protection." He raised a wickedly arched brow. "Unless you think we'll be too busy fucking?"

That statement went off with the force of a bomb and I drew a sharp breath, sure that they were going to attack each other, but Blane didn't take the bait.

"I was wrong," Blane said quietly. "I was wrong to not trust you and wrong to not trust Kathleen. And I've paid for that mistake in more ways than you could possibly imagine."

"Well, maybe you've paid enough for you, but I don't know if you've paid enough for her." This time there was no mistaking the cold menace in Kade's tone.

Blane's gaze drifted from Kade to me. "I'll go," he said. "Just please. Be careful."

My heart broke inside at the pain in Blane's voice and the haunted agony in his eyes.

Neither Kade nor I said anything as Blane left, the door closing behind him.

Kade glanced at me. "Well, *that* was awkward."

The unexpected remark broke the tension, making me give a little laugh in spite of the pain Blane had left in his wake.

Kade dug into the paper bag. "Chinese food. Just what the doctor ordered." He pulled out a prescription bottle. "And exactly what the doctor ordered."

My stomach growled as the aroma of kung pao filled the room. It looked like Blane had gotten enough for two people, which gave me a moment's pause. Had he thought we'd sit here and eat dinner like we used to? Yeah, that wouldn't have been uncomfortable or anything.

"You on a diet or something?" Kade asked as we sat down to eat.

"No, why?" I shoveled a forkful in my mouth.

He eyed me while he chewed. "You look like a stiff wind could blow you away," he said bluntly.

I shrugged, my cheeks heating. "Haven't been hungry lately, that's all." But that didn't seem to be the case now. I ate as though the food was trying to run away.

"Ah, the breakup diet," Kade said, watching me plow through the kung pao. "Let me guess, more vodka than food in your freezer, right?"

I swiped a napkin across my lips, avoiding his eyes. "Maybe," I mumbled. A thought occurred to me. "If you and Blane aren't speaking, then how'd you know we broke up?"

"Oh, we had a lovely heart-to-heart a few months ago," he said with a smirk. "I believe I told him what a fucking moron he was and he accused me of sleeping with you."

Now *this* was awkward.

Suddenly my appetite was gone and I tossed down my fork. "I tried to tell him, but he wouldn't listen," I said. "Blane said . . . awful things . . ." My eyes saw nothing as my mind replayed that horrible scene in Blane's office. I shuddered, pushing the memories away. "And that was it. I haven't seen him since. At least, not until last night."

"So this is my fault," Kade said.

I couldn't decipher the look on his face. "No, it's not," I said firmly. "I told Blane the truth and he chose not to believe me. If he can't trust me about something that serious, then he doesn't love me. Maybe he never really did."

And that was the first time I'd voiced that fear aloud. It had swum darkly in my mind for weeks and I'd been afraid to face it. Doing so now, uttering those words, felt freeing in a way. I could handle it. I didn't fall apart at the thought that Blane had never really loved me.

"I don't know if that's true—" Kade said, skeptical.

"It doesn't matter, does it?" I broke in, interrupting whatever he was going to say. I didn't want to hear anyone defend Blane, not even Kade. "What's done is done and there's no turning back."

"Princess, listen to me," he said, reaching over and lightly grasping my tightly fisted hand. "People make mistakes. Trust me. I'm the king of fucking up. But I don't believe that Blane never loved you, and I'm willing to bet he still does."

Anger flashed through me and I jerked my hand away. "If he loves me so damn much," I spit out, "then why did it take him three months and someone trying to kill me for him to come talk to me? Apologize?"

Kade put his hands up in a gesture of surrender. "Hey, I don't know why he does what he does. I'm just saying. Don't get your panties in a twist."

I was immediately embarrassed about lashing out at him. "I'm sorry," I said, pushing my fingers through my hair. "I'm not mad at you. I shouldn't have said that."

"Hey, no apology necessary. Give me your worst. I can take it." His telltale smirk was back.

I thought about asking Kade why he'd chosen to be absent all this time, too, but decided against it. I didn't want to bring up that painful argument we'd had the last time I'd seen him. It was too nice having him here, his easy company making me forget the gnawing anxiety in the pit of my stomach.

"Let's get out of here," Kade said abruptly. "Go see a movie, do something."

I hadn't seen a movie in months. That actually sounded pretty good. Normal.

"Okay," I said with a smile. "Let me grab my shoes." I set our plates in the sink and slid my feet into flip-flops.

"Princess, as much as I enjoy the view, I'd appreciate not having to beat the shit out of someone tonight." Kade's long-suffering drawl had me glancing at him in confusion. He pointedly looked at my chest. I looked down.

Oh.

My cami with no bra left little to the imagination. I hadn't even thought about it and now I was embarrassed. I had the kind of breasts that made my going without a bra extremely noticeable, not to mention tacky, but the thought of putting one on over my bruised ribs had me thinking twice.

"I'll just throw a shirt on over this," I said.

"Ribs hurt?"

I nodded.

"Let me see."

That had my alarm bells jangling, but I didn't resist when he lifted my shirt on my injured right side and raised my arm. I held the fabric to cover my breasts while he inspected the bruises that I knew would look worse in the morning.

"That has to hurt like a sonofabitch," he observed. His fingers gently touched me, brushing over my abused skin.

I couldn't answer. His nearness and his touch made my breath freeze in my lungs. I watched him, but his eyes were fixed on my injury, his dark brows drawn together in concern. I waited for him to make some sexual innuendo as usual, but he surprised me.

"You're lucky you didn't do more than bruise them," he said, dropping his hand and moving away. "You don't have any padding. Your ribs are right under the skin. And trust me, a fractured rib is a total bitch."

My breath finally came back and I dropped my shirt, giving him a wan smile. I was absurdly disappointed, which made no sense at all.

After I'd shrugged into a short-sleeved button-down shirt that I left unbuttoned, I followed him out the door. The shirt sufficed for modesty's sake.

Kade opened the door of his Mercedes for me. "You got a new car," I observed, sliding into the leather seat. Of course, the car was black. I doubted he'd ever buy a different color. It just . . . suited him.

"Got sick of the old one," he said before shutting the door and rounding the car to get in the driver's seat. It even had one of those new ignitions that you start by just pushing a button instead of turning a key.

Kade's two-door Mercedes coupe had seats that blew honest-to-goodness cold air on your ass. The interior was amazing, a little *Mercedes-Benz* etched into each windowsill lighting up when Kade opened either door. The engine was a gentle purr as Kade drove and I would've bet my next paycheck that the car had cost six figures.

Even if I didn't have money, it was nice to be with a man who did.

"So where's the Lexus?" he asked as we headed toward downtown.

I'd been dreading this. "I'm really sorry," I said, "but I had to sell it." Kade had bought me that car and it had hurt to let it go, but sometimes life necessitated doing things you didn't really want to do.

"Why?"

I couldn't tell whether he was mad—Kade was infuriatingly difficult to read—and I really didn't want to tell him why. But I wasn't going to lie, either.

"I-I just . . . had to," I stammered, looking away from him. "It was kind of expensive, you know? And I needed the money, so . . ." I shrugged, hoping he'd fill in the blanks.

"So you sold the car and used the money to go back to school?"

"Yeah." I looked over at him. "Thank you, by the way. I hated selling it, but it helped pay my tuition." Something occurred to me then. "How did you know I'd gone back to school?"

Kade's reply came easily. "Saw the books in your apartment."

Oh. Well, that made sense.

It was the height of the summer season, so we had our pick of movies. The latest superhero flick was my choice and Kade bought the tickets. I offered to pay for mine, but he just shot me a look, so I shut up. Movie tickets were expensive, so I wasn't all that bothered when he paid.

"I need popcorn," he said once we were inside. He headed for the concession stand and I followed in his wake.

"We just ate!"

"You can't watch a movie without popcorn. It's a rule."

"Whose rule?"

"Mine."

I laughed and stood next to him as he ordered a jumbo popcorn (extra butter), two Pepsis, and two boxes of candy. I had to bite my tongue so I wouldn't protest the cost. Good lord, it was more expensive than if we'd gone to a sit-down restaurant somewhere. On the rare occasion I went to the movies, I smuggled my snack and Pepsi in my purse. It had been years since I'd splurged on honest-to-God movie theater popcorn.

So if you went to the movies with a man and he paid, did that make it a date?

The errant thought flitted through my mind and I hurriedly shoved it away. How ridiculous. Kade Dennon wasn't the kind of man who went on dates. He was the kind of man who walked into a place, crooked his finger, and a dozen women came running, hoping for a chance to be in his bed. Dates were unnecessary.

Besides, he was . . . Kade, a drop-dead (sometimes literally) gorgeous man who had danger and sex oozing from his pores. He killed people for a living and enjoyed doing so. And when he wasn't hunting someone, he was hacking into something, usually highly secure, which was coincidentally, highly illegal.

He could definitely do better than me, just a bartender from Rushville, Indiana.

Kade made us sit in the very top row and stuck me in the corner seat.

"Why are we sitting way up here?" I groused. I liked to sit somewhere in the middle and close to the front.

Kade rolled his eyes as he sat, one ankle resting on the opposite knee. "Have I taught you nothing? Like I want someone sticking a knife in my back. Or yours."

Oh. I hadn't thought of that. I sighed, suddenly tired. I'd briefly forgotten that Gage was trying to kill me.

"Here, you hold this," Kade said, handing me the popcorn. He dipped his fingers in the bucket and extracted a handful, munching on it as his eyes scanned the theater.

I realized he wanted his hands free in case something should happen. Kade wasn't wearing his holster—the theater prohibited weapons—but I knew he had a gun on him somewhere as well as a knife that made me shudder to remember the last time I'd seen him use it.

Kade had killed a man in cold blood because he'd hurt me, threatened to kill me.

It wasn't something a girl forgot.

The movie was decent and I lost myself in it for a couple of hours. I had the feeling Kade only half paid attention, but that was fine. To my surprise, by the time the movie was over I'd eaten my box of candy and made a pretty big dent in the popcorn, too, though Kade hadn't eaten much more than a few handfuls.

It didn't escape my notice that Kade was trying to get me to eat. His carefully hidden concern was sweet, though he'd probably make me walk back to my apartment if I said so.

"That movie sucked," Kade said as we sauntered back to his car.

It was late, the heat of the day finally fading with the onset of night. The moon was full, dispersing the darkness with its silvery wash of light.

"I liked it," I said, somewhat surprised that he hadn't.

"That's because it had a happy ending and the hero got the girl," Kade said, opening the passenger door for me.

"Well, yeah. I like happy endings, so sue me."

Kade's smile held more than a trace of bitterness. "There's no such thing as a happy ending."

He shut the door before I could reply. When he got in his side and started the car, I said, "That's not true. Life is full of happily-ever-afters."

"Name one," Kade said.

I thought. "My parents."

"Both dead."

Ouch. "Well, they were happy before that," I argued. "It is possible and it does happen."

Kade just glanced at me before looking back at the road. "If you say so."

Staring at his profile, faintly lit by the glow from the dash, I began to doubt myself. Maybe he was right. Maybe there really were no happy endings.

I rested my head against the seat, turning my body more fully to face him. I watched him as he drove and if he noticed, he didn't say anything. The darkness gave me courage.

"Why did you leave?" I finally asked, hoping I wouldn't regret the question.

Kade's eyes flicked briefly to mine. "I told you why."

He'd told me he hadn't wanted to stay and watch me marry Blane, that it would be a huge mistake for me to do so.

"That doesn't explain why you didn't come back," I persisted. "Even after . . ." My voice faltered. "After Blane and I had broken up" was what I left unsaid.

Kade was silent, his only reaction the tightening of his grip on the steering wheel.

I cleared my throat and ventured out onto that shaky limb again. "I could have really used a friend."

Kade still didn't reply and I didn't have the courage to say anything more. An awkward silence descended.

After a few minutes, we pulled into my lot and he turned off the car. He shifted to face me and suddenly the inside of the car felt much smaller. The air between us was heavy, pressing on my chest. I wondered if I'd said too much, had again made myself stupidly vulnerable to a man who had the power to hurt me.

"Don't depend on me, princess," Kade finally said. "I'll disappoint you every time."

He went to get out of the car but my hand flashed out and grabbed a fistful of his shirt, stopping him. The look he gave me had me rethinking that move, but I swallowed hard and gamely held on.

"Stop saying things like that," I said. "You've been a friend to me, saved me, more times than I can count. I hate it when you talk about yourself that way."

"I'm not the hero, princess," he said roughly. "Hell, I'm not even the good guy. Don't try to pretend I'm something

I'm not." He untangled my fingers from his shirt and got out of the car.

I was out, too, by the time he rounded the car to my side.

"So am I staying or going?" he asked.

Apparently our conversation was over and Kade wasn't going to tell me why he hadn't come back.

That hurt.

I'd thought, perhaps irrationally given his absence, that Kade would be there for me when the chips were down, that we were really friends. But now he wouldn't even say why he'd come back only when I'd asked him to. Would he have ever stepped back into my life if I hadn't made that phone call?

Had I done it again? Did I care more about Kade than he did about me? I remembered how Kade had helped Blane when he'd gotten back from deployment.

"Made me go out, do things. Normal things. Go to a baseball game, see a movie, have dinner. He didn't pity me and he didn't baby me," Blane had said.

I suddenly wondered if that was what going out tonight had been about. And here I'd been hoping Kade had just wanted to spend time with me. What had I thought? That he'd come back because he'd missed me? What a pathetic idiot I was. Foolish, foolish Kathleen.

The thought had me slipping back inside my armor. I wished I hadn't let my guard down so much with him. It seemed I was doomed to allow men to keep hurting me.

"No, I'm fine," I said stiffly, wishing I had pockets so I'd have something to do with my hands. I felt awkward now, anxious to go inside.

Kade tried to catch my eye, but I glanced away. My earlier good mood had plummeted.

"Still have your gun?" he asked.

"Yeah."

"Okay, well, I'm gonna bug out then," he said. For the first time this evening, he seemed awkward, shoving his hands into his pockets and looking away from me.

"You're leaving again?" I couldn't stop from blurting out the question. My insides froze in dismay to think of him leaving again so soon.

He shook his head. "Nah. Got a new place. It's . . . not far from here."

I nodded wordlessly, relieved.

"I'll probably leave in a day or two," he said. "I have some business to take care of."

My stomach was in a hard knot again and I didn't speak.

"I'll stop by first, say good-bye."

I cleared my throat. "Um, yeah. But, I know you're busy, so, you know, if you don't get to it . . ."

If he didn't "get to it"—what? It was fine? Okay? I wouldn't care if I didn't see him? My throat closed up again.

"You should . . . ah . . . call Blane," he said out of the blue.

"What?" I was sure I'd misheard.

"You guys should talk, patch things up." He still wouldn't look at me as he said this.

"Isn't that the pot calling the kettle black?" I said. "You didn't seem like you were in any mood to 'patch things up' with him earlier."

Kade looked at me now. "I'm still pissed."

"So am I."

His lips twisted at my sharp retort.

After an awkward moment, I said, "So, I guess I'll see you when I see you."

"Guess so." Kade's face was unreadable.

"Thanks for the movie." I walked past him, noticing his hands were clenched in fists, but he made no move to stop me and said nothing more.

My steps were slow as I climbed the stairs to my apartment. When I reached my door, I glanced back at where Kade still stood in the parking lot, watching me. The sight of him reminded me too vividly of how he'd looked in Denver after he'd stuck me in a taxi bound for the airport.

I couldn't take seeing him get in his car and leave, so I hurried into my apartment. It was blessedly cool inside for a change, but I knew I needed to turn the air off. Mechanically, I went from window to window, opening each one wide. A slight breeze wafted in, which was nice, but it still got warm fast.

I brushed my teeth and washed my face before climbing into bed. I didn't bother changing, it was too hot to wear much, so I just shucked my shorts and the shirt I'd thrown on over my cami and lay on top of the sheets. I glanced at the bureau across the room. All my textbooks were stacked neatly on it. None of them had been in the kitchen or living room where Kade might have noticed them.

Huh.

As I lay there, I realized it was the first day in a long time that I hadn't had a drink. I decided that was a Good Thing. I was even mildly concerned about Gage and the threat he posed. At least, enough to make sure Blane's gun was fully loaded and within easy reach on my bedside table.

Which didn't help me at all when I was jerked awake sometime later by someone's hand covering my mouth.

My eyes flew open and I saw a man standing over me. I screamed, but the sound was muffled under his hand. I struggled, trying to pry his hand off me, only to freeze when he leveled a gun to my forehead.

"Don't make a sound," he said. "Scream and you're dead. Understand?"

I nodded ever so slightly, my eyes glued to the gun.

He slowly removed his hand and I took a deep breath, my brain working frantically.

"Now here's what's going to happen," he said. "You're going to slowly stand up . . ."

He moved back and I did as he said. My gaze flicked to my bedside table. The gun was gone.

"Now walk into the living room."

I could feel the gun pointed at my back as I walked. My hands were clammy with sweat and my heart raced.

"Who are you?" I asked.

"Doesn't matter."

"Are you going to kill me?" I'd reached the living room and saw the door to my apartment standing slightly ajar. He must have jimmied the lock and broken in.

The man grasped my arm, turning me back around in front of the couch.

"No. You're going to kill yourself." He motioned with the gun. "Sit."

My knees gave way and I sat heavily. Sweat trickled down between my breasts. The moonlight filtered through the open windows.

"I'm not going to kill myself," I said.

"Of course you are. I get a bonus if you do."

I could see the man more clearly now and he wasn't much to look at, though it was clear that meeting him in a dark alley would be inadvisable. Medium build with dark hair, his grip on the gun was steady and sure. I was willing to bet this wasn't his first time at murder.

"I could give a shit if you get a bonus," I gritted out, anger beginning to burn away the fear. How dare this bastard invade my home? "Tell Gage to go fuck himself."

"Now is that any way for a lady to talk?" he mocked. "But dressed like that, I'm guessing you ain't no lady. I'd give you a test drive myself, but the things they can do with DNA nowadays . . ." He shook his head forlornly, as though lamenting that he couldn't rape me before killing me.

"You should leave before I kill you," I threatened. Rage was making me tremble.

He laughed. "That's a good one. What you're really going to do is take this gun"—he held up my gun—"put the barrel inside your mouth, and pull the trigger."

"You'd have a better chance of getting me to suck your dick," I spat.

"Okay, let's try this," he said. "I suppose you know your friend—what's her name, Alisha? Well, she got home a little while ago, romantic weekend getaway, you know. They must have had a real nice time, too, because she let him sleep over tonight."

My blood ran cold at his words.

"So you either do as I say," he continued, "or I'm going to go over there and put a bullet in both their heads."

I swallowed. "How do I know you won't do that anyway?"

He shrugged. "Because I said so. It's messy, it'll make noise and attract attention, and I'm only getting paid for you, sweetheart."

I didn't see any way out of this. I couldn't let him go kill Alisha and Lewis. And I'd sent away both men who could have protected me, so no one was coming to the rescue.

In retrospect, probably not the best decision I'd ever made.

"Don't worry," he said. "It'll be quick and painless. You won't even know what hit you."

Gee, thanks, now I felt all better.

He holstered his gun and racked the slide on mine. Standing in front of me, he reached for my arm—

Tigger suddenly jumped up on the couch, startling both the guy and me. I used the split second of distraction to slam my arm into his, knocking the gun away. He fired reflexively, the bullet embedding itself in the couch.

I threw myself at him and we both went down. The gun flew from his hand and I fought dirty, shoving my knee into his groin and pressing my forearm against his throat. He grunted in pain, but his hand found my hair and yanked, forcing my head back. I lost my leverage and he threw me off. His fist crashed into my side and I screamed in pain from the agonizing blow against my bruised ribs.

He scrabbled to get on top of me, but I rolled, throwing my elbow out and catching him in the face. My gun was just a few inches away and I reached for it. He grabbed my waist, pulling me backward—

Then suddenly I was free. He was off me.

I leapt for my gun, grabbing it and rolling onto my back in one quick movement, then froze.

Blane had the man in a headlock and was squeezing his neck, slowly suffocating him. The man struggled, but he was no match for Blane. A few moments later, his body went lax and his eyes rolled back in his head. Blane dropped his body to the floor and stepped over it. He crouched down next to me.

"Kat, are you all right?"

I couldn't answer, so I just gave a jerky nod.

He reached out and carefully took the gun from my grip, ejecting the chambered round before setting it aside. He took me in his arms and pulled me onto his lap. I curled into him, my hands fisting his shirt.

I was shaking like a leaf, the fear and adrenaline leaving me an exhausted mess. It felt so good to be in Blane's arms again, which was a bizarre thought, considering the circumstances. I inhaled, the familiar scent of him comforting in ways I didn't examine too closely.

"Did he hurt you?" Blane asked.

"Hit me. Pulled my hair," I said, my voice barely above a whisper.

Blane's hand cupped my head and I felt his lips brush my brow, then he tucked me back into the crook of his neck. I sighed, my eyes slipping shut.

Blane's arms tightened around me. "I can't lose you," he murmured. "Not like this."

I didn't have anything to say to that, so I remained silent.

"Well, this wasn't what I was expecting."

At Kade's voice, my eyes shot open. He stood in the open doorway, gun in hand. His gaze took in the man on the floor and every part of me folded into Blane's lap. If I could have made myself smaller to fit inside Blane's pocket, I probably would have.

"Nine-one-one call on the scanner," Kade said. "Neighbor heard shots. Cops are on their way." His eyes locked on mine. "What happened?"

"He broke in. Told me to kill myself," I said. "Said he'd get a bonus if it looked like a suicide."

"Fuck."

I agreed with Kade's sentiment, as did Blane, judging by the way his muscles contracted around me, holding me even closer. My body felt like liquid against his.

"Why the *fuck* haven't you taken care of this?" Kade exploded, shoving his gun in the back of his jeans.

I started, his anger taking me by surprise. "What—"

"Not you. Him." He jerked his chin toward Blane. "Why is Gage still alive?"

"I don't go running around killing people just because it suits me," Blane ground out.

"So you'd rather that he keep sending people to kill Kathleen?" Kade's furious outrage made me wince. "Are you out of your fucking mind?"

It seemed time to move out of the line of fire between the two of them, so I eased myself off Blane's lap. He stood and helped me to my feet.

"She could be *dead* right now," Kade continued, berating Blane. "But hey, at least you could sleep at night, right?"

Blane had Kade by the throat before I could even blink. He shoved him up against the wall and a framed photo crashed to the floor, its glass shattering.

"Where the fuck were *you*, Kade?" Blane accused. "What, you don't bother protecting her if she's not mine?"

"I didn't think you'd be a fucking moron, *again*, and not take care of it," Kade hissed.

Both of my hands covered my mouth as I watched them argue, and I backed up until I hit a wall. The two men blurred in my vision.

"This is all my fault. This is all my fault," I kept repeating in broken whispers. My knees gave out and I slid down the wall to the floor. I stared at them as both Blane and Kade kept throwing accusations at each other. Kade had gotten free of Blane's hold and it looked like at any moment they were going to come to blows.

But Kade's eyes flicked to mine and he seemed to remember himself, tossing one last accusing look at Blane before crouching next to me. I looked up at him.

"It's not your fault, princess," Kade said gently. "None of this is. Come on, let's get some clothes on you."

He helped me to my feet and I blindly followed him to my bedroom. A few minutes later I had on shorts and a T-shirt over my cami. Kade slipped flip-flops onto my feet and took my hand.

"We're leaving," Kade told Blane once we'd returned to the living room. I couldn't stop looking at the dead guy on the floor, his eyes staring sightlessly at the ceiling.

"Where are you going?"

"Kathleen's coming with me," Kade replied. "Get this shit fixed with Gage, or I'll take care of it myself." The threat underlying his words was obvious.

"Kat . . . ," Blane said.

I tore my gaze from the dead guy.

"Are you sure?" he asked. "Are you going . . . with him?"

I glanced at Kade but couldn't read anything from his face. I couldn't tell if he wanted me to say yes, no, or didn't care one way or the other.

But I could feel his hand in mine, and it was warm and strong.

"Yeah."

And that was the last thing I said to Blane before walking out the door with Kade.

CHAPTER FOUR

Kade led me to his car and I slid into the passenger seat when he opened the door. My mind was a blank, processing only the physical necessities of putting one foot in front of the other and breathing in and out.

Coincidentally, that hurt like a sonofabitch.

It was the middle of the night and I had no clue where Kade was taking me, not that I cared. If not for Blane, I'd be dead. He'd saved me. Again.

That rankled.

I was grateful for Blane's extremely timely intervention. But it bothered me that I hadn't been able to save myself. I'd almost gotten to my gun, but what was it my dad used to say? Oh yeah.

Almost only counts in horseshoes and hand grenades.

It was just a few minutes later when Kade stopped the car in a parking garage.

"Where are we?" I asked, looking around.

"My place."

Well. That explained how he'd gotten to my apartment so quickly in the middle of the night. He couldn't live but five miles away. Of course, those five miles traversed the gap between the bad side of town and the nice side.

I got out of the car before he could open the door for me, anxious to show that I was all right. Now that I was snapping out of my panic and terror, I was embarrassed at my meltdown back at my apartment.

Kade again linked our fingers together as we walked to an elevator. Once inside, he punched the button for the top floor. A few moments later, he was unlocking the door to his apartment and I followed him in.

The space looked remarkably similar to his last apartment, prior to when it had gotten blown up. Hardwood floors, comfortable though expensive-looking furniture, all in creams, beiges, and warm ivories. Floor-to-ceiling windows took up one wall and I drifted toward them to look outside.

I heard Kade toss his keys on the countertop in the kitchen, then the more careful sound of him depositing his gun. I turned to watch him. He'd crouched down and lifted the cuffs of his jeans, removing a gun from one leg and a knife from the other.

He looked dangerous and raw. He'd gotten dressed in a hurry, it seemed, pulling on a white tank, dark jeans, and black boots. The muscles in his biceps flexed as he moved, the veins in his forearms—made prominent by pumping iron—stood out in stark relief under his skin. His black hair was tousled like he'd just rolled out of bed, which made him look even more appealing.

Kade stood, glancing my way. "You want a drink?" He took a highball glass out from a cabinet and opened his freezer, pulling out a bottle of vodka.

I shook my head. "No, thanks." I was still turning over that new leaf.

He shrugged. "Suit yourself." He poured a shot of the clear fluid and tossed it back in one swallow. He eyed me, one brow raised, and I suddenly realized I was staring. I flushed and looked away.

"How's the ribs?"

"Hurts."

"I bet." He set the glass down and disappeared into the bathroom I'd noticed near the entryway. When he came back, he was carrying something. "Come in here," he said, heading across the living room.

I followed him into an expansive bedroom. A king-size bed took up the center of the space and a leather wingback chair sat by a fireplace in an alcove. The colors were darker in here, the wood of the furniture a deep mahogany.

"Did you decorate this?" I asked.

He snorted. "Right. Please. I hire shit like that."

Of course he did.

"Lie down," he ordered, opening the jar he held. "Pull up your shirt."

My eyebrows shot up. "Excuse me?" I squeaked.

He rolled his eyes. "This will help with the ache," he said, holding up the jar.

Oh.

I slipped off my shoes and climbed up onto the bed. The covers were turned back and the pillows askew. Obviously, Kade liked to use the whole bed when he slept. The cotton sheets were of a thread count I'd never be able to afford, their color a deep coffee.

The pillow smelled of Kade and I had to resist the urge to bury my nose in it, instead turning to lie half on my back, half on my side. Kade raised my right arm above my head and I rested it on the pillow. His movements were impersonal as he pushed the fabric of my shirt up, exposing my abdomen and back.

Kade gave a low whistle as he examined the bruises. "Nice. They're even prettier now."

The gel was ice-cold and I hissed when it touched me, flinching away from him. But his touch was surprisingly gentle as he rubbed the gel into my skin.

We didn't speak, but the silence wasn't uncomfortable— and I watched him, his gaze intent on his task. The slow swipes of his hand relaxed me, the gel turning from cold to warm against my skin.

I wondered why he was doing this, bringing me here, defying Blane to do so. Kade wasn't the type of person to be kind just for the sake of kindness.

"You're being awfully nice to me," I said after a while.

"Don't let that shit get around," he quipped, his gaze flicking to mine, then away.

A smile tugged at my lips. Kade did that a lot, made me smile no matter the circumstances.

The bruising extended down to my hip and Kade pushed the top of my knit shorts lower, his fingers slipping under the cotton.

And abruptly I went from relaxed to . . . something else.

I didn't know what possessed me then. Maybe it was the fact that I was in his bed, or maybe it was the slow heat building inside my skin, or maybe it was just that this was Kade and he was touching me in a soft, slow way that made it seem he wasn't in any hurry to stop. Whatever it was, I found myself reaching for him, my hand and nails trailing a light path from his shoulder, over his biceps, to his forearm.

Kade froze. His piercing blue eyes lifted to mine and I tried to read what he was thinking, but it was impossible.

The moment became heavy and I was acutely aware of his hand, large enough to span the breadth of my side, as it rested just below my breast.

"Don't," he said.

The word was unexpected, as was the stiffly curt way in which it was said.

My face flushed hotly and I yanked my hand back, embarrassed to the marrow of my bones. I wanted to crawl under the covers and hide until he went away.

"I-I'm sorry," I stammered, yanking my shirt down. I couldn't look at him. I moved to sit up, to get off his bed, but he pushed me back down into the pillows. In the blink of an eye, he was on top of me, his knees braced on either side of my thighs and his hands pinning my arms over my head.

"Do you have any idea what it's doing to me, seeing you in my bed?" he hissed.

Kade's anger both frightened and thrilled me. His face was inches away, his eyes boring into mine. I couldn't blink, could barely breathe. I gave a tiny shake of my head.

"I've fantasized about this," he said. "It's taking everything I have not to rip your clothes off and make love to you, injured or not."

His words sent a bolt of heat through me, his body so close to mine that my chest brushed his when I breathed. My gaze dropped to his mouth and I licked my lips, remembering what it had been like when he'd kissed me before. His hold on my wrists tightened almost to the point of pain. My breath came faster and my pulse pounded.

Our eyes locked, the unholy fire burning in his making the blood pound in my veins. "So what's stopping you?"

"I'm not your rebound guy. You want to get back at Blane, use someone else."

Well, that was a douse of cold water if I'd ever felt one.

And just like that, he was up and gone from the room.

I wasn't proud of myself in that moment. As a matter of fact, I felt pretty much like a complete slut. I'd actually made a pass at Kade and been rejected because of my ex-boyfriend.

I groaned and buried my face in the pillow. This all had to be a nightmare and I'd wake up anytime now.

Well, I did wake up, several hours later, but nothing had changed. I was still in Kade's bed. Alone.

I'd been covered with a blanket and the duvet at some point during the night and now I pushed them aside. There was a master bath in the bedroom and I went in there. It was beautiful and luxurious. Knowing I didn't want to face Kade yet, I took a shower, taking an inordinately long time to sniff his shampoo before lathering it into my hair. Searching through the drawers turned up some extra toothbrushes, still in their packaging, so I chose one and brushed my teeth.

I wrapped myself in a towel and used Kade's brush on my hair, carefully cleaning the long strands caught in the bristles once I was finished. When I came out of the bathroom, Kade was sitting on the edge of the bed.

I paused outside the door, and our eyes caught. I felt my face heat as I remembered last night, and I was unsure what to say or do. Maybe he wouldn't talk about it and we could pretend it never happened. I was all for that.

"I brought you some things," he said, motioning to a suitcase sitting a few feet away. "And your purse."

I still didn't know what to say. Exactly how long did Kade plan on me staying with him?

"I'm leaving town," he said. "Thought you might want to come with me. Get you out of Indy for a few days until the mess with Gage is . . . resolved."

I think Kade's version of "resolved" included an obituary, but who was I to complain? It seemed it was going to be either Gage or me, the way things had been going the past couple of days.

So a trip, then. With Kade. "Where?" Not that I particularly cared. Getting away from my life for even a short time sounded heavenly.

Kade's lips twitched in a smirk. "Vegas, baby."

～

I'd never been to Las Vegas before. Well, actually, I hadn't been much of anywhere before. The heat of the Nevada desert took my breath away and I was glad for the AC blowing full blast in the Mercedes that Kade had rented.

I couldn't conceal my excitement as I peered out the window like a kid going to Disneyland for the first time. The ride from the airport to the hotel was barely long enough for me to get a glimpse of the looming hotels and casinos flanking the Strip.

"We'll take the tour later," Kade said as he pulled up to a hotel. I had a glimpse of a huge fountain as we passed by. "It's better at night."

A few days of relaxation sounded too good to be true, and I was grateful Scott had said he'd cover my shifts at The Drop. I'd miss a couple of classes but could get caught up without too much of a problem. Mona had happily agreed to watch Tigger for me, and though the trip was last minute, Kade and I had flown on a private jet borrowed from "a friend" of his.

Barely had Kade stopped the car before my door was being opened by a uniformed valet. Another was getting the luggage from the trunk, and I saw Kade hand his keys and a tip to a third and then pocket a ticket. Kade's hand settled on the small of my back as he guided me inside the hotel.

The moment my eyes adjusted from the brightness outside to the interior, I stopped short, my mouth gaping. The lobby was the most beautiful I'd ever seen, with a huge glass sculpture crafted into the ceiling, every color of the rainbow shown in gorgeous detail.

"Wow," I breathed, feeling precisely like Dorothy dropping from Kansas into Oz.

"You like that, huh?" Kade asked with a smile, hooking his sunglasses in the neck of his shirt.

"It's . . . amazing," I said. There were no words to adequately describe the sculpture, and I kept craning my neck to look up as Kade led us to the registration desk.

Although we didn't have a reservation, that didn't seem to matter once Kade gave his name. The woman behind the desk looked him up in the computer and said, "Welcome back, Mr. Dennon," then handed us a small packet. "Joseph will show you to your room."

Kade thanked her and we followed a uniformed man while another pushed our luggage on a cart behind us.

Joseph had to insert a key card into a slot in the elevator before we could access the correct floor, and a few minutes later he was opening the door to the kind of hotel suite I'd only ever read about.

There was an honest-to-goodness foyer in the hotel room, and I passed by doorways going to a bedroom on my left and another on my right. Kade had gotten us a two-bedroom suite. I filed that information away for later, my attention completely absorbed now in the view out the curved windows stretching the width of the wall in front of me.

I barely noticed as Joseph mentioned amenities to Kade and the valet placed our luggage in the bedrooms, my nose just inches from the glass as I tried to take it all in. A few minutes later I heard the door click shut and realized they were gone.

It occurred to me that rooms like this didn't come cheap. I turned to Kade, who was standing nearby, watching me.

"This has to cost a fortune," I said. "I won't be able to pay you back." Which I knew to be true. There was no way I could afford even my share of a place like this.

"No worries," Kade said with a shrug. "You're my plus-one. Besides, I don't pay for this."

I frowned. "What do you mean?"

"I did a favor for a certain friend a year or so ago. He was very grateful, and he offers accommodations when I'm in town."

"That must have been some favor," I said, wondering how illegal it had been to deserve free, luxurious accommodations. It must be nice to have "friends" like Kade's, I mused.

Kade just smirked at my thinly veiled fishing expedition. "It was."

"So . . . now what?" I asked.

"Now you're going to the spa for a while to relax, then you're going shopping," he said, heading to a nearby table to pick up the phone.

Alarm shot through me. "Kade, I can't afford—"

"Yes, can I get a spa appointment for my guest?"

I listened while Kade made spa and salon appointments for me, and when he hung up the phone I was all up in his business.

"Kade, I can't afford to do any of that and I'm not having you pay for it," I said. Even though it all sounded divine—a massage, facial, mani/pedi, the works—I wasn't about to be anyone's charity case.

Kade barely glanced at me as he fixed two drinks at the wet bar. When he had finished, he walked over and handed me one of them.

"Why not?" he asked, taking a sip of the clear liquid.

"Because," I insisted, "it's just . . . wrong."

"Consider it a belated birthday present."

I gave him a look. His lips twisted and he turned to go sit on the couch, an arm stretched along its back.

"I want to. I can afford it. So enough already." He cocked an eyebrow. "Unless you're ethically opposed to being pampered?"

I rolled my eyes. "Don't be ridiculous."

"Good," he said. "Besides, I wasn't kidding about the plus-one thing. I need you to look your best."

"Why?"

Kade smiled. "This is a business trip, princess. You can help enhance the image. Because in Vegas, image is everything."

He finished his drink and stood. "And get some new clothes. Swimsuits, a dress or two, something for clubbing—whatever you need. Charge it to the room."

I bristled. "What's wrong with my clothes?"

"I didn't bring you any."

And with that, he disappeared into one of the bedrooms. A few minutes later, I heard the shower running.

Sure enough, when I opened my suitcase I found toiletries, lingerie, and my peacock-blue stilettos. That was all. For a man who'd rejected my tentative advance last night, it was an odd assembly of items.

I chose not to analyze that. It was time to leave for the spa, and I couldn't help being excited. So I could either ruin my pleasure at the unexpected luxuries Kade wanted me to have by worrying about the cost, or I could just roll with it.

It took only a moment to decide on the latter.

~

The massage was divine, once I got over the uncomfortably awkward feeling of a complete stranger touching me. Then there was another awkward moment when the woman giving me the massage got an eyeful of the bruises darkening my skin.

"I got hit by a car," I tried to explain, but my voice was muffled by the headrest and I wasn't sure she understood me. She said a few words under her breath and carefully skirted the bruised area. The scent of eucalyptus was heavy in the air, the sounds of the ocean drifted over me, and I nearly fell asleep, I became so relaxed.

After I dressed, the woman brought me some water and I thanked her. She nodded politely and then said, "If you're having problems with your boyfriend, there are places you can go, people who can help you."

It took me a minute to cotton on to what she was implying. "Oh no, it's nothing like that," I said, my face burning as I realized she thought my boyfriend had beat me. "I really did get hit by a car."

Her smile was a little sad and I could tell she didn't believe me. "They never mess up the face, you know," she said. "Certain kind of men. Just where people won't see."

I didn't know what to say, how to convince her, or if it was worth the bother. It made me a little sad, though, to realize she saw enough women with bruises to know that sort of thing.

My mood a little darker, I went next to the salon where I was waxed and buffed and primped to within an inch of my life. Wax was put in places that had never before had it, and after today I was sure I wouldn't want it there again. I tried to argue with the tiny Japanese lady, but she was firm in her mantra: "Must do. Vegas. Bikini. Everyone do."

Speaking of bikini, my eyes nearly bulged from their sockets when a selection of swimwear was presented to me. I'd never in my life owned a swimsuit as daring as the ones I now tried on.

"Mr. Dennon said to come to the pool once you are finished shopping," the lady assisting me said. She'd popped in while I was half-naked, but didn't bat an eye, just held up the top for me.

"Um, okay, thanks."

So Kade was at the pool and I was supposed to "enhance" his image. And spend his money doing it. Okay, how did a woman enhance a man's image while in Vegas? Only one way that I could think of.

"I'll take that one," I said, pointing to a suit I'd previously ruled out.

An hour later I'd set Kade back several thousand dollars and was trying to ignore the niggle of guilt I felt. I'd seen some other women in the spa and salon. I figured I could hold my own with any of them, given enough money to dress the part. Lucky for me, Kade had the money. At least, I hoped he did.

When I walked from the hotel to the pool, I held my head high and pulled my shoulders back. I added a little extra sway in my hips and I could see heads turning as I passed. The sky-high stiletto sandals I wore were held to my feet by a thin strap of leather that snaked between my newly painted toes and then inched up to circle my ankles. I had on oversized mirrored sunglasses and my hair was left in expensively tousled waves down my back. But it was the bikini that seemed to seal the deal.

At least losing my day job had left me time to lay out some this summer, so my tanned skin contrasted nicely against the white bikini. The top was a demi-cup bra that pushed my rather ample assets up and together for the best possible display. Two ties kept it in place around my neck and back. The string bikini bottom was tiny and I was glad now for the Japanese lady's insistence on waxing. I carried a beach bag that held the matching white lace cover-up, a sleeveless dress that came to mid-thigh. I'd had the salon girl smear makeup over my bruises, so they were invisible against my skin.

I spotted Kade from some distance away—it was a big pool—and stiffened. He was sitting on a daybed under an umbrella, which was fine.

It was the topless woman sitting next to him that set my teeth on edge.

Kade didn't appear to be paying her much attention, which mollified me somewhat as I made my way toward him, my heels *click-clack*ing on the concrete. He lazily sipped the drink in his hand as the woman talked to him, her hand moving to rest on his thigh. My grip tightened on my beach bag.

I moved closer and could tell when Kade spotted me. His body went still for a moment. He slid his glasses down his nose to peer over the tops. Even from a distance, it seemed I could feel the touch of his gaze as it raked me from head to toe. His lips moved as he said something to the woman and he didn't even glance her way as she abruptly got to her feet and whirled, marching away in an obvious huff.

She spied me and made right for me. I stopped when she blocked my path.

"I guess you are zee something better," she sneered. Her accent was thick.

"Pardon me?"

"Ee say to 'beat it,'" she huffed. "Zat something better had come along."

My smile was thin lipped, the green monster digging its claws in deep. "He's right."

She cursed fast and fluently in another language. I assumed it was cursing, anyway. I'd heard plenty of cursing in English and thought I could tell when it was being done in another language, especially when I was the target.

I'd had enough by now and interrupted her tirade. "Move along," I said. "We're done here." The steel in my voice shut her up and I stepped around her, dismissing her entirely as I approached Kade.

"This spot taken?" I asked, lifting an eyebrow.

"It is now."

I hid a satisfied smile as I arranged myself on the day-bed. Kade watched me unabashedly as I reclined with a sigh. A beat passed.

"You're staring," I said. "Am I not helping to enhance your image?"

"Well, you've certainly drawn attention," he said dryly.

I tipped my head so I could see him. "Is that a bad thing?"

"No, but how the fuck am I supposed to concentrate with you wearing that?"

His obvious irritation made me laugh outright. "Just trying to do my job, boss," I teased. I was rewarded with a half smile, the corner of his lips tipping upward. I took the chance now that my eyes were hidden behind sunglasses to take him in. He'd obviously been in the pool, as his hair was still damp. Kade wore dark blue swim trunks and had thrown on a thin, white linen shirt. The shirt was unbuttoned, with the cuffs rolled up.

Kade raised a hand and signaled a waiter, who hurried over. "What do you want to drink, princess?" he asked.

"Just water," I said.

The waiter turned to go, but Kade halted him with a word before turning back to me.

"Water? Are you kidding me?"

I hesitated. "I've been . . . trying to watch my carbs."

Kade made a disgusted noise. "Bring the lady a mai tai," he said. After the waiter had departed, Kade said, "Spill it. What's going on?"

I resolutely refused to look at him when I replied. "I've just been drinking a lot lately, that's all. Trying to cut back." Blane's condemnations rang in my ears.

A moment passed. "Well, one mai tai isn't going to knock you on your ass, so I think you're safe. Now on to more important things." He grabbed a brown plastic bottle from the nearby table and handed it to me. "I need sunscreen." His grin was wicked and I couldn't help the small smile tugging at my lips.

"Fine," I said, rearranging so I sat back on my knees. "Turn around and take your shirt off."

"I thought you'd never ask."

Kade's teasing bothered me. After last night, I didn't really want to be reminded of the attraction between us, especially when it seemed nothing was going to come of it. I'd been fighting the draw I felt for Kade for months now and the one moment I'd tentatively made a move, he'd shut me down.

My mood worsened as I spread the sunscreen on his back. His nicely muscled, broad-shouldered, naked back. Even the scars from the abuse he'd endured as a child appealed to me. It had been months since I'd had sex and my libido was throwing a cranky fit.

I finished my task and snapped the lid back on the bottle. "Done," I said curtly, flinging myself back on my side and taking a long gulp of the mai tai the waiter had left for me.

"Your turn," Kade said, waggling his eyebrows suggestively.

I smiled sweetly. "I can do it myself, thanks anyway." My tone was pure bitch, but I didn't care.

Kade's eyebrow lifted, but he made no comment, simply lying back in the bed and folding his arms behind his head. I couldn't tell whether his eyes were open or closed behind the sunglasses.

I took my sweet time applying the sunscreen, some not-so-nice part of me wanting to get back at Kade for his unrelenting sexual teasing. And perhaps I achieved my goal because after a good five minutes or so, Kade snapped, "Are you done yet?"

"Don't want to get burned," I said breezily, swinging my hair to the side so I could apply the lotion to one shoulder. "The sun here is more potent than back home, you know."

Kade muttered a curse and abruptly got up, tossed aside his sunglasses, walked to the pool, and dove in.

I smiled.

The sun was hot, even in the shade of the umbrella, and I was glad for my cold drink. I sighed, perfectly content and relaxed, and feeling better than I had in weeks. I didn't think about Blane. I didn't think about the bills waiting for me. I didn't think about Gage wanting to kill me. I didn't think about anything, and it was wonderful.

"Hi there. May I sit down?"

I opened my eyes to see a very nice-looking man standing next to me. He was holding another mai tai and he offered it to me.

"I thought I might buy you a drink," he said with a smile.

"Thank you," I said, smiling back as I took the drink from him. He sat down next to me.

"I'm Trace," he said. "And you are?"

"Kathleen."

Trace was tall, with a nice build, sandy-brown hair, and deep-chocolate eyes. And he was looking at me as though he'd like to eat me up with a spoon, which I decided wasn't a bad thing. He was also easy to talk to and I found out he was in town on business, that he was from LA but currently lived in Seattle. He was just getting around to asking me to dinner when Kade reappeared.

Trace and I both glanced up at Kade and I sucked in a breath. His face was cold and hard, which I knew signaled dangerous territory on Kade.

"That's my seat," Kade said to Trace in a voice that managed to be calm and yet still reek with menace. "And that's my girl."

I opened my mouth to object to that last part, but Trace had already jumped to his feet.

"Sorry about that, man, she didn't say." Trace shot me an accusing glare before turning and walking away. Kade took his spot and sat back, sliding his sunglasses on again. Water droplets covered his chest and thighs while rivulets ran from his hair, trailing wet paths down his neck.

My jaw was still slack in astonishment at how quickly my potential date had been routed by Kade. Then I went from shocked to supremely pissed off in three seconds flat.

"What the hell, Kade?" I burst out. "He was asking me to dinner and you just scared him off! And for the record, I am *not* your girl. You made that pretty damn clear last night." My fists were clenched tightly in anger and my fingernails dug into my palms. "Besides," I finished snottily, "if you're not going to be my revenge lay, then stop scaring off other candidates."

I knew that last one was a low blow, but that didn't stop me from saying it. A part of me that I used to know was shocked and dismayed at my behavior, how horrible I was being to Kade. But I couldn't stop. It was as if I was daring him to do what Blane had done, reject me and leave me. Maybe him seeing the very worst of me would speed the process along so I wouldn't be so devastated when it finally happened.

Kade stared at me, his face serious, though his eyes were still hidden from view. The tension between us grew during our stare-down until I couldn't take it anymore. I swallowed hard and leaned back in the bed, my eyes stinging behind my sunglasses.

"I think it's fuckin' hot out here," Kade mused.

I jerked my head around. "What?" Where had that come from and what, if anything, did it have to do with what I'd just said? He was talking about the *weather?*

"You need to cool off."

Before I could say anything to that, Kade was up and had lifted me in his arms. I realized what he was going to do a split second before he did it.

"Kade, no—!"

He dropped me unceremoniously into the pool. I came up spluttering and spewing obscenities at him. He just laughed and slid into the water.

"You ruined my hair, asshole!" I cupped my hand and sent a spray of water his way. "And my shoes!" I splashed him again, but he just laughed and turned aside, which infuriated me more. I sprang at him, wanting to dunk him and maybe hold him underwater. Not for long, just maybe a minute . . . or three.

Kade caught me easily, holding my wrists behind my back with one hand and snagging me around the waist with the other.

"Those are four hundred–dollar shoes you just ruined," I snapped, trying to jerk away from him.

"Worth every penny," he retorted.

I managed to get free, then abruptly sank. I flailed my arms, realizing he'd moved us into deeper water where I couldn't touch the bottom. My new sandals made it impossible for me to swim. Kade pulled me up and I clung to his shoulders, coughing.

"Damn you, Kade," I gasped at last, blinking water out of my eyes. His shoulders were slippery from the sunscreen and I tightened my hold.

He took my sunglasses and perched them on top of my head. I was briefly glad the salon had used waterproof mascara on my lashes. Raccoon eyes was not the look I was going for.

"If you think I'm going to let you throw yourself at any man who buys you a drink, you're sadly mistaken," he said.

"What does it matter to you?" I retorted.

"If you want to go all self-destructive, be my guest," Kade said. "You're talking to someone who takes self-destruction to an art form. But I didn't bring you here to watch you implode. You're here on business, so destroy your life on your own time."

"So suddenly sleeping with a guy is self-destructive?" I fumed. "Isn't that a little judgmental, coming from you?"

"Absolutely."

I stared at him, no quick comeback springing to mind, which was always frustrating around quick-witted Kade. No doubt I'd think of something in about ten minutes, but by then it would be too late.

Kade's black hair shone like a raven's wing in the sunlight, the water and my own face reflecting back at me from his sunglasses. I was suddenly acutely aware of our bodies pressed together, my legs drifting next to his. My anger drained away as my pulse quickened. He was hard everywhere. Literally. And I felt an answering ache between my thighs.

Kade turned, moving us to shallower water before lifting me to sit on the side of the pool. I wondered for a moment what he was doing, though it became clear as he lifted an ankle and began undoing the strap that held the sandal in place.

Hormones screaming in frustration, I popped my sunglasses back on and leaned back on my elbows, not bothering to keep my knees together. Two could play this game.

Kade deposited the sandal next to me and went to work on the other.

"How's the ribs?" he asked.

I glanced down. The water had washed off a lot of the makeup, so the lovely black-and-blue marks were back in all their glory. I sighed.

"Looks like the makeup came off," I said. "Now more people are probably going to think you beat me."

"What?" Kade frowned and his hands had stilled on my ankle.

I shrugged. "The massage lady thought my boyfriend hits me. I tried to tell her the truth, but I don't think she bought it. So I made sure they put makeup on the bruises. I didn't really want to look like the battered girlfriend." My tone was wry. I was the battered ex-girlfriend all right, but my wounds weren't visible.

He resumed work on removing my shoe, placing it next to the first. When he was done, he stood between my spread knees, the water lapping at his waist.

"You realize that swimsuit is slightly see-through now," Kade said, his hands resting on the backs of my calves. They slid slowly up to the back of my knees, then back down to my ankles, then repeated their journey. The touch was as maddening as it was intoxicating.

"Is it?" I asked. "I hadn't noticed." Compared to the scraps of fabric some of the barely clad women around me were wearing, even a see-through white swimsuit was tame. I'd seen enough naked boobs today to last me a lifetime.

"I like this." Kade touched the thin gold chain the wardrobe lady had added at the last minute. It circled my neck like a loose collar, with a lone strand extending from the circle down between my breasts to stop at my navel, where it formed another loop that hung low around my hips.

His fingers lightly traced the chain as it lay against my skin, stopping just below my breasts. He tugged the chain and the gold strand pressed lightly into my skin. I obeyed the unspoken command and sat up, the collar suddenly having a different feeling to it than merely being pretty. And judging by the sudden rush of blood in my ears, it wasn't a bad feeling.

I couldn't look away from Kade, and the rest of the people around us seemed to fade away. His hands closed over my hips and he pulled me closer to him. With me perched on the edge of the pool, our height was about the same and for once I could look him directly in the eyes. My legs automatically circled his ribs.

He leaned forward, one hand brushing my hair back as his mouth settled near my ear. My breath caught somewhere in my throat as his lips grazed my skin.

"In a moment, I want you to look over my left shoulder to two o'clock."

His whisper made my eyes jerk open and I would have pulled away, but his grip tightened on my neck, stopping me.

"What are you talking about?" I hissed.

"My target," Kade said. "Do you see him?"

I glanced over where he'd said and sure enough, there was a man inside an open cabana, talking on his cell. He wore drawstring linen pants and a matching button-down shirt, left open at the neck. Two other men were in there with him. As I watched, he lifted his head and looked at me. I closed my eyes and leaned against Kade, running my fingers through his hair.

"I see him," I breathed in Kade's ear. My heart was still pounding, but now for another reason. "Are you going to kill him?" I had to force the words out. Yes, I'd always known what Kade did for a living, it had just never been as real to me as it seemed right now.

Kade pulled back until we were practically nose to nose. "What would you say if I said yes?"

I swallowed. "I'd ask you not to."

"And you think just because it's you who asks me that I'll do it?"

"Why would I have any influence over what you do?" It was a valid question. Trying to persuade Kade upon a course of action was like trying to coax a tiger into obedience. He had a mind of his own.

Kade didn't answer, and after a moment he cocked a half smile.

"He's paying me to hack him, not kill him."

"What do you mean?"

Kade's shoulders lifted in a shrug underneath my hands. "A new business venture I started," he said. "High-level security penetration testing. They hire me to make sure their business is really secure."

I lifted an eyebrow. "Well if he hired you, isn't he going to know what you're here to do?"

"Nope." Kade's smirk reminded me of a smug teenage boy who'd managed to steal a girl's virginity before delivering her back home to her overprotective father. "They don't know who I am or what I look like. They hire me through a representative, then get notified of the test results."

"How?"

"If I make it in, I take double my fee."

"Which is?" Tacky to ask, I know, but I couldn't help it. Curiosity got the better of my manners.

Kade leaned forward and whispered in my ear a number that made my jaw go slack.

"You like me a little more now, princess?" he said.

I drew back sharply. "It's been a while since you implied I was a gold digger," I snapped, hurt.

"What else do I have to offer?"

Kade's bitter reply made me frown and I wished I could see his eyes behind the dark glasses. His hands seemed to be touching me almost without conscious thought, one grasping the back of my neck while the other settled just above the top of my bikini bottom, his thumb brushing my lower back.

"Why would you say something like that?" I asked. "You're a good man, Kade."

"You make me wish that were true."

I opened my mouth to reply, but Kade had discarded his sunglasses and now his mouth was sucking lightly on my neck. My nails dug into his shoulders, his chest brushing against mine and making the blood heat in my veins. My eyes drifted closed at the soft touch of his tongue against my skin.

"Hit me."

My eyes fluttered open again. "What?" Surely I'd misheard him.

"My target. He's been keeping an eye on you. The bruises gave me an idea. So in a moment, slap me as hard as you can." Kade's words spoken in my ear made me swallow hard.

"I don't want to hit you," I said. "I . . . can't."

"You've done it before."

The reminder made me wince.

"Not a whole lotta time, princess," Kade said. "Let's fight. Make it look good. I'll drag you out of here and we'll make a nice big scene."

"I'm not hitting you," I repeated more firmly. I didn't care if it was playacting. I regretted the times I'd struck Kade and wasn't about to do it again.

Kade heaved a long-suffering sigh, his breath warm as it fluttered against me.

"Fine," he said. "Then I promise I'll pay you well if you make this look good and forgive me later."

"What—" The word was cut off on a gasp as Kade's hand fisted in my hair, tugging my head back sharply. It hurt. Not terribly, but it surprised me.

"Now flinch like I'm going to hit you," Kade hissed.

I did what he said, cringing away from him. He pulled again on my hair and I made a noise this time, a little cry of pain. A quick glance over and I saw Kade's target was no longer on his phone and was watching us.

Kade jerked me closer and I whimpered. His lips were at my ear. "Nice job. Is he watching?"

"Yes."

Then Kade was up out of the water and hauling me none too gently to my feet. He'd grabbed his sunglasses and put them back on, and the look of cold fury on his face would have terrified me if I hadn't known this was a setup. As it was, my hands still shook as he dragged me to the daybed to get my things.

"Put some clothes on, unless you want everyone to see you for the fucking whore you are."

Kade's scathing insult was loud enough for everyone nearby to hear, including the man in the cabana.

I dug my cover-up from my bag and jerked it on over my head, pretending I was hurriedly obeying out of fear.

"What the fuck is that? I hate it, and it probably cost me way more money than you're worth."

Kade reached out, grabbing a fistful of the fragile lace and gave a sharp tug. It ripped easily, parting down my front until it hung limply from my shoulders.

I stood in shock. That had cost a lot of money and Kade had just destroyed it. Granted, it wasn't my money, but still.

"I can't believe you just did that!" I exclaimed, anger making my voice shrill.

In a flash, Kade had me by the back of my neck and was in my face.

"Don't think for a second you can talk to me like that and get away with it," he threatened. His hold on me was firm and didn't hurt, but I made noises like it did.

"Everything all right here?"

The voice came from behind and Kade abruptly released me. I turned to see the target had come up to us. No wonder Kade had been laying it on thick.

The man looked me over carefully, his gaze pausing on the bruises decorating my torso, before glancing at Kade.

"Everything's fine," Kade said, his voice smooth and cold.

"I wasn't asking you," he said, turning back to me. "Miss? You all right?"

"She's fine, too," Kade said, and now I could hear danger in his tone. "So fuck off, friend."

Kade took my elbow and steered me back to the hotel. I glanced back once and saw the man staring after us, a frown on his face.

Once we were walking down the hall to our room, I chanced a question.

"How'd you know you'd get his attention that way?" Not every man cared when a woman was being pushed around.

"He has a daughter about your age," Kade replied. "It was a hunch." He unlocked the room and held the door open for me as I passed by him.

"Are you all right?" he asked as the door swung closed.

"Well, you ruined my shoes and my cover-up," I said with a sigh. "If I'd known you were going to do that, I'd have gone to Walmart for them." I could've bought groceries for months on what those things had cost.

Kade tossed his sunglasses on a table and stepped in front of me. "I don't give a shit about the clothes," he said. "I didn't hurt you, did I?"

My stomach twisted at the look of concern on his face and I couldn't answer right away, not that it seemed to matter. He was busy inspecting me himself, circling behind me to lift my hair. I guessed he was checking for marks. His hand brushed the back of my neck and shoulder.

"I wish you wouldn't be so cavalier with the stuff I bought," I said, trying not to think about his hands on me.

"I'll buy you new ones."

"It's not that," I said, turning to face him and forcing him to drop my hair. "It's a waste of money. Your money. And it bothers me."

He frowned. "Why are you so hung up on this?"

"I'm not," I protested, trying to figure out how to put into words the gnawing worry that I felt. "I just know how hard money is to come by and I don't like seeing you waste what you have."

Kade's blue-eyed gaze searched mine. "Until Blane came for me," he finally said, "I was dirt poor. Food was a luxury I never had enough of. Clothes and shoes that actually fit even more so. I get it, okay? I'll take care of it. Trust me."

I gave him a somewhat skeptical look, but the little knot of anxiety in my stomach eased.

"If you're this consumed with money, I'm guessing you've been living pretty close to the bone lately," he observed.

My face grew hot, my embarrassment acute at his perceptiveness. I shrugged and turned away so I wouldn't have to look at him. "It is what it is. It wasn't like I was going to beg Blane for my job back."

"You shouldn't have to beg Blane for anything."

The fierceness of his reply surprised me and I glanced at him.

"I meant what I said at the pool," he continued more calmly. "I'll pay you to work this job with me. You did good out there. We've gotten his interest and you have his sympathy. We'll play up the damsel in distress thing, let you distract him while I break into his room."

"How do we do that?" I asked, somewhat alarmed. Breaking into his room sounded dangerous.

"Let me figure that out," he said. "In the meantime, go shower and get dressed." His mouth lifted in a half smile and he waggled his eyebrows suggestively. "It's time to party, Vegas style."

CHAPTER FIVE

I stared at my reflection, suddenly consumed by second thoughts about the one clubbing outfit I'd purchased. The cost of clothes and shoes had been outlandish, so I'd limited my picks to one clubbing getup, a dress, a couple pairs of shorts, and the bikini.

The jeans I wore were practically painted on, they were so tight, and rested low on my hips. The top I'd bought was a champagne color that sparkled when I moved. It had spaghetti straps with a deep V of folded fabric between my breasts. It was nearly backless, the fabric draping down to my waist, exposing a lot of skin and a lot of cleavage. With my tan, it looked great. Not something I'd wear back home, but perfect for Vegas. I hoped.

I'd blown my hair dry and it lay in waves down my back, my makeup applied with a heavier and more dramatic hand than usual. I'd lightly brushed my skin with a glittery powder so I sparkled a bit, too.

The peep-toe four-inch sling-back heels that matched my top were the final touch.

"I'm as ready as I'll ever be," I muttered to myself, suddenly inexplicably nervous, which was silly. It was a job with Kade, that's all, no matter how much it felt like . . . a date.

I took a deep breath and emerged from my bedroom, and was immediately captivated by the view outside. I drifted to the windows to see more. The sight was amazing, with lights illuminating everything up and down the Strip.

"Beautiful."

I turned around, realizing Kade stood behind me. I hadn't even heard him approach. "I know, isn't it?" I enthused. He just smiled.

"Want a drink?" he asked, walking to the bar and grabbing two glasses.

"Sure." It was nice to have a drink as part of an evening out, rather than as an attempt to help me sleep, to forget, or both.

A moment later, Kade handed me a vodka tonic. I took a drink, covertly eyeing him. He looked . . . *mouthwatering* was the word that immediately came to mind. Expensive black slacks were paired with a black silk shirt that had one more button undone than what most men would have attempted—but most men weren't Kade Dennon. A look that would seem silly on another man looked sexy as sin on Kade.

The skin of his neck and part of his chest was bared by the open V of the shirt and begged to be touched. His square jaw was smooth and freshly shaven. His black hair curled slightly over his collar, a thick lock falling over his forehead. Just looking at him made the breath catch in my chest.

"I picked this up for you," Kade said, handing me a rectangular jewelry box.

My eyes widened at the Tiffany blue. I'd never in my life gotten something from Tiffany's. I glanced up at Kade and our eyes met. I thought I glimpsed just a shade of uncertainty in his gaze.

"Open it," he said, taking another drink.

I slowly pulled on the elaborate white bow tied around the box, trying to prolong the moment. I didn't get gifts very often, and certainly not ones like this.

I gasped when I lifted the lid. A sparkling diamond bracelet lay inside, the diamonds fashioned into four-petal flowers. The bracelet was a silver metal that I fervently hoped was white gold but suspected was platinum.

"Kade, I don't know what to say—" Why would he give me this? The bracelet was obviously very expensive. My chest tightened. Maybe I'd been wrong about the distance he was keeping between us. Maybe he still felt the way he had three months ago.

"You don't have to say anything," Kade replied, taking the bracelet from the box and fastening it on my wrist. "If you're not wearing something outrageously expensive, it'll look suspicious."

I couldn't breathe for a moment, the sharp disappointment I felt robbing me of breath. Then I immediately chastised myself. I'd been engaged to marry Kade's brother mere months ago, had dismissed the feelings Kade had confessed to me, and been angry with him for even feeling that way. Why wouldn't he have moved on? Why was I disappointed that he had?

"You're not going to sell it later, are you?" he asked, and I winced at his tone.

I shook my head. "No." I'd starve first before I sold anything else Kade gave me.

He finished fastening the bracelet and our eyes met. He was standing close enough for the scent of his cologne to tease my senses. His fingers lightly brushed my arm as our gazes locked.

"You ready?" he asked, breaking the spell.

I nodded. I needed to stop thinking about what might have been and just enjoy being here with my friend, someone who understood me more than I would have guessed—and who was giving me a really, really nice working vacation.

And it had been nice. I'd only thought about Blane about a dozen times today rather than the usual fifty or so.

"Good, because I'm starving."

A short while later, we were being shown to a table in the fanciest restaurant I'd ever been in. I followed the maître d' to a table in a private little alcove on the second floor. He graciously pulled a chair out for me.

"I'll do that," Kade said, taking the maître d's place as I slid into the seat. He moved my chair forward slightly, then sat down next to me.

"What was that about?" I asked, opening the menu the man had left.

"Didn't think he needed to see the view."

It took a moment before I got it, then glanced down and realized what "view" Kade was talking about. "Oh."

Kade ordered us cocktails and a first course. I wasn't sure what it was called, something with crab and avocado, but it was good.

"Where all have you traveled?" I asked him, reaching for another bite. I had the feeling Kade had been a lot of places.

"A little bit of everywhere," he said.

"Tell me?" I asked.

He thought for a moment as he took another drink, then said, "I think you'd like Hawaii."

"You've been to Hawaii?" It sounded incredibly exotic to me, and completely out of reach.

"A few times, yeah," he said. He went on to describe what it was like, how the moment you step off the plane on Oahu, the warm breeze of the tropics hits you. The way the island was divided into the wet and dry sides, and how when it rained, you could drive over the mountains and see water-falls.

I was captivated by his obvious love for the place and listened to him talk. He told me a funny story about a run-in he'd had with two huge Samoan guys and I laughed. Our food came, but I barely noticed, eating an occasional bite as I asked him questions and he answered. I didn't know why he was feeling chatty or when it would stop, so I took advantage.

Dessert was something chocolaty that Kade insisted on ordering for us to share, even though I told him I was full. He took a bite, his eyes sliding closed, and I watched, smiling a little at his obvious pleasure. I'd forgotten what a sweet tooth he had.

"You've gotta try this," he said, scooting his chair closer and holding the spoon to my mouth.

I obeyed, letting him feed me the bite. The decadent chocolate oozed over my tongue.

"Mmm," I said. He was right. It was worth eating even though I was full. I licked my lips, getting the last of the chocolate, and realized Kade's gaze was rapt on my mouth.

He scooped another bite and lifted the spoon to me again. My pulse sped up, but I didn't say anything and neither did he. I opened my lips and he fed me.

I don't know why he continued, but he did, slowly feeding me bite after bite until I'd eaten the entire thing. He watched my mouth with an intensity that made me acutely aware of his proximity. I self-consciously lifted my napkin, but his hand stilled mine.

Kade leaned closer and his fingers lightly brushed my chin, lifting my head, and his lips met mine.

The touch was electric, as though a shock had gone through me, and I didn't move, afraid that if I did, he'd stop. His mouth moved gently over mine, his touch maddeningly slow as he lightly licked and sucked on my lips. His tongue was soft, warm velvet.

Only his fingers under my jaw and his lips touched me. The scent of the cologne he'd worn tonight drifted to me, its alluring aroma mixed with his own scent, creating an aphrodisiac that, combined with his kiss, had me clenching my hands into fists to keep from touching him.

When he lifted his head, his eyes finally met mine, their brilliant blue intense beneath long, dark lashes. His face was inches away and it took every ounce of willpower I had to not pull him back for a real kiss.

"Chocolate tastes even better on you," he murmured.

My breath was shallow and quick, my pulse even more so. The effect Kade had on me was so profound and strong, and something I'd fought for so long. It seemed odd to think that I didn't have to anymore.

Or did I?

I'd been with Blane, engaged to him, still had feelings for him that couldn't be flipped off like a light switch, no matter how angry and bitter I was over how it had ended. Where did that leave anything I might feel for Kade?

I felt confused and unsure and excused myself to go to the ladies' room. I touched up my makeup, reapplied my lip gloss, and tried to regain the peace of mind I'd had earlier. Kade had kissed me before. It didn't have to mean anything more now than it had then. I was reading too much into it. Maybe because I was lonely, and hurting, and my ego could certainly use some stroking from a man like Kade.

I decided I wasn't going to allow myself to ruin the night. I'd been having a good time and getting lost inside my own confusion hadn't been part of the plan. I'd go back to Kade and just have fun doing whatever he had planned. I'd worry about my state of mind, and my life, later.

Kade had paid the bill by the time I returned, and when he ushered me outside it was into a waiting limousine.

"What's the occasion?" I asked, as he slid in after me.

"To see the Strip, of course," he said, moving to the seat across from the wet bar. "Champagne?"

I grinned, delighted at this turn of events. "Absolutely." Sip champagne while riding up and down the Vegas Strip in a limo with a gorgeous man? Yes, please.

Kade popped the cork and poured two glasses.

"What should we toast to?" I asked as he handed me a flute of the golden liquid. "To the future? New beginnings? World peace?"

Kade smirked at my teasing. "How about to how incredibly sexy you look tonight?"

That made me feel as though I'd swallowed a ray of sunshine and its warm glow was spreading through my body, melting me from the inside out.

I clinked my glass against his. "Ditto," I said, and drank.

Kade played tour guide and I was wide-eyed with amazement as he pointed out landmarks. We passed the MGM hotel and when I read who was performing there on the sign outside, I let out a squeal.

"Can we go?" I asked excitedly.

Kade shook his head. "Sorry, princess," he said with a grimace. "I'm banned from MGM for life."

I stared at him in surprise. "You're kidding."

"Nope. Blane and I came here once a few years back," he said, taking another drink of his champagne. "He's banned, too."

I was dying to ask more, but decided to let it go, especially when I saw the famous *Las Vegas* sign and hurried to snap a photo of it with my phone.

It seemed like barely any time had passed before I realized we'd finished the bottle of champagne and were pulling up to another hotel. Kade led me inside and we rode the elevator to the top floor. It opened into a nightclub that made me wish I had six pairs of eyes, there was so much to see. I abruptly decided that people watching could seriously be an Olympic sport in Vegas.

The club was rocking out to the DJ's tunes and the dance floor was crowded. Kade found us a spot, and a cocktail waitress took our order and brought us drinks.

You couldn't really talk, at least not if you wanted to be heard, so I just sipped my drink and watched the crowd. I could feel Kade's arm around my waist, his hand resting lightly on my hip, and for a moment, it seemed surreal. If someone had told me nine months ago that I'd be having a fabulous time in Las Vegas with Kade Dennon, I'd have laughed myself silly. But now, it didn't seem silly at all. It felt right somehow. I was the happiest I'd been in a long time, and I had Kade to thank for it.

"Dance with me," Kade said loudly near my ear, taking the drink from my hand and setting it aside.

I didn't resist as he took my hand and led me into the mash of people on the dance floor. It was hot, and crazy, and personal space was nonexistent, but I loved it. The music filled my ears and throbbed through my body. I closed my eyes and danced, moving to the rhythm of the pulse. All the alcohol I'd consumed had left me feeling pretty darn good, a little tipsy but not enough to make the room start spinning.

Kade's hands settled on my waist and I opened my eyes, smiling up at him. I raised my arms, lifting the heavy mass of my hair off my neck. The heat was making the strands stick to my skin.

People pressed in close and no one seemed to notice or care who they touched. It was just a mass of bodies moving in time to the music. Kade was even closer, one leg insinuated between mine. He caressed the bare skin of my back above my jeans. His touch felt good. Really good.

I let my hair go and rested my hands on Kade's silk-clad shoulders. The heat from his body soaked through the delicate fabric. The undone buttons exposed the skin that I'd admired earlier, only now it was right in front of me, glistening slightly with sweat. I didn't think, I just leaned forward and fastened my mouth to a spot right under the tantalizing dip between his collarbones.

Hot. Salty. Soft. Hard. Sensations filtered through my brain as I pressed against Kade, my tongue licking the addictive flavor of him from his skin. His fingers dug into my rear, dragging me closer until I could feel his arousal against my abdomen. I took this as encouragement and continued on my path, undoing another button or two to give his body the attention it most certainly deserved. Kade's hands slipped underneath my blouse, settling on my waist before sliding tantalizingly up my ribs. My breasts ached for his touch.

It felt good to be wanted.

The darkness of the club was punctuated by a swirl of lights that spun and sent rays of color over the dance floor, briefly illuminating Kade in shades of neon blue and yellow before plunging us back into the black. I closed my eyes, blocking out the mass of people surrounding us, many of whom were in similar clinches with their partner. Or partners.

The DJ switched tunes and I was abruptly jolted from my hypnotic reverie. I knew this song. It had played on the jukebox the night Blane had come to the bar for me, the night I'd met my three "fairy godfathers." He'd walked through the door, put me in his car, and then we'd—

I jerked back, horrified. What was I doing? I'd already come between them once over a lie, was I now going to make it a truth? Was I just using Kade to make myself feel better?

"I-I need some air," I stammered, pulling away from Kade.

The look of confusion on his face made more guilt swell inside me, and I hurriedly pushed through the crowd that now felt oppressive until I was outside.

A high fence barricaded the edges of the roof, but it was blessedly cooler out here and the music was muffled. Couples dotted the roof, though few appeared to be talking.

"What's wrong?"

I turned. Kade had followed me.

"Nothing." How could I possibly put into words how confused I was? How much I regretted that I'd come between him and Blane? How every moment I spent with him made it harder and harder to remember why I shouldn't want him?

"Liar," he said without heat. He advanced until my back was pressed against the fence, then took my hand in his. The wind blew my hair and he tenderly smoothed it away from my face. "Tell me."

His sweetness was my undoing, and I broke. "I don't know, Kade. I don't know what I'm doing or why. I feel guilty all the time for what happened with you and Blane—" My voice broke at the pain those words produced. "I came between you, you and your brother, and I never wanted that. Please believe me. I'm so, so sorry."

"Shhh, it's okay," Kade whispered. His brows were drawn together in concern as his thumb brushed my wet cheeks. "It's not your fault."

"It is," I insisted. "It really is. I never should have . . . have . . ."

"Been my friend? Is that what you regret?" Kade interrupted.

His eyes seemed to beg me to contradict him, to not deny what we'd built between us.

Did I regret it? If I hadn't spent time with Kade, Blane never would have had reason to suspect we'd had an affair. We wouldn't have broken up. We'd still be getting married. Kade and Blane would still be speaking to each other.

My hesitation was too long and Kade's expression turned cold.

"That's what I thought."

"Kade, that's not—"

"Turn it off, princess. Time to get back to work."

He was looking to my right now and I looked, too. The guy Kade was supposed to target stood nearby with a small group of people.

"I need you to keep him occupied for the next thirty minutes," Kade said. "Can you do that?"

I swallowed, nodding. "Where will you be?"

"Breaking into his room, of course."

Alarm shot through me. "What if you get caught?"

"I won't. After thirty minutes, excuse yourself to go to the bathroom and leave. Meet me back in the room. The key is in your back pocket." I felt him slide the card into my jeans.

I chewed my lip in worry. I hated that I hadn't gotten the chance to answer Kade's question. "Kade, I—"

"Not now," he interrupted. His tone was such that I immediately shut up. "Put it aside. We have work to do. Everything else will have to wait."

I gave a reluctant nod. "All right."

"Can you cry on demand?" he asked. "That would help."

That was an easy one since I was already fighting back tears. I looked up at Kade and allowed the tears to leak out my eyes. For a moment he looked stricken before he schooled his features into a grim mask.

"I'm going to grab you, shake you," he said. "Try to push me away as hard as you can. I'll let you go and you head in his direction, but not directly for him. Understand?"

"Yeah."

"You ready?" he asked, looking slightly skeptical.

"I'm fine," I said. "Just do it already."

Kade's hands closed on my upper arms and he shook me. "Start fighting me," he hissed. His face hard with anger. I tried to push him away, squirming, but he just held me tighter. "Try harder. He's watching." I put all I had into it, twisting to get away from where Kade had me pressed against the fence.

"Let me go!" I demanded, pushing at his chest. His arm was within reach, and I clamped my teeth around it and bit.

"Ow! You bitch!"

Kade released me and I wasted no time pushing past him toward the man, but was careful not to look at him. I hurried, glancing over my shoulder to see Kade was jogging after me. He reached out and I cringed away with a cry.

I was suddenly snagged around the waist and yanked toward someone. It was the guy. He'd grabbed me and had moved me behind him while he faced off with Kade.

"Get out of the way," Kade ordered.

"I don't think she wants to go with you," the man said.

"I don't give a shit what she wants," Kade snarled. He pushed roughly past the man and grabbed my arm.

The guy threw a punch at Kade, which I knew he could have blocked, but he chose not to. The crunch of bone on bone made me flinch. When Kade looked back at me, his mouth was bloody.

I decided I didn't like this job very much.

"Fine," Kade said, wiping his mouth on his sleeve. "I was through with her anyway."

He turned and stalked away, disappearing into the crowd.

"Are you all right?"

I swung my attention back to the guy.

"Yeah. I'm okay," I said. "Thanks for helping me."

He gave me a small smile and held out his hand. "I'm David, and you're welcome."

I shook his hand. "Kathleen."

"Can I buy you a drink, Kathleen?"

I forced a smile. "Sure. I'd like that."

David motioned to a nearby cocktail waitress and soon I was sipping a vodka tonic. Sipping because I certainly didn't need more alcohol, not when I felt responsible for keeping Kade out of trouble.

David asked me what I did and I told him I was a bartender. He didn't bat an eye at that. He didn't wear a wedding ring, so I assumed that though he had a daughter he must be divorced. Now that he was talking more, I could hear the trace of a British accent.

When I asked him what he did for a living, his answer was vague.

"I run security for a firm in Switzerland," he said.

"That sounds interesting," I said. "What kind of firm?"

His smile was enigmatic. "The kind of firm for which people pay a lot of money to retain their anonymity."

I took a drink to hide my dismay. I'd heard about the big, prestigious banks in Switzerland in movies and such. That was what Kade was trying to hack into? I broke out in a cold sweat.

"It's been lovely meeting you, Kathleen," David said. "But I have an early meeting tomorrow. Do take care and perhaps choose your company more wisely in the future." He turned to go.

I panicked. It hadn't been thirty minutes yet.

"Wait!" I said, latching on to his arm. He looked back questioningly. "I mean, we were just getting to know each other." I smiled and threw in a come-hither look for good measure. "Surely you can stay a little while longer?"

David paused, a slight frown crossing his face. "You seem awfully self-destructive, Kathleen. First you're with a man who mistreats you in a quite brutal fashion, and now you're flirting with a complete stranger."

Okay, well that was brutal honesty for you. And he didn't know the half of it.

"I'm sorry," I said, "I'm just . . . alone. And I don't know what to do now." I shrugged. That sentence was actually true.

David studied me. "Come with me, Kathleen," he said.

I followed him. Maybe I should tell him I was hungry, so he could get me something to eat? That should stall him long enough for Kade to finish up and get out of his room.

Two big men followed at a distance, then rode down in the elevator with us. I could tell they were some type of security detail for David. They had telltale bulges under their jackets and their eyes never stopped scanning in all directions.

A limousine was waiting downstairs and David motioned me inside. It was just the two of us then, the bodyguards riding in another car.

"Where are we going?" I asked.

"My hotel."

Shit. "I'm really hungry," I said, hoping he'd catch the hint.

"I'll order you something there."

Great. Kade had given me one job and I couldn't even manage it. We were going right where he'd asked me not to go. He was *so* going to fire me.

The bodyguards left us at the door to his suite when David dismissed them, which made me nervous. Why had he brought me back here? Hotel rooms with strange men hadn't worked out so well for me in the past.

"Where are you from, Kathleen?" David asked, gesturing for me to precede him into the suite, which was even nicer than the one Kade and I were staying in. I headed for the windows to take in the view. I figured if Kade was in here, the farther I could get David away from the door, the better the odds for Kade to get out. And moving across the room also put me out of David's immediate reach.

"The Midwest," I said vaguely.

"Runaway?"

"Orphan."

He poured two glasses of wine from the bar and handed me one. I took a sip.

"I'm sorry to hear that."

I shrugged and asked to use the bathroom. Maybe Kade was hiding. But when I went through the bedroom, it was dark and empty. I gave a sigh of relief. Perhaps Kade had made it out early. Going into the bathroom, I shut the door and flipped on the light, then immediately had to stifle a scream.

"Did you forget how to tell time?"

I spun around. "Jesus, Kade! You scared me to death!" I hissed. "What are you still doing here?"

"I said I needed thirty minutes," he reminded me. "Has it been thirty minutes?"

I immediately felt guilty. "I'm sorry. He wanted to come back here and I couldn't stop him."

"So you came along," Kade said. "Why?" His irritation was obvious. He reached behind me to turn on the water.

"I don't know. I thought maybe if you were still here, I could distract him or something, so you could get out."

"And how did *you* plan on getting out?"

I didn't have an answer. I hadn't thought that far.

Kade snorted. "That's what I thought."

I bristled. "Listen, I'm just a girl he brought back from the club. I'm not suspicious. But a strange man walking out of his bathroom *is*."

Kade's lips pressed into a thin line and I had a brief moment of satisfaction that he knew I was right.

"Did you get what you needed?" I asked.

"Do you even have to ask?"

How Kade could make arrogant sarcasm sexy was beyond me.

"Okay then. So, there are two bedrooms here. I'll get him into the other one and you get out. I'll meet you back in our room."

"I don't like that plan," he said.

"I'll be fine." And I really hoped that was the truth. I reached over and turned off the water. "See you soon."

I switched off the light as I left the bathroom, taking a deep breath before stepping back into the living room. David was still sipping his wine by the windows.

I picked up my wineglass and headed back over to him, walking slowly and putting enough sway in my hips to get his attention. "So, David," I said after taking a healthy swallow, "I didn't get a chance to thank you properly for your help tonight." Yeah, I was the same age as his daughter—oh well. Men were great at rationalizing inconvenient facts like that. And I noticed his eyes had dropped to my cleavage.

David cleared his throat. "Thanks aren't necessary," he said.

My palms were sweaty and my heart was jackknifing in my chest, but I tried to ignore all that. I needed to distract him enough for Kade to get out. The more time that passed, the greater the chance of discovery. I remembered the amount Kade had whispered in my ear. A cut of that would be very nice.

I set my glass down, my hands shaking. Making myself put one foot in front of the other when I desperately wanted to run in the other direction, I got close enough to David for him to get a whiff of my perfume.

"But," I said quietly, taking the wineglass from his hand, "I like to pay my debts." My voice was steady and calm, thank God.

It seemed any thoughts of maybe saving the lost and abused orphan were long gone, because he swallowed heavily. Turning, I headed for the bedroom and he followed

126

closely behind. "I mean, this is what you intended, bringing me back here, right?"

"Perhaps," he admitted.

That I was right didn't surprise me in the slightest. Gathering my courage, I gave him a little push and he sat down on the bed. Being in a bedroom with a complete stranger who obviously expected sex was unnerving. I wanted to get out of there as soon as possible.

David seemed willing to let me take charge, which was unexpected given his earlier behavior but gave me an idea. Opening his closet, I spied what I needed. Dragging a tie from the rack, I turned to face David.

"I like to play games. Do you like to play games?" I gave him what I hoped was a wicked smile.

"I . . . could be persuaded," he said, his gaze raking down my body.

Although I strained my ears, I didn't hear the door to the suite open or close. But then again, Kade was always as silent as a ghost.

I climbed onto the bed, straddling David and forcing him backward until I could stretch his arms over his head. My top gaped and his eyes were locked on my breasts, which was fine with me, as I was able to tie his hands to the head-board with no fuss at all. I made sure the knots in the silk were tight.

It felt strange, and more empowering than I wanted to admit, to be the one in full control of a sexual situation. I remembered the harrowing attack by Stephen Avery months ago and how powerless I'd felt. I'd learned a lot about my own sexuality since then, learned it could be one of the most useful weapons I had—though using it as such still left me feeling scared and uneasy.

Sitting back on my haunches, I could feel proof that David was way into this. I unbuttoned his shirt and had the brief, wayward thought that it was too bad this wasn't real—he was a good-looking guy who obviously took good care of his body. I guessed him to be in his late forties.

"I'm afraid I have to be going now," I said, climbing off him. He was tied up. He couldn't get me now. Relief flooded my bones. Please, God, let Kade have gotten away.

"Wait—what? You're leaving?"

"I did what I came here to do. Time to go."

"It was a setup," David said, his voice no longer friendly.

"Afraid so," I confirmed, more cheerful now that I felt safer.

"Who do you work for?" he asked.

"In a roundabout way . . . you." I smiled at his confusion and a bit of pride made me say, "When you hire the best to do a job, you should expect the unexpected. And Kade Dennon is the very best of the best."

Understanding lit his eyes. "So that's what this is about."

I nodded. "I'm guessing he's hacking your company even as we speak. Which reminds me, I'd better get going. Thanks for the drink. The maid will find you in the morning."

"Tell Dennon he can try all he wants, but he'll never hack into my system."

Gone was the affable British gentleman. David was heading toward seriously pissed.

I shrugged. "I guess you'll find out soon enough."

"Find out what?"

"Kade never fails."

With that parting shot, I left the bedroom, only to be grabbed and hauled against a man's chest.

"So I'm the best of the best, huh?" Kade's eyes glittered with an emotion I shied away from identifying. The breath caught in my chest.

"This is new information to you?" I asked, twitching an eyebrow upward.

"It is that *you* think so."

My stomach twisted, surprised and glad that Kade cared what I thought about his competence. "I'm not wrong, am I?"

His smirk made heat curl low in my belly and I was acutely aware of our bodies pressed together.

"Not about this, you're not."

I wondered what he *did* think I was wrong about.

He released me and took my hand. "Let's get out of here before he gets loose."

"He's not going to get loose," I insisted. "I tied him well."

Kade snorted. "Of course he's going to get loose," then he headed out of the room before I could retort.

Ten minutes later we were back in our room, and I was watching over Kade's shoulder as he typed on his laptop. It was gibberish to me, but it amazed me what he could do. His fingers flew over the keyboard.

"So what did you need from his room?" I asked.

"His fingerprints."

Kade did something with a little device attached to his computer, and more lines of text appeared on the screen.

"Aren't you tired?" I asked. It was getting late and the time change was catching up to me. "Can't it wait until tomorrow?"

"Tomorrow they'll have changed the algorithm," he said. "Besides, I don't quit when I'm tired. I quit when I'm done." He said this matter-of-factly and I knew he'd work all night if he had to, which actually made me admire him even more.

I decided he probably didn't need me hanging over him, so I retreated to the bathroom and showered. After wrapping myself in one of the hotel's satin bathrobes, I went back to the couch and lay down. Kade was still working.

He hadn't turned on any lights other than the little floodlight above the minibar and I didn't, either. It was easier to see the neon skyline this way, with the room darkened.

A while later—I must have dozed off—Kade woke me with a "Done." Yawning, I pushed myself up. "You got the money?" I asked.

"And sent your cut to your bank," Kade replied, coming to sit next to me on the couch.

I snorted, bending my knees so he could sit. "I hope it wasn't much. I didn't do anything but screw up."

Kade unfolded my legs to rest them on his lap. "You kept him occupied, kept him from calling his security down on our heads. Dead bodies left in my wake are bad for business."

I laughed. "I can't imagine why that would be," I teased.

His mouth curved in a half smile as he leaned back against the couch with a sigh. His eyes slipped shut and I knew he must be tired. It was really late. And yet . . .

"Kade," I said softly. "About earlier, I'm really sorry."

"Sorry for what, for telling the truth?" He didn't open his eyes.

"I don't regret anything, Kade," I said. "And most certainly I don't regret us being friends. But I hate it, more than anything, that you've lost Blane because of me. And if there were a way I could turn back the clock and change that, I would. In a heartbeat. He's all you have. You need each other."

Kade finally opened his eyes, their penetrating blue pinning me in place. "What do you know about what I need?"

I swallowed, wanting to look away, but I didn't dare. "I'm not trying to say that I do . . . ," I backtracked.

Kade closed his eyes, so I shut up. After a moment, he spoke.

"All I need is right here."

A lump grew in my throat and Kade's form blurred in my vision. Reaching down to where his hands rested on my bare knees, I took one hand in mine and laced my fingers through his. He opened his eyes again and lifted his head from the cushion.

"You're all shiny, you know," he said quietly.

I gave a little smile, chagrined. "Stupid glitter wouldn't wash off," I replied, my voice as soft as his.

"I like it. You sparkle like an angel on Christmas morning."

His words rendered me speechless, but he didn't seem to mind. With another soft sigh, he turned and lay down between my legs, resting on his side and nestling his head on my stomach. His hands rested on the curve of my waist in a loose grip as I leaned back against the arm of the couch. I was reminded of that night in the crappy motel room in Chicago, so long ago, when Kade had assumed a similar posture.

I wasn't wearing much underneath the robe—but Kade seemed to be behaving himself. My fingers combed through his hair, the dark strands as soft as silk. I didn't know if he was sleeping or just looking out the window at the lights. I did know it was quiet and peaceful, a moment to be savored, and made all the more special for its rarity.

Kade—letting down his guard.

"Do you want to know why I started this new business?" he asked after a while.

"Hmmm?" I was still idly combing through his hair.

"I did it for you."

My fingers stopped, my brows drawing together in confusion. "What do you mean?"

"When you and Blane broke up, again, I had this stupid, idiotic hope that if I changed, if I could make a life someone could share with me, that maybe . . . you would."

I was stunned. "Kade, I—I don't know what to say."

He shifted, turning so he could look up at me. "Don't say anything," he said. "Not yet. Just think about it. We're good together. We have fun, make a good team."

All that was true.

"You wouldn't have to worry about money anymore," Kade continued. "We could travel. I can find jobs anywhere and everywhere. You want to see the world, princess? I can give it to you."

"We're friends," I said. "You don't have to give me anything."

"I need you," Kade said. "I've never needed anyone the way I need you. You and I have something, and if this is the only chance I'm going to get to convince you of that, then I'm going to take it."

"Kade—"

"Just . . . think about it. We could be good, really good, together. And we could be way more than friends."

I went quiet as he settled back on my stomach, my mind spinning with what Kade was offering. Then I inhaled sharply. Kade had turned his head more and was now pushing between my legs, sliding aside the satin fabric of the robe.

"Don't—" I began, squirming backward. I didn't get far, though. His hands tightened on my hips, holding me in place.

Kade's mouth fastened to my inner thigh. His tongue traced warm, wet circles over my skin. Taking my legs, he hooked them over his shoulders and nuzzled the silk triangle at the apex of my thighs.

He groaned even as I let out a gasp, heat flooding the core of me.

More heat as he pressed his tongue flat against the thin fabric. My legs trembled in reaction, every sense acutely aware of the brush of his jaw, the warmth of his breath.

He nuzzled me again, inhaling deeply, and I felt my face grow hot.

"I thought you didn't want to be the rebound guy," I managed to say.

"I changed my mind," he growled. "I'll take whatever you'll let me."

There was the sound of fabric tearing, and then I was bare to him. Frantically, I reached down to cover myself, but he caught my wrists. Then his mouth was on me, his tongue inside me. My eyes slammed shut as rational thought flew out the window.

I felt like one of Kade's Moon Pies—no part of me was left untouched by the warm invasion of his lips and tongue. Fire licked at my veins the way Kade licked my body. Blood thundered in my ears as he teased me, my heart racing. My hands clenched into fists and Kade released my wrists, but instead of pushing him away, I buried my fingers in his hair.

He lifted his head, then slid a finger inside me. I gasped and choked at the new sensation, prying open my eyes.

Kade's head was shockingly dark against my thighs. His mouth was wet, his lips red—his eyes were the bluest I'd ever seen them, and he was watching me.

Holding my gaze, he lowered his head again between my legs. I was transfixed by the sight of him. His eyes never left mine as he kissed me in the most intimate way.

My conscience was screaming and part of me was aghast at what was happening. The other part of me, the part that had been frozen in ice the past three months, felt alive.

"Oh God, oh God, Kade . . ." I wasn't even aware of what I was saying—I just knew that despite my conscience I didn't want him to stop. My body tensed and I could no longer keep my eyes open as I shattered into a million pieces, a cry ripping from my throat. Gentle swipes of Kade's tongue prolonged my pleasure until it was too much. I pulled on his hair and he climbed up my body to take my mouth with his.

I could taste myself on his tongue. His kiss was deep and languid. I'd forgotten how well he could kiss. Kade didn't rush through kissing, he savored it like an alcoholic with the last drop of bourbon. My whole body trembled in the aftermath of what he'd done to me and my eyes were wet. Kade gentled me with his kisses until my heart rate had slowed and I breathed more easily. When he lifted his head, our eyes met.

"I could get addicted to you," he said.

He stood and lifted me in his arms, which was a good thing, as my legs were too unsteady to support me. I tentatively rested my head against his shoulder as he carried me into his bedroom.

After settling me on the bed, he stripped down to a pair of charcoal-gray briefs that clung to him and weren't of enough adequate material to hide how he was really feeling. Lust slammed hard into me and I couldn't tear my eyes away.

"Keep looking at me like that and I'll forget my resolve to take it slow," he said roughly.

Sliding into bed next to me, he turned and arranged us spoon style, my bottom nestled against his pelvis and his arm curved around my waist. My hands curled into fists as I fought not to turn around.

It was a long time before I fell asleep.

~

I don't know what woke me. I was just suddenly awake. The glowing clock on the nightstand said it was still the middle of the night, though it was pushing dawn back home. Maybe my internal clock hadn't yet adjusted.

Kade was sound asleep next to me, his breathing deep and even. I turned my head to look at him. Stretched out on his stomach, the sheet fallen to his waist, he looked like he was posing for a magazine's photo shoot. His face was smooth and peaceful in sleep, his dark hair tousled over his forehead, and I had to restrain the urge to comb my fingers through it.

I couldn't fall back to sleep, my mind beginning to spin as I looked at Kade. The words he had said, the offer he'd made, what he'd done—all of it replayed inside my head. He wanted to be with me but hadn't said anything about love, just that he needed me, wanted me. Could I do that—build a life with someone I didn't love, who didn't love me—and close the door forever on Blane and me? I hadn't realized until this moment how I'd still been hoping, in a tiny corner of my heart, that Blane and I weren't over.

Choosing to be with either one of them at this point would ruin their relationship forever, wouldn't it?

My stomach rolled and I couldn't breathe. I climbed out of bed, grabbed my robe, and stumbled from the room, hoping I didn't wake Kade. I couldn't face him yet. Not while my heart was in such turmoil over the tangled mess that ensnared all three of us.

What had I done?

I made it into the other bedroom, then just stood there. I didn't know what to think or how to feel. What would it do to Kade and Blane if I took Kade up on his offer? Kade had said he needed me, only me, but I knew that wasn't true. He needed Blane, too, even if he was currently pissed off and in denial about that.

I sank to the floor and wrapped my arms around my knees, pulling my legs to my chest and trying to ease the churning in my stomach. I rocked back and forth, staring unseeing out the windows. I was drowning . . . drowning in regret and confusion.

The muffled ring of my cell phone penetrated my cocoon. My purse lay on the floor by the bed. I reached for it without thinking, dug out my cell, and froze.

Blane was calling me.

CHAPTER SIX

My hand trembled slightly as I answered the call.
"Hello?" My voice was soft. I didn't want to wake Kade.

Silence for a moment, then, "Kat. It's me."

"I know."

"Did I wake you?"

"I was up."

A beat. "I guess you're wondering why the hell I'm calling you in the middle of the night."

He sounded tired, the deep gravel of his voice telling me he was in bed maybe, or had just woken up and was perhaps trying to fall back asleep.

"Yeah. I guess." My voice was thick as a great wave of sadness rose in me. I rested my head on my knees and stared out the window.

"I had a dream," Blane said. "About you. You were here with me, and we were curled up on the couch together, watching some movie. And it was so real, and God, it felt so good. And then I woke up."

Yeah, been there, done that. When I didn't speak, he continued.

"I was so wrong, Kat, my own doubts and insecurities made me think you'd do things that I should have known you never would. And I wanted so bad to call you, tell you, once I realized what a fucking dick I'd been. But I was afraid. Afraid I'd gone too far, afraid you wouldn't be able to forgive me or even *want* to forgive me."

They were words I'd wanted to hear from Blane for months, words I'd thought I never *would* hear. I waited for the surge of happiness that I'd thought I'd feel, but it didn't come. Instead, I just felt tired.

"Kat? Are you there? Please, say something."

"What do you want me to say?" I asked with a sigh. "After all we've been through, do you think you can call me, say you're sorry, and it'll all be okay? It seems to always be about you—what *you* want, what *you* need. Am I supposed to just forget what happened?" I paused. "How could we ever go back to the way we were?"

The question wasn't rhetorical—I was really asking. I couldn't see a path to a new life with Blane, at least not one where I wasn't constantly terrified that my next step would cause him to turn on me again.

"Kat," Blane spoke softly, "where are you? Let me come to you, see you, touch you. We can talk."

"You can't," I said without thinking. "I'm in Las Vegas." I wondered what my answer would have been if I'd been at home instead, and whether I'd have let him come over.

Silence. "Vegas?" Blane asked, a note of warning entering his voice. "What are you doing there?" A pause. "Are you with Kade?"

"Who else would I be with?" My reply was sharp, the change in his tone affecting mine.

"I see. And are you two still just . . . friends?" There was no mistaking his meaning or the leashed anger in his words now.

"What the hell is that supposed to mean?" I snapped, guilt hitting me hard. I knew exactly what he meant. "What do you care if I'm in Vegas with Kade or what we do here? In case you've forgotten, Blane, you and I broke up."

"That doesn't mean I stopped loving you. I just never imagined you'd come between Kade and me like this."

"That's not fair," I said. "You know that's the last thing I ever wanted. None of this would have even happened if you had listened to me instead of your uncle."

"Don't bring my uncle into this—he has nothing to do with it."

"Bullshit!" I exploded. "He has *everything* to do with it! He tried to buy me off months ago to stop dating you, and when that didn't work, he made up an affair between me and Kade that you never should have believed!" I was yelling now, seething with anger. "So don't you dare try and take the high road, Blane! The blame for all of this is staring you right in the mirror."

I ended the call, trying to get my boiling emotions under control. I was so angry and yet devastated. I buried my face in my hands.

Kade's hands on my shoulders weren't a surprise and I didn't resist as he pulled my body toward his chest to envelop me in his arms. His skin was warm against my cheek and he smoothed my hair as I cried.

I was struck by how wrong this was, crying on Kade's shoulder about Blane, and forced myself to stop. As cruel as

Blane had been, he'd been right. It wasn't going to get any better between them while I was still in the picture.

"Kade, I can't," I said thickly, looking up at him. "We can't. This"—I motioned between us—"can't happen. Things will never be right between you and Blane so long as I'm around."

"Is that what he told you?" His eyes were intense, even in the dim light, his expression grave.

"It's what I know," I said. "And you know it, too." I moved to get off his lap, but he stopped me, holding me close.

"I don't care," Kade said fiercely. "Stay with me. Just a little longer. You've been happy with me—could be happy with me. Just give us some more time."

His plea tore at me. I felt like I was standing on a precipice that held nothing but empty days and nights ahead of me, endless stretches filled with loneliness and despair. I had to let Kade go or risk the two of them being estranged forever.

Could we have just a little more time? Kade was right—I'd been the closest to content and happy in the past twenty-four hours with him than at any other time in the past three months. And I didn't want to give that up. Not yet. It was selfish of me, but I wanted just a little more happy, something to tide me over in the bleak near future that awaited me.

I gave a reluctant nod. "But you have to promise me that this won't go any further. I won't drive an even bigger wedge between you and Blane."

Kade kissed me, his palms cradling my face. "I promise," he murmured against my lips. I clung to him. His kisses were like a forbidden drug, comforting and sensual. His desire for me was a heady thing.

I allowed him to lead me back to his bed, where he again laid me down spoon style, his arm draped across my waist.

"Go to sleep," he murmured into my ear. His hand rhythmically stroked my hair, relaxing my tense body.

My eyes were heavy and I sighed, exhaustion and the emotional turmoil taking their toll. I felt safe and protected, cherished even, in Kade's arms. I yearned to close my eyes and wish all my problems away. But nothing's that easy.

∼

When I woke again I was still in Kade's arms. I turned to look at him, rubbing the sleep from my eyes. He was awake.

"Did you sleep?" I asked.

"No."

"Why not? Are you all right?"

"Why would I waste the time I have with you sleeping?" he asked with a lopsided smile. "I'll sleep when I'm dead."

I didn't smile. That remark may have been a joke for anyone else, but for Kade it had been a near reality too many times for me to find it funny.

I brushed my lips across his chest before pulling away. My eyes felt like sandpaper and I really wanted to brush my teeth. I rolled out of bed and walked to the bathroom, feeling Kade's eyes on me the whole way.

I showered, wrapping myself in a towel afterward. My clothes were in the other bedroom, but when I left Kade's to head that way, I smelled coffee and changed direction to peek into the living room.

Kade had thrown on a pair of jeans and was setting a tray on the dining table. He must have sensed my presence, because he turned around.

"Hungry?" he asked. The way his eyes raked me from head to toe told me he had more than food on the brain.

I had to be strong. What had happened last night—and I shivered just thinking about it—couldn't happen again, not if I wanted to be able to live with myself afterward.

"Is there coffee?"

"Of course." His smirk clearly signaled that he knew I had to have my coffee. He poured a cup and handed it to me.

"What time is it?" I asked, adding sugar and cream to the steaming cup.

"Almost noon."

I about dropped the cup. "Seriously?" I hadn't slept that well or that long in months, which explained why I actually felt rested this morning, even after the middle-of-the-night phone call with Blane.

Blane. My thoughts skittered away from him. I couldn't think about him right now, wouldn't ruin the moment by dwelling on how horrible our conversation had gone last night.

"I'm going to take a shower," Kade said. "You eat and get dressed. Let's go have some fun." His eyes widened suggestively, the way he said "fun" making it sound like an endeavor of the utmost importance.

I wasn't hungry but drank more coffee while I dressed and blow-dried my hair. Guilt gnawed at me even as I tried not to think about all of it.

I should be on a plane home. I shouldn't have agreed to stay. Blane knows I'm here, knows who I'm with. . . .

The coffee cup slipped from my shaking fingers and shattered on the marble sink. Coffee and porcelain went everywhere, including on me.

"Shit," I cursed under my breath. I didn't want Kade to see. He was so pleased I was staying, I couldn't let him know the guilt I felt. It didn't matter if I was happy with Kade, had been so thrilled to see him turn up on my doorstep. I was a selfish brat to still be there. But I couldn't leave. I promised him I'd stay.

I needed a drink.

I walked into the living room, listening to the distant sound of Kade's shower running. The bar had plenty of vodka and I reached for a bottle, then grabbed a glass.

Crap. No ice.

Taking one of the room keys and the ice bucket, I stopped by the door to Kade's bathroom.

"I'm going to get some ice!" I called out. I wasn't sure whether he heard me or not, but I'd be back in a few minutes anyway. Grabbing one of his white shirts, I took off my stained cami and pulled it on, tying the tails so it wouldn't be so long on me.

I padded down the thickly carpeted hallway in my bare feet, wishing I'd checked out the room's welcome packet so I knew where to find ice. Surely it couldn't be far. . . .

But damned if I wasn't wrong. I searched what felt like the whole floor and was about to give up. A detour down one last corridor and I was done—I'd drink bourbon instead.

I turned a corner, then stopped short. There, not twenty feet in front of me, was David. Looked like he'd gotten untied without a problem.

He spotted me and I didn't know what to do. Should I say hello or was there some other proper protocol for this particular situation? Did Hallmark make a card for it? Then David did something that made me rethink that.

Raising a tiny walkie-talkie to his mouth, he said, "Found her. Floor thirty. Northeast corridor."

I dropped the bucket and ran.

I chanced a glance behind me to see that David was in pursuit, and gaining. I'd gone quite a ways from our room and the identical hallways were a maze. Panic made me confused and I made a wrong turn. Backtracking wasn't an option, so I kept going.

Looking behind me again, I didn't see David. I slowed. Had I lost him?

Frantically struggling to get my bearings, I turned down another long corridor and ran right into David.

"Leaving me tied to the bed was a bad idea," he hissed.

Before I could say or do anything, he hit me, his fist slamming into my cheek with enough force to knock me to the ground. Pain exploded in my head and then, mercifully, everything went dark.

∼

When I regained consciousness, I wished I hadn't. My head throbbed and I could feel that my face was swollen. One eye wouldn't open all the way.

Raising my head, I realized I was tied to a chair. Each of my wrists was tied to an arm of it and each ankle to a chair leg. Nice.

Looking around, I realized I was in an office of some sort. There was a desk and a couch, both in mahogany and red leather. It reminded me a little of Blane's office, very professional, which was why it was so disconcerting to feel the ropes chafing my skin. The windows made it clear that it was still daytime, but also that I was no longer in our hotel. The view was different.

The door opened and I jerked my head around, then bit back a groan. Shouldn't have moved so fast.

David walked in, followed by the two other big guys from last night. They wore suits, but that did nothing to make them look more civilized. They were the muscle.

"Glad to see you're awake," David said, moving to stand in front of me.

"You really hold a grudge," I replied, meeting his eyes. "If I'd known you'd do this just because I tied you up and didn't screw you, I'd have gone all Lorena Bobbitt on you."

David's eyes narrowed. "Don't be ridiculous, stupid girl. I don't give a damn about you. That little trick Dennon pulled last night has my bosses breathing down my neck. I want the money back."

"You knew when you hired him what his fee was," I countered. "It's bad business not to pay someone for a job."

"I knew his fee, but he was supposed to fail," David hissed. "Now I'm out four million dollars with no fucking idea of how he got in."

"He's going to show you," I said. "That's part of the deal."

"You're right—he *is* going to show me," David sneered. "And he's going to give the money back. You're insurance against that."

"That's why I'm here?" I asked. "You're planning to threaten him with me?"

David's smile was cold. "Go after the Achilles' heel and even the smartest of them will fall."

"You have no idea who you're dealing with, do you." It wasn't a question. Somehow I doubted Kade had provided much of a résumé to this guy. "Taking me was a big mistake."

David turned away, ignoring me as he looked at his cell phone. "Don't worry, sweetheart. We won't rough you up too much, just a little if he doesn't cooperate. But we'll know here shortly."

"You've already told him that you have me?" I asked, panicking. "Are you insane?"

David glanced my way with a frown. "I don't appreciate your tone or insinuation," he said.

"You don't understand," I said. "You've got to listen to me. Let me go. Now. If he comes here, he'll kill you."

For a moment, I thought David understood, then he laughed outright. "A hacker's going to kill me? Good God, I must have walloped you a bit hard if you think a computer geek is capable of that."

My eyes slid shut in dismay. Kade was trying to turn over a new leaf and this asshole was going to screw it all up. "Please," I said, opening my eyes, "you have to listen to me."

David ignored me now, still on his phone. He headed for the door.

"Let me go!" I yelled. "Please!"

The door shut behind him.

Well, shit.

I sat there for I don't know how long, waiting. The ropes were too thick to break and I rubbed my wrists and ankles raw trying. The chair was too heavy for me to scoot to the desk to reach the phone or look for scissors. I was well and truly screwed.

The sun went down and the lights on the Strip came on. My back ached and my mouth was bone dry. I was starving, my stomach cramping with hunger pangs, and I tried not to think about how badly I had to pee. I knew Kade would come, hopefully sooner rather than later, and when he did it wouldn't be pretty.

Sometimes I really hate it when I'm right.

Darkness fell and with it came the inevitable.

I was dozing, my head drooping down to my chest, when the lights went out in the office, plunging me into darkness. I jerked awake as emergency lighting clicked on, a dull red glow. I listened hard, then started when I heard yelling and gunshots.

The door flew open and David barreled inside.

"What is this shit?" he gritted out.

"What's happening?" I asked.

"I don't fucking know. The lights went out, and when they came back on my men were gone. No one is answering their radio and the front desk security is silent." He looked panicked, his eyes darting around wildly. The gun in his hand shook slightly.

"Kade's here."

David's gaze whipped to mine.

"Untie me," I said, trying to get through to him. "Let me go. There's still time."

"No, there's not."

Both of us looked toward the door—in the direction the voice had come from—just as a gunshot sounded. David yelled in pain and dropped his gun. Kade was there in an instant, kicking the weapon away. It skittered across the floor.

"David, why'd you have to go and be an asshole?" Kade chastised him. "Our arrangement was working out so well. It's not my fault you're fucking incompetent."

David glowered at him, cradling his injured hand. I was glad Kade hadn't hurt him too badly.

"Fuck you, Dennon," David spat.

Kade ignored him and walked over to me, careful not to turn his back to David. I lowered my head, letting my hair obscure my face. I didn't want Kade to see, not yet. I just wanted to get out of there.

"You all right?" he asked softly, crouching down to cut through the bonds on my wrists. I hadn't even seen him pull his knife.

"Yeah, I'm fine," I said, flexing my freed arms. I winced when I rubbed my wrists where the ropes had scraped me.

I was grateful for the low light and kept my face averted as Kade finished freeing my legs.

"Let's go," he said.

But as I stood, my knees buckled immediately from having sat for so long. Kade quickly caught me around the waist, keeping me from falling. I turned my face away, but he was too quick. Catching my chin in his hand, he forced me to look at him.

Kade went very still when our eyes met. I didn't move, barely breathing, afraid of what he'd do. His gaze moved slowly from my swollen eye to my cheek.

"Go wait for me in the hall," he finally said, helping me to the door. His voice was quiet and calm, which was utterly terrifying.

"No, Kade, don't," I whispered. "Let's just go."

His fingers barely brushed my damaged face. "Do as I say," he said, and this time his tone was such that I knew better than to argue.

I walked out of the room and Kade closed the door behind me. The hallway was empty and I stood there, straining to listen, praying Kade wouldn't kill him.

A crash came from inside the office and my nails bit into my palms. I heard grunts and thuds, glass splintering, a man's scream. Was Kade all right? What if David got the upper hand? Should I do something? But Kade had said to wait here.

I was nearly hyperventilating when Kade finally emerged. I threw myself at him, relieved to find him unscathed. I wrapped my arms around his neck and his circled my waist.

"It's okay," he said softly in my ear. "You're safe now."

I drew back to look him in the eyes. "I was never worried that I wouldn't be."

Kade frowned a little at that, his thumb brushing my cheek, but I took his hand and stepped back. "Can we go now?"

He nodded wordlessly and moments later we were heading toward the front doors of the building. A black man, bigger than the other men I'd seen, stood nearby, holding a lethal-looking rifle. I froze in my tracks, my grip tightening on Kade's hand.

"It's okay," he said. "I know him."

I was still fearful and Kade seemed to sense that, pulling me closer as we neared the man.

"Thanks, Badger," Kade said, clasping hands with the guy. "Appreciate your help."

"Anytime," Badger said. "Did you leave the little fucker alive or is there a mess to clean up?" Badger had the same British accent as David.

"He's alive, but there's a mess," Kade replied.

"Did he shite himself?"

They both laughed at that, hardy-har-har, but I really wanted to leave. I pressed Kade's hand in a silent message.

"Gotta go, my man. Thanks again," Kade said, taking the hint and clapping Badger on the shoulder one last time. He helped me out the door and into his rented Mercedes. I relaxed against the seat with a sigh.

Kade took my hand again once he'd started the car, and he didn't let go until we were back at our hotel. I grabbed his sunglasses from the dash and put them on before I got out, using one hand to finger-comb my hair over the bruised side of my face. When Kade saw this, his jaw tightened, but he didn't say anything.

Once back in our suite, I headed straight for the bathroom. I was in there a long time. I knew I had to do damage control with Kade but was putting it off.

I showered and brushed my teeth and tried to avoid looking in the mirror, which wasn't easy. I put Kade's shirt back on when I was through, finding it somehow comforting to me in a way I didn't want to examine too closely.

After pawing through my makeup bag, I spent several minutes caking makeup on my bruises. It helped a little, but other than an icepack, there was nothing I could do about my swollen, bloodshot eye, so I put the sunglasses on again.

The smell of food made my stomach rumble and had me hurrying to finish brushing my hair. It had been twenty-four hours since I'd eaten and I felt more than a little shaky. When I came out of the bathroom, Kade was standing in front of the windows, his back to me, a drink held loosely in the hand at his side.

"Something smells good," I said with forced cheerfulness as I headed to the dining table. It was laden with dishes, the aroma making my mouth water. It seemed Kade had ordered one of everything on the menu for me. I grabbed a plate and started helping myself. "You don't mind if I start, do you?" I asked over my shoulder. "I'm starving."

"That's fine," Kade said, his voice flat.

I avoided looking at him, rounding the table to sit cross-legged in a chair before attacking the food piled on my plate. I heard the clink of ice in his glass as he made another drink.

Several minutes passed in silence that grew thick and heavy. I barely tasted what I ate, the churning in my stomach telling me what was coming though I resolutely tried to ignore it. Denial had become a favorite state of mind lately.

"It's good," I said. "You should come have some."

I felt more than heard Kade approach. He took the seat next to me and set his drink on the table. I caught a glimpse of his hand. The knuckles were raw and torn. I briefly wondered how well David had fared against Kade's rage, then decided I didn't really care. He'd hurt me and I was sure that now he was very, very sorry he had.

Kade sat on my injured side, which bothered me. I kept my hair hiding my face. I didn't want him to see, didn't want to talk about it. But he reached out and removed my sunglasses.

"No, leave it," I said, trying to grab the glasses back, but he'd already whisked them away. My fork clattered to my plate and I looked him in the eye. Time to tackle this head-on.

"I'm. Fine," I said firmly. "I know it looks bad, but I've been through worse. It'll heal in a few days, okay?"

"It's not 'okay,'" Kade said. "You could be dead—"

"I'm not," I broke in. "And thank you, for not killing him."

"I wanted to," he said matter-of-factly. "Nearly did."

"But you didn't, and we should focus on that." I smiled, but Kade didn't smile back. His eyes were bleak as he studied me, and my smile faded away, too.

"This is my fault," he murmured. "What was I thinking? That I could go legit and everything would be hunky-fuck-ing-dory?"

"It is not your fault. It's David's fault, the slimy asshole. You made a deal and he didn't keep his part of the bargain. You couldn't have known what he was going to do."

Kade's smile was bitter. "I'm like the kiss of death for you, princess."

"What? No! Don't say that." I was dismayed. I pushed back the midnight lock of hair that had fallen into his eyes, then cradled his cheek. "You rescued me," I said. "Like I knew you would."

"You shouldn't need to be rescued."

His words were so serious, and so final, that my breath caught.

"What are you getting at?" I asked, afraid of his answer.

His hand covered mine, the faint whiskers on his jaw softly abrading my skin as he turned his face into my palm and pressed his lips there. When his eyes again met mine, they were unusually bright.

"Tomorrow I'm taking you home," he said. "And then I'm leaving. You won't see me again."

I couldn't have heard that right. "What did you say?"

"It's not worth it," he said. "I won't risk you again." He stood, giving my fingers a squeeze before releasing my hand and heading back to the windows.

My hands turned to ice and I felt like the wind had been knocked out of me. I couldn't breathe. This couldn't be happening. Not again. I stood up so fast, my chair toppled behind me.

Kade turned around, his dark brows drawn, his mouth turned down in a frown.

"You are *not* going to do that," I gritted out. "How could you even say that? I thought we were friends, Kade, and friends don't just ditch each other when it's convenient."

"I'm not 'ditching' you," he retorted. "I'm saving your life. You were nearly killed because of me three months ago when Garrett broke in, and now this today. . . ."

"That doesn't matter—"

"It's done." Kade interrupted me. His voice echoed finality and he turned away, dismissing me as he walked toward the bar.

"So you're just going to give up? Just like that?" Anger masked my desperation. I didn't want to think about losing someone else, forever. I'd been so alone the past few months. Kade had helped me feel alive again.

"Sometimes you gotta know when to fold 'em," Kade quipped, flashing me a bitter smile as he poured more bourbon into his glass and took a healthy swallow. "Or at least that's what Kenny always said."

"Bullshit."

"You said it yourself," he said, lifting his glass as though in a toast. "Blane and I won't ever reconcile if you're still in the picture. That leaves only one option."

I sucked in my breath at that, his words cutting deep. It was one thing to blame myself for coming between them, but another thing entirely to hear Kade speak of tossing me aside so matter-of-factly. Guilt stirred within me even as my eyes filled with tears.

"Go to hell," I said, seething and hurrying past him to my bedroom. It was all I could do to not run. I slammed the door and flopped onto the bed.

My hands were shaking and I felt inches from falling apart. Everything I'd felt when Blane had dumped me came flooding back. The anger. The heartbreak. The loneliness. Even when Kade had been absent the past few months, I hadn't really thought it would be forever. I'd kept thinking that he'd turn up, sooner or later—that he hadn't abandoned me entirely.

Now it seemed he was prepared to do just that.

I had to get a grip. This wasn't me, this needy, weepy person. I'd withstood my father's death, my mother's illness and subsequent death, the breakup with my fiancé, being kidnapped—twice—and nearly dying too many times. Surely I could handle this.

But as logically as I reasoned out all that had happened to me, it didn't stop the deadening ache inside my chest. I wrapped my arms around my knees and rocked.

I don't know how long I stayed that way, my thoughts in a turmoil, wondering how I was going to get through the next few days, weeks, months. Alone. Again.

Hours passed and, eventually, I must have fallen asleep. Something woke me, though, and I jerked awake, cringing at the crick in my neck. Then I heard a thump and a crash.

Jumping to my feet, I hurried out of my room, afraid but still too sleep befuddled to reason. I stepped into the living room and halted, not fully comprehending the sight that met my eyes.

CHAPTER SEVEN

Kade was lying sprawled on his back on the floor, a half-empty bottle of bourbon at his side. A completely empty one lay a few feet away.

Shocked, I hurried to him and dropped to my knees at his side.

"Kade! Are you all right?" I grabbed his shoulder and he abruptly sat up, his eyes squinting as though the light hurt them even though it wasn't that bright.

"Pri*ncesss*," he slurred. "What're you doin' here? Thought you were 'sleep."

Oh God. He was drunk. I'd never seen him drunk, though I'd definitely seen him drink many times. Kade didn't strike me as the type to ever let down his guard enough to get drunk. I was surprised he'd done so tonight.

"Have you been out here drinking all this time?" I asked in dismay.

Kade's brow scrunched, as if he were trying to remember. "Um, yeah. Think so."

My gut twisted and I reached to take his arm. "Come on," I said. "Let's get you into bed."

Kade flashed a wicked smirk. "Tha's my line," he said. "But okay."

Getting him off the floor was a feat. He kept getting distracted. It was like trying to keep the attention of a two-year-old.

"Mmm, you smell good," he said, burying his nose in my hair when I leaned over to try to haul him upward.

"Thanks," I said, my good humor somewhat lacking. He was heavy. I tried pulling again, but he just sat there.

"Is that my shirt?" he asked. "My clothes look good on you, but I bet they'd look better *off* you." He began pulling at my buttons. I slapped his hands away.

"Stop that," I scolded. "Help me out here. Stand up."

After some stops and starts, Kade was finally on his feet, though I had a few scary moments when I feared he might topple over and take me down with him.

"C'mon," I said, heading to his bedroom. He leaned heavily on me.

"You're too little to carry me," he protested, trying to stand on his own. He immediately began listing to one side and I had to grab the front of his shirt to right him.

"Whoa there, buddy." I slid my arm back around his waist and drew his arm over my shoulders. "We're almost there, okay?"

"I forgot my bottle," he said, turning back halfheartedly. I had to turn with him or risk falling down.

"You don't need it. It's okay," I said, pulling him forward and shuffling him a few more steps closer to the bedroom.

"Course I need it," he scoffed. "She coulda *died*, you know. And it'd been *my* fault." Even with his slurring, I could understand he was talking about me. "I'm bad," he continued. "Bad for everybody."

"You're not bad," I insisted. "Just drunk." A few more steps and we'd be at the doorway to his bedroom, thank goodness. My shoulders were starting to ache.

"No, I'm bad," he said, narrowly avoiding taking out a table in the hallway. "She should be with Blane. He's the good one."

I wasn't sure I agreed with that.

"Told him, told him—not sleeping with her. Stupid fuck. Ruined it. Told me to get the fuck out. Done with me."

That made my ears perk up and distracted me from trying not to let Kade's flailing arm knock over what I was sure was an expensive flower-filled vase.

"What do you mean 'done with' you?" I asked.

"All these years," Kade mused, ignoring me. "Kept waiting for it, knew he'd be through eventu'ly. Still took me by surprise, though." His tone had changed from cheerful drunk to morose.

Blane had thrown Kade out? Told him he was done with him? Because of his stupid, idiotic belief in his uncle's lies? I gritted my teeth. As though this whole situation weren't complicated enough, Blane had to take away the one thing he'd tried so hard to give Kade all these years—his unconditional acceptance. Asshole.

I managed to get to the bed and was relieved to plop Kade down on it. He looked at me as though just realizing again who I was.

"Hey, you're here!" he said in wonderment, reaching out to clumsily pat my uninjured cheek until he saw the bruises on the other. "I want to kill him."

His tone was menacing, much different than how he'd been speaking previously.

"What?" I asked warily.

"The fucker who did this to you," he said, his eyes widening and blinking as he tried to focus. "I want to kill him."

"I don't want you to do that," I said, crouching down to remove his shoes. "You beat him up—that's enough."

"You bet your ass I did," Kade said. I had to hide a smile. He sounded like a kid who'd gotten a good grade on a report card and was proud of it. "Broke his fucking hand."

Okay, that was news.

I pushed the thought aside—there was nothing I could do about it anyway, and I didn't know if I would have if given the choice. It struck me then that I was more cavalier, and perhaps more bloodthirsty, than I used to be. Maybe I'd seen too many bad people doing too many bad things to turn the other cheek anymore. Punishment and justice seemed in short supply these days, and I found myself resolutely glad that Kade had meted out both, frontier style.

I stood up with a sigh, dragging Kade's T-shirt over his head. His arms fell back to his sides, like he didn't have the strength to lift them. He stared at me as I folded the shirt and set it aside.

"What?" I asked. "Did you need something?"

Kade grabbed my hand and tugged me between his spread knees, resting his head against my stomach. I took the opportunity to bury my fingers in his hair, always soft to the touch. His hands moved to settle on my hips.

"You okay?" I asked softly. "Tired, I bet." I remembered his raw knuckles and untangled myself to go get a washcloth. I came back and reached for his hand, carefully dabbing away the dried blood.

"This is a dream, right?" Kade asked, staring at me again, completely oblivious to what I was doing.

I smiled a little. "I hope not," I joked. "Surely you can do better."

"Don't call me *Shirley,*" he said automatically. I laughed at the joke, overused though it was.

He closed his eyes and tipped his head back slightly. "I love to hear you laugh," he murmured. "Makes me think of springtime, and carnivals, and being happy."

My smile faded. The things Kade said sometimes—they made my heart hurt.

"Aren't you happy?" I asked.

His eyes opened, their piercing blue captivating me.

"I am when I'm with you."

My heart seemed to skip a beat and the small smile I gave him was watery. "Me, too," I whispered, my throat clogged with emotion.

"No, no, no, don't cry," he said, his dismay evident. He got to his feet before I could react, though he seemed slightly steadier now. Cupping my face in his hands, he pressed light kisses along my cheeks and around my eyes. "Don't cry," he softly repeated, the words brushing across my skin.

My arms were trapped between our bodies and I tentatively rested my hands on his bare chest. Kade pulled back slightly to look at me, but I couldn't meet his eyes. My gaze dropped to his chest.

This close to him, I could see a thin white, jagged scar that was about four inches long, running in a slice down toward his abdomen. I traced it with my finger, wondering how he'd gotten it. If it, like the cigarette-burn scars on his back, was a bleak memento from a crueler time in his life.

Without warning he placed his hands around my waist to pick me up, then turned and laid me on the bed. Surprised, I tried to sit up but was trapped by him hovering over me. He was on all fours, his arms and legs a cage. Then he kissed me.

He tasted of bourbon and Kade, forbidden and sweet. I became lost in sensation, my mind replaying his declaration from earlier.

You won't see me again.

I wrapped my arms around his neck and pulled him closer, kissing him back with everything I had in me. Tears leaked from my eyes, trailing down my face to the pillow underneath my head.

Kade made a noise, the sound a low rumble in his throat. His hands began to fumble with the buttons on my shirt, but after a moment, he gave up and tore the fabric free. Buttons flew everywhere.

His mouth covered my breast with no preamble whatsoever, making me gasp even as he moaned. He licked and suckled my breasts as though starved and unable to get his fill. My nipples ached, sensitized to his slightest touch, while the flesh between my legs grew plump and moist.

I clutched his head to me, rubbing my thighs restlessly together to relieve some of the ache. Kade's fingers latched into the thin elastic around my hips and he tugged my panties down, sitting up on his haunches to pull them off my legs.

I had a brief moment of clarity. Was I really going to do this? Kade was drunk, but I had no excuse.

It was one of those moments that seemed frozen in time even as a barrage of thoughts raced through my head. I knew in my bones that what I was contemplating was probably wrong—knew that I should stop Kade and just leave. Guilt would no doubt consume me in the cold light of day, adding to that which already dogged my every waking moment.

And I was suddenly tired of it all. Tired of feeling guilty for coming between Blane and Kade. Tired of seeing my hopes and dreams vaporizing into dust. Tired of losing people I loved. Tired of the heartache I endured each and every day and the regrets I had for trusting a man who couldn't trust me in return. But mostly I was tired of doing what I was *supposed* to do, what I was *expected* to do, when I got *nothing* from it but pain and a broken heart.

And in the moment of time it took for Kade to strip off his jeans and settle back between my legs, I made my decision. I was going to be selfish and take this slice of happiness and not think about the consequences, just this once.

Kade lay between my spread thighs, his body covering mine. He kissed me again, cradling my jaw as though I were made of delicate porcelain. I felt him at the entrance to my body and I was more than ready. But he surprised me, sitting back while drawing me up onto his lap, all while still kissing me.

He pushed inside me in one strong thrust, settling me astride him. I tore my mouth from his, choking on a gasp. It had been a while and Kade wasn't a small guy. His shirt was still hanging off my shoulders so I let go of him long enough to push it off and fling it away. Kade took the opportunity to wrap his arms underneath mine and pull my shoulders back. I whimpered as his mouth closed again over my nipple, his tongue doing things that made me dig my fingernails into his arms.

I couldn't move. Everything overwhelmed me. The hard thickness of Kade inside me, his mouth tormenting me, his arms surrounding me. His hands moved to my hips, lifting me nearly off him before letting me slide back down. A sound I was sure I'd never made before escaped me.

I pried open my eyes, trying to focus on raising myself up. He was going to think I was completely inept at this if I just kept sitting there like I didn't know what to do. My legs trembled but somehow I managed to lift up before coming down again. We both moaned at the sensation.

Kade took my mouth again, his hands easily helping to raise and lower me as we found a rhythm. My breasts were crushed against his chest, their sensitive tips creating a delicious friction as we moved.

It grew heated between us and our skin grew sweaty. My hair was plastered to my neck and I had to tear my mouth from Kade's so I could breathe. He buried his face in my neck, licking the salt from my skin.

My orgasm crashed over me in a sharp explosion of pleasure. I cried out with the force of it, my body gripping Kade's, contracting around him.

"Ah God," he gasped, his voice choked. His hands dug into my hips, holding me still. "Not yet," he breathed. "Don't want it to end yet."

After a moment, he seemed to regain control. In a quick motion, he turned me so I was facing the other direction. My thighs were pushed even farther apart in this new position, angling him deeper inside me.

His lips brushed my ear. "You're perfect. Everything I'd imagined," Kade whispered. His hands roamed over my body as I rested against him, one at my breast, the other skimming down my stomach to touch softly between my legs.

His hips moved steadily beneath mine while his hand gently stroked me, and all the while he whispered things in my ear, things that made me blush, but I didn't want him to stop. He whispered about how beautiful I was, how my body was flushed and hot, how I tasted and how he wanted to put his mouth between my legs, how he'd dreamt of us like this, how much he loved me.

My eyes flew open.

"God, I love you. Waited for so long . . ." Kade swept my hair to the side and pressed openmouthed kisses to my neck. His hips moved faster, as did his hand, and I couldn't think anymore, my body coiling inside with tension. He thrust harder and I twisted so I could kiss him. Our tongues tangled as he jerked into me, his whole body seeming to convulse. Kade losing all control was a heady thing. I could smell his own distinctive scent mingled with mine, the combination tinged with our sweat. My fingers dug into his hair, holding him so our mouths stayed as connected as our bodies. The feel of him pulsing inside me sent me over the edge again.

I would have collapsed if he wasn't holding me up. My hair lay half covering my face and I was too weak to even lift a hand to push it out of the way. I sucked down air, my heart still thundering in my ears.

Kade was brushing kisses along my neck and shoulder, our bodies still connected. I leaned my head back on his shoulder and raised my arms to comb through his hair, now damp and clinging to his own wet skin. His hands cupped my breasts, gently rolling the sensitive tips in his fingers. I felt an answering quiver deep inside.

His finger dipped down to touch where we were joined, smearing some of the fluid there on my clit. I jerked in his arms, overly sensitive.

"No," I breathed. "I can't again."

"Yes, you can," he said, his voice dark as sin. "I want to feel your body reach that ecstasy again, watch your face when you come, and know I'm the one doing it to you."

His touch was expert, knowing, and just when I thought I wouldn't be able to handle any more, he would change it—harder, softer, faster—until I was panting in his arms. Impossibly, he grew hard again inside me. Sooner than I would have believed possible, I was coming again, more intensely than before.

Kade's moan was one of both pleasure and pain, then he was rearranging us, laying me on my back and moving my legs up until they rested, one on each of his shoulders. He entered me again, his hips driving hard as he leaned his weight on his hands, pushing my legs closer to my chest.

It was hard and fast, my positioning erotic and making me feel very exposed. He was deep inside me and his eyes were glued to mine, the look in them branding his possession and adoration. I couldn't blink, couldn't look away. The bond between us felt as though it were being forged in heat and sweat and flesh.

Only when his orgasm took him did he close his eyes, cries and gasps falling from his mouth in a moment of utter vulnerability. I watched, awestruck by how beautiful he was.

He collapsed next to me on the bed, sucking large gasps of air into his lungs. I couldn't help a smile. So I'd finally found out what made Kade Dennon out of breath.

His eyes cracked open just a fraction and he pulled me closer to him, his arm heavy on my waist. Slanting his lips across mine, he gave me another deep kiss before resting his head on the pillow of my breasts, his eyes falling shut again.

"Love you," he murmured, and I knew he was already half asleep.

I reached down and pulled the sheet up over us, though Kade was already out, and cradled him to me, my fingers running through his sweat-dampened hair. I felt content and safe, and I had no trouble finding my own way into slumber.

~

When next I woke, it was late morning. Kade was still out cold. I figured it would be a while before the booze he'd drunk would wear off. Getting out of bed, I grabbed Kade's torn and discarded shirt off the floor and went to shower.

I stood under the streaming hot water for a long time, thinking. Hearing Kade tell me he loved me was shocking, overwhelming . . . exhilarating. I'd known we were friends, known for a while that he wanted to sleep with me, but I never would have known or guessed that he loved me . . . or that he'd ever tell me so.

But did I love him?

I didn't think I had an answer for that question. I cared about him. A lot. I didn't want to lose him. Making love with him had been . . . incredible. My body still tingled and I blushed at some of the things we'd done.

But . . . Blane.

It always seemed to come back to him. The guilt, the pain, the heartache, the betrayal. He was still controlling my life even though he'd pushed me from his. What did I have to offer Kade except being the wedge that would constantly drive him and Blane apart? And I couldn't even tell Kade that I was no longer in love with Blane. I wouldn't lie to him.

Kade certainly deserved more than his brother's left-overs.

That cynical thought made me go still, the water streaming from my hair, over my shoulders and down my back.

The guilt I'd known I'd feel had returned and now threatened to swallow me whole. It hit me, really hit me, what we'd done.

What *I'd* done.

On autopilot, I got out of the shower and dried myself off. I couldn't change the past, couldn't change what had happened between Kade and me. And if I was really honest, I didn't know that I wanted to. I could live with the guilt, but I didn't know if I could have lived with turning away from the one chance I had to make love with Kade.

Nothing could come of it, I knew that. But one time with Kade, hearing him tell me how he felt about me—I wouldn't trade it for anything. And when he left and I never saw him again, I'd have it to remember. I wouldn't fight him leaving. It would be selfish of me to do that. The only way Blane and Kade were going to regain their trust in each other was if I wasn't in either of their lives.

I pulled on a pair of the shorts I'd bought and found another shirt of Kade's to wear. He was still dead to the world, so I ordered coffee and breakfast from room service.

I sipped my coffee and stared out the window at the Vegas Strip, which looked much different in the harsh light of the Nevada summer sun. What was I going to say to Kade when he woke? What would he say to me?

I heard the shower start in his bathroom and chewed a nail as I waited. I was as nervous as I'd been when I'd first met Kade, when his fallen angel good looks and the aura of danger emanating from him had overwhelmed me.

Kade emerged from the bedroom clad in jeans and an unbuttoned shirt, with bare feet. He walked toward me while toweling his hair dry. I couldn't help my soft smile or the stutter of my heart when I saw him, memories of how he'd been last night flashing through my mind.

"Good morning," I said cheerily, glad to see him despite my nerves.

Kade winced, glancing up at the windows and squinting. He didn't answer, just grabbed his sunglasses off the dining table and put them on. Shuffling toward me, he sat down heavily on the couch.

"What time is it?" he asked.

I glanced at the clock. "Pushing noon."

"Christ," he muttered, leaning forward to rest his elbows on his knees while he rubbed his eyes under the sunglasses.

I shifted nervously in my chair. Was I supposed to say something? What were the rules for the morning after? Were we not supposed to talk about it?

"My head feels like it's going to fall off my neck," he grumbled.

"Well, that's what happens when you drink too much," I replied mildly.

Kade heaved a sigh and leaned back against the couch. I tried, and failed, not to stare at his chest.

"Sorry about last night," Kade said. "I, uh, usually don't drink that much."

I frowned. Was he apologizing for being drunk—or for what had followed? "It's fine," I finally said.

"I didn't act like an asshole, did I?"

I stared at Kade, an inkling of horror dawning. When I didn't answer, he lifted his head to look at me.

"Did I?"

I swallowed. Hard. "You . . . don't remember?"

He shook his head. "I remember us arguing, then I started drinking. That's pretty much the extent of the replay."

Stunned, I just gaped at him, the familiar ache in the center of my chest returning with a vengeance. My stomach gave a hard roll and I thought I might throw up.

"What?" he asked, the expression on my face seeming to clue him in on my dismay. "I said something, didn't I." He shook his head and rubbed his eyes again. "Fuck. I'm sorry. I'm a bastard, you know that. I didn't mean it, whatever it was."

I shut my mouth with a snap. I should be glad about this. Kade had just punched the reset button. Last night never happened. I was the only one who knew we'd made love, knew Kade had told me he loved me, and I didn't have to tell a soul.

The thought made me want to cry.

"Um, no," I said, pulling myself out of my stupor. "It's fine. No worries." I forced a fake smile. "You were drunk. People do and say all kinds of things when they're three sheets to the wind."

The ringing of Kade's cell phone interrupted our conversation and I gladly got up to get more coffee. Anything to get a moment to compose myself, to realign my expectations and emotions with a reality I hadn't expected.

I was lost in my own thoughts until I realized that Kade had turned on the television and stood watching it while still on his cell.

"I'm watching," he said to the person on the other end.

Puzzled, I moved to his side so I could see the screen, too, then about spit my coffee.

A photo of Kandi Miller, Blane's ex-girlfriend and a member of a wealthy, politically connected family, was displayed on the screen. She was beautiful, with long blonde hair and a tall, willowy figure. As I watched, I processed the voice-over by the news anchor.

". . . found murdered in her home in Indianapolis. Police have not yet made an arrest, but sources inside the department say they're not ruling out anyone, including Indiana gubernatorial candidate Blane Kirk. Mr. Kirk and Miss Miller had a prior relationship and were no longer dating. However, anonymous reports say the two had recently rekindled their romance."

Video footage of Blane showed him walking from his house to his car. Over a dozen reporters mobbed him, shouting questions as he pushed through. Blane's eyes were hidden behind sunglasses and his face was expressionless.

He didn't respond to any questions, just got in his car and drove away.

My knees gave out and I sat heavily on the couch, staring at the screen. Kandi was dead? Murdered? And it seemed the police suspected Blane.

Kade muted the TV and spoke into his cell. "Yeah, I saw." A pause. "I'll be back in a few hours." He ended the call.

"Was that Blane?" I asked hopefully.

Kade shook his head. "Clarice. He doesn't know she called."

"Why wouldn't Blane call you himself?" I knew they were currently on the outs, but surely something like this over-rode the petty disagreement about me.

Kade's jaw tightened. "Because he's still being a fucking moron," he said bitterly. "Pack up. We're leaving."

I hurried to obey, my mind spinning with the news. It was killing me not to call Clarice, but I didn't want to take the time, not when it was obviously imperative that Kade get back to Indy as soon as possible.

I pancaked on some makeup as quickly as I could to cover the bruises, glad to see that my eye was no longer swollen. I then threw my stuff into the suitcase and was hauling it out into the hallway not ten minutes later. Kade was already waiting, his shirt now buttoned though sunglasses still hid his eyes. He was staring at something in his hand, but it was little and I couldn't see what it was.

"I'm ready," I said.

He looked up and his gaze fixed on me for a moment. I shifted my weight from one foot to the other, nervous under his scrutiny.

"What?" I finally said, somewhat testily.

Kade shook his head, putting whatever was in his hand into the pocket of his jeans. "Nothing. Let's go."

The flight back to Indianapolis seemed interminable. The same "friend" of Kade's who'd allowed him to use his private jet for the flight out was also letting us use it to go back. We'd boarded the plane and then I'd had nothing to do for hours except sit and dwell on what had happened, imagining every possible scenario.

The anchor's words kept replaying in my head. Sources said Blane and Kandi were back together? That surprised me. After we'd found out that Kandi's hatred for me had indirectly caused her to give a hit man all the information he needed to know to kill me, I'd assumed that Blane had cut all ties with her.

But now I reflected that that had been a naive notion. Blane and Kandi had grown up together, been chosen by their parents to make an advantageous political match. They'd broken up several times, but always seemed to get back together. Maybe after our breakup, Blane had reverted to the original plan that had included Kandi.

I finally ginned up the courage to ask Kade. "So were Blane and Kandi back together?"

Kade grimaced. "I don't know, but I wouldn't find it that hard to believe if they were."

That shut me up. Kade knew Blane better than anyone. If he thought Blane would go back to her . . .

It was nearly 8:00 P.M. in Indy, but the heat and humidity outside the terminal made my shirt instantly stick to my skin as Kade put our luggage in his car. I missed the pool in Vegas with a vengeance.

Kade had been driving for a few minutes when I realized he wasn't heading to my apartment.

"Where are we going?" I asked.

"Blane's."

Instant panic. "No way," I protested. "Take me home." He'd take one look at Kade and me together, another look at the bruises on my face, and then all hell would break loose.

"He needs you. I'm taking you there."

"Are you kidding me?" I couldn't wrap my head around this. Kade was offering me up to Blane? "The last thing he needs is more drama, which is exactly what will happen if I go there. Especially if I'm with you."

"He knew we were together. This isn't a surprise."

Of course, neither of them knew how "together" Kade and I had been. I rubbed my forehead, a sudden headache coming on. Short of jumping out of a moving car, which I wasn't too crazy about doing, there was little I could do. I sat in the passenger seat, fuming at Kade and worried about Blane.

A few minutes later, we pulled into the driveway of Blane's house. The reporters had left and the house was dark.

"Is he home?" I wondered aloud as I got out of the car.

"Let's find out."

I had no choice but to follow Kade inside. My nerves were shot. I swung my hair farther over my face and hoped I could stick to the shadows. Though Kade seemed sure that Blane would want me there, I wasn't convinced.

Mona was in the kitchen when we entered through the back door. She took one look at Kade and threw her arms around him.

"Thank God you're back," she said, her voice thick with tears.

Kade hugged her for a moment, then she caught sight of me. The tears came even faster now as she wrapped her arms around me, squeezing me so tight I could barely breathe.

"Kathleen!" she exclaimed. "I can't believe it. Thank you for coming. He needs you."

"How is he?" Kade asked.

Mona released me and I took a deep breath, my own eyes stinging at the warmth of Mona's heartfelt embrace.

Mona gave a frustrated shrug. "Who knows? He won't talk to me. Always keeps things to himself. He went to work today, but he wouldn't eat dinner. He's been in the library all evening."

"Has Robert been here?"

I stiffened. Robert. Blane's uncle. But Mona shook her head.

"I don't think Blane wants to draw him into this." Her eyes filled again. "What's going to happen, Kade?"

Kade gave her another one-armed hug and pressed a kiss to the top of her head. "Don't worry. It'll be okay."

She nodded, dabbing a tissue to her eyes.

"I could use some coffee," Kade said.

Mona immediately moved to the coffeepot. "Good idea," she said. "I'll make some."

I had the feeling Kade could care less about the coffee, but it gave Mona something to do, and it was perceptive of him to realize she needed that.

Something brushed against my legs and I reached down to give Tigger a scratch behind the ears. Poor guy. His mom had just up and left him, though it didn't look like he'd had it too rough. Scrutinizing him, it looked like he'd put on a pound or two.

We ran into Gerard in the hallway. He gave Kade a solid handshake.

"Good of you to come," he said roughly. When he saw me, he seemed surprised but gave me a hug. "I'm glad Blane didn't make you hate him forever, sweetheart. We've missed you, Mona and me." He drew back. "Blane, too," he added with a meaningful look.

"I've missed you and Mona, too," I said. I didn't know what to say about the Blane part.

"He's in the library," Gerard told Kade with a sigh.

"Thanks, Gerard," Kade said.

As we drew closer to the door, my anxiety ratcheted up. If nothing else, I was sure Blane was upset about Kandi's death. I had sincere doubts he wanted another ex-girlfriend to share in his misery.

Kade seemed to sense my encroaching panic, taking my hand firmly in his. He rapped once on the door, then pushed it open.

The room was relatively dark. A single lamp gave off a weak glow that didn't quite reach the far corners of the room. Blane was sitting in one of the matching leather chairs by the fireplace.

I hid slightly behind Kade, embarrassed to be intruding. It felt like Blane and I were strangers now. I shouldn't be there.

Blane glanced up as Kade stepped inside the room. He stiffened and immediately got to his feet.

"I didn't realize you were back," Blane said as Kade walked closer. I remained lingering in the shadows of the doorway.

"News travels fast." Kade stopped in front of Blane. "How are you doing?"

Blane took a drink of the amber liquid from the glass he held before answering. "Better than Kandi."

"What happened?"

"They found her, early this morning. Strangled."

I sucked in a breath at the image he painted, the pain in Blane's voice evident. I'd hated Kandi, but no one deserved that.

"Jesus," Kade breathed, turning to pace a few steps away. He shoved a hand through his hair. Then he seemed to recollect something and glanced around. Spotting me in the doorway, he crooked his finger, beckoning me. "I thought you might need somebody to talk to," he said to Blane, watching me reluctantly walk forward.

Blane turned around as I stepped into the light, the hand holding his glass freezing in place halfway to his mouth.

I managed to make it all the way over to him, each step feeling as though I was wading through quicksand. The pull of Blane like a black hole, drawing me in. After what felt like an eternity, I stopped directly in front of him.

"Blane," I said, "I'm really, really sorry about Kandi. I know she meant a lot to you." Once the words were out

179

of my mouth, I was glad I'd said them. Regardless of our tumultuous history, I wasn't the kind of person to turn my back when someone I loved was in need. If Blane needed me, I'd be there for him.

The expression on Blane's face was one of utter surprise. Perhaps he didn't expect that I'd meant it, or that I even wanted to be there. But where I came from, you put aside the hurts and history when tragedy struck.

Without even looking at him, Blane handed his glass to Kade, who took it without question, then Blane was folding me into his arms.

He pulled me so close and so tight, I felt my trepidation ease away like sloughing off an old, heavy coat.

I heard the door behind me close softly, and knew that Kade had left us alone.

CHAPTER EIGHT

I didn't know what else to do or say. What do you say in times like this? I remembered when my dad and mom had died. Multitudes of people had shaken my hand, told me how sorry they were, and I'd tried to be strong—first for my mom, then for myself. I had seen the pity in their eyes, but I'd made it through the funerals, waiting until I was alone to fall apart.

Chance had been with me then and I was reminded of that now. He was the only family I had left. It had felt so good to have someone to lean on, someone who I knew wouldn't pity me, but just loved me and would let me be vulnerable to my sorrow. Blane needed that kind of someone right now, and maybe he could allow himself to do the same with me.

We stood like that for a long time, in silence, wrapped in each other's arms. I closed my eyes and breathed in Blane's scent. I didn't allow myself to think of anything. I just savored this moment and being in his arms, a place I'd thought I'd never be again. Only when his grip finally loosened did I let go, too. My mom had always said to never be the first one to stop hugging.

Blane took my hand and tucked my arm under his, drawing me over to the sofa. We sat, him so close his thigh pressed against mine. He cradled my hand in his, intently studying my palm. But I had the feeling he was really gazing inward, which was confirmed when he began talking.

"They called me this morning," he said. "I have a few friends on the force. One of them was there and knew of our . . . relationship."

I pressed my lips firmly together to keep from asking if that was a past or present-tense form of "relationship." That was none of my business. Not anymore.

"When I got there, her body was still where they'd found it—" His voice cracked and he broke off. He cradled my hand now in both of his, hunching over to rest his elbows on his knees. After a moment, he seemed to regain control. "She wasn't always the way you knew her," Blane said. "She used to be sweet. Selfish and spoiled, yes, but not bitter. That came later. And I keep thinking that it's my fault. She was unhappy because I let her down."

His words tore at me. The blame game? Yes, I was familiar with that one. "Blane, no," I said. "You weren't responsible for Kandi's happiness. She was. She made her own decisions. And I know she thought you and her were supposed to be together, but it's not your fault that it didn't work out that way." I gave a small shrug. "People grow. People change. And what may have made sense when you were fifteen isn't the same when you're older and life has changed both of you."

Blane looked at me, his eyes wet and filled with pain and grief. My own eyes stung in sympathy.

"I haven't told you the worst part," he said, his voice thick. "When they called, told me my ex had been found murdered—at first I thought it was you." He swallowed, then seemed to have to force the next words out. "And when they told me it was Kandi, I was . . . relieved."

It seemed like he couldn't look me in the eye any longer and bowed his head again, bringing my hand to his forehead as though in prayer. I felt the wet streaks on his face against my skin.

My vision blurred with tears at Blane's confession, a confession of something he deemed reprehensible but was really just . . . human. But rarely did Blane get to be just human. Too many people counted on him and too much was expected of him by others as well as himself. Now he was punishing himself for feeling an emotion—relief—something he had no control over.

"Blane, please," I said, "don't do this to yourself. You can't control what you feel. It doesn't mean you loved Kandi any less. Please don't punish yourself." I wrapped my free arm around him the best I could, leaning into him as though I could convince him by my sheer physical presence.

He looked up at me, his eyes red and swollen, and my heart nearly broke. I swiped gently at his wet cheeks and leaned forward, pressing my lips to his forehead and pulling his head to rest on my shoulder. He wrapped his arms around my waist and leaned on me. It was the first time that Blane had ever shown that he needed me in this way or that he was anything less than in complete control.

After a few minutes, Blane lifted his head. I gave him a small smile. His hair was in disarray and I couldn't resist the temptation to push my fingers lightly through it, rearranging the blond locks into their usual place as if I could rearrange his emotions.

Blane lifted a hand to my cheek and I stilled. He was so close and now the air between us changed, making me acutely aware of him. The rustle of his clothes when he moved, the way his eyes stared intently into mine, the saline making their usually gray depths a clear, brilliant green.

His head lowered and I knew what was coming, but I didn't move away. I couldn't. And in another moment, he was kissing me, his lips moving gently over mine in the lightest of caresses.

Tears clogged my throat and I held in a sob. Kissing him again, being in his arms, just being near him, was so bittersweet it made my chest hurt. The familiar feel and taste of him was like finally being given a sweet after being denied for a long, long while.

When he lifted his head, I was flustered, unsure what had just happened, why he'd done that, what it meant . . . A thousand questions ran through my mind and I couldn't meet his eyes. Nervously, I pushed my hair behind my ear.

Blane's hold on me suddenly tightened and I glanced up at him. He was frowning, and as he looked at me, his expression changed to disbelief. I was about to ask what was wrong when he took my chin in his hand and turned my face toward the light. He sucked in a sharp breath. That's when I remembered the bruises.

Shit.

"What happened?" he asked, his voice rife with fury.

I tried to turn away, but his grip tightened on my face, preventing me.

"Did Kade do this to you?"

"You're. Hurting. Me," I gritted out. Blane immediately released me. "No," I said. "Of course Kade didn't do this.

How could you think that? It just . . . happened. How does any of the crap that happens to me happen? It just . . . does."

"It's precisely for that reason that you shouldn't be around either of us," Blane said.

"That's your opinion," I retorted.

"It's a fact," he shot back.

I bit back what I was going to say, the stark paleness of Blane's face reminding me that this wasn't about me, not really. He was bound to overreact, given what had happened to Kandi and the guilt he felt.

"When did you last eat?" I asked.

Blane just looked at me, no doubt knowing full well that I was changing the subject.

"Weren't you just chewing my ass out a few days ago for not eating?" I asked. "Come on. I'm hungry and I'm sure Mona has something in the kitchen." I got to my feet and tugged on his arm.

"I'm not hungry," Blane said, resisting my attempts to pry him off the couch.

"If you don't eat, I don't eat."

Blane glowered at me, but I stood my ground. Finally, the corners of his mouth tipped up slightly.

"God, I've missed you," he murmured.

I couldn't go there, not if I wanted to maintain my composure. Yet I found myself saying quietly, "Yeah, me, too." I glanced away, my cheeks burning with the admission. I released his arm, but Blane stood and caught my hand in his.

We went to the kitchen, and I could hear Mona's and Kade's voices as we approached. The moment we stepped into the room, Kade's eyes zeroed in on Blane's and my joined hands. I tried to ease mine from Blane's without making a big deal of it, but he kept a firm hold.

We sat at the small table, me between Blane and Kade, who sat opposite each other. I managed to free my hand from Blane's when Mona set a plate in front of me.

"I made sandwiches," she said. "But I can make something more substantial if you want."

"Sandwiches are great," I said quickly, my smile forced. Most of my attention was directed to how Kade and Blane were eyeing each other.

"Mona," I called as she was about to leave the room, "won't you sit and visit for a few minutes? I haven't seen you in a while."

Mona beamed at me and sat down at the table. "Gerard took your car to get it filled up," she told Kade.

"That's nice of him," I said. I wished I had a Gerard.

"He likes to do stuff for the boys," Mona said with a wave of her hand and an indulgent smile.

I took a bite of my sandwich to hide my own smile. It was just so funny to hear her refer to Blane and Kade, two dangerous men, as "boys."

"So what have you been up to, Kathleen?" Mona asked.

I swallowed and took a drink of the water she'd set in front of me, noticing that both Kade and Blane were now looking at me and waiting for my answer. "I decided to go back to school," I said.

"That's wonderful!" Mona said. "What are you studying, dear?"

I took a deep breath before answering. "Criminal justice."

"Why?" Blane asked.

I looked at him, surprised. "Why what?"

"Why would you pick criminal justice?" he clarified. "I thought you didn't want to become a lawyer anymore."

"A scum-sucking, bottom-feeding lawyer isn't the only career you can pick with a criminal justice degree," Kade interrupted. My eyes widened at his deliberate insult and Blane stiffened. "She can go into law enforcement, private investigation, the FBI—any number of fields."

"You mean, so she can know exactly how to evade and bend, if not outright break, the law? Just like you, right, Kade?"

"Looks like she won't have much choice, seeing as how you threw her out of your life and, just to add insult to injury, took her main source of income with you," Kade shot back.

"What, you didn't swoop in and save the day?" Blane sneered, leaning slightly over the table. "Didn't buy her another expensive car or leave twenty grand on her table again?"

Okay, news flash—I didn't realize Blane knew about that.

Kade leaned forward, too. "At least I did something about it," he said, his voice rife with anger and contempt. "Unless she dances to your tune and obeys your every whim, you could give a shit what becomes of her."

"Listen, you sonofabitch—" Blane began.

"Boys!"

Mona's sharp interjection cut through what Blane had been about to say, making me start in my seat at the tone of her voice. Both Blane and Kade shut up, but their eyes were glued to each other's and their body language screamed that they were a hair trigger from coming to blows.

Again.

Because of me.

"First of all," Mona said, her voice quieter but still edged with steel, "language. You know I won't tolerate language of that sort in this house."

Kade broke the staring contest with Blane first, glancing guiltily at Mona. Blane sat back in his chair and stared glumly down at the table.

"Second," Mona continued, "may I remind you that a dear friend of this family has died. I don't think I need to point out that your behavior is disrespectful to her memory. And last, I was having a pleasant conversation with Kathleen, which you rudely interrupted, and now your bickering has upset her." She gestured toward me.

The distress I felt at their fighting must have shown on my face, because Blane and Kade both looked at me, their expressions changing to an identical one of chagrin.

I cleared my throat and scooted back my chair from the table. "Um, I think it's best if I leave. Mona, can Gerard give me a lift home?"

"Of course, dear," she said a little sadly.

I stood but was stopped by Blane's hand on my arm.

"Please don't leave," he said.

I looked at him, surprised.

"We won't fight—I swear it," he continued. "Just . . . stay. Please."

It was a bad idea, I could feel it in my bones. But his eyes were pleading with me, saying things his mouth couldn't, and in the end I couldn't tell him no. Then again, when had I ever been able to tell Blane no?

"You promise not to fight?" I asked, looking to Kade as well. "Both of you?"

"Oh, am I invited to the sleepover, too?" Kade said, his tone laden with sarcasm and his eyes on Blane.

"Kade," Mona admonished.

"Of course," Blane said. He had his lawyer face back on and I couldn't read anything from his tone or expression.

"Blane," Mona said, "I would think, given his training, that Kade would be a big help to you in finding out who did those awful things to Kandi."

"We can talk about that later," Blane hedged.

"I'll just call it a night then," I said. "It's been a long day." I was desperate to get away, my nerves shot from too much happening too fast.

"I'll walk you up," Blane said.

I caught Kade's eye but didn't know what to say or do, if anything. His gaze was cold and nothing at all like the way he'd looked at me last night.

A flicker of the memories I'd been avoiding all day flashed through my mind and I felt my cheeks burn. Kade's brows drew together and he frowned before I hastily turned away. I felt Blane's hand settle on the small of my back as we walked toward the stairs.

"I know the way," I said quietly as we started upstairs. "You don't have to come with me."

"I know" was all he said.

It was silent between us the rest of the way to "my" room, but not uncomfortable. When we paused at the doorway, I turned to face Blane, suddenly reminded of the first time I'd stood outside this door with him looming over me.

He stood close, close enough for me to breathe in the scent of his cologne. Close enough that if I made the slightest move toward him, I knew he'd have his arms around me in the blink of an eye. I stayed very still, though the temptation to inch closer was strong. I remembered the kiss from earlier. I was confused and uncertain. What did he want from me? Hadn't I already given him everything? In spite of that, I was worried about him. Would I ever learn self-preservation when it came to Blane?

"Are you going to be okay tonight?" I asked.

Blane gave a bitter huff of laughter.

I stiffened. "What's so funny?"

"Even after everything I've done, how I've treated you, you're still worried about me," he said.

I frowned. "And that's funny?"

Blane shook his head, his expression turning grave. "Not a bit. It's tragic. For me. For you. For what we had. I knew you . . . know you . . . and I let myself believe . . ." He glanced away for a moment, then back. Our eyes met.

"I've wasted so much time," he said baldly, "made so many mistakes. I'm damn lucky you're even here at all, that you still care. But then again, that's the kind of person you are."

I was also the kind of person who had slept with his brother less than twenty-four hours ago and was desperately trying to pretend it hadn't happened. I decided not to mention that, but my silence didn't stop the guilt from rising like nausea in my stomach.

"I'm not a saint, Blane," I said, looking at the floor because my guilt made it impossible for me to look him in the eye any longer. "I just care about you—that's all. I don't like to see you hurting."

Reaching out, he fingers brushed my uninjured check and I reluctantly lifted my eyes. "You were always too good for me, Kat," he said. "It just took me too long to see it." There was the lightest touch of his thumb to my lips, then he was heading back downstairs.

But I wasn't too good for him. I was a horrible person keeping a painful secret.

My lips seemed to tingle from his touch and I just stood there, rooted to the spot, and berated myself for being too weak. Too weak with Kade, and too weak with Blane.

I took a shower and found the white nightgown I always wore when I stayed. My suitcase was sitting on my bed when I came out of the bathroom. I loved Gerard. I dug through it for my brush, pausing when I came across Kade's shirt, the one he'd ripped off me last night. I pulled it out. Almost all the buttons were missing, torn off by Kade. I brought it to my nose and inhaled. Kade's scent lingered on the fabric.

This was the first chance I'd had to be alone since realizing Kade remembered nothing about last night. Now I allowed myself the full range of my emotions. I didn't know what I'd been thinking, why I'd done what I'd done. Had I thought that just because Kade had said he loved me, that made all the difference? That my life would take a different turn, or that Blane would ever allow it? If so, I'd been very much mistaken, not to mention stupid. And it didn't really matter what I'd thought last night—all of it was gone, fizzled like morning mist in the unrelenting Nevada sunshine.

A shudder went through me when I imagined what Blane would do if he ever found out.

I refused to cry. It was my own fault for letting it happen. Regret played second fiddle only to the guilt, and on top of that was an overwhelming and unexpected sadness.

And I could never tell Kade. How would I even begin that conversation?

I know you don't remember any of it, but we made love last night, and it was amazing. Wonderful. A night I'll never forget. You said you loved me.

I wondered when Kade had last told a woman he loved her.

I should get rid of the shirt, I knew—it was evidence of a night best forgotten. Instead, I found myself carefully folding it, then putting it in my suitcase before setting the whole thing in the back of the closet and crawling into bed. I was lucky Kade didn't remember anything, I told myself. Seeing Blane and Kade still at such odds because of me was physically painful. Neither of them needed to know about my selfishness last night.

I'd stay here for a few days, do what I could to help Blane through this, then go home. Kade would leave, Blane would go back to campaigning, and I'd . . . be alone.

The pillow under my cheek grew wet, my self-pity all the worse in light of what had happened to Kandi. A good person? I felt like the good had been rubbed out by all the bad now inside me.

∼

I didn't go downstairs the next morning until I had on my full armor: makeup, hair washed and blow-dried, clothes. I'd found a little white denim skirt in the closet and a

navy-and-white polka-dot blouse with little straps, both in
my size. When Blane and I had dated, he'd been adamant
about buying clothes for me to keep at his house, hiring the
same man who did his suits to stock my closet. I was glad of
it now, as the clothes I'd bought in Vegas were woefully inappropriate for here.

The skirt was maybe a bit too big, given that I'd lost some
weight, but I also found a belt to cinch it with. The shirt was
made of a sheer, lightweight material, so I wore a thin cami
underneath. A pair of strappy white, wedge-heeled sandals
fit me perfectly.

My bruises looked better. The ones on my ribs were
still dark, but the one on my cheek could be covered with
enough makeup and my curtain of hair to hide it.

I didn't know who I'd find in the kitchen. It was Thursday
and Blane should have already been at work, but I had a feeling he'd be taking a few days off to deal with Kandi's murder and funeral. I heard voices as I approached and when
I stepped into the sunny, cheerful room, I saw that Mona
and Kade were the sole occupants. The aroma of coffee and
bacon permeated the air and I sniffed appreciatively.

"Good morning," Mona said with a smile. "Hungry?"

My stomach growled. "Starving," I said.

"Well, sit down. I'll get you some breakfast. Blane left for
work earlier but said he'd be back after lunch."

While she busied herself at the stove, I poured myself a
cup of coffee, catching Kade staring at my legs as I walked
over to the table where he sat. His gaze moved to meet mine,
but I had a hard time looking him in the eye. I gazed at my
coffee instead.

He was wearing jeans, boots, and a T-shirt. His only concession to the heat outside seemed to be that the shirt was short-sleeved, which I could appreciate. Seeing Kade's arms on display was never a bad thing, and I eyed them covertly from under my lashes.

"Good morning, princess," he said, giving me a half smile. "Sleep well?"

My dreams had started with a replay of the night in Vegas, which wasn't bad at all, but ended with Blane and Kade beating each other to a pulp, which was. I'd shouted at them and cried. Gee, I wondered if I could get someone to interpret that one for me.

I forced a fake smile. "Like a baby," I said.

He rolled his eyes. "You are such a shitty liar."

Mona set a plate of food in front of me, distracting me immediately. I loved breakfast food and didn't give another thought to Kade's comment as I dug in to the eggs, bacon, and toast. After a few minutes, I glanced over at Kade, who was sipping his coffee and watching me.

"Aren't you going to eat?" I asked around a mouthful of food.

"Already did."

"Mona, this is amazing," I said to her. "Thank you so much." It was such a treat to have someone cook for me. It never got old, and since my mom had died, I'd never again taken it for granted.

"You're welcome, dear," she said with a soft smile, giving me a little hug around my shoulders before leaving the room.

My nerves returned with a vengeance without Mona nearby as a buffer, and I didn't try to talk to Kade anymore while I ate.

"I have class this morning," I said after I'd cleaned my plate, getting up to put it in the dishwasher. "Can I borrow your car? Or can you drive me to mine?" A reprieve from both Blane and Kade would significantly decrease my stress level.

"I'll take you to class," Kade said.

I frowned as I turned back to him. "What? Why?"

"Blane can't say for certain if the Gage situation is resolved," he replied, his tone conveying exactly how he felt about that. "He delivered a warning, but neither of us is willing to risk it."

"I don't want a bodyguard," I objected.

"Too bad."

I glared at him, crossing my arms over my chest. "So you're just going to tag along with my every move?" I didn't know if I could handle that. Not now. Not with the weight of my secret pressing so heavily against my chest that it took effort to just draw breath.

"That's the plan."

"I don't like that plan," I retorted, echoing his words in Vegas.

He smirked appreciatively. "Consider me your private tutor," he said.

I thought of the other girls in my class and how quickly they'd decide they needed "tutoring" once they got an eyeful of Kade.

Kade found a place to park on campus, then walked me to class. I caught more than one pretty passerby taking a second look at Kade and wondered if he was checking them out, too. Not that I cared if he were.

Right.

"You can't bring your guns in here," I said in an undertone as we stepped inside the air-conditioned building. A sign was plastered to the door about no firearms allowed.

Kade raised his hands. "I don't see a gun. Do you see a gun?"

His innocent act didn't fool me for a second, but he just gave me his telltale smirk and followed me to class.

The summer session was nearly over, so the class wasn't as full as it would have been during a fall or spring term. Kade and I found seats in the back of the small auditorium. Since I'd missed class on Tuesday and the final was next week, I asked a student nearby if I could copy her notes. She and I had spoken a few times before and she readily agreed. I began writing while waiting for the class to begin. Kade slouched in the seat next to me, his long legs splayed in front of him and his sunglasses hooked on his shirt.

His pose got me thinking and I asked, "So what kind of person were you in high school?" I glanced at him before resuming my copying. "I'm imagining you to be the guy in the back of class who was always smarting off to the teacher."

Kade raised an eyebrow. "I'm hurt," he said, pretending to take offense. "I was a model student."

I stopped copying and just looked at him until he cracked.

"Okay, that might not be precisely true," he amended.

"Shocker," I teased. "You were that guy the girls whispered about, the one who never followed the rules, which only made you more exciting and dangerous. How many teenage hearts did you break, Kade?"

He laughed lightly. "I think your imagination of me is much more interesting than reality."

Somehow I doubted it.

"And you were the good, quiet, shy girl," he said, his eyes narrowing as he studied me. "Always sat in the second row. Not the front—that would attract too much attention. Made good grades, but not like the cutthroat genius types who loaded up on honors classes. Went to the homecoming football game, but not the dance. Never had a curfew because you didn't need one, because you weren't the rebellious kind."

I smiled a little at his perceptiveness. Spot-on so far.

"Your mom was your best friend," he continued, leaning over his desk toward me as his voice grew quieter. "And you couldn't stand to be in the same house, the same town, all alone without your parents, which is why you did something so utterly out of character as to sell the house you grew up in and move away from the only home you'd ever known."

I wasn't smiling now. It was no secret to me why I'd left home the way I had, but it was jarring to hear Kade spell it out like that and to realize . . . he knew. He knew exactly how it felt to be alone and lose everything that meant anything to you.

My wide eyes were locked on his and he frowned at whatever he saw in mine. His next words were barely more than a murmur.

"What aren't you telling me?"

My breath froze in my chest and I felt the blood leave my face in a rush. How? How could he possibly know?

I was saved by the professor entering the room to start class. I could barely concentrate on what was said, though—Kade's too-close-to-home psychoanalysis had me rattled. Not to mention his comment about what I wasn't telling him. Kade had always been able to see through my lies. How was I going to keep the secret?

"What class is this again?" Kade whispered in my ear. His warm breath fanned across my skin and I instinctively jerked away, his proximity reminding me too much of when he'd been even closer in Vegas.

He gave me a what-the-hell-is-the-matter-with-you look as I stammered back, "Um . . . Criminal psychology."

"This guy is full of shit," Kade snorted.

The girl I'd borrowed the notes from glanced back at us with a frown.

"Keep your voice down," I hissed at Kade.

"Are you listening to this guy?" Kade asked, making somewhat of an effort to be quieter.

I hadn't really, no. My mind was occupied with other things. But apparently the question was rhetorical because Kade kept talking.

"All this crap about why criminals do what they do—it's all bullshit. The whole my-daddy-hit-me-therefore-it's-okay-if-I-abuse-little-kids or I-get-depressed-sometimes-so-let's-kill-some-people."

"Then how do you explain it?" I asked. If Kade had personal insight as to why people did bad things, I certainly wanted to know.

Kade looked at me. "Some people are born bad, and that's just the way it is."

I remembered what he'd said about himself while he was drunk in Vegas. We weren't talking about your average bad guy. We were talking about Kade.

"Or maybe," I said, "some people just think they're born bad, but that's not who they are. Not really."

"And you think you can tell the difference?"

The way Kade had touched me, made love to me, told me he loved me—all of it went through my mind. "Yes," I replied with absolute certainty.

Kade's eyes studied mine before he at last looked back toward the still-speaking professor. "You're delusional," he muttered.

I hid a smile at his disgruntlement. I didn't care what he persisted in believing about himself, I just wanted to make sure he knew I refused to think that of him.

Kade refrained from making any further comments on the course material and soon we were heading back to his car. He slipped his sunglasses on and I caught myself taking way too many covert glances at him as we walked.

It was so strange—the intimacy we'd shared made me want to walk closer to him, touch his arm or shoulder, but I couldn't. It started to hurt when I thought about it too much, so I made a conscious effort to push the memory aside, forcing myself to put a little more space between us and to stop looking at him. As far as he knew, yes, we'd had a brief interlude in Vegas, but he'd decided to end things between us permanently, even our friendship.

I had to remember that part and forget the rest.

He held the car door for me and I slid inside. When he got in the driver's side, I said, "I need to go by the bridal shop. My fitting for Clarice's wedding is today."

He winced as though I'd asked him to donate a kidney. "How long will that take?" he asked.

I shrugged. "I don't know. Maybe an hour? You can drop me off and come back if you want."

"Like that's not a recipe for disaster," he quipped.

"So how long are you going to be on bodyguard duty?" How much longer did I have with him before he was gone for good?

"Until there's no longer a threat," he replied. "I'll check around, see if there's a contract out on you."

"Contract?" I squeaked. That sounded very . . . *Godfather*. It wasn't like I was a mob boss or something.

Kade's mouth twitched into a sly smile. "Relax. If there is, I'll find out about it."

And I believed him. I knew, without a doubt, that Kade would find a way to keep me safe.

I gave him directions to the little bridal boutique where Clarice had bought her gown and ordered the bridesmaid dresses. He parked and followed me to the door.

I stiffened my spine and took a deep breath before entering the store. I hadn't gotten a chance to shop for my wedding gown before Blane had broken the engagement. In retrospect, I was glad. A nonrefundable deposit would have been wasted if I'd found the dress I wanted, not to mention that I hadn't particularly wanted to have the image of my wedding gown in my head when it turned out I wasn't getting married.

The boutique wasn't busy this afternoon. Kade and I were the only customers, and I gave the saleslady my name and Clarice's. She went in the back to get the dress and seamstress.

Kade looked decidedly uncomfortable, and I couldn't help a little smile. He was most certainly out of his element, surrounded by mannequins dressed in billowing clouds of white satin and lace. The boutique had plush rose-colored carpet and flower arrangements advertising the florist next door were displayed throughout the shop, perfuming the air with their delicate scent.

"You really don't have to stay," I offered again, taking pity on him.

He was looking around, eyeing the wedding gowns as though they were going to gang up and attack him, and his gaze swung to meet mine. He cleared this throat. "I go where you go," he said simply.

I gave a little sigh, then the saleslady returned and we followed her to the dressing rooms. Kade perched carefully on a delicate-looking chair upholstered in pink velvet. I hid a grin and disappeared into a changing room to try on the dress.

Clarice had great taste and I loved the dress she'd chosen. It was strapless, the hem ending a couple of inches above my knees, and was the palest of pinks. A delicate ruffle ran from the neckline to the hem on one side, and a filmy length of sheer black organza tied around my waist and hung down the other. It was beautiful and very feminine.

I walked out to stand on the dais in front of a three-way mirror so the seamstress could check the alterations she'd made. I'd had to go up a size to accommodate my chest, which had made the rest of the dress too big. Now it fit perfectly and the seamstress agreed. She and I had a quick discussion about when they would steam the dress for pickup, then she was called to the front of the store.

I turned toward Kade. "So?" I prompted. "What do you think?" He hadn't said anything or even seemed to move much during my discussion with the seamstress, though I'd felt his eyes on me.

"It looks expensive," he said.

Not the words I'd been hoping to hear. I shrugged, hiding my disappointment. I wasn't searching for compliments, but a girl liked to hear she looked nice in a dress like this.

"It was, but they have a payment plan here, so . . ." I turned back to the mirror, admiring the dress. I thought it suited me and, thankfully, I had a tan. If it had been a winter wedding, the color would have washed me out completely. Idly, I twisted my hair into a makeshift updo, turning my face this way and that to see if my hair should be up or down for the wedding. Clarice had said she didn't have a preference.

In the mirror's reflection, I saw Kade stand. His expression was somewhat pained and I wondered if he'd had enough and was going to tell me he'd wait outside. To my surprise, he approached, not stopping until he stood behind me on the dais. His hands moved to rest gently on my shoulders, the touch sparking underneath my skin like electricity. I dropped my hair, my arms falling to my sides.

"What I meant to say," he said in my ear, "is that you're beautiful, no matter what you're wearing, and that dress makes me wish I had another man's soul."

My eyes widened as I stared in the mirror, our gazes locked. His thumbs brushed my skin as he held me, and my breath caught.

Kade bowed his head, his eyes closing as he pressed his lips to my bare shoulder. My pulse quickened as I watched our reflection, the contrast of Kade all in black stark against my strawberry-blonde hair and fair skin. He was a good head taller than me, maybe more, and broader. I ached to ease into him and have his arms envelop me, but I stayed rooted to the spot.

He brushed my hair to the side, his mouth trailing a heated path toward my neck, and my eyes slipped shut. I tilted my head to give him better access, reaching up to push my fingers into his hair. A shiver ran across my skin under his touch.

"Ahem."

The sound of someone clearing her throat shattered the spell and I jumped, startled. In the mirror, I could see the seamstress standing behind us, an indulgent smile on her face.

"Pardon me," she said, "I'm sorry for interrupting, but are you pleased with the alterations?"

"Oh, um, yeah," I stammered, moving away from Kade. *And the Excellence in Bad Timing Award goes to . . .*

Kade stepped off the dais. "I'll wait outside," he said, his expression unreadable. Before I could protest, he was gone. I stared after him in dismay.

"Don't worry," the seamstress said with a twinkle in her eye as she untied the fabric from around my waist and started the zipper for me. "He's probably just embarrassed. I'm sure you'll get him to the altar soon. The way he looked at you, I'm guessing before the year is out."

I didn't bother correcting her that, first of all, Kade was impossible to embarrass and, second, he had absolutely no plans to marry me.

When I emerged from the boutique, Kade was leaning against his Mercedes, his ankles crossed and hands casually tucked into the back pockets of his jeans. Shades once again shielded his eyes. I stopped in front of him.

"Any other errands?" he asked, pushing himself off the car and digging the keys out of his pocket.

So we weren't going to talk about what had happened. Again. I got that he'd changed his mind, that the offer to be with him had been rescinded, but I couldn't take this. It was bad enough to carry around the secret of what had really happened between us in Vegas, I couldn't handle his two-steps-forward, three-steps-back behavior any longer.

"You've got to stop, Kade," I said.

He frowned. "Stop what?"

My eyes stung behind my sunglasses but my temper was in my voice. "Stop kissing me. Stop touching me. In short, stop leading me on when your only intention is to leave—" I choked back the *me* that wanted to end that sentence.

"I'm surprised you noticed," Kade shot back with unusual venom. "You think I didn't see what was going on last night? That I don't know you're going to go back to Blane? It's just a matter of time."

"Isn't that what you want?" I asked, exasperated.

"It's for the best," he said, his voice cold. He turned away from me to open the car door.

Fury and hurt hit in equal measure and I reached out and grabbed a fistful of his T-shirt. He stopped and glanced down at me.

"I'm so *sick* of everyone thinking they know what's best for me," I fumed. "And I'm sick of you playing this game with me. How dare you? You've been throwing me at Blane one second and the next you're kissing me or telling me you—"

I stopped. I'd been about to blurt out that he'd said he loved me. That would be a disaster. I pressed my lips tightly closed.

"Telling you I what?" Kade asked, his tone dangerous. Of course he'd latch on to the one thing I wished he hadn't heard.

"Nothing," I said quickly with a wave of my hand. "Forget it. My point is I can't do this anymore! I don't know what to think, or feel, or who to trust. And every time you do or say something that makes me think you feel more for me, you take it back!" Exasperated, I turned away, trying to regain my composure. I swiped angrily at my wet cheeks and when Kade didn't say anything else, I rounded the car and got in.

Kade got in the car after me, slamming his door so hard I jumped. He started the engine, jabbing his finger at the button, while the silence between us grew thick and oppressive. He put the car into gear but then hesitated before slamming it back into park.

I looked at him. Was he going to talk to me? But he just stared straight ahead, his jaw locked tight. I squirmed nervously, plucking imaginary lint from my skirt and smoothing the fabric down my thighs.

"Stop fidgeting," he said.

I stilled, glancing uneasily his way, but he still stared out the windshield, his hands clenched in fists on the steering wheel.

"You're not the only one who can't do this anymore," he finally said, turning to look at me.

I swallowed, ignoring the knot of nausea in my stomach his statement had produced. "What do you want from me, Kade?" I asked.

He shrugged and gave a long sigh, his gaze returning to the windshield. "I don't know. I want you to be happy. I don't want you to worry about money anymore. I want you to be safe. I want your dreams to come true."

It took me a moment before I could speak. "I want the same for you."

Kade reached over and took my hand, threading our fingers together and giving it a squeeze. He didn't say anything more, just pulled out into traffic.

I cleared my throat. "Can you run me by my apartment, please?" I asked. "I need to get my mail and work uniform." And pay some overdue bills so they wouldn't shut off my water.

A short while later, Kade was parking in the lot. I got out and so did he.

"You can wait here if you want," I said. "I won't be long."

Kade shook his head. "I'll come with."

He followed me up the stairs and I tried not to think about his presence behind me as I unlocked my door. I twisted the knob.

Kade's hand suddenly caught my wrist in a painful grasp. "No—!"

But it was too late.

CHAPTER NINE

I was jerked hard to my right and shoved to the ground. Kade fell on top of me a split second before the explosion.

A wave of heat washed over me as terror licked my veins. My hearing was muffled, the explosion still ringing in my head, and Kade was a dead weight holding me down.

Oh God.

"Kade!" I struggled to move, the concrete biting into my hands and bare legs. "Kade!" He didn't move and didn't respond in any way. I started to panic. He'd been protecting me. What if he was hurt? Or worse?

"Oh my God!"

It was Alisha.

"Help us," I said, thrusting an arm out from beneath Kade.

"Kathleen?" Alisha grabbed my hand. "Are you okay?"

"Yes. Please, just help Kade."

I felt Kade's body move as she rolled him carefully off me. I sat up in a rush. His eyes were shut, but he was breathing.

"Call nine-one-one," I ordered. Alisha ran to make the call.

The fire was still burning inside my apartment. I could feel the heat and smell the smoke.

"Kade," I said, pushing his hair back from his face. "Kade, wake up." It didn't look like he was hurt. Splinters of wood and plaster covered him, but I couldn't see any blood. "Please, Kade. Please wake up!" I was close to hysterical, crying and shaking his shoulder to try and wake him.

Kade shifted and his eyes fluttered open.

"What the fuck?" he groaned.

A small laugh escaped through my tears and I bent my head to his chest, wrapping my arms up over his shoulders and hugging him tightly.

"You're okay," I said. "Thank God, you're okay."

His hand cupped the back of my head and I felt his chest rumble as he spoke. "I'm fine," he said. "You?"

I couldn't speak and just nodded, my cheek scrunching his shirt.

Sirens wailed in the distance and Kade got to his feet, wincing as he did so. My hands and knees were scraped from hitting the concrete. We rounded up Alisha and her dog, Bacon Bits, and scurried down to the parking lot. Lucky for them, the people in the apartment below mine weren't home.

It was only as we were watching the firemen climb the stairs with the hose that I saw Kade's back. His shirt had been burned away in spots, some as big as my palm, the skin underneath an angry red. His hair was singed, too.

"Kade, you're hurt," I said stupidly, staring at him.

He glanced at me, then looked over his shoulder. "It's not bad. Could've been worse. Glad I had the jeans on. I know my ass is hot, but I don't need it to be literal." He waggled his eyebrows at me, but I didn't think it was funny. I was angry, and scared, and I took it out on Kade.

"Why did you do that? You could've been killed!"

"Better me than you, princess."

"Stop saying that!" I cried, getting in his face. "It's not true! I hate it when you do that!" I was crying and yelling and I didn't care what kind of scene I was making. I fisted his shirt in my hands, trying to make him listen to me.

The mischief faded from Kade's face, a look of concern replacing it as his brows drew together and his lips twisted in a frown. "Calm down. It's okay. Everything's okay," he said. He tried to wrap his arms around me, but I jerked away.

"Everything is *not* okay! Everything I own is up there burning. I was nearly killed. *You* were nearly killed. And I'm sick of it!"

I ran to where I'd dropped my purse and dug my keys out. This had to stop. I couldn't take it anymore.

"Kathleen, wait—!"

I heard Kade calling after me, but I ignored him, running to my car and getting in. I slammed my hand down on the door lock just as Kade got there.

"Kathleen, where are you going?" he asked, trying fruitlessly to open the door.

"I'm going to make him stop," I said, jamming my key in the ignition.

It only took a second for Kade to catch on.

"No," he said, his face hard. "You are not going over there, Kathleen. Don't be stupid."

I really didn't like being called stupid. I glared at him through the window. "Watch me," I said, and tore out of the lot.

I drove fast—traffic rules optional. My whole body still shook, though whether it was from shock or fear or fury, I didn't know. But I was mad. Maybe madder than I'd ever been in my life. And I knew just the person who I wanted to see.

William Gage lived in a two-story brick mansion just north of downtown, off Meridian. I wouldn't even know where he lived if I hadn't had to go by his house occasionally to pick up a few things when I'd first started at the firm. My memory supplied the address and soon I was squealing to a stop in the big semicircle driveway.

I jumped out of the car, not even bothering to close my door, just as Kade's Mercedes skidded up next to me. He vaulted out, but I was already heading to the front door. He caught me around the waist at the foot of the stairs.

"Let me go!" I pulled at his arm, but it was like an iron band around my middle.

"You're not doing this," he said, his voice implacable.

"You can't stop me," I fumed, twisting in his arms as I tried to break free.

Kade lifted me off my feet. "Actually, I can," he said.

That just sent me to a whole new level of pissed off. I kicked and fought him with everything I had, which only resulted in his other arm crossing over my chest to hold my arms down.

"Let me go! I swear to God, Kade!" I knew I was making contact with some of my hits because he grunted a couple of times, but still he wouldn't let go. I channeled my anger and twisted around, getting my arms in between us so I could push against him. "I said, *let me go.*"

"Stop it, Kathleen," he barked, pressing me tightly against him so my arms were immobilized. "I said stop!"

His words finally penetrated my haze of rage and I went limp, sagging against him. I couldn't hold back the sobs that now engulfed me. I hid my face against Kade's chest, my shoulders shaking.

"Shhh, you're okay, I'm okay," he said softly, cradling me. His lips brushed the top of my head. "Everything's going to be okay. I promise."

His hand slipped under my hair to the back of my neck when I pulled back slightly. "But it's not okay, Kade," I choked out. "Look at your back. What if—"

"No," he interrupted. "No what-ifs. I'll take care of it. Right now." He stepped away, but took my hand and started for the stairs.

I followed him. When we reached the door, he turned to me. "Let *me* do the talking," he said. Reluctantly, I nodded.

Kade rang the doorbell. I nervously shifted my weight from foot to foot as we waited.

"Stop fidgeting," Kade murmured. I stilled.

The door opened and an old man, clad in a butler's uniform, stood there.

"May I help you?" he asked.

"I'm looking for William Gage," Kade said.

The man glanced from Kade to me and back, then said, "I'm sorry, but he's not accepting visitors right now—"

"That's all right," Kade said, moving past the old butler. "This won't take long. Where is he?"

Kade's voice was like steel and I knew the coldness in his eyes well. The butler took a good look and didn't question him, but just pointed to a doorway down the hall.

Our footsteps echoed on the hardwood floor as we walked down the hallway. I couldn't take my eyes off Kade's back, belatedly realizing my abrupt departure had caused him to forgo getting medical attention for his burns.

Nice one, Kathleen.

Kade pushed open the door at the end of the corridor and stepped into the den. It would have been a bright, cheery room if heavy drapes hadn't been drawn over the windows. The air was stuffy and too warm. But I noticed and then forgot all that in a flash, my attention drawn to the man sitting in a wheelchair behind a behemoth of a desk.

Gage had changed since I'd last seen him, his body withered and bent. The disease was obviously taking its toll. I wished I could feel sympathy. Instead, I found myself only sorry it was taking so long to claim his life.

He looked up when the door opened, surprise evident on his face before he could conceal it. "Dennon," he said carefully, "to what do I owe the pleasure?" Gage glanced at me and it took him a moment to recognize me, his eyes narrowing before realization struck. Then his thin lips pressed together and his face grew mottled with anger. "What is *she* doing here?" he hissed.

I gritted my teeth and moved forward, but Kade stopped me in my tracks, his hold unbreakable.

"She's with me," he said, walking right over to Gage. "I hear Blane Kirk stopped by to give you a warning about this obsession you have." He let go of my hand to press his palms flat on the desk and lean closer to Gage. "And today you went too far."

Gage's smile was cold. "Oh, I wasn't trying to kill her." He leaned forward. "I just want to hurt her, terrify her, and make her regret the day she was born."

I shivered, a chill spreading across my skin at his words.

"That's nice," Kade said, nonchalant. "It's good to have goals. But here's the problem. Today you hurt *me*." Menace dripped from his voice and Gage blanched. "The girl is under my protection now, and I would take it *personally* if something were to happen to her."

Gage recovered, his gaze hardening. "This is none of your business, Dennon," he said.

"I'm making it my business," Kade bit out.

"Then I suggest you watch your back," Gage said.

Kade straightened and once again took my hand. "Your choices are your own, Gage," he said. "But hear this—if anything else happens that so much as harms a hair on her head, my face will be the last one you see." He tugged on my hand, pushing me in front of him as we left the room.

"You don't scare me, Dennon!" Gage called after us. "I'm already at death's door."

Kade paused. "Just say the word, old man, and I'll shove your ass right on through."

Gage spluttered in rage, grabbing a paperweight from his desk and throwing it at us. It bounced harmlessly off the wall as Kade hustled me down the hall and out the front door.

I got back in my car, sliding behind the wheel and taking a deep breath.

Kade leaned into the open door. "Go straight to Blane's," he ordered. "Nowhere else."

I frowned at him. "But you need to go to the hospital. I can come with—"

Kade was already shaking his head. "I've got to give a statement to the cops. We kind of ran out on them, you know."

"Then will you go to the hospital?"

He rolled his eyes. "Fine. If you'll do what I say."

I nodded. "To Blane's. Nowhere else. Got it."

Kade stepped away, but something occurred to me and I called out to him. "Kade, wait!" He turned. "How did you know?" I asked. "You tried to warn me. How did you know?"

"It's a trick I've seen before," Kade said. "Rigging the door. They were just a little messy or I wouldn't have seen it."

"Where have you seen it?" I asked. I hadn't seen a thing and even now as I searched my memory, I came up blank.

Kade seemed to hesitate before finally saying, "I guess it's not so much that I've *seen* it before as that I've *done* it before."

I stared at him, unable to conceal my dismay. "You've . . . blown somebody up?" I asked. I wasn't stupid, I knew what Kade did for a living, it just rarely smacked me in the face like this had.

Kade just looked at me, resignation in his eyes, until I glanced away, unable to hold his gaze. Guilt ate at me for what I'd said. It wasn't my place to judge him; he couldn't change his past.

"I'll see you at Blane's later," he said before closing my door. I watched him as he walked to his Mercedes, his shirt in tatters across his back, the burned skin showing through. Then suddenly I was up and running after him. I was breathless when I reached his car and knocked on his window. He rolled it down. He'd already donned his sunglasses and I couldn't see his eyes.

"What's wrong?" he said with a frown. "You okay?"

I nodded. "Yes, I just forgot something."

"What?"

I leaned inside, kissing him hard on the mouth for a long moment. When I pulled back, I said, "Thank you."

I was gone, heading back to my car, before he could reply.

∼

I called Alisha while I drove to Blane's.

"What the hell happened?" were the first words out of her mouth.

"I'm sorry," I apologized. "I kind of . . . lost it for few minutes."

"Can't say I blame you," she replied. "I'd lose it, too, if someone blew up my apartment."

I winced at the reminder. "So what did the firemen say?"

"It was localized in your apartment," she said, "and they managed to put it out before it spread back into your bedroom, so it's not as bad as it looked."

Well, that was good news. All my family photo albums were in the bedroom closet. I felt a little better. I hadn't had a lot of personal things in my living room and kitchen, just furniture and appliances. My memories were all in the bedroom.

"Thanks for your help," I said.

"No problem. You need someplace to stay until they repair the damage?"

I hesitated. Staying with Alisha was tempting, but I didn't want to bring more trouble or danger into her life. "Um, that's okay. I have a place to stay."

"Where?"

"Um, yeah. I'm, uh, staying with Blane for now."

Silence, then, "Are you out of your mind?" she screeched. I winced, pulling the phone slightly away from my ear. "Don't you remember what he did? The things that piece of shit said to you—"

Alisha had been with me, had comforted me, when Blane had broken our engagement. She'd seen my heart-break and her animosity toward Blane had reached a new high.

"It's not what you think," I broke in to her tirade. "We're not getting back together. Kandi Miller—remember her?—she was murdered."

"Oh." Alisha's voice betrayed surprise now. "I saw that on the news. That was her? His ex?"

"Yeah."

"Wow. Geez. I'm sorry."

"It's okay," which was an absurd thing to say—it wasn't okay, but what do you say? "So, anyway, Kade and I are staying with Blane for a little while, until after the funeral and stuff."

"Kade *and* you?" she asked, disbelief edging her voice.

"Yeah."

"Wow."

"What?"

"Isn't that going to be a little . . . awkward?"

She didn't know the half of it. The desire to tell my friend what had happened between Kade and me was strong, but I held my tongue. "Yeah, it's been a little . . . tense." Understatement of the century.

"Do you need anything?"

I smiled to myself. Alisha was a good friend, OCD and all. "No, I'm okay. Thanks for asking, though."

"Well, just let me know," she said.

"Thanks, I will. Tell Lewis I said hello."

We disconnected and a few minutes later, I pulled up to Blane's house. It was late afternoon and I thought Blane would probably be back home. Glancing down I saw that my once-white skirt was now smeared with dirt, the delicate blouse I had on was torn, and my knees were streaked with dried blood.

Lovely.

I headed inside, hoping not to encounter anyone on the way to my bedroom. A shower and change of clothes sounded good. I felt grungy and my hair smelled like smoke, which made it darn inconvenient to run into Blane in the hallway upstairs.

"Hey," I said, trying to ignore how I looked. "How are you doing?"

Blane didn't answer, his astonished gaze sweeping me from head to foot. "What the hell happened? I thought you were just going to class?"

I sighed, knowing I had to come clean. "I did. But then we went by my apartment, and someone had rigged a bomb."

"We?"

"Kade and me."

Blane glanced behind me. "Where's Kade? Is he all right?" The anxiety in his voice was good to hear. No matter how mad he was at Kade, blood was blood.

"He's okay. He got some burns on his back, was going to go to the hospital."

"And you? Were you injured?" He stepped closer now, his hands running from my shoulders down my arms as he inspected me.

"No. Kade saved me. If he'd been a little slower . . ." I shrugged, not really wanting to finish that sentence. I felt like a cat whose nine lives were running dangerously low.

Blane turned my hand palm up and I winced, the scrapes on my skin burning.

"Come on," he said, lightly grasping my arm. "I've got some salve for your scrapes."

I expected him to take me downstairs, instead I found myself being led to his bedroom.

If it wouldn't have looked completely and utterly childish, I'd have dug my heels into the carpet and refused to follow him. Blane's bedroom held way too many memories, and I found all of them assailing me with the force of a wrecking ball as I walked in the door.

The room smelled strongly of Blane—his cologne, his aftershave, and just him. My step faltered and Blane glanced quizzically at me. I couldn't look at him, not with images of him and me writhing naked on his bed streaming through my mind like a highlight reel.

He gave me a gentle push to sit me down on the bed and I immediately sprang back up.

"I can stand." My voice was a little squeaky.

Blane's jaw tightened. "I'm not going to attack you," he said flatly.

"It's not that," I protested. "It's just—" *Something I really didn't want to say.* I pressed my lips closed and resumed my seat, perching awkwardly on the very edge of the bed.

Blane looked at me for a moment, but I couldn't read the look in his eyes, then he disappeared into the bathroom. I heard the water running and a moment later, he returned with a washcloth and a small plastic tube.

He sat beside me, taking one of my hands in his, and began gently cleaning the dirt and dried blood.

"Was your apartment destroyed?" he asked.

I focused on my hand as I answered. "Alisha said the back is okay, that just the front part was burned."

"I'll go talk to Gage again," Blane offered.

"That may not be necessary," I said. "Kade and I went by."

The pause in Blane's ministrations was nearly imperceptible. "I see."

"You have enough going on right now," I said, hoping to placate him. I didn't need him and Kade getting into another pissing match. Time to change the subject. "Have you heard anything about the funeral?"

Blane switched to my other hand, reaching across me and moving closer. "They're holding her body for evidence right now. I imagine the funeral will be next week sometime."

"And they've cleared you, right?" I was sure the only reason Blane had been on their list was because they always went after the boyfriend, husband, or ex in these things.

Blane took a moment to respond, setting aside the washcloth and squeezing some salve into my palm. He started rubbing it in, the calluses on his fingers a gentle abrasion against my skin.

"No, they haven't."

I jerked my gaze to his, but he was looking down at our hands. "What do you mean, 'they haven't'?"

"They have an eyewitness who says I was there that night," he said.

He seemed so calm, in stark contrast to the sheer panic flooding me. I fisted my hand, clutching his fingers, and he finally looked up at me.

"How could anyone think you would do something like that?"

"I'm a defense attorney, Kat," he said. "I've made my share of enemies in this town over the years."

"But you would never . . . hurt someone, anyone, like that! You wouldn't do that to Kandi and you certainly wouldn't have killed her." I was horrified, my mind trying to wrap itself around the fact that the police would consider Blane a serious suspect. "What's going to happen?"

Blane gently pried open my clenched fist and resumed rubbing the salve on my palm. "If my source at the precinct is correct, they'll work with my lawyer first and then come by here to question me. If I go downtown, it'll be all over the news. We'll see if they'll agree so we can avoid the media circus getting any worse."

Stunned, I couldn't think of what to say. This was rapidly turning into a nightmare.

"Could they arrest you?" I asked.

Blane's eyes met mine and he didn't answer. He didn't have to.

I couldn't wrap my head around it. They suspected Blane strongly enough to question him, possibly arrest him?

"Your hands are like ice," he murmured, squeezing my hands inside of his.

"I can't believe this," I whispered. "It's . . . insane." And I was scared. Scared for Blane.

"Everything will be okay," he said.

Kade had said that, too, but I didn't know if I believed either of them.

"Kat, the last time we talked, while you were in Vegas, you were really angry," Blane said carefully. "And I deserved everything you said. I . . . underestimated my uncle's aspirations for me. And the thing is, I believed the lies because I've seen you and Kade together. I know my brother better than anyone, and I've never seen him fall for a woman. Not like he's fallen for you."

I listened, barely breathing.

"So I need to know." He raised his eyes to meet mine. "Are you and I truly finished? Is what we had gone for good?"

My heart was racing as though I was running a marathon and panic made me break out in a cold sweat. I couldn't deal with this right now. Kade and I had nearly gotten burned alive. The police were coming to question Blane about Kandi's murder. And Blane wanted to have a talk about the status of our relationship? It seemed absurd to me.

I jumped to my feet. "Blane, I don't think now is the right time to talk about this," I said, pulling my hands from his and backing toward the door.

He stood, moving closer until he towered over me. I swallowed, memories threatening to overwhelm me. Given the path the conversation had suddenly taken, I wondered if

Blane bringing me into his bedroom had been intentional, if he knew exactly how much standing inches from where we'd first made love would affect me.

"Give me something, Kat," he rasped. "Please. Just tell me if you still love me."

His gray eyes held me captive and I couldn't look away, their depths filled with pain and sorrow. Another woman might have been glad to see Blane hurting. He'd hurt me, after all. But I couldn't stand it, so I told him the truth.

"I wouldn't be here if I didn't."

Relief flashed across his face, then he wrapped his arms around me and pulled me close. I held him around his waist and rested my head against his chest, listening to the strong sound of his heart beating.

My emotions were teetering on a ledge, my love for Blane warring with the guilt I was carrying around inside. It was wrong of me to lead him on. But if he knew what had happened between Kade and me, he'd never forgive me. And I couldn't face that yet. I'd just gotten him back in some small degree and couldn't handle the thought of another fallout between us—one that, this time, would be permanent.

The guilt gnawed at my heart, which made me hold him even more tightly. His shirt grew damp beneath my cheek and when he forced my chin to tip up, I couldn't look him in the eye, so stared at a spot on his neck instead.

"Don't cry, Kat," he said, his words a pained whisper. "It'll be okay. I promise."

But it wouldn't be okay. It really, really wouldn't. Not with Kade, who was determined to disappear from my life, and not with Blane, who I loved but couldn't trust.

My anger and bitterness over what Blane had done had finally dissipated, but without it, I felt even emptier than I had before.

~

I had to be at work soon, and my uniform was in my burned-out apartment. I called Tish to see if she had an extra I could borrow.

"Oh, not to worry—we have new uniforms for the Fourth," she informed me.

My heart sank. "Oh no."

"Oh yes."

"Are they as bad as the Santa ones?"

"Think Daisy Duke meets Wonder Woman."

I groaned. Good Lord, I couldn't even imagine what that was, and it turned out that even if I'd been able to, it wouldn't have come close to the real thing.

I turned around to see exactly how much of my ass was hanging out of the cut-off denim shorts Romeo had bought for us. They were even shorter than the ones he usually made us wear in the summer. The employees' bathroom mirror said way too much. The shirt was like Daisy's, tying between my breasts, but one side was red-and-white striped while the other was navy blue with little white stars. At least the shirt had short sleeves, so I knew it would stay on, but the plunging neckline left little to the imagination. Though the bare midriff and stomach didn't bother me—my broken-heart diet had taken care of that—my chest appeared immune to weight loss.

I sighed. Well, here was hoping the getup helped with tips.

It was a good hour or more into my shift when I turned from one side of the bar to work the other and saw Kade walking in the door.

He'd changed into jeans and another of his ubiquitous black T-shirts, and he was just taking off his sunglasses when he spotted me. His hand paused for a fraction of a moment, then he was heading my way.

A stupid grin spread across my face and my pulse quickened. Ridiculous, how glad I was to see him, but I couldn't help it.

"Hey," I said as he slid onto an empty barstool. "How's your back?"

"I told you to go to Blane's," he said. "Nowhere else."

His voice was hard and flat, his eyes sparking with anger.

My smile faded. "I did, but I had to come to work."

"I would have brought you, or Blane."

"You weren't there." And I wasn't going to relate how I'd snuck by Blane's den to avoid an uncomfortable car ride. I was getting angry. Here I'd been all happy to see him and he had to go and ruin it. "Stop yelling at me and have a drink." I popped the top off a beer bottle and set it in front of him.

Kade glowered at me and I raised an eyebrow, waiting. At last he sighed and reached for the beer. Taking a swig, he eyed me.

"Looks like your ribs are better," he said.

I looked down at the expanse of skin revealed by my "patriotic" uniform. "Yeah, guess so." The marks were yellowish now, hardly visible in the low light of the bar.

"Better not come home in that outfit," he said. "Blane will have a shit fit." The words were said casually, but his eyes were keen.

I stiffened. "It doesn't matter what Blane thinks," I said. "He doesn't control me." I felt absurdly like a rebellious teenager: *He's not the boss of me.*

"Doesn't he?"

"Is that what you think?"

Kade gave a deceptively casual shrug and took another drink of beer. "I brought you back because he needed you."

His words stung. "What about what *I* need?"

Kade's eyes held mine. "That's something only you can decide."

I had to go back to work then, but Kade stayed. He switched to coffee after the beer, and I could feel his eyes on me as I worked. Too vivid memories of his hands on me—of all we'd done in his bed—made me acutely aware of him.

I tried not to think about it.

I was delivering drinks to a table with three guys when one of them put his hand on my ass. I cursed Romeo in my head while hurriedly putting down the drinks.

"No touching," I said through a forced smile, pushing his hand away.

"Sweetheart, I've got a hard-on just lookin' at you," the guy said. He wasn't drunk but was well on his way. His buddies laughed, both of them staring at my chest.

"Well, that's just great," I said sweetly. "I hear men your age often have trouble with that."

His smile faded pretty quick and I headed back behind the bar.

I grabbed the coffeepot and went to refill Kade's cup.

"Should I break his arm or just his hand?"

I glanced at him, surprised. "Neither," I said. His face was cold and he was staring at the guy who'd put his hand on me. "It's just part of the job. Especially when Romeo has us dress like this. You get used to it."

"I don't like it," he said, swinging his gaze back to mine.

I shrugged. "It is what it is," I said. "You didn't tell me how your back was. What did the doctor say?"

"He said I'm fine. Don't change the subject."

"Fine. Then I'll just get back to work then." I spun away and spent the rest of the evening ignoring Kade. Well, at least I pretended to. He was a hard man to ignore, especially when I felt his gaze on me the entire time.

"So what's with tall, dark, and gorgeous?" Tish asked as we were cleaning up. She gave a small jerk of her head toward Kade. "Wasn't he the guy you left with that one night a few months back?"

She meant when I'd pretended to pick Kade up from the bar. It felt like forever ago, so much had happened since.

"Remember how Blane and I broke up because he accused me of sleeping with his brother?"

She nodded.

"That's him."

Her mouth fell open and she took another look. "Well, if you weren't sleeping with him, you should fix that right quick."

I avoided that one, reiterating instead, "He's Blane's *brother*."

Tish shrugged, tugging the overflowing trash bag from the bin. "So? Stuff like that happens all the time. It's not like you're doing a threesome." She grinned. "Though that sounds awesome."

I couldn't help but laugh at her irreverent humor, though I was sure the image that flashed unbidden through my mind had me turning bright red. I glanced at Kade, who was watching us, and quickly looked away.

At last it was time to leave and I went to grab my purse from underneath the bar.

"I'll walk you to your car," Kade said, sliding off the stool.

I gave a curt nod, following him out the door.

"I called a company to start cleanup on your apartment," he said as I locked the door behind us. "They moved your stuff into storage for now."

"Thank you," I replied. That was one less thing to worry about, though I wondered how badly my clothes reeked of smoke.

The night air was thick and humid. Sweat broke out immediately on my skin. Fishing an elastic band from my pocket, I pulled my hair up into a high ponytail as I walked beside Kade. Not even a slight breeze stirred.

"Feels like a storm coming," I said absently, glancing up at the sky. A flash of lightning lit up the horizon.

"Not pissed at me anymore?" Kade asked.

I sighed. "I'm tired of feeling. Angry, sad, hurt, bitter, disappointed, afraid. I'm just sick of it all." I desperately wanted a drink, something to numb the tumult and confusion inside me.

We'd reached my car and Kade's Mercedes was right next to it, which was an apt paradigm for how I felt standing next to him. Like his elegant car, he was beautiful and drew the eye. From the wave of his inky black hair to his clear blue eyes, square jaw, lean biceps and shoulders encased in thin cotton, he looked like an expensive luxury. My lips curved in a sardonic smile at the analogy.

Kade leaned against my car, blocking the door. "What's so funny?" he asked.

I shook my head. "Just a stray thought."

He raised an arched brow, waiting.

I sighed, feeling stupid. "I was thinking that our cars look like us."

Kade frowned in confusion.

"You know," I said, waving a hand toward the Mercedes, "yours is gorgeous and perfect, and mine is cheap and forgettable." So forgettable, he didn't even remember making love to me. Yeah, it was for the best, but it was still a blow to my pride whenever I thought about it, which was way too often.

Now his lips twitched in a near smile even as I wished I'd just kept my mouth shut. The comparison had sounded ridiculous when I'd said it out loud.

He reached out and snagged a finger in the band of my shorts. "C'mere," he said, tugging lightly. The roughness of his voice made my stomach tighten. I let him pull me closer until we were nearly touching.

"So you think I'm gorgeous and perfect?" he said, settling his hands on my hips.

I deliberately recalled the image of his face as he lost all control, his body inside mine. "You're beautiful," I blurted. Kade's ego didn't need stroking, but I couldn't help it.

His smirk faded. "I wish you were as forgettable as your car."

Kade's eyes searched mine as though trying to read what I was hiding. My hands were clenched in fists at my sides so I wouldn't touch him, and I was hypersensitive to every brush of his fingers against my bare skin.

"Come on," he said, stepping away and taking my hand.

"Where are we going?" I asked, following as he led me to his car.

"There's something I want to show you."

"But what about my car?" I protested.

"We'll get it tomorrow. Get in."

I thought I should probably say no, should just get in my car and drive away, but I couldn't. I didn't want to miss a single moment I might have with Kade, not when they were numbered.

I got in the car.

A half hour later, Kade was pulling into a deserted high school parking lot. It was a big school, one everyone in Indiana knew about. He turned off the engine and pocketed the keys.

The sultry night air hit me again when I emerged from the air-conditioned car. You could almost feel the wetness in the air, it was so thick and heavy.

Kade took my hand and we started walking. The night was moonless, the clouds obscuring the night sky, but he seemed to know where he was going, his steps sure.

We left the parking lot and walked across grass toward a gentle hill dotted with trees. A breeze had picked up and I could hear the rustle of the leaves around us. We didn't speak, and the gradual incline combined with the humidity had me sweating after a few minutes. We eventually broke through a copse of trees and I halted in surprise.

The hill had crested, and spread out below us was the heart of the town, nestled among the trees. Lights blinked in the darkness, warm and friendly. It seemed like something out of one of those Thomas Kinkade paintings.

Kade sat on the grass, drawing me down next to him. The grass was cool and soft on the backs of my thighs. I leaned back on my elbows with a sigh.

"I used to come here when I was a kid," he said. "It was quiet, peaceful. I could think here, and just . . . be."

"It's beautiful," I said.

We sat like that, in companionable silence, for a while. I deliberately didn't think about anything. I just wanted to enjoy being there, in the moment, with Kade.

"I came here when Blane told me he was joining the Navy," Kade said. He turned on his side to face me, propping himself on one elbow to rest his head in his hand.

It was too dark to see his features clearly, though I tried.

"I was . . . angry. Scared. Hurt. I felt betrayed," he said.

My heart went out to the younger version of Kade, one I could see in my mind's eye, who wasn't as self-assured as the Kade before me now. That Kade was unsure and just learning to trust his brother.

"Did you tell him?" I asked.

"He knew."

"What happened?"

"He had about three months before he left for basic, and he spent nearly every waking moment with me. He taught me to shoot and took me to the range to practice. We played basketball, went to the arcade, the batting cages. All kinds of shit."

Of course Blane had done that. He loved his brother, and as much as he'd wanted to join the Navy, he would have hated leaving Kade.

"I asked him one night, why he was spending so much time with me instead of Kandi," Kade continued.

"What did he say?"

"He said, 'Because you mean more to me than anybody else, and you always will.'"

The tightness in my chest spread, making my stomach ache.

"Why are you telling me this?" I managed to ask. Regret clawed at me, guilt making me nearly nauseated. Too disheartened to even hold myself up any longer, I lay back on the ground and looked up at the black sky.

"Because it's not true, not anymore, for either of us. Blane or me." He moved closer and rested a hand on my stomach, sliding it around until he gripped my waist. I gazed up at him, trying to see his eyes in the darkness.

"You're part of us now," he said softly. "And somehow, we all have to find a way to live with it. Even if I thought I could stay away from you, I'd just be lying to myself." His thumb brushed against my ribs and my skin seemed to tingle at his touch.

I shook my head. "When this is over, I'll go home. It's the only way for you and Blane to fix this between you. That's the way it should be." I moved to get away from him, but Kade's grip tightened and he braced himself over me, pushing a denim-clad leg between my thighs to hold me in place.

"Like we'd let you go," he scoffed. "One of us will have you, that's for damn sure."

I shook my head again, more vehemently this time, but my throat was closed off and I couldn't speak.

His arms were on either side of my head, his weight resting on his palms. I could barely breathe, anxiety and pain combining in my chest to smother me.

Almost of their own volition, my hands crept up to his shoulders. I could feel the heat of his skin through the thin cotton of his shirt. My fingers brushed the nape of his neck. His skin was damp from sweat, just like when we'd made love.

Kade didn't move, didn't seem to even blink as my fingers threaded slowly through his hair. My body thrummed as though an electric current was passing between us, from him to me and back.

Lightning flashed, briefly illuminating his face, his expression tortured as he looked at me. I curled my arm around his neck, urging him down. He resisted, his arms locked in position. I licked my lips, unable to tear my gaze from his mouth.

Lightning split the sky again, then the heavens opened up. I gasped in surprise as the first icy drops hit my overheated skin, then let out a high-pitched squeal of dismay as the torrential downpour began.

Kade pulled me to my feet. "Come on, princess," he said, taking my hand in his. "You won't melt."

I could barely see a foot in front of me and latched myself onto Kade's arm. He led us down the hill, catching me twice when I slipped and would have fallen. When we finally reached the car, we were both drenched to the skin.

"I don't want to mess up your seat!" I protested when he opened the passenger door for me.

"Feel free to strip naked," he said, leaning against the car and crossing his arms over his chest as though he was getting ready to watch. The lights illuminating the empty parking lot were a welcome change from the dark.

I laughed at the incongruity of the moment, both of us standing in the pouring rain with me not wanting to get his seat wet. I shoved my dripping hair back from my face. The rain was letting up a bit now, becoming gentle and steady as opposed to a stinging torrent. I tipped my head back and shut my eyes.

After the sweltering heat, this felt good, washing the sticky sweat from my skin. I laughed again in sheer pleasure, stretching my arms up as though to catch the droplets in my hands. God, I couldn't even remember when I'd last stood outside in a summer rain.

When I opened my eyes, Kade was watching me.

"What?" I asked, self-consciously dropping my arms. I knew I had to look a disaster. My mascara was probably running in rivulets down my face. "I look awful, I know. Damn rain." I scrubbed at my cheeks and under my eyes, hoping the makeup was gone.

He stepped close to me, catching a finger under my chin and tipping my face up to his.

"I'll always remember tonight," he said, "and the way you look right now."

I gave him a watery half smile. "I look like a drowned rat."

"You look *happy*."

My smile was wider this time, because he looked happy, too, which made his face appear younger and less cold.

"And that outfit was sexy before," he said, moving us until I was backed against the car. "Soaking wet, it's downright . . . indecent." The last word was a sibilant hiss in my ear. Then he was kissing me, his lips and tongue a slick heat that contrasted sharply against the chill of my skin.

My arms curved around his neck, holding him tight. His hands cupped my rear, pulling me against him. We kissed and kissed, until I lost track of time and space, like we were teenagers forbidden to be together and had to squeeze in as much as we could before we got caught. Or in this case, before either of us came to our senses.

A crack of thunder made me jerk my lips from his in startled fright. I began to shiver.

"Let's get you home," he said in a voice so low I barely heard him. This time, I got in when he opened the car door for me.

My teeth chattered and I kicked off my sodden shoes and socks, pulling my knees to my chest so my feet rested on the seat. Kade turned on the heat and soon my chills subsided. I held my icy hands in front of the vent.

"This kills me to do this to your car," I said. "Water and leather don't mix."

"You worry too much," he said.

"Aren't you freezing?" I asked. He had to be. Jeans were a bitch when they got wet.

"I'll admit to some chafing in areas that I prefer to be treated more gently," he said, making me laugh.

The seat warmer, combined with the heat wafting over me and the stress of the day, had me nodding off. I woke, still groggy, then realized the car had stopped and Kade had turned off the engine.

"Shall I carry you?" Kade teased when I made no move to get out of the car.

"I'm going, I'm going," I groused. "Maybe *I* should carry *you* to ease your 'chafing.'"

He smirked, his blue eyes twinkling at me, the sight making me feel warm from the inside out. "I'd like to see you try."

I laughed. The idea of me carrying Kade was an absurd one. He had to outweigh me by nearly a hundred pounds.

It had quit raining and the stars were coming out. I carried my shoes in my hand and walked barefoot to the darkened house. Kade fished out his key and was unlocking the door when it was suddenly flung open.

Blane stood there and the look on his face made me immediately take a step back.

"Where the hell have you been?"

CHAPTER TEN

Blane appeared to be livid, his gray eyes flashing fire as he looked at Kade.

"I've been worried sick," he snapped. "Kat got off work hours ago. You said you were going to get her. Where the hell were you?"

Okay, now I felt *exactly* like a teenager, complete with a pissed-off "father." A chill racked me and I shivered.

"Can we come in before you start the interrogation?" Kade snapped.

Blane's jaw clenched and he backed up, allowing Kade and me into the house. As we walked down the hallway, I could feel Blane's eyes on me, especially when we stepped into the light. And when I stopped and turned, his gaze raked me from head to foot and back. I remembered what Kade had said about Blane throwing a fit and raised my chin. I wasn't about to be looked down on for having to wear a uniform to work, even if it did make me look trampy.

"Romeo had Fourth of July uniforms for us," I couldn't help explaining.

"You're soaking wet."

My cheeks burned. "Got caught in the rain," I said with a shrug.

Blane seemed to let that go, thank God. He turned to Kade. "I've been worried about you, both of you. I tried calling a dozen times. I was just heading out to find you when I heard you at the door."

"I said I'd get her and I did," Kade retorted. "No need to check up on me, brother. Or was it something other than her safety you were concerned about?" He gave Blane a cold smile, turned, and walked up the stairs. I heard a door open and close, then Blane and I were alone.

Blane pushed a hand through his hair, heaving a sigh. The muscles of his shoulders and neck looked tight and I suddenly felt bad. He had enough on his mind.

"Listen," I said. "I'm sorry. I didn't realize you were waiting up for us."

"You didn't think I'd notice you sneaking out of here?"

Crap. Busted. "I didn't want to bother you," I hedged.

"Didn't want to be alone with me, you mean," he corrected.

"That's not true."

"Isn't it?"

The look on his face was so pained, I couldn't stop myself from going to him. I rested a hand on his arm.

"I'm here now," I said. "What can I do to help? Did the police agree to come here?"

He nodded. "Tomorrow morning."

The anxiety that had lifted while I'd stood in the rain came roaring back. "Are you all right?"

Blane didn't answer. Instead, he glanced down to where my hand rested on his arm. Self-consciousness kicked in and I pulled back, but he caught my fingers in his and held them.

"I don't want you in the room tomorrow when they come," he said, his eyes catching mine.

"But I don't want you to be alone—"

"I won't be," he said. "Charlotte will be here."

My heart seemed to skip a beat. "Oh?" *Coming to hold your hand, is she?* My cattiness and instinctive desire to claw her eyes out surprised me.

Blane didn't seem fooled by my oh-so-nonchalant response. "She's my lawyer, Kat, that's all," he said.

"I see." Uh-huh, sure she was.

Blane's lips twitched like he was thinking about smiling. "That's not jealousy I hear in your voice, is it?"

"Of course not—don't be ridiculous," I sputtered, trying to tug my hand from his, but he held on, inching closer to me until I had to tip my head back to look him in the eye.

"Because if you were jealous, that would mean I still have a shot." His voice was a gentle rasp that seemed to run right through me.

"I'm not," I lied. "I just want this to be over, that's all."

"When it's over, will you still be around?"

His hand slid down my arm to cup my elbow. The backs of the knuckles of his other hand ran in a gentle path up and down my stomach, softly brushing my skin. He stood much too close and I realized my back was against the wall. He loomed over me, his gaze holding mine.

Blane's touch made it hard for me to breathe. It was too familiar, had too many memories associated with it. I couldn't think, could only feel his skin against mine, gradually moving up to the edge of my top, then ever so slowly down my ribs, across my stomach, dropping beneath my navel to where the wet denim of my shorts clung to me.

I swallowed. "I've already come between you and Kade," I said. "I think it's best that, once this is over, we all go our separate ways."

Blane's hand paused fractionally, then resumed its seductive path, now tracing the top edge of my shorts. The brush of his fingers made me tremble, and it wasn't from the cold.

"Tell me you don't mean that," he said. "There's still something between us. I can feel it and I know you can, too."

"It doesn't matter what's between us," I managed to say, grabbing his hand to stop him touching me. "The bottom line is you broke my trust, Blane, and that's not something you can just get back."

I slid out from between him and the wall and hightailed it to my room before I did something I'd regret.

~

I tossed and turned, unable to sleep. My mind was in turmoil as anxiety for Blane ate at me, and behind all that there was an overwhelming sadness. But I didn't want to think about the future. Right now I was with both Blane and Kade, and I didn't want to squander any of my remaining time with either of them.

Blane's question and behavior made it obvious that he wanted to get back together. I'd been honest with Blane—I didn't trust him. He'd burned me too many times for me to consider getting back together. But getting my heart and emotions on the same page as my brain and common sense was impossible.

And then there was Kade.

Alone in the dark silence of my bed, I closed my eyes and relived that night in Vegas. All day every day, I had to keep the memories at bay, but at night they crept back in. Being with him tonight, having him kiss me, touch me—it made every one of those memories replay inside my head. It wasn't something I should indulge in, but I couldn't help it.

He'd opened up to me tonight, told me something about his past and what he was feeling now. Those moments with him were rare and I couldn't bring myself to regret them.

My head was spinning and I knew I wouldn't be sleeping anytime soon. Blane kept bourbon in the library. Maybe a shot or two would help.

I climbed out of bed, my bare feet padding on the floor as I crept downstairs. I didn't hear a thing as I passed by Kade's room, and no light showed from under the door to Blane's room at the end of the hallway.

Guilt and a little embarrassment washed over me. Was I really going to sneak booze in the middle of the night? Blane's chastisement last week about my drinking still echoed in my head. But I was a grown woman. I could have a drink if I wanted one. It's not like I needed permission.

A dim glow splashed into the hallway from the library door, open a scant few inches. The light wasn't unusual. Blane often forgot to turn off all the lights when he went to bed.

But I didn't expect the voices. I froze in place outside the door, listening.

". . . cops will be here in the morning," Blane was saying.

"You still haven't answered my question," Kade replied. "Why are you a suspect?"

The clink of ice in a glass. Blane was drinking. "A neighbor saw me go in that night. And they don't know it yet, but they have something even more incriminating."

"What?"

A long pause. "Semen."

The breath left my lungs in a rush and the room seemed to tilt. Blane had slept with Kandi on the night of her murder.

"They don't know it's yours."

"No. Not yet. They don't have my DNA and won't get it without a court order or arresting me, neither of which they're prepared to do. Yet."

"Tell me you didn't bareback with Kandi."

Blane snorted. "I'm not that stupid. I always use a condom. The only time I haven't was with—"

He cut himself off and there was silence for a moment. It seemed Kade knew what he'd been going to say, because he didn't ask Blane to finish his sentence.

"But the condom's still there. I'm sure they grabbed the trash. I'm guessing it's already in evidence."

"Was this just an incredibly badly timed reunion?" Kade asked.

"We weren't back together again, if that's what you're asking," Blane said. "We fucked a few times. It didn't mean anything." More ice clinked.

My eyes squeezed shut. This couldn't be happening.

Kade snorted. "How long had that been going on?"

"I wasn't cheating on Kat," Blane bit out. "This was after we . . . broke up. Kandi must have found out about Kat and me—who knows?—but she came by one night. I was angry. She was available and willing. End of story."

"Apparently not, if you kept fucking her," Kade retorted.

Silence.

"Did you kill her?"

My legs gave out and I sank soundlessly to my knees on the floor. The fact that Kade was even asking the question had me reeling, as apparently it did Blane, too.

"You'd think that of me?" he asked in a pained but angry rasp.

"No, but shit happens. And if you did do it, then I need to know. You're not going to jail—I don't care what I have to do. That's not going to happen."

"Wouldn't my being out of the picture solve a big problem for you?" Blane was angry now.

"What the fuck are you talking about?"

"You think I don't know you're in love with Kathleen?"

There was a long silence and I covered my mouth with my hands so they wouldn't hear my ragged breathing. My knees ached from being pressed against the hardwood floor.

"She picked you, brother," Kade said quietly. "Long before she knew me. That doesn't just go away because you fucked things up."

"She's better off without either of us."

"Yeah, that's not gonna happen and you know it."

A pause. "Did you sleep with her?"

"What do you care, Blane? You tossed her aside and fucked Kandi. Who else have you fucked the past few months? Yet you expect her to be a nun, waiting for you to come to your senses?"

Glass shattered and I started. My hands trembled, still covering my mouth.

"Can we get back to what the fuck you're going to do about this?" Kade's irritated voice cut through the sudden silence.

"What do you think I'm going to do? I'll do everything in my power to fight it, call up every favor anyone has ever owed me."

"Will that be enough?"

"I don't know."

They were quiet then and somehow I managed to get off the floor and creep back to my bedroom. I crawled underneath the covers, wishing I hadn't heard everything I had. Images in my head of Blane and Kandi making love wouldn't go away, though it sounded like it hadn't really been making love, at least not from his perspective. And I didn't know if that was better, or worse.

Two things became clear as I finally drifted to sleep. One, Kade hadn't answered Blane's question about whether or not we'd slept together, and two, Blane hadn't said whether or not he'd killed Kandi.

≈

I was awake, dressed, and downstairs before 7:00 A.M., but even that early start wasn't enough for me to beat Charlotte's arrival.

Both Charlotte and Blane were sitting at the kitchen table when I walked in. They looked up and I halted for a moment. Charlotte looked as surprised to see me as I was to see her. She recovered first.

"Kathleen," she said in her come-fuck-me accent that put my teeth on edge. "I—it's good to see you again." She smiled and the smile I returned was just as fake.

"Same here," I lied, heading for the fresh pot of coffee Mona had brewed. I poured myself a cup and took my time fixing it the way I liked. When I turned around to face them, Blane and Charlotte still hadn't resumed their conversation.

"Kathleen is staying with me for a while," Blane explained. His eyes devoured me from head to foot, and although it was vain of me, I was glad I'd taken pains to look good this morning. I'd figured the younger and more innocent I looked sitting at Blane's side—because that's where I was going to be regardless of what he said—the better it would look for him with the police. If I wasn't afraid of him, then how could he possibly have done something like that to Kandi?

To that end, I'd chosen a navy sundress with a sweetheart neckline and cap sleeves. The bodice was fitted and hugged my waist and hips, then flared out into a flirty skirt that stopped a couple of inches above my knees. I'd blown my hair dry, then added some curls so it lay in soft waves down my back. I'd painted my toes I'm Not Really a Waitress red and slipped on a pair of white sandals with three-inch heels.

"When will the police be here?" I asked, taking a sip of coffee.

"Shortly," Charlotte replied.

Blane's eyes narrowed. "Don't you have class today?"

I smiled and said, "Not today. I thought I might be able to help."

"I said I don't want you here for this," he said, his words clipped.

I looked at Charlotte. "Would it help if I was there?"

She hesitated, then said, "Well, yes, and maybe more so if you and Blane were back together." A pained expression had flitted across her face as she said this, then was gone, leaving me to wonder if I'd imagined it. "Are you?"

Blane's gaze was steady on mine as I processed this information, then he turned to Charlotte.

"I don't want her involved," he said.

Damn it. That just pissed me off. Blane had risked his life to save mine too many times for me to turn my back on him now, and if saying we were back together was what it took to give him an edge with the police, then that's what I'd do.

"Yes, actually," I said, directing my words at Charlotte. "We're back together."

Her face was carefully blank as she glanced at my left hand. "You'll need a ring."

I looked at Blane as my stomach did a flip-flop. I hadn't touched the ring he'd given me since I'd set it on his desk those many months ago. For all I knew, he'd returned it.

Blane's jaw was set in steel bands as he looked at me, but his voice was calm when he said, "Charlotte? Would you please give us a moment?"

Charlotte excused herself and left the room, though neither of us looked at her—our eyes now locked in a battle of wills. Blane got up from the table and approached me. I stood my ground, tipping my head back to look him in the eye when he stopped.

"I don't want you doing this," he said flatly. "I know you're trying to help and I appreciate that, but you've been through enough."

"There's no record of my flight to Vegas or my stay there," I said. "I can be your alibi." I set down my coffee. "You've saved my life too many times for me to turn my back on you now."

Blane gripped my arms. "Kathleen, be realistic. You're not going to lie to the police for me! I am *not* getting you involved in a *murder* investigation!" he said, giving me a shake. His voice was louder than he'd ever spoken to me. I flinched but my resolve didn't waver, though I couldn't say the same for my knees, which were practically knocking together. "Do you have any idea of what that entails?"

I gave a slight shake of my head, my lips pressed tightly closed.

"It means," he said, "that the police will crawl into every aspect of your life. Your work, your friends, your finances. They'll question your character, your motives, make you feel like you're guilty of something you didn't even do. And through it all will be the press, documenting and overanalyzing everything. It'll destroy you!" His voice wasn't as loud but was just as intense, pushing me to capitulate, to give up.

"Then what's it going to do to you?"

Blane didn't answer. He didn't have to. I knew as well as he did that what happened in the next few days could ruin everything he'd worked his entire life for—his career, his reputation, everything that meant anything to him.

"Where's the ring?" I asked. His hands still had a hold of my upper arms, the grip tight but not painful.

Something flashed in his eyes and his jaw clenched. The tension between us was thick, a war between his stubbornness and my determination to help him.

"Blane."

Both of us turned to see Mona standing in the doorway. Her eyes flicked to where Blane held me, then back to his face. "Blane, the police are here. I put them in the library with Charlotte."

"Thank you," Blane said politely, utterly controlled again.

Mona nodded and disappeared.

Blane released me but took my hand and led me out of the kitchen. To my surprise, we didn't go to the library but headed upstairs, to Blane's bedroom.

"What are you doing?" I asked. "Shouldn't we be downstairs?"

"I thought you wanted the ring?" He let go of my hand and went to his closet.

I swallowed, my mouth suddenly dry. I didn't know if I was ready to put that ring on my finger again, even if it was just a charade.

Blane emerged from the closet, holding the same velvet box he'd given me four months ago. Walking over to me, he opened it and took out the ring.

"This was always yours," he said, taking my hand in his. He turned it palm up and placed the ring in my palm, closing my fingers over it. "I bought it for you and want you to have it, no matter what happens between us."

I could barely breathe, the cold metal of the ring pressing against my skin. Blane's eyes searched mine and I wondered what he saw in them. My feelings were so confused and conflicted, I didn't know what to think or say.

Blane glanced at his watch. "We'd better get downstairs. Do you want to freshen up before we go?"

I nodded wordlessly, welcoming a moment to regain my composure. I brushed by Blane into the bathroom, closing the door behind me.

I stared at the ring for a moment before sliding it back onto my finger. I remembered when they'd taken it from me on that island, and how Blane had somehow gotten it back. He'd rescued me. Saved me. I straightened my spine. Now it was my turn to do what I could to rescue *him*.

Coming out of the bathroom, I realized Blane was no longer in the bedroom. I frowned, wondering if he'd gone downstairs without me. Then I saw the bedroom door was shut. Afraid that I already knew what he'd done, I ran to it and twisted the knob.

Locked.

He'd locked me in his fucking bedroom.

"Goddammit!" I yelled, slamming my palms against the door.

Furious, I yanked on the handle again. Why did he have a door that locked on the outside? Never mind, that wasn't important. What *was* important was that the cops were downstairs with Blane while I was stuck up here.

Okay, I had to get a grip. Being mad and yelling wasn't going to get me anywhere. I thought of calling Kade, but my cell wasn't on me. Plus, I had no idea if he was still in the house or gone. Considering how he and Blane liked to keep their family ties a secret, I assumed he was making himself scarce this morning.

I bent down and studied the lock on the knob. It had been a while, but maybe . . .

Ten minutes and a lot of cursing later, the lock clicked and the knob turned. I wanted to squeal with satisfaction. Tossing aside the tiepin I'd used to pick the lock, I got to my feet and smoothed my dress. I'd go downstairs and do what I could to help save Blane, then I'd kill him.

My heels clicked on the hardwood floor as I walked toward the library, and I could hear voices. Taking a deep breath and squaring my shoulders, I walked in.

The look on Blane's face would have made me laugh if the circumstances had been different. My smile was perfectly real as I greeted the two plainclothes detectives seated across from Blane and Charlotte.

"I'm so sorry I'm late," I said, holding out my hand to each of them in turn and ramping up the Southern belle. "Blane thinks my disposition is such that this might be too unpleasant for me, but I assured him that I'm not going to let him go through this alone."

I sat next to Blane and took his hand in both of mine, settling it in the folds of my skirt, then dug my nails into his palm. He didn't flinch, but his hand fisted, capturing my fingers and stilling them.

"Please continue," I said, crossing my legs.

One of the detectives glanced at my legs, then cleared his throat. "I'm sorry, miss. You are—?"

"Kathleen Turner," I replied. "Blane's fiancée."

Both men wrote that down in the little notebooks they held.

"And were you with Mr. Kirk the night Miss Miller was murdered?"

I frowned. "I'm so sorry about that poor woman. It was awful what happened to her."

"Yes, it was," the detective said. "Were you with Mr. Kirk that night?"

I took a deep breath and did something I'd thought I'd never do to a police officer—I lied. "Yes. Yes, I was." My dad had to be turning over in his grave.

Blane's grip on my hand tightened to the point of inflicting pain.

The detective consulted his notes again. "Miss Miller was involved with Mr. Kirk for a while. When did you and he start seeing each other?"

"Last fall," I said. "Kandi never got over the fact that Blane chose me and not her."

The detective seemed uncomfortable as he asked his next question, but his gaze was steady on mine and I braced myself.

"You are aware that Mr. Kirk has admitted that he and Miss Miller were having an affair for the past few weeks?"

Blane went utterly still next to me and I avoided the impulse to glance at him. His hand still held mine in a vise-like grip. I was suddenly glad I'd overheard him and Kade talking last night so I was prepared, otherwise my shock would've given away the game.

My expression turned into one of regret and sorrow. "I'm sure you of all people, Detective, would know that every relationship has its problems. Blane and I had a disagreement that kept us at odds for a short time, but we've worked through our differences."

"And why me 'of all people'?" he asked.

"I'm sorry. I didn't mean to assume. It's just that my daddy was a cop and I know from firsthand experience the toll that can take on a relationship."

The detective gripped the notepad with his right hand, his left hand clenching in a fist. I'd noticed the faint mark of an absent wedding ring on his finger. He was recently separated or divorced and judging from the mark that was still there, I guessed the former.

"Was a cop?"

"He died in the line of duty when I was fifteen," I explained. This time I didn't have to fake the sadness in my voice.

"And how would your daddy feel about you marrying a man who regularly gets criminals acquitted?"

Ah. A personal ax to grind? Lovely.

I gave the detective a look my mother used to give me when I sassed her, a mix of disappointment and patience. "I think he would be proud that I'm marrying a man who spent several years serving his country in war. I think he would be grateful to Blane for risking his own life several times to help me and others. I think he would be glad I found someone with the strength of his convictions and a strong sense of justice and loyalty, a good man who loves me and wants to spend the rest of his life with me."

It took every ounce of self-control I had to keep my composure after that little speech. It was exactly how I'd felt after Blane had proposed and the memory made my heart ache.

The detective's smile was devoid of humor. "Well, Mr. Kirk is lucky to have a woman like you standing by him at a time like this."

I stiffened. I could tell by his tone that he was already convinced of Blane's guilt and pitied a woman who would stand by a murderer.

The detective focused again on Blane. "So let's just go through the events of that night one more time," he said.

I turned to Blane and our eyes caught. His mask was firmly in place and I couldn't read what he was thinking or feeling. I could only feel the pressure of his hand gripping mine.

Blane cleared his throat before answering. "Kandi had called me, wanted me to come by. Said she wanted to talk to me. I arrived around 9:00 P.M."

"And you didn't mind him going to see her?" the detective asked me.

"Kandi is . . . was . . . a longtime family friend," I said impassively. "No, I didn't mind."

"What did you and she talk about?" he asked Blane.

"Our relationship, such as it was. She'd been drinking and was . . . highly emotional."

"What does that mean exactly?"

"Kandi was angry one moment, crying the next."

"What was she angry about?"

"That's speculative," Charlotte interjected.

"This is an informal questioning, Counselor," the detective snapped. "Not a court of law."

"It's okay," Blane murmured to Charlotte.

"She was angry about us," Blane answered. "She didn't feel like we were going anywhere. She said I was just using her."

"Weren't you? After all, it wasn't as if you were planning to marry her, was it?" The detective sneered in contempt.

"That's neither here nor there, is it, Detective?" Blane avoided the question.

"Did you have sex that night?"

"No."

It looked like I wasn't the only one lying to the police today.

"Did anyone see you arrive at her home?"

"A neighbor was walking their dog when I got there."

"Anyone see you leave?"

"Not that I'm aware."

The detective wrote that down. "Then what happened?"

Blane sighed. "That's all. Kandi's temper tantrums weren't an unusual occurrence. I told her we'd talk about it when she calmed down and I left."

"And what time was that?"

"A little after ten."

"Did you go anywhere after that?"

"No, I came straight home."

"And you can verify that, Miss Turner?"

"Yes."

"Mr. Kirk, you're trained in many forms of hand-to-hand combat, are you not?"

"Yes."

"Ever strangle someone before?"

"No."

"Ever kill someone with your bare hands?"

It took a moment for Blane to answer, and when he did, his voice was cold. "I spent five years in the Navy deployed in Afghanistan and Iraq. Yes, I've killed without a weapon."

The detective turned to me again. "Have you and Mr. Kirk ever argued?"

"Of course we have," I said stiffly.

"Has he ever hit you or injured you in any way?"

I had a flash, my memory conjuring the time Blane had smashed his fist into my jaw when he'd been having a nightmare and I'd tried to wake him. "No," I said. "Absolutely not." But I could tell he'd noticed my hesitation and I wanted to kick myself.

"If you don't mind me saying so, Miss Turner," he said, motioning to my face, "it looks like you've had an accident recently."

The bruises where David had hit me had faded and I'd used makeup to cover the yellowing spots, but apparently the detective could still see them.

I smiled tightly. "I'm afraid I was clumsy."

"It occurs to me," the detective said, sitting back in his chair and directing his attention to Blane, "that having a governor who casually cheats on his fiancée wouldn't be something most people would appreciate. Did Kandi threaten you, Mr. Kirk? Did she say she was going to go public with your affair and that's why you killed her?"

"Don't answer that," Charlotte ordered. "Detective, you're out of line."

He smiled as he put his notepad into the pocket of his jacket. "It was just speculation, Ms. Page." He stood, as did the other detective. "We'd like a DNA sample as soon as possible."

"You'll need a court order," Charlotte said. "Mr. Kirk has already admitted to being present the night of the victim's death."

"A warrant is public record, you know," the detective said. "The news media will likely have a field day with that."

"My client has an alibi for the time of death," Charlotte replied. "I'd like to see you try to get a warrant."

Blane got to his feet but remained quiet, letting Charlotte handle it. He kept hold of my hand and I rose as well.

The detectives turned to go, but before they reached the door, the one who'd led the questioning turned. "By the way, it seems that whoever killed Miss Miller also raped her." He paused, his eyes flicking to mine. "Postmortem."

Nausea rose like a wave in my throat. My knees threatened to buckle and I clutched Blane's arm for support. His arm slid around my waist, holding me up as the detectives left the room. I heard the front door open and close.

Charlotte glanced at Blane and me. "I'll wait outside," she said, her face carefully blank.

I barely noticed her leaving, my mind busy trying not to imagine the horrible things that someone had done to Kandi. Someone so sadistic I had trouble wrapping my head around it.

Blane coaxed me to him and I let him wrap his arms around me, resting my head against his chest. My hands fisted the fabric of his shirt. I took a deep breath and closed my eyes, listening to the sound of his heartbeat. My anger at being locked in the bedroom had evaporated into sober grief as the reality of what Blane was facing set in.

He could never, ever do something like that. Sleeping with Kandi was one thing, but Blane would never physically harm her, nor was he capable of violating her dead body in such a way.

"Are you all right?" I asked, leaning back so I could look up at him. I couldn't imagine what he must be feeling. He'd been there with her, argued with her, just a short while before she'd been murdered. What if he'd stayed? Would she still be alive? Those thoughts had to have gone through Blane's mind a dozen times at least.

Blane was pale under his tan, the lines around his eyes more pronounced than usual. "You see why I didn't want you around," he said. "I didn't want you to hear, to know, any of that. I didn't want you to lie to them."

"I know you could never do something like that," I said. I thought about asking why he'd lied about having sex with her that night but decided not to. He'd wonder how I knew, then I'd have to admit eavesdropping on him and Kade last night.

He looked at me for a moment, then leaned forward, brushing his lips over my cheek before settling his mouth by my ear.

"I'm so sorry, Kat," he whispered.

I didn't have to ask to know what he meant.

"We were broken up," I managed to say, my voice soft as a wave of sorrow washed over me. "Why would I think you wouldn't be with her, or anyone else, after that?" The words made sense, were logical, but it took a massive amount of will to say them. My heart felt something else entirely, which seemed hugely hypocritical of me, but I felt what I felt.

I thought perhaps I should step back, put some space between us, but Blane had both arms wrapped tightly around me, pressing us close together so I felt every inch of him from chest to knee.

Blane's face was etched in regret and grief. "God, I wish I could turn back the clock," he murmured. "So many things I would change."

"Things happen for a reason, Blane," I said. "Maybe you and me were never meant to be together."

His eyes squeezed shut as though what I'd said pained him, and maybe it did. It had hurt to say it.

"Don't say that," he said, his eyes brilliantly green when he opened them. "Please. You're all I have to hold on to right now."

I looked him in the eye. "I'm not the only one standing by your side. You have Kade, too."

"I no more want Kade to be involved than I want you to be," Blane said. "It's too dangerous. Whoever did this to Kandi is still out there."

"Then I guess we'd better get to finding them."

I started at the sound of Kade's voice behind me and jerked guiltily out of Blane's arms. Kade was leaning negligently against the doorjamb, his arms crossed over his chest. He didn't look at me.

"There's no 'we,'" Blane said. "You don't need to be involved in this."

Kade rolled his eyes. "Still trying to do everything on your own, I see," he sneered. "God forbid anyone should help the great Blane Kirk."

Blane didn't take the bait but instead turned away, going to his desk and pocketing his wallet and cell phone. He grabbed his keys. "I have to go to the firm with Charlotte. I'll be back later."

His fingers lightly brushed mine as he passed, then he was gone. I chewed my lip, worrying about what was going to happen. Kade was right, we needed to figure out who had killed Kandi. That was the only sure way to save Blane.

"You look like sugar wouldn't melt in your mouth," Kade said with a smirk, his gaze moving from my face down to my red-tipped toes and back.

I shrugged. "Just trying to help Blane out if I can. I thought it might put him in a slightly better light if I was there this morning." I needed more coffee to handle Kade, I decided, heading toward the door to pass by him.

"And looking like an untouched virgin will help?"

I definitely didn't want to discuss anything related to sex with Kade, and I lightly smacked him on the chest.

"Don't say things like that!" I admonished.

Kade suddenly gripped my left hand, his mischievous smirk fading. He was staring at the engagement ring on my finger.

"What the hell is this?" he demanded. "Are you fucking kidding me?" He appeared livid, his grip on my hand way too tight.

I tried in vain to pull my hand away. "It's to help Blane," I said. "Charlotte said it would look better if we were back together, so I said I'd do it." His hold finally loosened and I snatched my hand back. "What does it matter anyway? You *told* me to get back with him."

"I know, it's just—" He turned away, shoving a hand through his hair.

"Just what?" I prompted, nearly holding my breath, though why, I couldn't say.

He spun around and gripped my arms, hauling me close to him. "Just that I can't get you out of my head," he hissed. "I think about you all the time. Hell, I even dream about you."

I stared at him, my eyes wide, not knowing what to say.

259

"And you know the worst part?" he continued, his voice low and intense. "It's the dreams—God, the dreams." He gave a huff of bitter laughter. "It's like you're trying to make me lose my fucking mind. They're so real." His grip loosened, his palms skimming lightly down my arms. "Why are they so real?"

My heart was hammering in my chest, my mouth as dry as dust. I shook my head. "I—I don't know what you're talking about."

"Don't you?"

I was saved from answering by Mona stepping into the room. "Kathleen," she said, "you have a phone call."

I knew I must have looked like a deer in headlights. First she'd seen Blane with me this morning, and now Kade. I cringed to wonder what she must think of me, but her face showed nothing except a friendly smile.

"Um, okay, thanks," I said.

She pointed behind me to a telephone sitting on the table. "You can take it there."

I picked up the receiver automatically. "Hello?"

"Strawbs, what the hell happened to your apartment?"

Chance! I hadn't talked to my cousin in weeks, not since he'd gone back to Atlanta after finishing his part in the human trafficking case he'd been working.

"Hey!" I exclaimed, a huge smile breaking across my face. "How are you?"

"I'm fine—now what's going on with you that someone's firebombing your apartment? And Alisha tells me you're shacking up with Kirk?"

I winced. Chance's hostility toward and suspicion of Blane hadn't waned, even though Blane had rescued me.

The ensuing breakup that I'd had no choice but to tell him about had wiped away any goodwill Blane had generated with Chance. I'd had to talk Chance down from a towering rage when I'd told him; he'd wanted to confront Blane to tell him what a "fucking dick" he was.

"William Gage is out of prison," I said, "and he's carrying a grudge. The bomb was courtesy of him. Kade spotted it in time to—"

"Kade?" Chance interrupted. "As in Dennon? Christ, Strawbs, when I left town I thought both of them were out of your life. And good riddance."

I bristled. "Are you through?" I asked coldly. "Or should I just hang up and I'll talk to you again in six months?"

Chance sighed. "I'm sorry. It's just that I get to your apartment only to find it burned out, which was nearly enough to give me a heart attack. Then Alisha tells me you're staying with that sonofabitch. I kind of flipped out."

My irritation faded. My cousin loved me and I could understand his worry. "I'm okay," I said. "Really."

"Well, I'm in town and I want to see you," he said. "Can you meet me for lunch?"

"Yeah, sure," I said.

We settled on a time that he would pick me up and I hung up the phone.

If I'd hoped Kade would leave while I was on the phone, I was disappointed.

"Saved by Barney Fife?" he asked. I let his nickname for Chance pass. Blane, Kade, and Chance were never going to get along, much less like each other, and that was that.

"He's going to come by and take me to lunch," I said. "I probably should get some studying done before he comes.

I have a couple of finals next week." I glanced nervously at Kade, hoping he'd let what we'd been talking about drop.

Kade walked over to look out the window. He was playing with something in his hand, though it was too small for me to tell what it was. I couldn't say whether or not he was seeing anything through the glass as he stood there; he seemed lost in thought.

"I, um, I guess I'll see you later," I said when he didn't reply.

That seemed to rouse Kade from his contemplation and he turned around, shoving whatever he held into the pocket of his jeans.

"Yeah," he said somewhat absently. "I'm going to check into Kandi's phone records. See who she was calling."

"Anything I can do to help?"

"Stay alive," he said curtly. "Tell Barney to keep a close eye out and his gun on him."

I frowned. "You think Gage will still try something? Even after yesterday?"

"I'd just rather *you* be safe than *me* be sorry."

Peachy.

∾

Chance was right on time and I didn't give him an opportunity to come inside—I really didn't need a run-in between him and either Blane or Kade. I met him halfway up the sidewalk, where he grabbed me in a big bear hug.

"God, it's good to see you!" he said.

I hugged him just as tightly. There was nothing quite like how family could make you feel.

Chance set me back on my feet and stepped back to take a look at me. "Well, you look better than you did the last time I saw you," he said.

Yes, the last time he'd seen me, I'd resembled a walking zombie.

"You look good, too," I said with a smile.

"So is Mexican okay with you?" he asked as we walked to his car.

"Sure."

I told him about William Gage and his obsessive vendetta against me as he drove. "But Kade paid him a visit yesterday," I said, "and I'm hoping that'll be enough to get him to stop."

"What kind of visit?" Chance asked.

I hesitated. Chance was a cop and I didn't want to get Kade in trouble. "It's not important," I said, brushing off his question. "So tell me what's been up with you?"

Chance shot me a look, but I just blinked innocently back at him. He sighed.

"Well, actually, I do have some news," he said, parking the car in the lot of a little restaurant.

"What is it?" I asked after I got out of the car.

He held up his left hand and I gasped.

"You got married!"

CHAPTER ELEVEN

I threw my arms around Chance again. "Oh my God! You're married! That's fantastic! Wait a minute—" I abruptly pulled back, frowning. "Who did you marry and why wasn't I invited?"

Chance didn't answer, he just smiled and pointed behind me. I turned.

Lucy and Billy stood at the entrance to the restaurant. She waved when she saw me and Billy took off toward us. I grabbed him up when he reached me, his little arms going around my neck.

"Billy!" I exclaimed, hugging him tight. "It's so good to see you!"

He pulled back so he could talk to me. "I got a new Batman. Wanna see?"

"Absolutely."

Billy squirmed and I set him back on his feet. He dug in his Spider-Man backpack, pulling out the famed caped crusader. "See?"

"He's fabulous," I agreed.

"C'mon," Chance said, taking Billy by the hand. "Let's eat."

I gave Lucy a hug, too, before we sat down at a table. She and I hadn't known each other as more than passing acquaintances before we'd both been taken by human traffickers. An experience like that tends to form bonds, though, and it was good to see her again. She looked healthy and happiness practically beamed from her.

A tiny brunette, she made an attractive partner to my cousin, who was tall and broad shouldered, his hair a thick, wavy chestnut. Chance and I didn't look much alike except for the Turner family blue eyes.

Chance ordered a round of margaritas to celebrate and I began quizzing the two of them on exactly when and how this had happened.

"When it's The One, you just know," Chance said, his face softening as he grasped Lucy's hand.

Huh. I wondered if that was true for everyone. Was that how I'd felt about Blane? A soul-deep conviction that he was The One? Was there only one man for me and we'd blown our chance to be together? Or could a person have more than just one soul mate?

"Well, I'm so happy for you both!" I said, pulling myself out of my thoughts.

"The wedding was a quick, private ceremony," Lucy explained.

"No worries," I said. "I'm just so glad you found each other." Lucy and Billy deserved someone who loved them and could take care of them, and Chance seemed to be that man. I also thought they'd be good for him, judging by the adulation in Billy's eyes and the love shining in Lucy's.

"So how long are you in town?" I asked.

"Actually," Chance said, "we've decided to move here."

My jaw dropped in surprise, but then I recovered and said, "Wow! That—that's wonderful!" To have family close by again? I couldn't imagine how that would feel. My eyes started to tear up.

"Now don't start crying on me," Chance ribbed good-naturedly while I dabbed my eyes with my napkin. "We just thought it would be good to be with family. The Indianapolis Metropolitan Police Department approached me after the Summers case, so I decided to take it."

I cleared the lump out of my throat. "I'm so glad you did." My smile was watery but genuine.

"Plus, we have a built-in babysitter here, right?" he asked, grinning.

"You bet." I ruffled Billy's hair while he chowed down on a taco.

"So . . . ," Chance said, and from the tone of his voice, I knew what was coming. "Want to tell me why you're living with Kirk?"

Lucy politely averted her eyes, murmuring something to Billy as she wiped a smear of sour cream off his cheek.

"It seemed the safest place to be right now," I said with a shrug. "I told you about Gage."

"You're aware he's being investigated in the murder of Kandi Miller, right?"

"No way would he do that, Chance," I said. "Somebody else killed her. Not Blane."

"Either way, do you really think being with him is the best thing for you?"

"I'm not 'with' him," I protested. "He just needs some-one to lean on. He rescued me, you know. Me, Lucy, and Billy. So how about cutting him some slack?"

"He also broke your heart and treated you like shit," Chance shot back.

My appetite was gone and I took a gulp of my margarita. There wasn't anything I could say to Chance's accusation. It was the truth.

"And Dennon is there, too, huh," Chance said, disgust in his voice. "He's bad news, Strawbs. The stuff I've heard whispered about him would give you nightmares for a week. You wouldn't listen to me before, but I'd hoped you'd listen to me now."

"He's my friend," I said. "And I don't care about what he's done. He's been there for me when I needed him."

"Oh really? Where was he three months ago when his brother dropped you? Blood's thicker than water, you know that."

I felt cold suddenly, my hands clammy, and it wasn't from the air-conditioning.

"Chance, give it a rest, will you?" Lucy's gentle admonition had him glancing her way, the hard set of his jaw easing. She gave him a pointed look and he sighed.

"I'm sorry," he said to me. "I just worry about you, that's all. I love you and I don't want to see you hurt any more."

"I know."

Lucy changed the subject, asking me about school, and we chatted for a while. She was going to start looking for a job once they got everything moved up from Atlanta. Billy would be in school in the fall and she thought a part-time job would help out.

After lunch, I gave Billy a kiss on the cheek and hugged Lucy good-bye. They were heading to meet a real estate agent to look at houses and Chance would join them after he dropped me back off at Blane's.

I hopped out of the car when we pulled up, but Chance got out as well.

"I'll walk you inside," he said.

"That's really not necessary," I protested, a sinking sensation in my stomach.

His smile was thin lipped. "It'll be fine, Strawbs."

I had no choice but to follow him to the front door. He watched as I fished out the key Mona had given me and unlocked the door. I breathed a sigh of relief when I saw that the hallway was empty.

"Thanks for lunch," I said.

"You're not going to invite me in? What, he doesn't allow you to have company? Just wants to cut you off from everyone who cares about you?"

I bit my tongue to keep from snapping at him, stepping back so he could come inside.

"So, you're inside," I hissed. "Happy now?"

"Kat?"

I squeezed my eyes shut. Damn it. Blane was here.

The man himself stepped out of the den, halting when he saw Chance and me in the hallway.

"Chance," he said, smiling a bit and coming forward with hand outstretched. "Good to see you again."

Chance ignored Blane's proffered hand. "Wish I could say the same, Kirk."

I winced as Blane lowered his arm. "Can I do something for you?" he asked, his expression a polite mask now.

"You can stay the fuck away from Kathleen."

"Chance!" My temper soared, but he wasn't done yet.

"You and Dennon," Chance continued. "I'm glad you were able to get her back from Summers, but she doesn't need the shit you're dealing with and you know it. And hanging out with Dennon will only get her killed—"

"I completely agree," Blane calmly interjected, stopping Chance mid-tirade.

"You do?"

"Absolutely," Blane said. "However, I'm not going to make Kathleen leave if she doesn't want to. She's welcome here for as long as she likes."

"That's what you say now," Chance retorted. "But you can't be trusted. I know it and I hope to God she does, too."

That seemed to have struck its mark, the barest hint of a wince crossing Blane's face.

"That's enough!" I shoved my way between them. "Don't you dare start in on this, Chance," I said, poking my finger hard at his chest for emphasis. "You were out of my life for years. Just because you've suddenly reappeared does not give you the right to tell me how to live it, no matter how much you care about me!"

"You're blinded by your feelings for these guys," Chance hissed at me.

My face heated with embarrassment, but I stood my ground. "I'm a grown woman and I make my own choices. Now go. Lucy and Billy are waiting for you."

Chance gave one last glare to Blane, then headed for the door. I followed him, sullenly allowing him to give me a kiss on the cheek before he left.

I sighed. Maybe having family nearby wouldn't be such a great idea after all.

I could feel Blane behind me and I turned around. "Sorry about that," I said.

Blane was wearing gray slacks and a light-blue button-down shirt with the cuffs turned back. All that was missing was the jacket and tie. His hands were in his pockets, his feet shoulder-width apart as he surveyed me. I squirmed under his gaze.

"It's fine," he finally said with a shrug. "He cares about you. Doesn't want you hurt. I get that."

"He doesn't understand why I'm staying," I tried to explain.

"Neither do I," Blane said bluntly. "I'm just glad you are."

Time for a change of subject. "How's the investigation going?" I asked.

"As well as could be expected."

Vague much?

My cell phone rang. I dug it out of my purse. "Hello?"

"Hi, Kathleen?"

I didn't recognize the number or the male voice. "Yes. Who's this?"

"It's Luke, ah, from the grocery store?" He huffed a nervous laugh. "Wow, that sounded awful."

And it clicked. "Luke, yeah, from the produce aisle." Luke with the sun-kissed surfer blond hair and blue eyes.

"Oh, good, you remember," he said, sounding relieved. "You said to give you a call, so I was hoping, if you aren't busy, that you might want to have dinner tonight? I know it's last minute . . ."

My instinctive reaction was to say no, especially with Blane standing there staring holes into me. His arms were crossed over his chest now and I glanced away. But a night out sounded like just the thing, especially with a cute guy who knew nothing about my life and had no prior relationship baggage with me. Maybe I could just relax and have a good time.

All this went through my head in the span of a second or two. "Absolutely," I said, making a decision. "I'd like that."

"Great! Can I pick you up?"

After a brief hesitation, I gave him Blane's address because, obviously, he couldn't pick me up at my place. We decided on a couple of hours from then and I said good-bye.

"What was that about?" Blane asked as soon as I hung up.

"I, um, have a date tonight," I said, giving him a sideways glance as I brushed by. "That guy from the grocery store, remember?"

"Yes, but I don't think it's a good idea for you to go out with him," Blane said, clearly irritated.

"I'm not dating anyone, Blane," I said. "So I fail to see the problem." I headed upstairs.

"You don't even know his last name," Blane called after me, and now I could hear anger in his voice. "Do you really think you should be going out alone with him?"

I paused, retorting, "Who are you, my father?"

"No, I'm your brother, remember?" he bit out.

This time, Blane got the last word, disappearing back into the den, the door slamming behind him with enough force to shake the house.

∽

I crept by the closed door of the den when I came back downstairs. I really wanted to avoid another confrontation with Blane. We were over. There was no reason why I shouldn't have dinner with a nice guy.

Right.

But it might be a good idea to wait for Luke outside.

My relief at Blane's absence was abruptly crushed when the door to the den flew open just as I neared the front door, startling a cry from me.

"You scared me!" Surprise made me snappish and I held a hand to my chest as though to get my hammering heart under control.

"Sneaking out, Kat?" Blane asked, one brow raised.

"Don't be ridiculous," I spluttered. "I just didn't want to . . . distract you."

"Is that what you're wearing?" he asked, nodding at my clothes.

I had on a strapless dress, backless except for laces that crisscrossed my back to hold it on. It was made of a filmy aqua material, the skirt fitted to a couple of inches above my knees and with a short slit up one side. My hair was up in a ponytail.

"Aren't you pushing the whole 'father' thing a little far?" I quipped. "It's creepy, even for you."

Blane was in front of me in two long strides. I gasped, automatically retreating until my back hit the wall. Blane followed, pressing his palms against the wall on either side of my head. He leaned down.

"Let's get one thing clear, Kat," Blane said, his voice low and dark. "I'm not your brother, or your father. I love you and want you"—he paused before adding—"to be safe."

"Your version of me being safe feels an awful lot like controlling every move I make."

The doorbell rang and neither of us moved, our gazes locked. It rang again.

"I'd like to get that," I said.

Blane eased back but didn't go far. I pasted a smile on my face and opened the door.

Luke looked as good as I remembered—slightly better, actually—and he was dressed in khakis and a polo.

"Hi," I greeted him, holding the door to hide Blane. Unfortunately, I felt Blane moving the door inexorably out of my grip, opening it wide.

Luke's smile faded a bit when he saw Blane and I winced, guessing Blane had put on his best I-could-crush-you face.

"You remember my . . . brother?" I asked.

"Yeah, sure," Luke said. "Nice to see you again." He directed his attention back to me. "Are you ready?"

"Yep!" No one was more chipper than me. My cheeks hurt from smiling. "Let's go."

Luke settled his hand on the small of my back as we walked to his very shiny black pickup truck. It took a little doing to get into the cab with the short dress I was wearing, but finally Luke just picked me up around the waist and gave me a boost.

He took me to a little restaurant that was small and cozy. I found out Luke had graduated from IU with a finance degree and was working at a place downtown, doing something with money and the stock market. I was a little fuzzy on the details, but that may have been because of the wine.

"So," he began once we'd ordered, "your brother seems like a, ah, real protective guy."

I was glad politics must not be Luke's thing, since it seemed he hadn't recognized Blane.

"Yeah. A little too much, if you ask me," I said.

"You live with him?"

I broke off a piece of the bread the waiter had brought. "Just for now. My apartment is being repaired from some . . . water damage."

The lies were kind of stacking up and I covered my discomfort by asking for another glass of wine.

Luke liked to talk about himself. A lot. So not much was required of me except to smile and nod every once in a while. But he was real pretty to look at, so I didn't mind. It was relaxing, in a way. I had to be so on guard with Blane, not to fall under his spell again, not to give in to how easy it would be to go back to the way things were.

And Kade. Being with him was bittersweet. I loved when he opened up to me, when I got an inkling of his feelings and thoughts. But there was no possibility of a future with him, even though it seemed he was coming closer each day to remembering what had happened between us in Vegas.

What would I do if and when he did?

Well, he just couldn't remember, that's all. It had been a mistake. One that should never and would never be repeated.

Which was too bad . . .

Whoops, that was the wine talking. I tuned in briefly to Luke again, just to get a feel for where we were in the one-sided "conversation." He was recounting his achievements on his high school's swim team.

Nod. Smile. Have a bite of salad. Tune back out.

I was feeling pleasantly tipsy and started mentally comparing Luke to Blane and Kade, which was a bad idea but one I couldn't help. Luke was an attractive, normal, nice guy with a normal, boring, nice-guy job. I should like him. He wasn't a public figure, apparently had little to no interest in politics, judging by his monologue—and he didn't kill people for a living. Always a plus.

He also didn't have the raw edge to him that both Blane and Kade had, more apparent with Kade because he didn't bother to disguise it, as Blane did, under a veneer of civility.

Both Blane and Kade were older than Luke, and both carried an air of maturity, though maybe it was more an air of don't-fuck-with-me. I wondered if Luke carried a gun or had a knife strapped to his leg. I considered asking, then thought better of it.

Luke was built, though, the muscles in his arms and chest filling out the polo shirt he wore in a very nice way. Blane and Kade had incredible bodies, too, each with strength that I relied on, took for granted. And they were smart. Luke was smart, too, obviously, since I couldn't even understand exactly what he did for a living.

But he'd never been a Navy SEAL, and had never hacked into a government agency or Swiss bank.

I sighed a little as I ate a mouthful of angel hair pasta, murmuring in agreement at something Luke had said.

"So," he said, finally coming up for air, "what do you do?"

That yanked me out of my pasta and wine-induced lethargy. "Oh, well, um, I go to school right now, and bartend."

"What are you studying?"

"Criminal justice."

He smiled. "That's cool. So what are you going to do with that?"

"I haven't figured that out yet," I answered honestly. "I just know I want to put bad guys behind bars. Maybe as a cop."

A look of skepticism crossed Luke's face and his smile turned indulgent. "You'd be the most beautiful cop I've ever seen," he said.

My smile was tight. I knew when I was being patronized. Suddenly, Luke didn't seem quite as attractive as he had been before.

And that was the extent of the questions about me. My career choice launched Luke into another story, about how he'd been pulled over by the cops but had gotten out of a ticket, blah blah blah.

I abruptly decided I was spoiled, spoiled by Blane and Kade. Yes, Blane was overprotective and controlling, and yes, Kade confused me utterly with his going hot and cold on me, but they listened to me when I talked. They'd never made me feel like an ornament who was supposed to sit in silent adulation at their awesomeness.

I passed on dessert. Luke suggested we go to a bar for a drink and a dance or two, but I pleaded a long day so he took me back to Blane's house. He walked me to the front door.

"I had a really nice time tonight," he said, taking my hands in his. I hadn't been quick enough getting my keys out of my purse.

"Me too," I lied with a smile.

"May I call you again?"

Ack. "That would be great," I said. Just because he called didn't mean I had to answer. I knew I should really let him down right then, but maybe he wouldn't call and I could avoid that whole unpleasantness altogether.

Luke moved closer and I knew what was coming. My first thought was to step away, but then I wondered—had Blane and Kade spoiled me in every way for other men? So when Luke leaned down and pressed his lips to mine, I didn't pull back.

It was okay. He was a good kisser as far as technique goes, but I felt nothing. No spark, no shiver of arousal in my veins, nothing. It was okay, and that was all.

"What the fuck is this?"

I jerked back, spinning around to see Kade and Blane standing in the driveway. Kade was the one who had spoken and he continued walking toward us even after Blane stopped by Kade's Mercedes, leaning against it with his arms crossed over his chest.

They were both dressed in jeans and black T-shirts, and I could see Blane was wearing his holster at his side, the Glock firmly wedged into it. Kade was armed as well. It was obvious they were going somewhere, and wherever it was, they expected it to be dangerous.

"Where are you going?" I asked as Kade reached past me to unlock and open the front door. Luke stared at him.

"Nowhere special," he said. "Go inside. We'll be back later."

"Um, who is this?" Luke asked me.

Kade had been ignoring Luke, but now he fixed him with a stare. "Back before eleven? I'm guessing she thought you were less than impressive." His smirk was cold, and if Luke had any sense, he'd shut up.

"No one asked you, asshole," Luke shot back, his ears turning red. "Kathleen, who is this guy? Is he your brother, too?"

"Brother?" Kade interjected before I could answer. "She doesn't have a brother, dipshit." He turned to me. "Really? You told him Blane was your brother?" His tone spoke volumes about what he thought of that idea.

My face heated as Luke's gaze landed on me again. "I'm really sorry," I said quickly to Luke. "It just . . . came out."

"So who is he then, if he's not your brother?" Luke asked, angry. Not that I blamed him.

"Her fiancé," Kade said.

"Ex-fiancé," I shot back.

"You're living with your ex-fiancé?" Luke was incredulous.

"Yes, but it's over now," I protested, though the part of my mind not completely aghast at what was happening was wondering why I'd bothered. It wasn't like I wanted to go out with Luke again.

"Then who's this guy?" Luke jerked a thumb at Kade.

Kade slung his arm over my shoulders. "I'm the brother," Kade explained. "His brother." He nodded at Blane. "And her friend," he said, which would have been fine. But then he added in a conspiratorial whisper, "With benefits."

My embarrassment was now complete. Luke looked at me like I was insane, a slut, or possibly both. I covered my burning face with my hands, wishing the ground would open up and swallow me whole. Maybe I should say something? But what on earth would I say?

"Um, yeah, I-I'm not really . . . in . . . to that," Luke stammered. "I'll catch you later, Kathleen." He hurried back to his truck without a backward glance and a moment later was speeding away.

"I can't believe you said that!" I rounded on Kade, forcing him to drop his arm.

"You should thank me," he said with a snort. "Did you see the size of that truck? Textbook overcompensation."

I just looked at him, my mouth agape, utterly speechless. Then a laugh bubbled up from my throat. Really, the whole situation must have seemed ridiculous when seen through the eyes of a stranger. And I probably didn't need to worry about having to turn down that second date with Luke.

Kade's eyes crinkled slightly at the corners, his smirk transforming into a soft smile.

"So now that I ruined what would have been a very disappointing evening," he said, "you want to come along?"

"You have to ask?"

"Go change. You've got three minutes."

I ran upstairs, unlacing my dress as I went and jerking it off when I hit my bedroom. Thirty seconds later, I had on jeans and rummaged in my closet until I found a black tank. I pulled it on over my head and grabbed a pair of tennis shoes before heading back downstairs.

Kade's eyes flicked appreciatively over me. "I love it when you dress badass. Let's go then."

Blane was still leaning against the car, smoking a cigarette, when we came back out of the house. I remembered that he smoked only when he was incredibly stressed-out. When he saw me, he flicked the cigarette to the concrete and ground it out with his boot. He didn't seem to bat an eye at my presence, though I'd been preparing myself for an argument.

"How was your date with surfer dude?" he asked as Kade rounded the car to the driver's side. Blane's eyes seemed to glitter in the faint light.

I lifted my chin. "It was great," I lied.

Blane just looked at me.

I huffed in exasperation, caving. "Okay, it wasn't great. But it doesn't matter because after that little scene I doubt I'll hear from him again. Are you happy now?"

His mouth tipped up at the corners, like he was thinking about smiling. "Very."

He opened the back door for me and I climbed into the car. Blane got in the front as Kade started the engine and we pulled away from the house.

I leaned forward between the two men, bracing my arms on the tops of their seats. "So where are we going?"

"Kandi's house," Kade answered.

"Why?"

"Check out the crime scene."

"I thought you'd already been there?" I asked Blane.

"It was right after she was murdered," Blane said, glancing at me. "I was in shock. There were lots of people around. I didn't get a good look."

"So why all the firepower?" I asked.

"Whoever did this is still out there," he explained. "And he's a sick fuck. I'd rather be armed, just in case."

"So what's with the date?" Kade asked.

I abruptly leaned back in my seat. "Nothing. Just some guy I met."

"And his last name was . . . ?" Blane prompted.

I shot a glare to the back of his head. "I don't remember."

"Well, he looked like a barrel of laughs, so I'm sure you had a great time," Kade teased. "And how thoughtful of him to get you home so early."

"He had to work tomorrow," I said, making up an excuse for my short date. I really didn't want Blane and Kade to know how boring Luke had been.

"I see," Kade said. "And what did he do for a living?"

Shit. "Um . . . something with numbers?"

Blane snorted a laugh at me.

"I wasn't paying a whole lot of attention, okay?" I protested. "He talked a lot."

Now Blane laughed outright, turning a bit so our gazes caught. His eyes twinkled at me.

I hid a smile and said loftily, "Okay, I'll admit it wasn't exactly a love connection. But hey, he bought me dinner, so it wasn't a total loss."

"I would've bought you dinner," Blane said, his voice a low thrum of sound.

Kade made a too-sharp turn and Blane was suddenly plastered against the passenger door.

"Sorry about that," Kade said easily.

I sighed. Maybe that maturity thing I'd been thinking they both had earlier was really just wishful thinking on my part.

Kade parked a block away, under the looming darkness of an overgrown oak tree. I followed Blane through the yards, Kade bringing up the rear. When we reached the rear of the darkened house, Blane paused, handing both me and Kade a pair of latex gloves.

"No fingerprints," he said, pulling on a pair himself.

My heart was pounding as Blane took out a key and unlocked the back door.

The house was still and silent, making the hair stand up on the back of my neck. I followed Blane as he left the kitchen, entered the foyer, and then climbed the stairs to the second floor. The last door on the left was ajar and Blane flipped on the light in the room.

None of us spoke, and I was painfully conscious that a woman's terrifying last moments had occurred in this very room. Flecks of dried blood stained the ivory satin sheets on the bed, which was where my eyes were inexorably drawn.

Blane paused for a moment, his gaze on the bed, too, then he seemed to shake himself. Moving to the dresser, he began opening drawers and pawing through them.

"What are we looking for?" I asked.

"Whoever did this was someone she knew," Blane said. "There's no sign of forced entry and no evidence of a struggle. She let him in, let him come up here. There's got to be something around here that can help us figure out who he is."

"Her phone records show repeated calls to an unlisted number, including one the night she was murdered," Kade said. "I traced the number to a burner phone, so dead end there. Was she dating anyone else?" He started on the dresser drawers.

I flinched at the "anyone else" part of that question. Opening her large walk-in closet, I started looking through her things, trying not to think about how much Kandi would have hated me touching her belongings.

"She said something," Blane answered, digging through another drawer, "about a man who, quote, 'appreciated' her. She was trying to make me jealous, I think. I didn't care enough to ask who it was."

Sometimes the coldness Blane was capable of rivaled Kade's.

"Shouldn't the police be looking for that guy?" I asked.

"The police have all the evidence they need," Blane said. "I'm not sure how much longer Charlotte can hold off an arrest."

"Shouldn't your uncle be helping you?" I asked, trying and failing to keep the bitterness from my voice. Regardless of how much I hated Senator Keaston, he had always had Blane's best interests at heart, no matter how misguided his actions.

"I've asked Robert to keep his distance," Blane replied. "No need to take him down with me."

I didn't have anything to say to that, so just kept on searching. My mind worked the puzzle as I searched through Kandi's clothes. Whoever had done this was sick and twisted. Maybe they were also the kind that liked to play rough in the bedroom? If so, he and Kandi would have needed . . . accessories. If they'd used any, maybe there would still be DNA. Where would she have kept stuff like that?

A woman like her would have hidden them, I decided. But where?

I looked up at the stacks and stacks of shoeboxes lining Kandi's closet. Hmm.

Reaching up, I pulled a box carefully from the stack, but it was high and I watched in horror as the whole stack teetered. I squealed in dismay and covered my head with my arms at the shower of boxes that tumbled down on me.

"What are you doing?" Kade asked in bewilderment, suddenly appearing at my elbow.

I cautiously lowered my arms. It looked like the avalanche was over. "I'm looking for her . . . toys," I explained.

"Her what?"

My face burned. "You know . . . her personal things. I just thought maybe if she was seeing someone else, they might have left some DNA, or something . . ." My voice trailed off at the look of amusement on Kade's face. "What?"

"So you're looking in shoeboxes?" He snorted. "Why don't we just ask Blane where she kept them?"

He turned away, but I grabbed a fistful of his shirt. "Don't you dare ask Blane—" I hissed.

"Ask me what?"

Now Blane had ventured into the closet behind Kade.

"Where did Kandi keep her sex toys?"

Kade's bluntness made me hurriedly turn away. I didn't want to think about the images going through my head now of Blane and Kandi—

"How the fuck would I know?" Blane retorted with some surprise.

"Figured you were sleeping with her, you'd know," Kade said with a shrug.

"Listen," Blane sneered, "you may need stuff like that, but I don't."

"So you're boring in bed," Kade said with a smirk. "It's nothing to be ashamed of. You can't be good at everything."

Good lord. I was trapped in a murdered woman's closet with two grown men acting like fifteen-year-old boys.

"Can we just drop it?" I snapped. "Or should I get out a ruler and start measuring?"

Both men looked at me, and I knew my face was flaming, but I just cocked an eyebrow at them. Blane's lips finally twisted in a near smile.

"It's too cold in here for that," Kade deadpanned.

"Well, they're not going to be in here," Blane said, glancing around the closet. "They'd be by the bed, right? In the nightstand?"

I shook my head. "No. Kandi probably had a cleaning lady and I bet she did the laundry. Kandi would've hid them from her." I crouched down and started taking lids off shoeboxes.

The men seemed to consider this statement for a moment, then Blane reached for more boxes off the shelf, looking into them one by one. Kade did the same.

"So . . . ," Kade said after a few moments of blessed silence.

I braced myself. I knew that tone and whatever was coming next was probably going to be wildly inappropriate.

"I can't help wondering," he continued. "Where do you keep your . . . personal things?"

Sometimes I hated being right.

"I am so not answering that," I shot back, digging through another stack of boxes and cursing that Kandi had so many freaking pairs of shoes.

"So is it like a collection? I mean, do you have enough to fill a shoebox? Some of these seem kind of . . . small . . . for that sort of thing." He picked up a box, eyeing its dimensions doubtfully.

Oh my God. I was going to kill him. To my dismay, I heard Blane smother a laugh.

"I do not have a collection," I protested.

"So you admit you do own items of a personal nature?"

"Every woman does. It's not a big deal." I tried to shrug it off.

At my admission, both men paused in their search, their heads turning toward me. I studiously avoided their gazes and prayed they weren't imagining me with . . .

"Found it!" I crowed. And not a moment too soon, considering where the conversation had been headed.

The box contained a few things I recognized, and a few I didn't. But what immediately caught my eye was the navy blue, patterned silk tie. I carefully drew it out of the box.

"Really hoping that's not yours, brother," Kade said softly.

Me, too, I thought but didn't say.

"It's not."

Blane produced a plastic baggie and I slipped the tie inside. There were a couple of silk scarves, too, and I put them in another baggie.

"We've been here a while," Blane said, glancing at his watch. "It's pushing it. Let's go."

Kade offered me his hand and I climbed out from the mountain of shoeboxes. Blane watched, flicking off the bedroom light. I saw Blane and Kade removing their gloves as we walked down the hall and I did the same, shoving them in my pocket.

We were almost to the stairs when we heard the front door open. All of us froze.

A cold rush of adrenaline poured through my veins. Who could be here at this time of night? Was it a friend of Kandi's? A relative? Or was it the murderer, returning to make sure he'd left no evidence behind?

Blane grabbed my arm, jerking open the nearest door and shoved me inside. Kade followed, then Blane, who eased the door shut behind him.

We were in some kind of closet, maybe a linen closet, I thought, and it wasn't big enough for the three of us. I was sandwiched tightly between Blane and Kade and couldn't see a thing, the blackness utterly complete.

CHAPTER TWELVE

Blane and Kade were still and silent, Kade at my back and Blane in front. I strained my ears, hearing the faint sound of footsteps on the stairs, coming closer and passing by our hiding place.

The closet was warm, too warm, it was stifling. I couldn't move. I was trapped. How long would we have to stay in here?

"Take it easy," Kade breathed in my ear, his voice a bare whisper of sound. His hands settled on my hips. "Breathe."

I closed my eyes—not that it made a difference in what I could see, it was so dark—and tried to concentrate on breathing. I felt Blane's fingers curl over mine as he took my hand. Only then did I realize that tremors shook my whole body. I was breathing too fast and too shallow. Hyperventilating.

I felt the same way I had in the ambulance. It was hard to concentrate. And when I opened my eyes, I kept seeing the faces of the men who'd taken me, felt the horror of being utterly at their mercy. In some detached way, I knew I was fighting a flashback and panic attack, but that didn't mean I could stop it.

Kade's arm curved around my stomach, holding me tight. "Don't think about it," he whispered. "Think about something else. You know how many women would sacrifice a limb to be stuffed in a closet with two hot guys like me and Blane?"

His words penetrated my haze and my lips trembled in a faint smile.

Blane had both my hands in his now, then took my arms and wrapped them around his waist, as though to ground me in the present. He rubbed my arms, gently and methodically moving up to my shoulders and back down to my elbows. I rested my forehead against his chest and closed my eyes, breathing in and out. Rinse, lather, repeat. Kade pressed his mouth to my bare shoulder, the kiss gentle and silent. His hands lay low across my abdomen as he held me.

Blane's scent clung to his skin, leaching through the thin fabric of his T-shirt. I inhaled greedily. Breathe in. Breathe out. But it was still too fast. My head swam.

Fingers lifted my chin, turning my face upward, and I felt the barest brush of Blane's lips in a kiss. His palm cupped my cheek, a thumb brushing my cheekbone as his mouth moved gently over mine. It was unexpected and I gasped in surprise. Blane took the opportunity to deepen the kiss, forcing my breaths to slow.

Kade's touch was warm against my shoulder, the slide of his tongue on my skin sending a shiver through me. His hand had crept under my tank, the heat of his palm like a brand.

I couldn't see a thing, I could only feel. And gradually, as I stood wedged between the two men whose entire focus was on me, who made me feel the safest and most protected that I'd ever been, my tremors eased and breathing was no longer a chore.

Distantly, through the haze of forbidden desire they'd woven around me, I heard footsteps pass the door, heading back downstairs.

Blane slowly eased back, our lips clinging together. I was breathing fast again, but this time for a completely different reason.

"I'm going to see who it is," Blane whispered. His lips brushed my temple. "Keep her here."

My heart shot into my throat and I clutched at Blane's shirt. What if he got hurt?

"I should go, not you," Kade protested.

"No time to argue." Blane gently but firmly disentangled his shirt from my clenched fingers, then he was out the door, closing it behind him.

"We should go after him," I said, turning to face Kade. His hands slid around my back.

"No can do," he replied. "We'll wait here. Neither of us wants you hurt. Blane will be fine. He's good at this, remember? Have a little faith."

I chewed my lip, my anxiety easing somewhat.

"Why do I feel like we're in a grown-up, slightly more dangerous version of spin-the-bottle?" Kade murmured. His voice was close to my ear now, his breath warm against my skin. "In which case, my time is short." His mouth began searching in the dark, trailing kisses along my jaw.

I turned my head away, trying to keep my wits about me. Kade's lips drifted down my neck to where my pulse was pounding.

"You should stop," I managed to say.

"I don't want to," Kade murmured against my skin. "Blane kissed you. Now it's my turn."

Cradling my head, he held me still as his lips found mine.

Kade kissed like he needed me more than he needed air to breathe, as if it was agony to have been apart these past few hours. He overwhelmed me, his tongue tangled feverishly with mine until I was lost to everything but him.

A sharp whistle pierced the silence and Kade pulled back with one last brush of his lips against mine. "That's our signal."

I was reeling, but Kade didn't seem fazed as he opened the closet door and carefully peered into the hallway. He had his gun in his hand when he turned to look back at me.

"You all right?" he asked.

Sure. I was hunky-dory. Making out with Blane, and moments later, Kade—I'd absolutely lost my mind. Guilt and self-loathing crept over me. What kind of person was I to do something like that?

I followed him down the stairs to where the glow of lights showed Blane with someone else. A woman. Older, perhaps in her mid-forties, she was Hispanic and was wringing her hands. Her face was lined with worry as she watched Kade and me approach.

Blane's gaze drifted over me, banked desire in his eyes. My cheeks flooded with heat, remembering what had transpired in the closet with the two of them.

"This is Maria," Blane said. "She's Kandi's housekeeper."

"Why is she here at this hour?" I asked.

"Kandi hadn't paid her," Blane answered.

"She pay every month," Maria answered, her accent thick over the broken English. "Now this horrible thing happen to her." Her eyes filled with tears. "I know is terrible, but

I must have pay. I have grandchildren. Rent is due, bills."
She shrugged helplessly. "I was hoping maybe Miss Kandi
have money here somewhere."

She started crying in earnest now, covering her face with
her hands. "I should not have come. Is dishonoring the dead
to steal from them. Here." She rummaged in the pocket of
the long skirt she wore, handing something to Blane. "I am
sorry."

It was some kind of jewelry. Blane looked at it, then
handed it to me. He pulled out his wallet. "It's okay, Maria.
How much did she owe you?"

"Three hundred dollars," she said.

Wow. Kandi had gotten off cheap for a housekeeper.

Blane dug twice that amount from his wallet and held it
so Maria could see it. "Can you tell me if Kandi's been seeing anyone recently?"

"Other than you, Mister Blane?" she asked.

Ouch.

Blane's fist clenched. "Yes," he said stiffly, "other than me."

Maria nodded, wiping her eyes. "Yes, but it was secret.
Kandi told me not to tell."

"I need you to tell me," Blane said.

Maria's eyes started leaking again. "But if I do, he said
he would send me back to Mexico. My grandchildren are
here. Who will take care of them if I go?"

"I promise, no one is going to send you back," Blane
assured her. "We need to know who it is. Who was seeing
Kandi?"

Maria hesitated, her indecision apparent. I waited, barely
breathing.

"It was Mister James," she finally said.

I sucked in a breath. It couldn't possibly be—

"James Gage?" Blane asked.

She nodded.

"How long had he been seeing her?"

"A while," she replied, "on and off."

"Okay. Thank you, Maria. You've been a big help." Blane handed her the money. She gave him a nod, glanced at Kade and me, then hurried out the front door. A moment later, I heard a car start in the driveway.

"Oh my God," I breathed, sinking down into a nearby chair. My legs wouldn't hold me any longer. James Gage was a bad guy, I knew that. He and I'd had several run-ins and he'd not hesitated to use violence and force to get what he wanted.

But murdering Kandi? Why? And what he'd done to her after she was dead? It didn't make sense, even for someone like him.

"Well, that was unexpected," Kade said. "I wonder if we'll find his DNA on the tie and scarves."

"I have a buddy on the force," Blane said. "He's supposed to come by in the morning and bring the case file. I can see if he can get the tests run. In the meantime, we need to go." His eyes met mine, then flicked away as he headed for the kitchen.

I avoided Kade's gaze as I hurried after Blane. What had we been thinking? What had *I* been thinking? Did Blane know Kade had kissed me, too?

The ride back to Blane's was filled with tension, and guilt turned my stomach into a pit of churning acid. Kade parked the car in the driveway and turned off the engine. I was slow in climbing out as they both loitered by the car.

I felt as though I was suffocating, the weight of their gazes made me want to cringe. Did they expect me to choose? How could I choose between a man I loved but didn't trust, and a man I wanted but didn't love?

"I-I think I'll stay out here for a while," I stammered, backing away slightly.

Hurt flashed across Blane's face before he masked it. He said nothing, just gave a curt nod, throwing a quick glance at Kade before turning to disappear inside the house.

Someone nearby was shooting off fireworks. Illegal, at this time of night, though it was technically the Fourth of July. I wandered over onto the lawn to get a closer look. It seemed like a better idea at the moment than going inside.

Kade followed and I felt his eyes on me as I gazed upward at the sky. The *whoosh* of a rocket launching reached my ears, then the sparkle and crackle of the firework as it exploded.

"I won't say I'm sorry, because I'm not," Kade said.

I shrugged. "It's not a big deal. It doesn't mean anything, right?" Hell, we'd done more than kiss in Vegas and that hadn't done a thing to change our relationship.

No. I wasn't being fair to Kade, after all, he had no idea how far things had gone between us. But I did, and my body did. Maybe that was why it had taken little more than a furtive encounter in a closet for me to fall under his spell.

I felt dangerously close to bitter, which was not how I wanted to remember Kade.

Another firework was launched, exploding into a brilliant show of color, then fading to ashes. Kind of like Kade and me, I supposed.

"I think we both know that's not true."

I jumped, not realizing Kade had moved directly behind me, his voice in my ear.

"Then what does it mean?" I asked, turning and looking up into his eyes. "Enlighten me." And perhaps part of that bitterness I was feeling leached into my voice.

Kade's fingers caressed my jaw. "It means you're beautiful. Desirable. That I can't keep my hands off you any more than I can tell my heart to stop beating. It means I listen for your voice when I know you're near and love it when I can smell your perfume on my clothes at the end of the day."

I couldn't breathe and the knot in the pit of my stomach grew to the size of my fist.

"Stop it!" I cried, shoving at his chest. I'd taken him off guard and he stumbled back a few steps. "Stop saying things like that! You can't . . . *tell* me all of that and then walk off like it's no big deal! You're killing me."

He stared at me, silent.

I took a breath and swallowed the lump in my throat. "Offer me something or offer me nothing, but stop trying to play both sides." Because that's what he was doing. Pushing me at Blane, telling me we should reconcile, then getting upset when he saw the ring on my finger. Kissing me, touching me, then saying it could lead nowhere.

Yes, he'd told me he loved me in Vegas, but he'd been drunk at the time and didn't remember saying it. Unless it was an emotion he was willing to own up to sober, it didn't really matter, did it?

I searched his eyes, not breathing, and hoped for . . . I didn't know what. To my disappointment, Kade turned away without a word. I watched his form be absorbed by the darkness as he walked to the house.

Two steps forward, three steps back.

I remained outside, unable to bear the thought of going inside just yet. I slumped down on the grass and watched the fireworks. I could hear the people laughing and talking as they shot off rockets. The frugal part of me cringed at every explosion, adding up the dollars in my head. I'd never seen the point of buying fireworks—it was literally like setting your money on fire. But I liked watching them, and if other people wanted to blow their money in that fashion, who was I to judge?

I thought about Kandi. She'd been having sex with Blane . . . and James. Why? Had she been hoping to make one of them jealous? Had she known how much James hated Blane? What if she hadn't told James and he'd found out she was sleeping with Blane, too? Could he have flipped out enough to kill her? Maybe accidentally?

My eyelids were heavy when I finally decided to call it a night. I brushed the grass off my jeans and went inside. I showered and wrapped myself in a towel, my wet hair clinging to my shoulders. I hoped I was tired enough to sleep. Part of me ached for my own apartment, but another part of me was glad to be here, glad to be with Blane and Kade, despite the tension between the three of us.

I walked out of the bathroom and froze.

Blane was sitting on my bed, the dim glow of the bedside lamp casting pools of light and shadow on his body.

He was silent, his gaze steady on mine before it dropped lower, taking in the damp towel I wore. Memories of our kiss earlier tonight assaulted me. My breath caught in my chest and I had to swallow before I could speak.

"What are you doing in here?" I asked.

"I'm sorry," he said. "I didn't mean to intrude. I just . . . need to talk to you."

I shifted my weight from one bare foot to the other, acutely conscious of my nakedness. Was this about Kade, or about us? I didn't know if I was ready for either conversation.

Yet, if it was important enough to make him invade my room at this hour, then I should probably hear him out. "It's okay. What is it?"

He approached me, stopping when he was close. "I wanted to tell you that you were right about my uncle. I confronted him with what you told me while you were in Vegas, that he had tried to pay you off. He admitted it quite openly."

Vindication. It was a good feeling.

"I'm so sorry, Kat," Blane said, his voice a husky whisper. "I had no idea, never thought for a moment that he would do something like that. Which also explains why, when you didn't take the bribe, he resorted to lying to me about you."

Yes, I could have told Blane all that months ago. Too bad he wouldn't have listened.

"But how could you do that to me, Blane?" I asked, unable to stop the question from tumbling out. "How could you believe I'd cheat on you? The man I was supposed to marry?" It was a question I'd wanted an answer to for months. "You risked your life to track me down and rescue me from Summers. How could you think I'd betray you?"

"I have no excuse, Kat," Blane said. "I could stand here and tell you I've never loved a woman before, not like I love you, and it terrified me. I could tell you that I was too afraid to believe we could be happy, that it all wouldn't disappear in smoke and lies. So when I saw those photos, it was almost a relief after waiting for my dreams to shatter, when they finally did."

His voice was choked, his eyes too bright and vividly green, but he kept talking.

"But those are just excuses," he said. "I believed the wrong thing. I made a horrible mistake. I thought the two people I loved the most had betrayed me in the worst possible way, and I couldn't handle it. I couldn't see or hear anything but what I thought was the truth. I sabotaged our happiness. My uncle had never lied to me before. Why would I doubt him?"

"Neither had I, but you doubted me," I said.

My stomach churned and my chest ached. I hadn't felt this much pain since the day it had gone so wrong between us.

"Can you forgive me?" he asked.

I looked at him. Who was I to withhold forgiveness? Everyone made mistakes, hurt the ones they loved, and I was no exception. If the situation were reversed, I'd want absolution, too.

"Yes," I said. "I forgive you."

Relief swept his features, and it felt like something inside me had echoed that feeling, like a knot tied too tight finally loosened. Forgiveness was good for the soul, my soul.

Blane took my hand in his, glancing down at the ring on my finger.

"How do you live with a regret so deep it cuts through every part of you?" he murmured.

I didn't know what to say, and perhaps wouldn't have been able to speak even if the right words had come. The lump in my throat felt as though it would strangle me.

Blane leaned down and pressed his lips to my forehead for a long moment, then he was gone.

Somehow, I knew sleep wouldn't come easy tonight after all.

~

The doorbell rang as I came downstairs the next morning, and I swung by to answer it. A man stood on the doorstep with a large manila envelope in his hand.

"Can I help you?"

"Is Mr. Kirk available?"

"Hey, Jared, come in."

Blane had come up behind me. Apparently, he knew the guy. I stepped back to let him in.

"Jared, this is Kathleen, my . . . fiancée."

That was like a punch to the gut.

"Kathleen, this is Detective Jared Jones."

Ah. Blane's friend in the department. We shook hands.

"Let's meet in the den," Blane said, gesturing to the door. Jared headed that direction. Blane turned toward me.

"You don't have to come," he said. "The photographs . . . I'm sure they won't be pretty."

"I want to," I said simply.

He searched my eyes, then nodded and took my hand, following Jared into the den. Kade was already in there. Blane introduced Kade, mentioning that he was a private investigator rather than his brother.

"What do you have?" Blane asked.

Jared handed him the envelope. "It looks bad," he said.

Blane dumped the pile of papers and photos onto the table. Kade picked up a few and started reading.

The photos were what jumped out at me. I picked one up. Kandi's eyes were open, staring sightlessly. I'd never seen her without makeup and she looked softer, younger without it.

The livid marks on her neck drew my eye as Jared spoke.

"Initially, we thought the cause of death was strangling," he said. "Turns out she was smothered."

I glanced up at him, then back at the photographs, choosing another that showed bruises on her upper arms, like someone had grabbed her. I was more interested in a close-up of her neck, visible in one corner of the photo.

"What is that?" I asked, pointing.

Blane peered over my shoulder and frowned, taking the photo from me to look more closely. He handed it to Jared.

"Those two marks," he said, pointing to what I'd seen on her neck. They were tiny, maybe only a quarter of an inch long, and close together.

"The ME thinks they're from a stun gun," Jared said. "It would have immobilized her, then he smothered her."

More photos, some I couldn't look at, of injuries and bruises on more intimate parts of her body.

"The killer was dumb, though," Jared said. "Left semen, so we have DNA."

Blane's head jerked up at that, which confused me. He'd told the cops he hadn't slept with Kandi that night, although he had, but he'd used a condom so the semen couldn't be his. It had to be James's.

"Who are they thinking did it?" Blane asked.

"Well," Jared said with a sigh, "you. They're working on a warrant for your DNA."

"It's not mine," Blane told him.

"I believe you," Jared replied, "but like I said, it looks bad."

Blane went to his desk, retrieving the tie and scarves from last night and handing them to Jared. "We found these last night among Kandi's things," he said. "Can you test for DNA against the semen you found?"

Jared nodded. "I'll get this cataloged as evidence, say I found them or something. You think the guy was someone she was seeing?"

"Yes, and she'd been secretly seeing James Gage."

"The district attorney?" Jared asked with surprise.

Blane nodded. "We're not sure exactly how long, but it had been going on for a while." He hesitated, then added, "James has a track record of violence, especially against women."

Yeah. I could vouch for that.

Jared's eyes got even wider. "You're kidding."

"I wish I were."

"Well, even if the DNA does match, we have no way of proving it's his," Jared said. "He's not in the database."

"If we got a sample from him, you could match it," Blane said.

"Yeah, but how do you plan on doing that? You're the prime suspect in a murder that he'll no doubt prosecute. Everyone knows there's no love lost between the two of you. He won't let you within three feet."

"I'll think of something," Blane said.

Jared left a few minutes later, leaving Blane, Kade, and me studying the file.

I took a deep breath before speaking, already knowing how this was going to go. "I could get the DNA."

The "No" was resounding and simultaneous from both men, neither of whom even glanced up from the papers and photos they were studying.

I blew out a frustrated breath. "I'm not going to just sit around and do nothing while James does all he can to ruin you," I said to Blane.

"He's not going to ruin me," Blane said, flipping a page of the report in his hand.

"I want to help," I insisted.

"You've already helped. You lied to the police to give me an alibi." Blane's tone said he didn't appreciate that overly much.

"You let her lie for you?" Kade interjected.

Blane looked up. "I didn't 'let' her do anything. I locked her in my bedroom to keep her away, but she got out. I don't suppose you know who taught her how to pick a lock, do you?"

Kade flipped him off and Blane gave a disgruntled snort before resuming his study of the case file.

I waited a moment before adding in an undertone to Blane, "By the way, I really didn't appreciate being locked away like the crazy aunt. That really ticked me off."

"Did it? I hadn't noticed." The eye roll was implied.

I kicked off my shoes and tucked my feet up under me as I thought. There had to be a way to get DNA from James without it being too dangerous. I just needed some bodily fluid or hair.

"Do you work tonight?" Kade asked.

I nodded. "My shift starts at six," I said, and I had an idea.

It was a holiday, so the bar would close by 9:00 P.M. Romeo bitched about it every year, saying people wanted to have a drink after watching fireworks, so why should he close? But Kade and Blane wouldn't realize the bar closed early.

"Whatever you're thinking about doing, forget it," Kade said.

I shot him a dirty look. "I'm not thinking of doing any-thing," I lied. I jumped to my feet before either of them could read anything more from my face. It was unnerving to realize just how well Blane and Kade knew me. "I'm going to go help Mona in the kitchen." Surely she needed help doing . . . something. So long as it wasn't actual cooking, I'd be fine.

Blane glanced up, his lips curving into a soft smile. When I walked by, he reached out to brush his fingers against mine, pressing a quick, gentle squeeze to my hand.

Mona was in the kitchen when I got there, thank good-ness, busy making something with peaches. Maybe a cob-bler. I loved peach cobbler.

"Can I do anything to help?" I asked.

She glanced at me with a smile. "That's sweet of you," she said. "I have some green beans that need snapping, if you don't mind."

"I can do that." No cooking required, right up my alley.

Mona handed me a large brown bag of fresh green beans and an empty bowl. I glanced outside. It was beautiful and sunny. "Do you mind if I snap these on the patio?"

"Not at all," she said, wiping her hands on a towel. "I think I'll join you for a short while."

Mona and I went out to the patio and settled onto a wicker loveseat situated in the shade of a large oak tree. A slight breeze was blowing, so although it was hot out, sitting in the shade was relatively comfortable. I had on a pair of cutoff denim shorts and a red baby-doll T-shirt.

My mom and I had spent many summer evenings shucking corn and snapping green beans. Those memories came back to me as Mona and I sat in companionable silence, snapping beans and enjoying the weather. Neighborhood kids were setting off fireworks, illegal bottle rockets from the sound of it, but I doubted anyone would turn them in. Shooting bottle rockets was one of those rites of passage in Midwestern adolescence.

"It's good to see you and Blane back together," Mona said after a while. I caught her looking at the ring on my finger. "I was afraid he'd driven you away for good."

I hesitated, unsure what to tell her about the reasons behind my wearing Blane's ring again. "Mona, we're not back together," I said. "I'm Blane's alibi for the night of Kandi's murder. It's more believable if the police think we've reconciled."

She stopped snapping beans for a moment, glancing at me with some surprise. "Oh," she said, "I didn't realize . . ."

Now the silence wasn't quite as comfortable. After a while, I couldn't take it anymore.

"I'm sorry, Mona," I said. "Blane and I have talked and we're friends, but I don't know if we'll be . . . more . . . again."

Her smile was a little sad. "No need to apologize, Kathleen. It's just too bad, that's all. He loves you, you know."

I swallowed, reaching into the bag for another handful of beans and avoiding her gaze. "I do. I love him, too."

"And Kade?" Mona asked quietly. "How do you feel about him?"

My eyes flew to hers, but her gaze was steady, sympathy written on her face.

"Kade and I are friends," I said carefully.

"I've never seen Kade quite like this before," Mona said.

I snapped another bean, dropping it into the rapidly filling bowl.

"What do you mean?"

Mona continued working on the beans as she spoke. "Kade has always been . . . difficult to reach. I remember when Blane first brought him home. He was just a little thing. Too thin for his age and wearing clothes that were too big. I could tell he was terrified, but he always could put on a brave face. Show no fear. He's lived by that ever since his momma died, God rest her soul."

It wasn't hard to picture Kade as Mona described him. Sometimes it seemed, if I just looked hard enough, I could see that same scared little boy in his eyes.

"He kept us all at arm's length for so long," she continued. "If he didn't care about us, then we couldn't hurt him. Caring about someone left him vulnerable. And he's never forgotten that." Mona looked at me. "Now I see him with you, the way he looks at you, and I realize how in love he is, though he may not yet know it himself. And I cry inside, for him and Blane and you, because I don't know how this can end well."

I looked at her, stricken. Mona and Gerard had worked so hard for years to build a family with Blane and Kade, and now I was destroying it. What had I done? "I-I'm so sorry," I stammered, dropping the beans I held back in the bag and clenching my fists to stop them from shaking. "I'll go. Right now." I made to stand up, but she grabbed my wrist, holding me firmly.

"No, Kathleen," she said kindly. "I didn't say those things to make you leave. You're a part of this family, I'm just not sure yet what path you'll take. My heart hurts for you, too. I know you didn't intend for any of this to happen." She shrugged. "Who can say when or where love will grow? It's no more your fault than Blane's or Kade's. I don't blame you."

The ache in my chest eased a little. I'd been afraid of what Mona had been thinking all this time, seeing me with Blane one moment and Kade the next. But she was right. The future terrified me.

Her hand reached down to grasp mine. "I just want you to know that I've grown to love you like I would a daughter, so I'm going to give you some advice, if that's all right."

I cleared the lump out of my throat. "Yes, ma'am," I said softly, reminded strongly of how my own mother would have talked to me.

"It sounds trite, like a cliché, but follow your heart. Don't let anything else—the past, the future, the what-ifs or ramifications, mistakes made or past hurts—don't let any of it stop you from going where love leads you. Love is the only thing worth living for, and you'd be surprised at how love can heal all wounds, if given some time."

I didn't have the heart to tell her that love wasn't in the cards, at least not for me. Fear made me shy away from Blane, and Kade had already made his decision. If I was less selfish, I'd go stay with Alisha rather than soaking up being here with both of them for as long as I could.

"I'm sorry, am I interrupting?"

I turned. Charlotte stood at the edge of the patio.

"No one answered the front door," she said, her gaze falling to Mona's and my clasped hands. She looked back up to Mona. "Is Blane around?"

"He should be," I said, getting to my feet. "I'll take you to him."

Charlotte's smile was stiff.

I felt her eyes boring into my back as I led her inside through the kitchen. "Would you like a cup of coffee or something?" I asked to be polite.

"You don't have to play the fiancée for me," she replied. "I know the truth."

The curt words took me aback. "I wasn't trying to 'play the fiancée,'" I snapped. "I just have manners. Something you obviously lack."

Charlotte stood right in front of me. "I saw what you did to Blane," she hissed. "You broke his heart, and it doesn't matter if you weren't sleeping with Kade. There was obviously enough going on that he didn't consider the possibility that it wasn't true." She paused, raising one perfectly arched brow. "That tells me all I need to know about you. Why he'd ever want you back is beyond me."

Now that we were alone, Charlotte didn't bother to hide her venom and contempt. All my roiling emotions boiled over into fury at this provocation, and I lashed out.

"You've tried everything, and he still won't sleep with you, will he?" I sneered. I moved closer, my next words low and said with a cold smile, "It takes more than a fancy law degree."

Her dark skin flushed and her eyes flashed. I stood my ground. If this was going to descend into a catfight, I could hold my own.

"Should I get some popcorn?"

We both turned to see Kade leaning against the door-jamb, a crooked smirk on his face. Blane stood behind him, his face unreadable. I really hoped he hadn't heard what I'd just said to Charlotte, but there was no way to tell.

Kade cocked his head, saying in an aside to Blane, "I got twenty on the redhead."

"Blane," Charlotte said, taking a step away from me, "I was looking for you. Is there somewhere we can talk?"

"In the den," Blane replied evenly.

Charlotte nodded, preceding him out of the kitchen. Blane glanced back at me before following her but said nothing.

I released a pent-up breath when they were both gone. "I really don't like her," I said. "I know she's supposed to be helping Blane, but I don't trust her."

"You don't trust her because you know she wants to fuck him," Kade said, pushing himself away from the door and grabbing a can of Coke from the refrigerator.

"Don't be ridiculous," I snorted, taking a loaf of bread from a cabinet. "Blane can have sex with whoever he wants. I don't care."

"Sure you don't."

"I'm not talking about this anymore," I said, getting some deli meat from the fridge. "You want a sandwich?"

"Sure." He popped the top on the Coke and took a long gulp. "So where are we going to watch fireworks tonight?"

I looked at him strangely. "I have to work."

"After that."

"There won't be any fireworks that late."

"Then I'll go buy some," he said.

I set two plates on the table, grabbing my own Coke before I sat down, a little disappointed there was no Pepsi in the fridge. "Don't," I said. "It's a total waste of money."

"But you like them."

I took a bite, shrugging. "So?"

Kade wolfed down his sandwich, while I cut mine and ate half of it. He eyed my other half until I pushed it toward him.

"You don't want it?" he asked, already picking it up.

I shook my head, smiling as he ate the rest of it in a few big bites. Glancing at the clock on the wall, I said, "I'd better go study. Finals are next week."

"I could help you study," Kade said, leaning back in his chair. He wore a white T-shirt and it clung to him in a way that made my mouth water. His hand rested on his stomach as he sprawled, drawing my eye. My gaze fell lower, lingering, until I realized it and hurriedly looked back up.

His blue eyes were staring into mine, the tilt of his lips saying he knew exactly where I'd been looking and exactly what I'd been thinking.

But he was wrong. I hadn't been imagining . . . I'd been remembering.

I jumped to my feet. "That's okay. I'll be fine on my own." Which felt patently untrue, but Kade probably thought I meant studying, because he just shrugged and took another drink of his Coke. I watched his throat move as he swallowed before I caught myself staring, then turned and hurried upstairs.

~

I went downstairs when it was time to go to The Drop, but sneaking by the den didn't work this time. The door was open and I heard Kade call my name. With a sigh, I walked into the room, straightening my spine, anticipating the disapproval I was bound to get from Blane.

"Seriously. That outfit never gets old." Kade's appreciative once-over had me glaring at him, even though a dozen or more men would probably do the same thing to me tonight as they checked out my "holiday" uniform.

Blane's expression wasn't disapproving. I couldn't read what it was, exactly, but his gaze lingered on my thighs, bare midriff, and breasts before our eyes met.

"I'm going to take you to work," he said.

I was quick to protest. "That's not necessary." Just thinking about being locked in a confined space with only me and Blane, no one else for a buffer, had my nerves on edge.

Blane's jaw grew tight. "It *is* necessary. Kade would do it, but he has to go break in to James's house tonight."

"What? Why?"

"Need DNA," Kade replied. "Blane's lawyer came by to say that James is pushing hard for the cops to arrest Blane."

"A friend of Robert's, a judge here, is holding off on signing the warrant, but he can't stall much longer," Blane continued. "We need to tie James to the crime or they're going to arrest me."

And Blane's entire career, maybe his life, would be destroyed. No one said it, but it hung in the air like a prophecy.

"Who's going with you to James's?" I asked.

Kade cocked an eyebrow. "I work alone, remember?"

How could I forget?

Kade walked toward me, and as he made to pass by, I grabbed his arm. Under my fingers, his skin was warm, the muscles hard. He paused.

"Be careful," I said quietly.

His mouth lifted in an almost smile. "Kiss for good luck?"

I felt Blane's stare like a weight pressing against my back, and Kade must have as well, because his eyes flicked from mine to look behind me at Blane. His smile turned cold.

"Maybe later," he said. Then he was gone.

Great. Now I was going to be a nervous wreck, worrying all night.

"C'mon," Blane said, taking my elbow. "Let's go."

His touch made me shiver, but we both ignored it. I sidled away from his hand and we walked in stiff silence to his car.

We'd only been on the road for a few minutes when Blane spoke.

"I want you to do something for me," he said, glancing my way.

"What?"

"If I get arrested—"

"That's not going to happen," I interrupted. It just . . . couldn't. Anxiety poured through me at the thought and I fidgeted in my seat, chewing on a nail until I tasted the tang of blood.

"Just hear me out," Blane said quietly. "If I get arrested, and the worst should happen—if I go to prison—I want you to stay. In my home. For as long as you'd like."

I stared at him, stunned. Finally, I found my voice. "Stop talking like that, Blane," I said, not sure what else to say. "Everything's going to be fine. You'll see."

"It's better to prepare for the worst," he said. "You know that. And I don't want you to have to worry about where you're going to live. My estate will take care of the house and grounds. Mona and Gerard will still be there, too."

I swallowed hard. "I couldn't do that, Blane," I said, my voice thick. "I couldn't live there, not without—"

The *you* got stuck and I broke off, turning to look out the window so he wouldn't see the tears in my eyes. This nightmare had to end. Kade had to get that DNA so Blane could clear his name.

His hand gently grasped mine, which lay on the seat between us. Blane slotted our fingers, pressing our palms together. I didn't look at him, but I held tightly to his hand.

A few minutes later, we pulled up at The Drop. Blane had driven around to the back door, where the employees entered. He let go of my hand to turn off the car and we sat there in a silence that wasn't uncomfortable.

I didn't want to get out of the car, didn't want to let him out of my sight. What if they came and took Blane away when I wasn't there?

"If I get out of this," Blane said roughly, "if I still have a name worth giving to you, please tell me you'll give us another chance."

Our eyes met, blue to gray. Regret and guilt were twin knives tearing me apart from the inside out. I'd put the final nail in the coffin of Blane's and my relationship the moment I'd decided to sleep with Kade. I couldn't take that back, and neither could I form the words to tell Blane. I couldn't bear to see the look in his eyes turn to one of loathing and disgust.

I shook my head. "We—we can't," I stammered. "I— Vegas . . . It's too late." I couldn't manage any more, my throat had closed up. I jumped out of the car before I broke down completely.

"Kat, wait!" Blane called, but I ignored him, hurrying for the entrance. He followed me and was quicker, slamming the door closed just as I started to pull it open. He spun me around until my back was against the metal door, his hands closing on my upper arms to hold me in place.

"Listen to me," he said, his voice low and intense. "I don't give a damn about what happened in Vegas. I know you still love me. Don't give up on us because of Kade," he implored. "Let me back in. Let me prove to you that I've changed, that I still love you. I can offer you more than Kade ever can or will. Please, Kat."

His desperation leaked into me. I couldn't breathe, couldn't think.

Then he kissed me.

CHAPTER THIRTEEN

Blane's lips were warm and soft, his hands moving up from my arms to cradle my jaw. His mouth moved over mine, not demanding a response but close. The scent of his cologne teased me, invoking too many memories. The feel of his body against mine made my knees weak and butterflies quivered in my stomach.

Thoughts of resisting faded away as my lips parted beneath his, our tongues entwining. My arms slid around his waist to pull him closer. Blane groaned, his kisses growing more heated.

"Don't go into work," he whispered against my lips. "Come home with me."

It was tempting, God, it was so tempting, but I pulled back. His lips glided smoothly down my neck.

"I can't," I said, breathless. "It's not that simple."

"I love you. You love me. What could be more simple?"

If only he'd believed that three months ago, instead of the lies about us. Yes, I'd forgiven him, but my heart wasn't healed. Not yet.

And then there was Kade. As the fog of desire lifted from my brain, I thought of him, abruptly remembering that he and I had stood in this exact spot a few months ago and put on a "show" for the madman stalking me.

"I-I need to get to work," I stammered, pushing against Blane. He seemed reluctant to release me but did so.

"I'll come back for you," he said.

I nodded, glancing away from him. "I'll see you later." I hurried inside, the compulsion to look back nearly overwhelming.

Tish was working tonight and I waved to her as I stuffed my purse under the bar. It was really crowded and Scott, also bartending, was glad to see me. I dived in, grateful not to have to think about all Blane had just said.

I couldn't keep my thoughts at bay for long, though.

I had no idea what to do. I felt torn, almost literally, in two.

I still loved Blane, that was true. I loved him, was attracted to him. When we were together, I felt like it was how we were supposed to be, that fate had determined our destiny. He was my first love, my first real lover.

Then there was Kade. Even though we couldn't be together, that it was wrong on so many levels for me to want him, I couldn't stop. When I was with him, I felt alive. He challenged me, brought out more than I thought I had in me. And although he pushed me away with one hand, he still clung to me with the other, needing me, wanting me. Kade was a drug I couldn't seem to give up. An addiction that had me craving more.

Where did all that leave me? Confused and so anxious, I was nearly sick with worry, fear, and guilt. What would become of the three of us? Blane said he didn't care about what had happened in Vegas, but could that really be true?

And Kade didn't even know we'd made love. Would his feelings for me be different if he did?

The Drop was busier than I thought we'd be for the Fourth, and it wasn't until almost closing that Tish and I had a chance to chat.

"The cops came by my house yesterday," she said, grabbing a peanut from the snack bowl on the bar.

I frowned. "That's weird. What for?"

"They were asking about you."

My eyes went wide. Was this what Blane had meant about the cops looking into every part of my life?

"What did you say?" I asked.

She shrugged, shelling the nut and popping it into her mouth. "There wasn't a lot to say. They wanted to know if you and Blane were back together, if you were living with him, if I'd ever seen you with some girl named Kandi or heard you talk about her.

"Of course I told them you weren't back with Blane, that piece of shit," she continued with a disgusted snort. "And that the last time you mentioned Kandi was months ago when she broke you and Blane up."

I closed my eyes in dismay.

"What's wrong?" Tish asked anxiously. "Did I say something I shouldn't have?"

I shook my head. I couldn't blame Tish. She'd told the truth, as far as she knew. "It's fine," I said. "I'm sorry they bothered you."

"Why are the cops asking me about you?" she asked. "What happened?"

I gave her a quick recap of Kandi's murder and how Blane was a suspect. It had been on the news, but I knew how little attention Tish paid to things like that.

"So they're asking me because they think maybe you were involved somehow?"

I gave a helpless shrug. "I have no idea. Maybe." Which was a lovely thought to dwell on the rest of the evening.

Scott and Tish were just as eager to leave as I was once we'd closed. I said good-bye to them, promising to lock up when I left. I had to go back to the storeroom for more liquor to stock. If I'd been the one scheduled to work tomorrow, I wouldn't have bothered, but I hated to leave the bar in that state for the next person to deal with.

Once I was in the storeroom, I scanned the shelves for what I needed. The air-conditioning couldn't keep up with the heat out front, so I felt sticky and hot, but it was cooler in there.

I wanted to hurry. If I could get to James's house, maybe I could help Kade. Not that he likely needed help, especially mine, but that's what I told myself to justify going over there.

I heard the door open behind me and I spun around in surprise. I should be alone now, no one else was here. When I saw who'd entered the room with me, my heart lodged in my throat.

James. How the hell had he gotten in?

"I'm so glad to have a moment alone with you, Kathleen," he said.

"What are you doing here?" I asked with more bravado than I felt.

James took a step closer. "I thought I'd stop by your fine new working establishment and check in on you, seeing as how your boyfriend's going to be arrested for murder." His fake sympathy was grating. "The cops say you two are back together, though if you ask me, hooking up with a murderer can't be good for your health."

"Blane didn't murder anyone," I said. James took another step forward and it was all I could do not to back away.

"How sweet, standing by your man," he sneered. "Or stupid." He moved closer until he stood right in front of me. "For all you know, you could be next."

My heart was hammering in my chest and I swallowed hard. Was that a threat? The last time I'd been alone with James, he'd attacked me. I'd gotten away only because of the stun gun I'd borrowed from Alisha. I had no such weapon now.

James reached out to trail a finger from my neck down inside my cleavage. I slapped his hand away and his eyes narrowed in menace.

"You know," he said softly, "I could maybe be . . . persuaded . . . to go easy on your guy. Involuntary manslaughter instead of murder one. Ten years, but he'd be out in five."

Blane. I could help him. My mind spun. If things progressed far enough for him to be arrested, this would be better than the alternative. On the other hand . . .

"You forget," I said, "I still have a rather incriminating recording of you threatening me, remember?"

"You mean this one?" He held up a familiar flash drive. "I was so sorry to hear about your apartment burning, so I went by," he said. "The restoration people were very cooperative once I told them who I was. They were impressed that the district attorney would take such an interest in one of my . . . constituents." He pocketed the drive. "You should find better hiding places, Kathleen. It took me all of ten minutes to find it."

Okay, well, this was an unfortunate turn of events. I swallowed. How far was I willing to go to help Blane? I loved him and didn't want to see his life destroyed for a crime he didn't commit. But the price for what James offered was steep, and I didn't know if I could pay it.

"How could I . . . persuade you?" I forced the words out, feeling sick to my stomach.

James's smile was triumphant. His hand slipped inside my shirt to cup my breast, pinching the nipple hard. I stiffened, wincing, but didn't move or make a sound of protest.

His other hand circled my throat as he shoved me against the brick wall at my back. His grip tightened and he forced my head to turn. "I thought you'd come around to my way of thinking," he hissed in my ear. "You'll do anything for Kirk, won't you. Stupid cunt."

I shut my eyes tight, struggling to breathe. His hold was painful but didn't completely cut off my air.

"*Won't you?*" he demanded again, squeezing harder.

I tried to nod, spots starting to appear before my eyes.

His grip loosened and I sucked in a lungful of air.

"That's a good girl," James said. "Now you just do as I say, and I won't hurt you. Much. Understand?"

I nodded again, suddenly all the more glad I hadn't told Kade or Blane about getting off work early. I didn't want either of them to see this.

He yanked on my shirt and it bit into my shoulders before the fabric tore. "Take it off," he said, letting go of me.

My hands shook as I shrugged out of the shirt. James's gaze dropped to my breasts.

"Kirk may be a killer," he said with an appreciative sigh, "but he knows how to pick 'em."

He fished something out of his pocket, and flipped open a pocketknife. My breath caught at the sight of it. I was abruptly reminded of what James had done to Kandi. Was he going to do that to me?

"Hold still now," James said, his tone too nonchalant for how close the knife was to my skin. "I don't want this to slip. That would be a real shame."

James slid the blade under the elastic of my bra, twisting upward, then tugged. The knife cut easily through the fabric. I didn't breathe as the blade again touched my skin.

"How about a souvenir?" James said. "I don't want you or Kirk to ever forget this."

I stood frozen as he sliced a thin cut down between my breasts. "It's such a treat, to have you finally minding your manners," he mused.

I could feel the warm trickle of blood trailing down over my stomach. Terror gripped me. I sucked in my breath to scream.

"Don't even think about it," James bit out, whipping the knife up to my throat. "I'll have your throat slit before you can manage a whimper."

I looked in his eyes—the steady, calm gaze of a sociopath—and knew there was nothing too horrifying for him to do.

"You're not worth fucking," he sneered. "But you can suck my dick. Get on your knees, you fucking bitch."

"If I do this," I managed to say, "you promise you'll only charge for manslaughter?"

James's fist closed around a handful of my hair and yanked me toward him. I gasped in pain.

"If you do this . . . and maybe a few more things," he said. The darkness in his voice made a shudder run through me.

"You don't need to hold the knife on me. I said I'd do it." My free hand searched blindly behind me, closing around the neck of a bottle.

He jerked my hair again and this time I cried out. "Maybe I just like you better if you're scared," he hissed.

I swung the bottle I held, but James reacted faster than I thought, jumping back so it only glanced off his shoulder. I slammed the bottle against the metal shelf and it broke, spewing booze everywhere but leaving me with a jagged weapon.

"Come on, you piece of shit," I taunted him. "You're not afraid of a girl, are you?"

"Like you know how to use that," he scoffed. "When I'm through with you, you'll wish I'd killed you."

"I may not know how to use it, but I bet it can cause some real damage. Let's see, shall we?" I smiled and leapt for him.

James jumped back again and grabbed my arm that held the bottle. His knife flashed toward me and I just managed to latch onto his wrist, deflecting the slash he'd intended for my face. We were in close quarters now and I brought my knee up, but it missed its mark, hitting him on the inside of a thigh instead of his crotch.

I twisted my wrist, breaking his hold on me, and slashed at him, tearing through his shirt to his chest. He let me go with a yell.

The door to the storeroom flew open, jerking my attention away from James, which proved to be bad.

He knocked the bottle out of my hand and punched me in the stomach. I doubled over in gut-wrenching pain, retching.

But then James spun around and I heard the crunch of bone against bone. He dropped to the floor, out cold.

I straightened, ignoring the pained ache in my stomach, and turned to see who'd entered the storeroom.

Blane.

But he wasn't looking at me, he was looking at James—and the expression on his face sent a jolt of terror through me.

Blane crouched next to James and grabbed the knife he'd used on me. He flipped the blade up with a practiced hand. Without a word, he took a fistful of James's hair and jerked his head back, exposing his throat.

"No!" I cried, tackling Blane.

I had enough momentum and motivation that I knocked him to the side, toppling both of us. I scrambled on top of him, holding on even as he sat back up and tried to push me off his lap.

"Are you out of your mind? You can't kill him!"

Blane was shaking with rage, and for a moment, I wasn't sure he was going to listen to me. But then he closed his eyes and took a shuddering breath. When he opened his eyes again and focused on me, the Blane I knew was there, not the murderous stranger from before. He wrapped his arms around my waist and pulled me tight against him.

"God, Kat," he breathed into my hair. "When I came in here and saw him hit you, I just . . . lost it."

"I'm fine," I said, squeezing him tight. Leftover fear and adrenaline were making me shaky, but I couldn't think about that right now.

After a moment, I got off Blane, grabbed my shirt, and put it on, tying a makeshift knot to keep it closed. I didn't want to imagine how ridiculous I must have looked fighting James with my boobs hanging out. I kept my back to Blane, embarrassed at being nearly naked and hoping I could hide the cuts James had made. I didn't think Blane had seen them.

My bra was useless, so I picked it up and knelt next to James. Blood seeped from the gash on his chest. I used my bra to mop up some of James's blood before folding it carefully into the pocket of my shorts.

DNA? Check.

"What are you doing here anyway?" I asked Blane while I worked. "Not that I'm not glad you were." He'd stood watching me as I got dressed.

"This place closed thirty minutes ago," he said. "I was waiting outside for you. When you didn't come out, I came in."

"How did you—" I began, then cut myself off at the look on his face.

"Do I look like an idiot?" he said, raising an eyebrow. "I knew you would try to run off and help Kade."

Couldn't deny that one. I changed the subject. "Help me get James out of here."

Blane reached down and hauled James up and over his shoulder in a fireman's carry. "Where do you want him?" he asked. "Trash goes in the dumpster, right?"

TIFFANY SNOW

I shook my head. As much as I'd love for Blane to dump James's ass in the dumpster, I didn't want to antagonize him further. Like it or not, James was the one who'd be trying the case against Blane, if it came to that.

I grabbed my purse from under the bar, hit the lights, and locked the door on the way out. James's car was parked in the front.

"Let me get his keys," I said, going to Blane and digging a hand in James's jeans pocket.

Blane deposited him none too gently in the backseat and tossed the keys onto his chest before shutting the door on James's unconscious body. He took my elbow and walked me to his car.

We weren't driving thirty seconds before the interrogation began.

"How long was he there?"

"Just a few minutes."

"Were you alone?"

"Yes."

"What did he say?"

I hesitated. "He offered a deal. Involuntary manslaughter instead of murder one."

"In exchange for what?"

I looked at Blane, then out the window. He was a smart guy. He'd figure it out.

I jumped when Blane suddenly slammed his hand on the dash.

"Goddammit!" he yelled.

I laid my hand on his arm and the muscles were like iron bands underneath my fingers. I could feel his rage like it was a living thing.

325

"I didn't do it," I said. "Surely you know me better than that."

"I don't want James anywhere near you," Blane ground out. "You know what he's done. You've seen the pictures. I want to kill him for even breathing the same air you do."

Blane was driving fast and we were back at his house before I could think of what to say, so I tried to change the subject.

"Is Kade back yet?"

"No, but he will be. And if you think he's going to have any other reaction to what happened tonight than I did, you're wrong."

"It's done," I said. "I'm fine and I have the DNA." I dug in my pocket, handing the folded bra to Blane. "Here. Give this to your guy and have them compare it to the semen."

I hopped out of the car and walked fast to the door, hoping I could make it inside before Blane got a closer look at me. No such luck.

"Kathleen!" he called, the car door slamming behind him.

I pretended not to hear, rushing inside the house and heading for the stairs.

"Stop!" Blane commanded, his voice thundering in the hallway.

My body locked in place on the second stair, the tone of his voice not one to be disobeyed. I heard his footsteps on the hardwood floor as he walked toward me.

"Turn around."

I crossed my arms over my chest before I did so, raising an eyebrow at Blane. We were eye to eye now. "Anything else?" I asked. "Should I roll over? Fetch?"

He ignored me, reaching over to flick on the overhead light. Shit.

Blane reached out, tugging my arms down. I tried to resist, but he was too strong.

I could have sworn his face paled under his tan.

I'd already gotten a look at what James had done, so didn't need to look down.

"He . . . carved a *J* into your skin?" Blane choked out, his eyes glued to my chest.

"It's not deep," I said. "Just a scratch. It'll heal."

Blane swallowed so hard, I saw his Adam's apple move up and down.

"So let me ask you this," he said. "Was he planning to rape you? Or did you agree to the deal?"

I looked at Blane, refusing to answer.

"Answer me," he demanded, his voice loud in the empty foyer.

My fists clenched at my sides as I stared at Blane. "Yes," I bit out. "I agreed to the deal, because I thought, maybe, just maybe, he would do it. That he'd go with a lesser charge and not murder one." My face was burning, but I didn't look away from Blane. "But it doesn't matter, because I couldn't go through with it. When it came down to it, I didn't have the guts."

Blane looked as shell-shocked as I'd ever seen him. "Why?" he asked. "Why would you even consider—"

"Because you don't deserve this," I interrupted, exasperated. "He's framing you, and you're too good a man to let something like this take you down."

"He won't win," Blane said. "We'll get him. I promise."

"And what'll you lose until then?" I asked. "If they arrest you, it's over. Your political career is over. Even if they let you go. Those photos of you in handcuffs, your mug shot—all that will be used every time your name comes up."

"Maybe I don't care anymore," Blane said quietly.

I frowned, sure I'd heard him wrong. "What?"

"I don't know if I care anymore," Blane repeated. "I feel like I've been so focused, for years, on achieving in my career that I've let it affect how I want to live my life. I've let it affect you. Us." He paused. "If I hadn't been so single-minded, maybe I would have seen how much my uncle wanted you out of my life—and I wouldn't have bought in to his lies. I just wish it hadn't taken losing you for me to realize that."

I stared at Blane, unable to believe what I was hearing.

He leaned forward, his arms sliding around my back to hold me close. My breath caught in my throat when his tongue traced the cut James had made. Blane gently licked the blood from my skin, the warm heat of his mouth soothing the burning slice. My fingernails dug into his sides as I held on to him.

"I'll avenge this," Blane murmured, lifting his face to mine. "I swear it."

His lips moved over mine, the faint tang of my blood on his tongue. When we parted, I rested my head against his shoulder.

I was still sick with worry about what was going to happen to Blane, but being wrapped in his arms calmed me. His hand brushed over my hair and his lips pressed against my forehead.

"Don't let me interrupt."

I jerked away from Blane with a gasp and turned to see that Kade had silently entered the hallway. His face was cold and blank. I took an uncomfortable step backward up the stairs, putting some space between Blane and me.

"Did you get it?" Blane asked.

"Of course I did," Kade said, stopping at the foot of the stairs. "He wasn't even home. Piece of cake."

"He wasn't at home because he was busy assaulting Kathleen at work," Blane said.

Kade's head whipped around, his blue eyes locking on mine.

"What happened?" he asked.

"I was able to get his DNA," I said, locking my arms tightly over my chest again. "Other than that, I don't want to talk about it." I wouldn't put it past Kade to slit James's throat like Blane almost had—only I wouldn't be able to stop Kade as I had Blane. "I'm tired. I'm going to bed."

I turned and jogged up the stairs, hoping that would put an end to any more questions. I just wanted to forget the whole thing. It had scared me, not only the threat from James but the realization of how far I'd been willing to go to help Blane. What did that mean? I loved him, that was true, but did it mean I was still *in* love with him? Or did it just mean I was colossally stupid?

I didn't want to answer that question.

I got a good look at James's handiwork in my bathroom mirror. Livid cuts formed an uppercase *J* between my breasts. But it would heal. And I chose to think of the *J* as standing for *Justice* rather than *James*. I hoped I'd done my part in helping bring Kandi's killer to justice. That made me feel better. Sort of.

The red imprints of James's fingers stood out around my throat, easier to see if I pulled back my hair. And my stomach was sore from his punch. I sighed.

Was being in constant danger and getting hurt worth it if I got to be with Kade and Blane? And did it mean I had a death wish if my answer to that was a resounding *Yes*?

The shower I took was long and hot, and if there was more than water wetting my cheeks, what did it matter? There was no one there to see. I didn't want to look at the cut on my chest again, so I shrugged into a button-down shirt to sleep in rather than my pajamas. I could button it up nearly to my chin.

I crawled under the covers and stared at the ceiling. I couldn't sleep. In my head, I kept replaying everything I knew about the night Kandi had died. Something didn't fit, but I couldn't put my finger on what it was.

She'd been secretly sleeping with James but had also been available for God-knew-how-many booty calls with Blane. Blane had gone to her home that night and had sex with her, though the cops didn't know that. It couldn't be his semen on her body because, as he'd said, he'd used a condom. So James must have stopped by after Blane left. He'd found out about Blane—maybe she'd told him—then what? He'd gone crazier than he usually was? Strangled and smothered her, then raped her?

I shuddered, remembering the feel of his hand around my throat. James had certainly seemed to enjoy hurting me. It wasn't that far of a stretch to see him doing all that to Kandi.

If the cops could match the semen to James, then it would be proof that someone else had been there that night. If nothing else, that was reasonable doubt.

My thoughts were interrupted when the door to my room opened. I knew who was there and didn't move as Kade stepped inside, silently closing the door behind him.

He moved to my bedside, gazing down at me. He must have seen I was awake, because he asked, "Are you all right?"

"I'm fine," I said. I could make a drinking game out of how often I said that phrase.

Kade reached over and flipped on the bedside lamp. I squinted in the sudden glow, but it wasn't that bright. He sank down onto the bed next to me.

"Where's your nightgown?" he asked, toying with the collar of the shirt I wore.

I shrugged. "I'm glad you didn't run into any trouble at James's," I said.

"Easy in, easy out," he replied absently, but his eyes were on my throat.

His fingers moved to the buttons of my shirt, sliding them through the holes. He'd already undone three when I grabbed his wrist.

"What are you doing?"

"Blane told me what James did," he answered, swiftly undoing the shirt's buttons despite my hold on him. "Show me."

I swallowed hard but couldn't disobey. Keeping my eyes on his, I slowly parted the fabric of the shirt just enough so he could see the cut. His gaze dropped.

"It's not that bad," I said, swallowing hard again at the look on Kade's face.

"You're one tough chick," he said finally.

"I don't feel like one," I confessed.

"Did you smear some bacon grease on his dick, dump him in the alley, and blow a dog whistle?" he asked.

I huffed a laugh. "Wish I'd thought of that."

Kade's shoes thudded to the floor and he pulled back the covers. "Move over," he said.

"What are you doing?" I asked, even as I scooted over to make room for him.

He turned off the light and lay down next to me. "I'm tired," he said with a sigh, draping one arm carefully over my middle. His breath was warm against my neck.

"You have your own bed, you know," I gently reminded him, not that I was overly upset that he was in mine.

"Need to have you near me," he said. "Know you're okay."

Yeah, I knew the feeling.

I started to button my shirt again, but his hands stilled mine. "Leave it."

Probably not a good idea. But his hand was warm and reassuring against my skin, and his body, stretched alongside mine, made me feel safe. I smiled and closed my eyes.

~

"I promised you fireworks," Kade whispered in my ear.

"Hmmm?" I said drowsily. I was really relaxed, though I could tell from the brightness against my eyelids that it was morning.

"I promised you fireworks and I didn't deliver," he said.

I patted his arm still wrapped around me. "S'okay. Next year."

"I can't promise you next week, much less next year," he murmured. The warm heat of his mouth brushed my neck, my shoulder.

"Don't say that," I said automatically.

He paused. "Tell me what happened in Vegas."

My eyes flew open and I stiffened, coming fully awake now. "You know what happened in Vegas," I said, pretending ignorance.

"I mean, why did I find buttons from my shirt you wore on the floor of my room?"

My pulse shot into overdrive. "I-I don't know what you're talking about," I stammered.

Kade's hand disappeared for a moment. I heard the rustle of cloth. Then he was placing something in my palm.

"I've carried this with me since Vegas," he said, "trying to remember."

He'd given me a button. I realized that must be what I'd seen him looking at several times since we'd gotten back. I squeezed my eyes shut. This couldn't be happening.

"Please tell me. It's driving me insane," he rasped. "I have these scenarios in my head, and I'm terrified that I hurt you, or forced you—"

Oh God, I couldn't talk about this. If I did, even to alleviate his concerns, it would all come out. Panic struck. "I'm going to shower," I said, jumping out of bed and hurrying to the closet. I grabbed a pair of short denim cutoffs and a white tank before disappearing into the bathroom.

Over half an hour later, when I came out dressed for the day, I was hoping Kade would be gone. No such luck. In fact, things were much, much worse.

Kade sat on my bed, my open suitcase on the floor, with his torn shirt—the one I'd worn in Vegas—in his hand.

I nearly turned around and went back into the bathroom.

He held it up in his clenched fist. "When were you going to tell me? Ever?" His anger was palpable and I flinched.

My voice was weak when I replied, "There's nothing—"

"Stop lying to me!" He was up and in my face now. My back hit the wall. "I remember," he hissed. "I remember *everything.*"

I could feel the blood leave my head in a rush. I stared at Kade, afraid of what was going to happen now.

"You weren't ever going to tell me?" he asked, pain in his voice and betrayal in his eyes. "Did it mean so little to you?"

"Mean so little?" I echoed in disbelief. "You didn't even remember!"

"I was drunk!"

"Which is supposed to excuse it?" I fumed. I didn't care that I didn't make sense. The hurt I'd felt since that night now had an outlet.

"I don't recall you saying no," he hissed.

"I'm talking about how easily you forgot," I retorted.

"Well, I remember now," Kade said, his voice low and intent. "I remember how it felt to be inside you, the feel of your body against mine, the taste of your sweat on my tongue."

I could hardly breathe. His face was inches away, his eyes boring into mine, when he dropped the next bombshell.

"I remember telling you I loved you. But what I don't remember is you saying it back."

My heart felt torn into pieces at the anguish in his eyes. "Kade," I began quietly, "you know I care about you—"

"But you don't love me," he interrupted. "You love him." Kade jerked his head toward the door and it didn't take a rocket scientist to know who he meant. "He used you, lied to you, betrayed you. And you're still in love with him?"

I was too stunned by his anger to speak and so just looked at him, my eyes wide.

"I saw you two last night," he continued, stepping away from me. The cold mask I knew so well turned his expression forbidding. "So tell me, have you slept with him since we've been back? Did you go straight from my bed to his?"

"I—"

"Or does he even know? Did you lie to him like you lied to me?"

Anger boiled up inside me. "He knows," I spat. "And he doesn't care. He wants me back. What do *you* want me for, Kade? An easy lay when you're in town?"

I could tell by his eyes that I was treading on dangerous ground, but I was too mad to care.

"You want to know why I didn't tell you?" I asked, advancing on him. "Because *there was no point.* You told me you were going to drop out of my life and I'd never see you again. So what would knowing that we slept together have changed?"

"Maybe you just regret it so much you were glad I didn't remember," he accused.

"And you don't regret it?" I asked.

"The only thing I regret is not waking up beside you the next morning."

With that he was gone, slamming the door behind him. My stomach seemed to drop to my toes and I ran to jerk open the door, only to see Blane and Kade facing off in the hallway.

Chapter Fourteen

"What the hell are you doing?" Blane snapped at Kade. "After what she went through last night, you're fucking yelling at her this morning?"

"Oh, excuse me, am I supposed to be taking advice on how to treat her from *you*?" Kade shot back. "In that case, let me crush her dreams and publicly humiliate and betray her. Am I missing anything?"

"At least I make my intentions clear. I want her back. You just screw with her head and put her in danger."

"You mean like Gage trying to kill her? Or you holding sleazy Uncle Bob in higher esteem than your own fiancée?" Kade accused, his voice laced with contempt. "How many women, besides Kandi of course, have you slept with over the past three months? I'm sure Kathleen would love to know where your dick's been."

Blane grabbed Kade by the shirt and slammed him against the wall. "You were just waiting, weren't you," he snarled. "You think I didn't know that the moment I was out of the picture, you'd try to fuck her?"

"Who said anything about try?"

Kade moved, so fast I couldn't see what he did, but he was out of Blane's hold now, his back no longer to the wall.

"Why are you doing this to me?" Blane asked. "Are you still so angry that I took too long to come get you? For all you went through? Are you trying to get back at me?"

"Give me a fucking break," Kade scoffed. "Don't try and blame this on some psychobabble bullshit about my childhood."

"Then why?"

Silence from Kade as they glared at each other.

"Tell me why!" Blane shouted, making me jump.

"Because I love her!"

The silence in the wake of Kade's outburst was deafening. Blane looked how I felt—stunned.

"I love her, too," Blane finally said, his voice much quieter.

"I know," Kade replied, the defeat in his voice painful to hear. "And she loves you. Not me. Congratulations. You win."

He turned then, and our eyes met. Blane looked over at me as well. I stood, frozen, under their steady gazes. I imagined they were accusing me.

I swallowed. "This has to stop," I managed to force out. "You're tearing each other apart and I'm to blame. It never should have gotten this far." And I didn't know if I was referring to myself and Blane, or me and Kade.

The sound of the doorbell precluded anything they might have said. I took it as my opportunity to escape and hurried to look out the window in my bedroom. When I saw who was parked outside, my heart jumped into my throat.

"It's the police," I called out, heading back to where Blane and Kade still stood in the hall. "Two patrol cars and an unmarked car." There was no way they were sending that much manpower without a good reason, a reason I was afraid I already knew.

"I'll go down," Blane said.

"I'll come with you," I added.

"You should stay up here," he said with a frown.

I shook my head. "No way. And don't even think about locking me up again."

The ghost of a smile crossed Blane's lips and was gone. He took my hand and turned to Kade. "Don't you dare come downstairs," he said. "I don't need the cops sniffing around you."

Kade's lips were pressed in a thin line. "Like I give a shit," he scoffed. "I'm not letting them take you."

"There's nothing you can do about it," Blane said. "And you'll only get yourself hurt or arrested if you try. I won't have it." His tone said he was not to be argued with.

Kade's lips twisted in a bitter smile. "Still under the delusion that you can tell me what to do?"

Blane grasped Kade's shoulder in a firm grip. "I'm still protecting my little brother. Nothing's ever going to change that. So stay out of it and keep your ass hidden, or you're going to be in deep shit with me."

Kade didn't say anything, his eyes on us as Blane led me downstairs.

He held my hand tightly as we walked to the front door, and I had the sense we were walking to our doom. Blane put his hand on the knob, then took a deep breath before he opened the door, schooling his face into a polite mask of indifference.

A plainclothes cop was standing there along with two uniformed men. He flashed his badge and ID, which proclaimed him to be Detective Walker. "Blane Kirk?"

"Yes."

The cop's eyes flashed to me. "Kathleen Turner?"

I swallowed. "Yes," I confirmed, but my voice was thready. I tried again. "Yes."

"Ma'am, we'd like to take you downtown for questioning in the murder of Kandi Miller."

My jaw fell open and the blood rushed from my head so fast I saw spots dance before my eyes. Blane's grip on my waist tightened. "Wh-what?" I stammered in disbelief.

"Why do you need to talk to Miss Turner?" Blane asked, his voice curt as he slipped into lawyer mode.

"We have reason to believe Miss Turner had motive and opportunity," Walker said. "That's all we need." His gaze didn't falter as he looked at Blane. "You of all people should know that, Mr. Kirk."

He and Blane were locked in a staring contest, the tension thick between them as the cops hovered in the background. I glanced from one to the other, confused. Was I missing something?

Finally, Blane's lips curved in a cold smile. "Well played, Detective," he said calmly. "There's no need to take Miss Turner in for questioning. As I'm sure you know, she was out of town the night Kandi was killed."

"Blane!" I exclaimed in dismay. He'd just blown the alibi I'd concocted for him. His hand tightened painfully on mine and I shut up.

"Do you have another witness who can vouch for your whereabouts that night?" Walker said, looking wholly unsurprised by Blane's confession.

"I do not."

"Then I'm afraid you'll have to come with us," he said, motioning to the two uniformed cops. They moved forward to flank Blane.

I panicked. "No! You can't arrest him!"

"Give us just a moment, if you would," Blane said to Walker, who nodded, a flash of sympathy or maybe pity crossing his face as he glanced at me.

Blane took me by the elbow, moving me a few steps away from the door and out of earshot. "It's okay, Kat," he said softly. "I knew this was coming."

"Y-you can't—they can't!" I stammered, tears flooding my eyes. "You didn't kill her!"

"Shhh, Kat, it's okay," he said, folding me in his arms. "Be strong. I need you to be strong."

I swallowed the sob building in my chest, nodding and clutching his shirt. I inhaled deeply, memorizing the scent of him, the warmth of his body, the strength in his arms, the press of his lips to the top of my head.

"Stay here," Blane whispered in my ear. "I can't think of you anywhere else right now. Promise me."

I nodded again, unable to speak.

"Kiss me."

I obediently tipped my face up to his.

Blane's lips met mine with a sweet tenderness that sent a shaft of pure pain through me. He cupped my jaw, lightly brushing my cheek with his thumb. There was the softest touch of his tongue against mine, then he was pulling back.

"I love you," he whispered in my ear.

It took every ounce of willpower I had to stand there and do nothing as they cuffed his hands behind his back. Blane never took his eyes off me while Walker read him his rights, as though he were memorizing me the same way I was him. Then they turned him, leading him out the door and into one of the squad cars. I watched, standing silently in the doorway, as they took Blane away.

Hands settled on my shoulders and I turned to lean into Kade, the tears flowing freely now. His arms circled me in a tight embrace.

"What now?" I asked, raising my tearstained face to look at him.

"We need to call that chick, his lawyer," Kade said, gently brushing the wetness from my cheeks. "And the cop, Jared, who said he'd help Blane."

I nodded, trying to push away the despair I felt and concentrate on how to best help Blane.

"Did he tell you how to reach that guy?"

I shook my head. "No."

"Go call the lawyer," Kade said. "Tell her Blane's been arrested. She needs to get over there ASAP and make sure they keep him in isolation."

"Why?"

Kade's face was stark when he answered. "If they put him with other inmates, they'll kill him."

I stared at Kade, horrified. "They wouldn't . . . he's running for governor . . ."

"That won't matter. I'll scour the den, find that guy's number—he may be able to help. Now go."

"Okay." I scurried off to the telephone, terrified of what was going to happen to Blane. A few minutes later, I was punching in Charlotte's phone number. She answered on the second ring.

"Charlotte, it's Kathleen," I said. "The cops—Blane's been arrested."

It took only a few moments to give the details of how Blane had confessed my fake alibi and the subsequent arrest.

"Kade's worried Blane may get hurt if they don't put him in isolation," I said. "Please, can you get down there?"

"I'll go right away," she said, "but I don't know whether there's anything I can do if they decide to 'accidentally' put him in with other prisoners."

"What do you mean?" I asked.

"Cops sometimes have their own idea of justice. A murder like Kandi's—they might put him with other inmates just to teach him a lesson, prod him into confessing."

Oh God. I felt nausea rise in my throat.

"Do what you can," I said.

We hung up after she said again that she would go downtown immediately. I went back to the den, where Kade was searching Blane's desk.

"Did you find it?" I asked.

"Not yet," he answered, pulling open the desk's bottom drawer and rifling through it.

My throat had a lump in it that felt the size of a golf ball, but I forced the words out. "Charlotte said she can request isolation but that the cops sometimes will ignore it and put him with other inmates anyway."

"I know."

"What are we going to do?" My voice was too shrill, but I couldn't help it.

"One thing at a time," he said, shoving the drawer shut and yanking open the top drawer. He paused.

"What is it?" I asked, peering over the desk, but I couldn't see what he was looking at.

Kade pulled out a photograph. Curious, I rounded the desk, then sucked in a breath.

It was one of the photos Keaston had given Blane. Kade and I were at Bar Sinister in Denver, me in my leather prostitute ensemble, standing between his knees as he sat on the barstool. His hands were nearly hidden, they were so far up the back of my skirt.

The obvious heat between us in that photograph made my cheeks burn.

"Where did Blane get this?" Kade asked, and the ice in his voice made me look at him in surprise.

"Keaston," I said. "That's what he gave Blane to prove to him that you and me . . ." I couldn't finish that sentence.

"Didn't you wonder how Keaston could possibly have had photos of us in that bar? No one knew we were going there."

I stared at him, wide-eyed. It had never occurred to me, the circumstances of my and Blane's breakup overshadowing everything else.

"The only person who knew was Garrett," Kade continued, "and he never said who he was working for before he died."

"You don't think—"

"What other possible explanation could there be?"

"But . . . he's your uncle, too," I spluttered. "Why would he try to kill you?"

"Because he knows I can tie him to Sheffield," Kade said.

Ron Sheffield. The former CIA agent who'd masqueraded as a Navy JAG officer. He'd threatened and killed witnesses, nearly killed me, all to coerce Blane into losing a trial. "But . . . you're family!" I couldn't comprehend it. Keaston would knowingly send Garrett to kill his own flesh and blood?

"Not to him," Kade said flatly. "He tolerates me because of Blane. That's all."

Kade pulled out a booklet and started flipping through it. "Ah," he said, "here's his numbers. Should've known. Only Blane would be so cliché as to keep a literal little black book. Here it is."

Kade pulled out his cell and dialed. After a moment, he said, "Jared—it's Kade. They've arrested Blane. I have evidence I need tested for that DNA match."

I listened as they arranged when and where they were going to meet. When he hung up, he said, "Get me the DNA you got off James."

I ran upstairs to Blane's bedroom, catching sight of the baggie with my bra stuffed inside. I grabbed it, then hurried back to the den and handed it to Kade. He looked at it, then seemed to realize what it was.

"Why is James's DNA on your bra?" he asked.

"It was all I had at the time," I answered with a shrug, watching as he pulled the piece of red lingerie out of the bag. He examined the fabric, paying particular attention to where James had cut the elastic.

"He cut it off you."

It wasn't a question, so I didn't answer. I knew that tone of voice, and I could only be grateful that Kade hadn't been the one to walk in on James and me last night. If he had, James would be dead.

Kade looked at me and our eyes caught. Suddenly, all that had been said upstairs between him, me, and Blane came rushing back.

"Kade," I began, not even sure what I was going to say, just that I wanted to fix things . . . somehow. "About earlier—"

He cut me off mid-sentence. "Now's not the time." He stuffed the bra back in the baggie.

I persisted. "Just listen to me—"

"I've gotta go," he said, interrupting again. He brushed by me, but I grabbed a handful of his shirt and hung on. He stopped, but the blue of his eyes was cold when he looked down at me, all emotion wiped from his expression.

I hated it when he did that, when I couldn't read anything from him—when he looked at me the way he had months ago, like he couldn't stand the sight of me. I instinctively knew it was a defense mechanism, Kade's way of dealing with his emotions, but I still hated it.

"I want you to know that I never would have done what I did in Vegas if I didn't care about you," I said. It had to be said, it was the truth, and Kade deserved that.

"But now that you and Blane are back together, you regret it," he replied, matter-of-fact.

"Blane and I aren't back together," I said. "But regardless, I . . . I just shouldn't have done that. You were drunk and I . . . Well, I have no excuse." Unless finally giving in to the overwhelming temptation of Kade counted as an excuse.

His steady, penetrating gaze made me nervous and I glanced down, realizing I still had hold of his shirt. I let it go, smoothing the wrinkles I'd made in the fabric.

"We'll discuss this later," he said. "I have to go make sure no one kills my brother."

Anxiety knotted in my stomach. "How can you do that?"

Kade smiled. "I've got friends in low places, princess. Don't worry. I'll be back." And he was gone.

I stood staring at the empty room, feeling like I'd just been hit by a truck. In the span of thirty minutes, Blane had been arrested and was possibly in danger, depending on the whim of the police. Kade had figured out that Senator Keaston had been behind the attempts on his life, and consequently mine, while we were in Denver, and he had also been involved with the intimidation and coercion of Blane during the Waters trial.

Then I realized that Mona and Gerard didn't know. They didn't come over on Sundays so had no clue what had happened.

I ran upstairs and slipped on a pair of flip-flops before hurrying outside to their home, which adjoined Blane's property. It was already over ninety degrees out, even at mid-morning, and as I walked I pulled my hair up to get it off my neck, wishing I'd thought to grab an elastic band to hold it in a ponytail.

Mona and Gerard's house was a homey white ranch with a deep porch. Two identical Adirondack chairs sat in the shade of the porch and a white hammock hung between two large maples in the yard. Petunias bloomed in a huge flowerpot at the foot of the stairs leading up to the porch. It looked like the home I'd always imagined I'd have when I got married. Someday. Maybe.

I knocked on the front door and after a moment, Gerard answered.

"Kathleen," he said with a genial smile. "This is a nice surprise. Come in!"

"Hi, Gerard," I said. "Is Mona around? I need to talk to both of you."

His smile faded to a look of concern as he took in the tone of my voice. "Of course. Let me go get her."

The foyer had a hardwood floor and a table held framed photos of Blane and Kade when they were young. I picked one up. It was a candid shot and must have been taken when Blane had returned from a deployment, as he was wearing fatigues. He stood next to Kade, showing him something the camera couldn't see. The sun was setting behind them, casting a golden glow. Kade wasn't looking at what Blane was showing him, instead gazing up at him with something close to awe on his face. I tried to guess his age from the picture. Maybe seventeen? Eighteen?

I put the photo back, glancing at the others. There was a posed photo of Blane in his dress uniform that took my breath away. School photos of Kade, culminating in his senior picture. The smirk I'd come to love curved his lips, a knowing glimmer in his blue eyes as he posed, as though he already knew the effect his looks had.

I was still perusing the many photos of Blane and Kade on one wall when Mona appeared, Gerard following her.

"Kathleen," she said, frowning with worry, "what's going on? Are you all right?"

"I'm fine," I said before taking a deep breath. "I came to tell you that the police . . . arrested Blane this morning." The words were harder to get out than I'd anticipated, nearly choking me.

She stared at me, shock obvious on her face. Gerard put his arm around her shoulders.

"Did you call Charlotte?" he asked.

I nodded. "Kade's also going to see what he can do." I decided not to tell them about the danger Blane was in. "I just thought you should know."

Mona's eyes grew bright with tears, which made my eyes sting as well. She reached for me and we held each other tight for a moment.

"It'll be okay," I found myself comforting her. "He'll get out of this."

Gerard patted me on the shoulder, giving me a gentle squeeze.

There was a knock at the door. I pulled back from Mona, quickly swiping a hand over my eyes. "I'll get it," I said. I headed back to the door, but before I got there, it flew open and I halted in surprise.

A man stood in the doorway, about six feet tall, dressed in dark slacks and a polo shirt. Sunglasses obscured his eyes, but the most important detail was the gun in his hand. When he saw me, he smiled.

"Thought I saw you heading this way."

I spun around, only to see a second man had entered from the back and now stood behind Mona and Gerard. The gun he held was pointed at Mona.

"I wouldn't try and make a run for it, if I were you," he said. "Not unless you want to be responsible for these good people dying."

I raised my hands in a gesture of surrender, turning sideways so I could see both men. Gerard held tightly to Mona, warily eyeing the man next to them. Mona's face was tearstained, but she'd stopped crying. Her lips were pressed tightly together.

"What do you want?" I asked.

"Why, you, of course," the man at the door said. "Honestly, I didn't think it'd be this easy. It seems you've a talent for surviving when other people would turn up their toes and die. Now be a good girl and come along."

"You're not taking Kathleen," Gerard said angrily, reaching for me.

The man behind him moved fast, slamming the butt of his gun against the back of Gerard's head. Mona let out a cry of dismay as he slumped to the floor, falling to her knees next to him.

I took an instinctive step toward them, but was brought up short by a firm hold on my arm. I tried to wrestle my arm away, but couldn't. The man's grip tightened on me until it hurt.

"Don't make us do something you'll regret, sweetheart," he threatened from behind me.

"Fine, I'll come!" I snapped. "Just leave these people alone. They have nothing to do with this."

"Then let's go."

I gave Mona one last look, sending up a prayer that Gerard would be okay. Tears stung my eyes. She looked like she was about to start crying again, too.

"I'm sorry," I managed to say before the guy dragged me from the house.

A sedan was parked out front, and when we got to it, he popped the trunk.

"Get in," he said, motioning with his gun.

I stared at the trunk's empty expanse. "It's nearly a hundred degrees out!" I protested. "I'll die in there."

He just smiled. "Let's hope you're tougher than you look. Now get in or you'll be hot *and* bleeding from a gunshot wound."

No, didn't really want that, and I didn't want them going back inside hurting Mona and Gerard, either, which left me no choice.

The dark metal of the car was already burning hot to the touch as I scrambled inside the trunk. Once I was in, the man with the sunglasses wasted no time in slamming the lid down.

It took my eyes a moment to adjust to the sudden darkness. When they did, I started looking for the usual glow-in-the-dark trunk release. All newer cars had them—surely this one wouldn't be an exception. I felt the car start and we began moving.

The heat became stifling fast, the air thick, and I felt the familiar panic creep over me that I'd felt in the closet with Blane and Kade. I struggled not to succumb to my memories. If I didn't keep thinking straight, I had no shot at getting out of this.

It seemed I could almost hear Kade's voice in my head: *Take it easy. Breathe.*

I was hyperventilating. I could feel it. I closed my eyes, concentrating on what it had felt like to have Kade's arms around me, Blane's body against mine, the two of them surrounding and protecting me. Their strength shoring up mine.

Gradually, my breathing slowed and I opened my eyes. My hand was fisted tightly over the locket around my neck.

Sweat dripped off me and I started looking again for the trunk release. I found it at last, my slick fingers grabbing hold as I waited to see if the car would slow. If I could pop the trunk at a stoplight or something, surely there would be someone nearby who would help a woman climbing out of a car trunk.

The car slowed and then stopped, the engine idling. Figuring this might be my only chance, I pulled the lever.

Nothing happened.

I pulled again. Still nothing. I pulled again and again, not wanting to face the truth.

They'd disabled the release.

The car started moving and I frantically searched in the dark for any kind of cables or lines that connected to the trunk, but I'd never examined the inner workings of a trunk latch before, which left me ill-equipped to figure it out in this situation.

My eyes burned from the sweat dripping in them, my bra and tank now soaked. I'd never been this hot in my life. The car ride seemed to go on and on, though my frame of reference was probably skewed since every moment inside the trunk felt like an eternity.

My hands faltered in their blind search as I struggled to breathe. My thoughts were fuzzy and after a while I realized my arms were still. I had no energy to move them. It felt like I was going to die, locked in a car trunk that was more like an oven. I could hear my own struggling gasps over the sound of the car.

I thought about Blane and prayed he'd be okay, that the evidence we'd collected would be enough to convict James and set Blane free. I thought of Kade and hoped he'd keep trying to turn his life around with the new business he'd started.

I wished I'd gotten to say good-bye, which was my last coherent thought before I sank into darkness.

∼

I didn't expect to wake up, which is why I was so surprised to open my eyes and find that I was out of the trunk. Unfortunately, my new location wasn't much better, though at least there was more air.

It seemed I was in some kind of a metal shed and not a very big one at that. The floor wasn't the usual concrete slab but just hard-packed earth. There were four small, dirty windows, all of them tightly closed.

I sat up with a groan, holding a hand to my aching head, and heard the rattle of a chain. I jerked around, afraid someone was in there with me, but then I realized the chain was attached to a thick metal collar around my neck. My fingers scrabbled at the chain and collar for several minutes before I allowed myself to recognize the futility of trying to remove either of them.

The sun was high in the sky—I could tell by the shadows on the floor—and the inside of the shed wasn't much cooler than the trunk had been. My hair was matted to my sticky skin.

Getting to my feet, I followed the chain to a metal rod stuck in the ground. The chain was rusty, as was the rod, but both were still heavy and solid. I pulled at the rod in the ground, but it didn't budge. It looked like it had been in that spot for a very long time. I tried to push and wiggle it, but it held firm against my sweat-slicked grip.

The chain's length allowed me only a few feet of movement and I couldn't get close enough to the windows to open them. From what I could see through them, I was out in the country somewhere. I didn't see any other houses around.

The shed itself was nearly empty, with only a couple of workbenches attached to the walls and an old sawhorse. The smell was musty and old, as though it hadn't been used or opened up for fresh air in a while.

Exploring kept my fear at bay, but as time passed, I couldn't help but grow more terrified. I was so thirsty, so hot, and the metal on my neck cut into my skin. I went back to working on the steel rod in the ground, though it seemed useless.

The shadows had grown long when the door finally rattled with the sound of a lock being slid back. I braced myself as it opened, revealing the guy with the sunglasses, only he was no longer wearing them and his eyes were cruel and cold. He was carrying two boxes.

"What do you want?" I asked, my voice coming out a rasp.

"I don't want anything," he said, setting down the boxes just inside the door. "I'm just doing my job."

"Which is?"

He smiled. "Torturing and killing you."

I swallowed, my mouth nearly too dry to make saliva. "I have friends," I said, "people who would pay you a lot of money to let me go." And I prayed Kade had whatever it took to make that a true statement.

He laughed. "I'm already being paid a lot of money to make you suffer"—he paused—"and . . . I enjoy it."

A cold chill went through me. "Who's paying you?"

"You already know the answer to that one, I reckon," he said. "He hired me to make sure it's done right this time, with a bonus for every day I can drag it out. He really hates you, sweetheart."

William Gage.

One of the boxes moved, a scratching sound coming from inside. The guy reached for it.

"I felt kind of bad, leaving you all alone out here, so I brought you some company." He opened the box and dumped it. Two dozen or more rats scurried out, scampering into the shed and toward me.

I screamed, scrambling backward until the chain jerked on my neck.

"Now don't worry," the man continued calmly. "We don't want the rats taking over the place, so I brought them some friends, too." He opened the next box, then used his foot to carefully tip it over. Horrified, I saw a tangle of reptiles. Two, no, three big snakes slithered out of the box.

"It's gonna be getting dark soon," he said, backing out the door. "If I was you, I might try to stay awake. Those rats are hungry, and those snakes'll probably send them into a bit of a tizzy. But watch yourself. A copperhead bite won't kill ya"—he smiled—"but I hear they hurt like a sonofabitch. You have a good night now, ya hear? I'll see you in the morning." He shut the door and I again heard the slide of the lock. After a moment, there was the distant sound of a car engine, which then faded away.

I stood, shaking, in the center of the shed, my eyes glued to the snakes. The rats had scurried to the shadowy corners of the shed. There were three copperheads, two adults and a young one by the looks of them. You didn't grow up in Indiana without being able to identify that particular snake. I'd never been bitten by one, but a neighbor kid had when I was about ten. He'd said it had hurt like hell, and by the way he'd yelled, I'd known he hadn't been exaggerating.

They weren't aggressive, though, and even as I watched, they slithered into nearby pools of light to sun themselves.

My heart was racing and my palms were slimy with sweat. I tried to think. The rats, I knew, would come around when it got dark. I didn't think there was reason to fear the snakes, unless I accidentally got too close. Given where the shed seemed to be located, it was going to be pitch-black inside when night fell.

And if I survived the night, he would be back in the morning to finish the job.

I eyed the sawhorse. It stood near a corner but within reach of my leash. Unfortunately, a snake was now curled around one of the legs, basking in the sun.

I took hold of the wood and slowly, very slowly, tipped the sawhorse backward. The snake was only about a foot away from me, and every time it twitched, I froze. It took an eternity, but eventually the leg was free of the snake's coils. I carefully dragged the sawhorse toward myself inch by inch.

I had two choices. I could try to tear apart the sawhorse so I had some kind of weapon when he came back in the

morning, or I could use it to stay up off the floor. Being bitten by rats and snakes held no appeal, but both were surviv-
able. Another encounter with the guy wasn't.

Decision made.

The sawhorse had seen better days, thank God, but the
splinters bit into my hands. After the third splinter and
scrape, I pulled off my tank top, using it to cover the wood
as I tried to pull it apart. The inside boards at the bottom
seemed to be slightly looser than others, so I concentrated
my efforts on them.

My stomach growled for about the fiftieth time, which I
tried to ignore. I was so hot and thirsty, I decided that if I got
out of this, I'd never again take air-conditioning or water for
granted. I was getting tired and weak, and had to take fre-
quent breaks. I wished I'd taken the time to put tennis shoes
on this morning instead of flip-flops.

The wood finally cracked just as twilight was fading. The
copperheads were moving now, sensing prey in the dark corners where I couldn't see. I heard rustling and scratching
and wondered how long it would be before the rats came
closer.

I shuddered. I wasn't afraid of rats, not exactly, but
wasn't real thrilled about being locked up with them all
night, either. I picked my way carefully to the closest bench
nailed to the wall, but my chain brought me up about six
inches short. Damn it.

I made my way back to where the pin rested in the floor.
Holding the heavy two-by-four like a bat, I swung, hitting the
side of the pin. The blow reverberated up my arms like they
were piano strings, but to my relieved amazement, the pin

moved just slightly. I took a deep breath, steadied myself, and swung again.

Something scurried over my foot and I screamed, jumping back. My scream echoed inside the shed, as if mocking me. I gasped for air, trying to get my breath back, before creeping back toward the pin. I swung the two-by-four again and again, missing it because of the dark as often as I hit it. My hands grew numb and my arms ached, each blow taking more and more effort.

A flurry of squeaking and hissing erupted a few feet away. There was more scurrying and something touched my feet, making me leap back again with a choked sob. It was so dark now, I couldn't see a thing. I held on to the wood and followed my chain until I came to the pin. Praying I'd touch nothing but metal, I reached down and grasped it, pulling and wriggling it for all I was worth. I was unprepared for it to suddenly fly free from the ground, sending me lurching backward to fall flat on my ass on the floor.

A hiss that was too close for comfort made me freeze in place. I couldn't tell exactly where the snake was or how near. Too afraid to move, I stayed exactly where I was. I couldn't track how much time passed, but long enough for my legs to cramp from not moving and for my head to bob from sheer exhaustion. Then something furry brushed against my leg, jerking me awake, and it took everything I had not to move.

The night was the longest night I'd ever endured. Time passed with agonizing slowness. I stayed where I was, not knowing where the snakes were, if they were coming closer or staying put. After the first rat brushed against me, they grew bolder, scampering right up to me. None bit, thank God, but the smell of them, the feel of their sharp little claws as they climbed on me—all while I was unable to see them—combined to keep me in a constant state of terror. Creepy things crawled up my arms and legs, some kind of bugs, maybe spiders, but I dared not move to brush them away. Chills racked my body, but they were from fear, not cold.

I was so tired, so thirsty and dirty. Though the sun had gone down, it was still at least ninety degrees in the shed. I'd stopped sweating, which I took to be a bad sign, and I knew that meant I was extremely dehydrated. Every sound seemed amplified in the pitch-black silence, and every horror movie I'd ever watched came back to replay itself inside my head.

I'd never been as glad to see dawn as I was when morning came at last. The first lightening of the sky had me searching the shed. I caught my breath when I saw a copperhead was only about a foot from me. I was sure that if I'd tried to get up or move at all during the night, it would've bitten me.

The rats had disappeared back into the dark recesses of the shed and I couldn't see the other two snakes. Hoping they weren't nearby, I inched backward. It wasn't until the sky had lightened considerably that I felt far enough away from the snake that I could chance getting to my feet.

My legs were practically numb and it was only through sheer will and perseverance that I remained standing. I stumbled to the workbench and climbed up on it, dragging my chain with me.

More than anything, my body begged to lie down. My back was cramped from me sitting all night and my ass was numb. But I didn't know when the man was coming back. I had to be ready, not sacked out.

I tucked my feet up under me and waited, the two-by-four lying next to me. I worked on the chain, trying to get it off the pin, but it wouldn't budge.

The sound of someone approaching had me setting the chain aside. My path to the door was clear and I grabbed the two-by-four, holding the chain so it wouldn't drag, as I took up a position just inside the doorway in the shadows. It was still really early and it surprised me that he'd come back so soon.

My arms shook with fatigue as I held the plank of wood like a baseball bat, ready to swing. My shirt was still wrapped around the base of it so I could get a good grip. I had no doubts that if I missed, I wouldn't get a second chance.

The bolt slid back and the knob turned.

CHAPTER FIFTEEN

I held my breath, closed my eyes, and swung.

The plank of wood stopped, midflight.

Aghast, I opened my eyes to see he'd grabbed the two-by-four as it had swung toward his head. And I was glad he had, because it wasn't the guy from last night.

It was Kade.

I choked in a breath, my mouth agape as I stared, wide-eyed, at him. My shaking hands dropped their grip on the wood.

"Kathleen," he said, looking as stunned as I felt.

"Oh God, Kade," I blurted before flinging myself into his arms. I sobbed with relief, though my tears were dry.

His arms were tight around me and I held on as though for dear life, which was actually true. My whole body shook with the force of my reaction, and I couldn't speak.

"Shhh, it's okay now. I've got you," he said.

I got a hold of myself with a massive amount of effort, swallowing down my emotions. I eventually pulled back slightly and he released me, angling me into the sunshine to get a better look. When he saw the chain, the look on his face was one of horror before turning hard and cold.

"Hold still," he said, the gentleness of his voice belying the fury in his eyes.

Kade reached for my neck, working at the collar. I tipped my head to the side, wincing as the metal cut more deeply into my skin. A moment later, Kade pulled hard at something, there was a loud snap, and the metal fell away.

I nearly started sobbing again to have that thing off me but instead took a deep, shuddering breath.

"Who did this to you?" Kade asked.

"I don't know," I croaked, my throat dry. "A man. Gage hired him."

Pain shadowed Kade's face at the sound of my voice.

"Get me out of here," I whispered in a hoarse rasp. "Rats . . . snakes . . . inside."

At the mention of rats and snakes, Kade's eyes flashed up to look into the recesses of the shed. His lips thinned and his arm supported my back as he led me outside.

The adrenaline had vanished, leaving me in an even more feeble state than before. I had barely taken four steps before my knees gave out.

Kade caught me, easily hoisting me in his arms. I was too weak to even hold on to him and my arms hung loose while my head lolled limply backward. Everything seemed to be spinning now, going in and out of focus. My eyes slipped closed.

I heard Kade's sharp intake of breath and inwardly winced, knowing I probably looked awful and smelled worse, not that I cared much at the moment.

A shadow fell over my face and I managed to open my eyes a sliver. Kade was carrying me into the trees. He walked until we reached a small glade, then I heard the sound I'd been dreading.

The sound of a car.

"Him," I rasped. "He's back." I flailed with my hand to try to point, but Kade shushed me, carefully laying me down on a bed of soft green grass. It was blessedly cool against my bare skin.

"Stay put," he said softly, brushing my tangled hair back from my face.

I panicked and tried to grab on to him. "Please, don't leave me," I gasped, starting to cry again, though my eyes were dry.

Kade paused, his brow creasing as he looked at me. His hand cupped my cheek. "Shhh, I'll be back. I promise." He leaned down, gently pressing his mouth to my cracked and bleeding lips. "Trust me, baby," he whispered. "I'll always come for you."

I don't know how long I lay there, drifting in and out of consciousness. I knew that if something happened to Kade, I'd probably die in that spot. I could no longer dredge up the will to save myself.

I woke when Kade lifted me in his arms, my overwhelming relief at seeing him again made my lips stretch into a smile, cracking the tender skin even more. Then there was nothing as I passed out. I didn't have to be strong anymore. Kade was there.

~

Someone was holding something cold to my lips, pressing against them until I opened my mouth. A trickle of liquid touched my tongue. Water. It tasted better than anything else, ever—better than my first cup of coffee in the morning, better than the first chilled cocktail on a summer Friday night.

Gradually, I woke up enough to realize I was in the backseat of Kade's Mercedes. He was holding me in his lap, cradled like a baby, as he carefully dribbled water into my mouth.

"Drink some water, princess," he cajoled. "Drink and then I'll get you to the hospital."

I didn't really process what he'd said, I was too busy swallowing as fast as I could.

It was several minutes and two bottles of water later before I took a break. Kade's hand traced the contours of my face, brushing my closed eyes, my nose, my cheek. I felt safe, when I'd thought I never again would be, and didn't want to move from his arms.

"How'd you find me?" I asked tiredly.

"Gage owns that property," he said. "He used to use it for hunting. I took a shot when I couldn't find you at his house."

I nodded, then saw that I'd smudged dirt on Kade's white T-shirt. I pulled back.

"I'm getting you dirty," I said.

"I can't decide if it's cute or irritating that you think I'd give a shit," Kade replied.

My smile was weak.

"I need to get you to a hospital," he said.

I shook my head. "No. There's no way I can explain this. And Blane doesn't need another scandal in the papers about me. Just take me home."

"You need medical attention," he insisted.

"I'm fine. Just dehydrated. I didn't get bitten by anything."

At the mention of being bitten, his jaw clenched tight, though his touch remained gentle.

"Did you get anyone to help Blane?" I asked.

"Blane's fine," he answered. "Let's worry about you for right now."

He arranged me on the seat before he got out and slid behind the wheel. I fell asleep to the motion of the car as he drove.

I woke up when we stopped. I felt better from the water, though still weak, but had enough strength to get myself up and out of the car.

"Let me help you," Kade said, wrapping an arm around my back. His solid strength was like a warm blanket as we made our way slowly to the door. Now that I wasn't worrying about rats, snakes, or killer psychopaths, my body ached from my ordeal.

Mona met us at the door, her face creased in lines of worry.

"Is Gerard okay?" were my first words to her.

"He's fine, sweetheart," she said, taking up a position on the other side of me and also lending support. "Nothing an icepack and a little painkiller wouldn't fix."

"She needs some food," Kade said.

"I'd rather be clean," I said. The water was still sloshing in my stomach and had taken the edge off my hunger. But I stank so bad, I could smell myself.

"I'll help her," Mona said to Kade, who seemed reluctant to let me go.

Mona helped me up the stairs to Blane's room.

"Why are we in here?" I asked.

"The tub is bigger," she said. "Now wait here while I run a bath."

She sat me on the edge of Blane's bed while she went into the bathroom and soon I heard the water running. I couldn't take my eyes off of Blane's pillow as I wondered where he was and how he was doing. I intended to quiz Kade on the status of things as soon as I could think straight.

Mona came and got me. I winced as I moved my arms, the punishment they'd taken last night coming back to haunt me.

"I can do that," she said, helping me push off the dirt-encrusted shorts and unhook my once-white bra. She took my hand and held me steady myself as I stepped into the steaming water. I sank down with a sigh that felt like it had come all the way up from my toes.

The memories of last night, of the snakes and rats, made me shudder. Mona picked up a washcloth, soaping it before taking my hand and gently washing my fingers and palm, then all the way up my arm.

"You don't have to do that," I protested, embarrassed.

"Gerard and I were scared to death for you," she said quietly, rinsing the cloth and soaping it again. She reached for my other hand. "I don't know what we would've done if Kade hadn't brought you back. I don't know what Kade would have done if he hadn't found you."

Our eyes met, and the look of genuine love and affection in hers made tears start leaking from mine.

"Shhh," she said, wrapping an arm around my shoulders. "Don't cry. You're home now." Her voice sounded as though she, too, was fighting tears. We stayed like that for a while, the tightness of her hold on me making an ache bloom in my chest.

Finally, she sat back on her heels and wiped her eyes. Taking the cloth, she again soaped it before washing my back and shoulders. When I lifted my arms to wash my hair, I gasped in pain.

"Lean back," Mona said, and she proceeded to wash my hair the way she would a child's.

After toweling my hair dry, she helped me put Blane's robe on, then made me sit down while she gently brushed my hair out, combing through the tangles one by one.

"Thank you, Mona," I said, and the words seemed inadequate for how I was feeling. Our gazes met in the bathroom mirror. She smiled.

"You're welcome, dear. We're just happy you're all right." She set the brush down. "I'm going to go fix you something to eat."

After she'd gone, I found a toothbrush and brushed my teeth. When I came out of the bedroom, my gaze lingered on the bed. I was strongly tempted to sleep there, knowing it would help me feel closer to Blane, but decided against it, heading down the hall to my room instead.

I lay down on the bed, then immediately sat back up when the door opened to reveal Kade carrying a tray laden with food.

"That was fast," I said. "Thanks for bringing it up."

He set the tray on the bed and sat down next to me. "I figured you'd be pretty hungry, and you still need to drink more water."

I didn't mind doing that and chugged some more from the glass on the tray. Mona had sent up a mix of cheeses, cured meats, and fruit. I wasn't shy about eating my fill.

After watching me for a while, Kade asked, "So you want to tell me what happened?"

I shrugged. "Not much to tell," I said around a mouthful of grape. "They stuffed me in a trunk. I passed out. When I woke, I was chained up. The sonofabitch dumped a couple dozen rats and a few copperheads in there with me and left. You showed up in the morning." I left out the part about how terrified I'd been in the pitch-black, with things crawling on me and a snake too close for me to chance making a move. But from the look on Kade's face as he watched my shaking hand snag another grape, I figured he already had a good idea of that part.

I sighed, my stomach full, and leaned back against the pillows. "Now tell me what I missed."

Kade moved the tray to the dresser and resumed his position beside me. "Jared is getting the DNA tested on what you got against what was found on Kandi. Blane's arraignment is set for tomorrow morning. I managed to work a few strings to hopefully keep Blane out of harm's way." As he spoke, he coaxed me into his arms and I went willingly, lying between his legs with my head resting on his chest.

His hand stroked my hair and I closed my eyes, exhaustion consuming every muscle in my body. I knew I should probably move away, but I couldn't seem to make myself. I needed him, needed to breathe in his scent and savor the warmth of his body through the layers of fabric between us.

"I thought for sure you'd be dead when I found you," he said after a while. "*If* I found you." His voice was quiet.

"I thought I would be, too."

"You're the most vulnerable part of me," he mused, his fingers threading through my hair. "A year ago, I would have killed you myself if I'd known."

I swallowed hard and didn't doubt him for a moment. "And now?" I asked, tipping my head back to look at him.

Our eyes met. "And now," he murmured, "now I can't let you go, no matter how much it costs me." He pressed his lips to my forehead and I closed my eyes at the contact.

Kade cradled my head against his chest and I relaxed, thankful down to my bones for his presence in my life. And it was only then, as I was drifting off to sleep, that I realized I loved him.

≈

When I woke it was dark outside. I'd slept the day away.

I sat up, realizing Kade was gone. He'd tucked a blanket around me, which I pulled away as I stood.

Fear crept over me in the dark room. Where was Kade? Was I alone in the house? What if that guy came back for me once he saw I'd escaped?

I groped for the light, feeling slightly embarrassed at the relief that flooded through me when I flicked on the switch and a warm glow dispelled the darkness. I shed Blane's robe and pulled open the closet door. I really didn't want to raise my arms above my head to dress and I searched frantically through the clothes. I saw a little summer dress with buttons down the front and grabbed it, but even pushing my arms through the short sleeves made me wince. I hurriedly buttoned it before going to the door.

I paused, opening the door just a crack and peering through. I wondered where Kade was and why he'd left me alone.

I knew Blane kept his guns in a cabinet in his den. Maybe it was unlocked.

Seeing no one in the hallway, I crept silently downstairs, my heart pounding so loudly I was sure it could be heard. Glancing at the grandfather clock as I passed, I realized it was late. I'd slept over twelve hours.

The den was empty and the gun case was locked tight. I muttered a curse, trying to think of what to do now.

Knives. The kitchen.

I headed that way, relief flooding through me when I heard Kade and Mona talking quietly. I heard my name and paused, unable to resist the temptation to listen in.

". . . stay with Kathleen tonight," Mona was saying.

"I'd planned on it," Kade replied. "Leaving her alone right now is a bad idea."

"Did you take care of the awful men who took her?"

"Yes. They won't be back."

"What about Gage?"

A pause. "He won't be a problem, either."

"Thank goodness," Mona said with a sigh. "He was such an evil man."

"And I'm not?"

"Don't be silly. Personally, I don't see anything wrong with protecting those you love when the police can't or won't help." She paused. "And I know you love her, Kade."

"She loves Blane," Kade dismissed.

"Does she? Things have been so crazy around here the past couple of weeks, I'd be surprised if she knows how she feels anymore."

"She's amazing, what she endured," Kade said. "You should have seen where he left her, that fucking piece of shit."

"Language," Mona said mildly, "though I don't disagree. And I don't want to know—it'll only upset me. I just thank God you found her." I heard the rustle of fabric, as though she were hugging him, and decided I needed to stop eaves-dropping.

I walked into the kitchen. "There you are," I said to Kade a little breathlessly. "I was afraid everyone had gone."

Mona looked pleasantly surprised to see me. "You're up!" she said with a smile. "How are you feeling?"

"Better," I said. "Thirsty."

She went to the refrigerator and took out a bottle filled with a blue sports drink. "Here," she said, handing it to me. "Gerard went to the store and got these for you in every flavor of the rainbow. Said he wanted to make sure there was one you liked."

My heart squeezed and I took a big gulp of the fruity liquid, trying not to cry. I was sick of crying.

"Speaking of which," she said, untying and removing the apron she wore, "I think I'll head home. I'll be back in the morning." She gave me a hug. "Good night, dear."

"Good night," I said, hugging her back. "And thank you."

She smiled and left through the kitchen door. I glanced at Kade, who was leaning against the counter. He frowned as he looked me up and down.

"What?"

"Why are you wearing that at this hour?" he asked.

I looked down at my dress. "I thought I was alone, and if that guy came back, I might need to run, or fight, or . . ." My voice trailed away. It had seemed like a good idea to get dressed at the time, though after sleeping so long, perhaps I hadn't been thinking too clearly.

"You thought I'd leave you?"

"You were gone when I woke up," I said with a shrug.

Kade stared at me, his expression unreadable.

I glanced away, taking another swallow of the sports drink. Suddenly, all I could think about was the revelation I'd had before falling asleep. I loved Kade, and maybe had for longer than I wanted to contemplate. And I could never, ever tell him.

I forced those thoughts from my mind. Now wasn't the time to dwell on it. I could fall apart some other time. "Will that guy be back?" I asked. "The one who took me? Or his partner?"

"No, they won't." Kade didn't elaborate.

"What, um—what happened to them?" I asked, still not meeting his eyes.

"You don't want the details," he said dryly. "Just know that if they came back, it'd be as ghosts." There was a drink on the counter and he took a swallow. Vodka, I guessed.

"Hungry?" he asked, pushing himself away from the counter. "Mona made dinner and saved you a plate." He went to the refrigerator without waiting for my answer and pulled out a dish, which he stuck in the microwave.

I stood awkwardly in silence, drinking until I'd finished the bottle.

Kade took the dish from the microwave and set it on the table along with a fork and knife.

"Thanks," I said, sitting down. Mona had made some kind of chicken with a sauce and potatoes. It was awesome, as was everything she made.

Kade sat down opposite me with his drink in hand. After a few minutes of silence, he spoke.

"Why won't you look at me?"

I glanced up from my nearly empty plate, my face heating. I didn't know what to say, how to act after everything that had happened between us. How did I deal with the fact that I loved two men? Two *brothers*? It was a disaster that left me reeling, my heart breaking inside. Two men who were far better to me than I deserved, and I loved them both. Mona had been right, there wasn't going to be a happy ending to this.

"I'm not avoiding looking at you, if that's what you're suggesting," I lied. "It's . . ." I stopped because I had no clue what to say.

". . . that we're just now having that awkward morning after," he supplied, his eyes narrowing.

Well, yes, there was that.

I got up to take my dish to the sink so I wouldn't have to answer right away. Unfortunately, Kade was still waiting when I finished, and he wasn't sitting at the table anymore but was standing right behind me.

I turned off the faucet, staring at the window above the sink. I watched our reflection while his eyes were solely on me. His hands settled on my shoulders, his brow creased as though he was in pain. His palms skated down my bare arms to my hands where he slotted our fingers together.

Mona had been right. I hadn't even realized that my feelings for Kade had grown so much. Though if I was honest, I should have realized I never would have slept with him in Vegas if I hadn't known, deep down, that I loved him. I just hadn't wanted to face it then, any more than I wanted to face it now.

Kade pressed a kiss to my shoulder, crossing my arms in front of me so he could hold me. His lips moved toward my neck and I closed my eyes, leaning back against him and tipping my head to the side. A soft sigh escaped me at the touch of his tongue, warm and soft, to the skin that had been scraped and abraded by the metal collar.

"Let's get you to bed," he said softly in my ear.

My pulse jumped, though I knew he didn't mean anything by it.

Kade kept my hand in his and walked me upstairs to my room. Even after sleeping all day, I was still tired. I worried about Blane and what he'd endured since they'd arrested him. I worried about what would happen when, and if, this was all over. If I'd thought it best for me to leave before I'd realized how I felt, now it was imperative.

"Has it been on the news?" I asked. "About Blane?"

"Yep," Kade answered, turning the bedside lamp on. "It got leaked almost immediately."

"Damn it," I said with a sigh.

"Don't worry. The public has a notoriously short memory," Kade said. He dug in my dresser drawer, pulled out my white nightgown, and handed it to me. "Here you go."

"Turn around," I said.

Kade's smirk made my heart beat faster, but he did as I said. I unbuttoned and shed the dress, not bothering to try and put on panties or a bra before donning the nightgown. It was enough of an ordeal to raise my arms to put through the straps and pull the gown over my head.

"You really should be more aware of your surroundings."

I jerked my head up. "Wh—?" I began, then I saw that he'd been watching me in the mirror. I flushed as he turned around, not a trace of remorse on his face.

"You're shameless," I said with a raised brow.

"You're gorgeous."

I flushed even more and quickly looked away as I climbed into bed. I pulled the covers up over me.

"I guess I'll flunk my classes," I said. "I missed a final today and have two tomorrow that I won't be able to take." I knew I wasn't going to miss Blane's arraignment, no matter what—and besides, it wasn't as if I'd spent a lot of time studying the past few days. All the money and time I'd spent on those classes had been wasted.

"Don't worry about that," Kade said, flicking off the overhead light before lying down next to me on top of the covers. He bent his arms behind his head and stared up at the ceiling.

Easy for him to say.

Kade reached for the bedside lamp.

"Wait," I said, grabbing his arm. He looked at me, questioning.

"Um, do you mind leaving it on?" The thought of being in the dark terrified me enough to swallow my embarrassment at asking for a nightlight like a child.

I couldn't read the expression that crossed Kade's face, but he gave a nod and lay back down.

"Will you stay with me?" I asked, hating that fear had prompted the question but unwilling to face the night alone. Or without Kade.

Kade looked at me. "Absolutely."

I abandoned any pretense that I didn't want to be close to him, scooting over until I was pressed against his side. His eyebrows climbed, but he didn't say anything, just wrapped one arm around me as I rested my head on his shoulder, my arm lying across his chest.

What would become of him? He'd said he couldn't stay away from me, but us being together wasn't an option. How could I possibly be with Kade when my feelings for Blane were still so confused? Blane said he wanted me back, but how could I go back to him when I also loved Kade?

I loved them both, but Kade had been wrong when he said one of them would have me. That wasn't going to happen. Not when I knew it would drive them apart for good. I couldn't—I wouldn't—be the catalyst for that.

Convincing them was going to be another story.

~

The next time I woke, sunlight streamed through my window. I glanced at the clock. It was early, which was good since I needed to get ready to appear at Blane's arraignment.

With a pang, I noticed Kade was no longer in bed with me. I figured he had probably known I'd be okay once the sun came up, but it still would have been nice to have him by my side.

I showered and blew my hair dry, my aching arms making it take longer than usual, then stood in front of my closet in a towel, trying to figure out what to wear. Though they were healing nicely, there were still the cuts on my chest from James. So something to cover up the scabs would be good.

A knock at the door interrupted my perusal. I opened the door to find Mona standing there with a tray.

"Breakfast," she said with a smile.

"That's so sweet of you," I said, stepping back so she could come in. "Thank you."

"It's no trouble," she said, setting down the tray. I saw her eyes flick over my neck and chest when she turned around and I self-consciously hitched the towel higher to hide the *J*.

"What are you going to wear?" she asked, brushing by me as she headed for the closet.

"I'm not sure," I confessed. "Do you have any suggestions?"

She picked out a deep pink tea-length dress with fitted elbow-length sleeves. It had a vintage feel to it and, though it wasn't something I'd normally wear, it would probably work well for where I had to be today. "And you can wear this, too," she said, opening a drawer and pulling out a pale nylon scarf printed with pink flowers.

I thanked her and she left. I drank the water she'd brought, only had one cup of coffee, and ate some of the yogurt and fruit she'd brought for me. Half an hour later, I was adjusting the scarf around my neck, glad to see it concealed the marks from the metal collar.

I headed downstairs and found Kade in Blane's den, sitting in front of the muted television. He was dressed nicely, too, and my breath caught at the sight of him in black slacks and a black button-down shirt. He didn't wear a tie and had left the top button of his shirt undone.

"How do I look?" I said stepping in front of him and doing a pirouette. "Am I suitably pure and innocent enough to be Blane's fiancée?" I smiled wryly at the joke, since the last thing I felt was pure and innocent.

The look on Kade's face was enough to wipe the smile from mine.

"What's wrong?" I asked, my heart plummeting. "What's happened?"

Kade didn't answer for a moment, then he said, "Your friend Tish called you."

I frowned. "She did?" That reminded me. "Where's my cell?"

Kade pulled my phone from his pocket and handed it to me. "She wanted to let you know that your boss, Romeo, was going to go to the cops with something he'd found."

I looked up from the phone, alarmed. "What did he find?"

"Apparently, unbeknownst to you or the other employees, he's had video cameras installed for monitoring. And one of them is located in the storeroom."

I stood in shock, staring at him.

"In reviewing the footage," Kade continued, "Romeo felt it should be turned over to the police, but he thought you should make that call. He felt uncomfortable, given the content, about talking to you himself, so he had her bring this by." He picked up a DVD that I hadn't noticed was on the table.

Shit.

"So does everyone know?" God, that would be awful. No, James hadn't raped me, but the realization that everyone I worked with might know I'd been cornered like that—attacked like that—made me want to crawl into a cave and not come out.

"I have no idea," he said. "She didn't say."

I eyed Kade. "So what's the matter?" I asked. "You already knew what happened between James and me."

Kade stood, coming so close to me that I had to tip my head back to look him in the eye. "Arriving after the fact," he said stiffly, "or hearing about it from someone else, isn't the same as watching every moment on a fucking video." The anguish was stark in his eyes. "Blane should have killed him."

"No, he shouldn't have," I said. "Or else that would be on the video, too, and then where would we be?"

Kade turned away and I caught sight of the television. William Gage's photo had flashed on the screen and I frowned, reaching for the remote control and unmuting the TV with a sinking feeling.

". . . found deceased in his home this morning," the voice-over was saying, "from an accidental fall down the stairs while in his wheelchair. He'd been ill with terminal pancreatic cancer . . ."

I muted the television again, not wanting to hear any more. Kade had completely ignored the story, pouring himself another cup of coffee from the carafe on the sideboard.

I thought I knew what had happened and who had done it, but I couldn't bring myself to feel remorse, only relief.

"Did you do that?" I asked. "Did you kill him?"

"Don't ask questions you don't want to know the answer to," Kade said.

I swallowed hard. While I didn't regret William Gage's death, I did regret that Kade had killed him because of me, but I knew that was the last thing Kade would want to hear.

"If James gets arrested for what he did to me," I said, changing the subject, "won't that provide a pattern of behavior that will help us prove what he did to Kandi?"

"Yes, but you'd need to file a complaint."

"I can do that."

Kade turned around, fixing me with a piercing stare. "You're going to file an assault charge . . . against the district attorney? Don't you realize what they'll do to you? The press will rip you apart. They love James, and now his poor daddy just bit the dust. As Blane's fiancée, they're going to paint you as the conniving slut, no matter what that video shows."

I raised my chin and squared my shoulders. "If it'll help Blane, then it's worth it."

Kade shook his head. "Your loyalty is admirable . . . and stupid."

"I don't ditch my friends just because it's convenient," I said, stung.

"Is that what you and Blane are? Friends?" He walked over and grasped my left hand, holding it up so I could see the diamond sparkling on my finger. "Is this just for show, or is that just what you keep telling yourself?"

"Are you two ready to go?"

I turned to see Mona peeking in the doorway. "Gerard and I are heading out now."

I pulled my hand from Kade's. "We were just leaving," I said, picking up my purse and tucking my phone inside.

"We'll see you there."

I turned to Kade. "Are you driving me or what?"

He was and we pulled up to the courthouse thirty tense minutes later.

My stomach was doing flip-flops while we waited inside the courtroom. Reporters had snapped photos of me and shouted questions outside, but Kade had hustled me past them, dark sunglasses hiding his eyes.

Charlotte had stopped briefly on her way to the front of the courtroom to tell us not to worry, that she was sure the arraignment would go fine and the judge would set bail.

There were several other cases ahead of Blane's and I grew more anxious as we waited, chewing a nail and shifting in my seat. Kade took my hand, lowering it to my lap and holding it there. He was a solid presence at my side and I gripped his hand tight with both of mine.

When Blane at last stepped into the courtroom, my breath left my lungs in a choked gasp. His hands were cuffed in front of him, which seemed incongruous with the suit he wore, but the bruises and cuts on his face were what caught my attention.

"It's okay," Kade whispered to me. "He's all right."

"But . . . he's not," I whispered back. "Look at him."

"A few bruises, that's all," Kade said. "He's alive and nothing's broken. He's fine. Trust me."

As though he felt my gaze on him, Blane glanced up and our eyes met. Something close to shame crossed his face before his expression smoothed and he turned to face the judge.

I couldn't take my eyes off him as the hearing commenced. Charlotte entered a plea of not guilty and the judge initially declined to set bail. Charlotte argued the point, citing circumstantial evidence and Blane's place in the community, and the judge relented, setting bail at five million dollars.

Blane didn't look back as they led him away, and I realized I was squeezing Kade's hand hard enough to leave fingernail marks, though he hadn't said a word.

"Now what?" I asked Kade.

He was already on his cell phone. "Now we post bond and get him the hell out of there," he said. "I'll be just a second."

Kade left the courtroom so he could hear on his cell while I paused to hug Mona, who looked as relieved as I felt, though I was working hard to hold it together. I assured her we'd bring Blane home. Gerard put his arm around her shoulders and led her out the doors.

I picked up my purse and turned to go as well, only to find James standing much too close.

He grabbed my arm and jerked me toward him. "That getup isn't fooling anyone," he hissed in my ear.

A few people stood talking nearby, but I didn't want to make a scene. I could imagine how my attacking the DA prosecuting Blane's case would play in the news, and it wouldn't be good or helpful to Blane at all.

"Let go of me," I gritted out.

"You were supposed to suck my dick, bitch," he hissed. "Now I'm going to put Kirk away for life. You can count on it." His grip on my arm was painfully tight.

"Is that what you said to her? Because I was real curious."

James turned to see Kade behind him. Though Kade's lips were twisted into the semblance of a smile, the look in his eyes was deadly. His gaze fell on James's hand on my arm.

"Let her go, dickhead."

"Dennon," James sneered, "on bodyguard duty?" He let go of me and got in Kade's face. "You know, she's a real spitfire, but her tits are fantastic."

I was absolutely sure that if we hadn't been in a public place, Kade would have killed James right then and there. As it was, I could already see James's death sentence in Kade's eyes. He was just biding his time.

"It's a real shame about your dad," Kade said with mock sympathy. "Fell down the stairs, didn't he? Such a tragic . . . accident."

The subtext of Kade's comment seemed to slam into James and his face turned red with rage. "You motherfucker," he spat. "You killed him."

"I don't know what you're talking about," Kade said with a shrug. "Accidents happen." His voice matched the ice in his eyes when he said, "You should be real careful one doesn't happen to you."

It was unmistakably a threat. James seemed to know it, too, because he shut his mouth, the red in his face fading.

Kade placed his hand on the small of my back and guided me out of the courthouse and to his car.

"Thanks for your help," I said, still shaken from the unexpected confrontation.

"James is like a rabid dog," Kade said. "He needs to be put down."

"Not by you," I said quickly. I couldn't shake the feeling that with each person Kade killed, a little of his soul was eaten away by darkness. I was afraid that eventually the darkness would consume him.

"If not me, then who?"

Kade's eyes met mine, but I didn't have an answer.

The police station was only a couple of miles away and we drove there quickly. "How are you going to pay them five million dollars?" I asked as we walked inside.

Kade snorted. "It's not five million. It's ten percent of five million."

Oh. In defense of my ignorance, I'd never had to bail someone out of jail.

We'd arrived before Blane had even been brought back and Kade went to pay the bail while I waited in the lobby. The blue plastic chairs were no more comfortable than the other times I'd sat in them. The minutes seemed to crawl by as I watched the clock.

"I see Kade's taking care of the bond," Charlotte said, sitting down next to me.

"Yes. Hopefully, it won't take too much longer." I put aside my antipathy for her only because she was Blane's lawyer and was trying to help him. Regardless of how much she disliked me and how heartily that animosity was returned, it didn't matter because both of us were after the same goal— to prove Blane's innocence.

Just then, Blane walked around the corner, Kade at his side. I jumped to my feet, but he was already headed my way, his long strides eating up the space between us. In the span of a breath, he had me in his arms.

He'd been gone for only two days, but it had felt five times that. I clung tightly to his neck and swallowed down the lump in my throat. The warm, familiar feel of him was so dear to me.

"Save the reunion for later," Kade said. "Police stations make me nervous."

I pulled back from Blane, but he didn't let me get far; his arm stayed locked around my waist, anchoring me to his side.

Kade handed Blane a pair of sunglasses. "Ready?"

Blane gave a curt nod. "You take that side," he said, sliding the glasses on.

Kade moved to my other side so that they flanked me. Charlotte led the way as we went out the doors.

The bevy of reporters made me falter in surprise, even more of them than had been on the courthouse steps this morning.

"Keep moving," Blane said. "Don't stop."

Charlotte was speaking to the crowd, which drew some but not all of the attention away from us. Flashes went off continuously, blinding me with their light as questions were fired at us from every direction.

"Mr. Kirk, how do you see the future of your campaign now that you've been charged with murder?"

"Was Kandi Miller aware that you'd reconciled with your fiancée?"

"You say you're innocent despite the evidence. Who do you think could have done this to her?"

"Miss Turner, how does it feel to be engaged to a man accused of murder?"

There was a car waiting at the bottom of the steps and Blane opened the door for me. I climbed in as quickly as I could and saw him say something to Kade before getting in as well. Kade closed the door behind Blane and me, cutting off the shouting reporters. The driver stepped on the gas and we shot down the street.

The tinted windows gave us privacy and I released a pent-up breath. Then my breath was gone altogether as Blane dragged me onto his lap, tossed his sunglasses aside, and kissed me.

It wasn't a gentle, tender kiss, but one filled with the ache of being parted as his tongue slid hotly against mine. Blane crushed me to him, his hands touching me everywhere he could reach—as though to reassure himself that I was really there.

I tore my mouth from his. "Blane," I gasped.

Both of us were breathing hard. His hand cupped the back of my neck as his forehead pressed against mine.

"I'm sorry you were there, that you had to see me . . . like that," he said.

"What do you mean? Like what?"

"Handcuffed. In court."

The shame I'd seen on his face earlier made sense now.

I leaned back, but he wouldn't look me in the eye. I laid my hand along his smooth cheek. "Look at me," I said softly.

His gaze reluctantly lifted to mine, and I could read the anguish in their depths. If there were two things Blane prided himself on, they were his honor and his reputation—and both were being called into question with this case.

"I know you," I said, "and I know you didn't do this. Nothing is going to change that, and nothing is going to change the fact that you're a man of courage and integrity."

I surveyed the bruises on his face, lightly brushing a finger over the cut on his lip. "What happened in there?" I asked. "Kade said he was going to help. We didn't want you to get hurt."

"It was what I expected," Blane said evasively. "Kade's help was very . . . timely."

And I knew he wasn't going to say anything more about it.

I thought I should probably get off his lap, but I couldn't make myself let go of him and his hold on me didn't let up.

"Were you all right while I was gone?" he asked. "Did you stay at my house?"

I ignored the first question and evaded the second. "I promised you I would."

Blane's fingers toyed with the scarf at my neck and I stiffened, hoping he wouldn't try to take it off. No way did I want to tell him what happened. He had enough going on and it didn't matter anyway.

Kade was waiting at the house when we arrived. Mona greeted us at the door. She didn't say a word, just hugged Blane. His face softened as he hugged her back, brushing a kiss to her forehead. She let him go and gave my hand a squeeze as we walked by, a look of shared understanding passing between us: Blane belonged here, not in a jail.

Blane led me to the den, where he tossed his jacket on a chair as he walked behind his desk.

"Where are we?" he asked, loosening and then removing his tie.

Kade sat in one of the leather wingback chairs facing Blane, who remained standing. "Jared said he has news. He's going to be by any minute."

Blane nodded. "What happened while I was gone? What's Kathleen hiding from me?"

"What—nothing!" I spluttered. I should have known that Blane, an expert at reading people, would have seen through my vague answers.

"Gage tried again," Kade said, ignoring me. "We're lucky she's alive."

The *we* seemed deliberate and the two of them locked eyes for a moment, something passing between them that I didn't understand.

The doorbell rang and a few moments later, Mona showed Jared into the room.

"We've examined the phone records for both James and Kandi," he said as he took a seat. "The number of calls between them should be enough to prove they had a relationship."

I frowned. Kade had said the calls Kandi had made were to an unlisted burner phone, untraceable. Now there were documented calls between the two of them? But I kept my mouth shut.

"Any calls the night of the murder?" Blane asked.

"Not that I'm aware of," Jared said.

"You probably want to have that checked again," Kade interjected. "I have it on good authority that not only is there a call from James to Kandi, there's also the fact that the cell tower his phone used is within a half mile of Kandi's house."

Blane sent a sharp look Kade's way but said nothing.

Jared's expression was grave as he handed Blane a folder.

"The DNA tests are complete," he said. "Unfortunately, there was nothing to tie James to the scene, but these came back positive."

"What are they?" Blane asked, thumbing through the folder.

"The semen tested as a positive match for you."

CHAPTER SIXTEEN

No one spoke. The look of shock on Blane's face echoed, I was sure, the one on mine.

"Well, that sucks."

I looked at Kade, thinking that was the understatement of the century. He seemed unfazed by the information, but the set of his face was grim.

"I managed to destroy the results," Jared continued. "But when they can't find them, I'm sure they'll test again."

"How did they get my DNA?" Blane asked.

"The Navy," Kade answered, getting up and going to the sideboard to pour a drink. "I bet they took your DNA when you joined the SEALs, in case they needed to identify your remains at some point."

Nausea rose in my throat at the thought of there not being enough of Blane's body left to identify him while he was in combat.

"Fuck." Blane's hands were clenched in fists. "They would have needed a court order for that."

"Maybe not if someone has friends in high places," Jared speculated. "The point is, the results match you, not James. What are we going to do about it?"

"Why are you putting your job on the line for Blane?" Kade suddenly asked, taking a swallow of the scotch in his hand. His eyes narrowed suspiciously. "What's in it for you?"

"Kade—" Blane broke in.

"No, it's okay," Jared interrupted. He addressed Kade. "Blane was deployed in Afghanistan at the same time my brother was there."

"Your brother's a SEAL?" Kade asked.

"No, he was in the Army. But he was part of a team that got trapped by insurgents. It was too hot—no one could get in to get them." He tipped his head toward Blane, who'd gone to the window, his hands braced on his hips. "Except Blane here. He and another guy got in to where my brother was holed up and fought their way out. He saved my brother and two of his buddies."

I glanced over at Blane, but he was looking out the window. He didn't respond to Jared's story, not that I thought he would, and the account of what he'd done didn't surprise me.

"So now if he needs something, I'm here to do it," Jared finished.

"Not if it costs you your job," Blane said, turning around to face him.

Jared stood. "You let me worry about that. I'll check into those phone records, but we need a break in this case—and soon."

"Thanks, Jared," Blane said.

Jared walked out, leaving me with Blane and Kade. Still reeling from the results of the DNA tests, I sat down heavily on the sofa.

"Kade, give us a minute, please," Blane said, his tone filled with quiet resignation. His hands were in his pockets as he stared again out the window.

Kade tossed back the rest of his drink in one swallow, his gaze resting on me. "No problem," he said, closing the door on his way out.

That's when I remembered. Blane didn't realize I knew he'd lied to the police about sleeping with Kandi the night of her murder. What I still didn't understand was how the DNA matched. Blane had told Kade that he always used a condom.

Silence reigned for several minutes, and I didn't break it. Blane had something he wanted to say, obviously, so I forced myself to wait and tried not to fidget. Finally, Blane turned and approached me, stopping a few feet away.

"When you and I broke up," he began—which I thought was a nice way of saying, *When I accused you of cheating and dumped you*—"I realized after talking with Kade that I'd made a huge mistake." He grimaced. "Though we didn't really talk, I guess. More like he kicked my ass, which I deserved."

Couldn't disagree with that.

"I thought about what I'd said, what I'd done, and I knew I couldn't take it back. You had to hate me. I'd lost the one person who loved me for me, and I couldn't face it. So I threw myself into work, but I felt dead inside."

A sob was building in my chest, but I held on, not knowing if I wanted to hear this or not.

"Kandi came by one night for some reason or other I don't remember, and . . . I slept with her. I realize you know that she and I continued having this . . . relationship right up until the night she died. And I know you heard me tell the cops I didn't sleep with her that night—"

"But you did," I finished for him.

His face was unreadable. "Yes."

I bowed my head, unable to look at him. "And you didn't use . . ." I couldn't say the word. Had he lied to Kade? I had no idea why the thought of him not using a condom with Kandi bothered me so much, it just did. Maybe it was because he'd told Kade he'd only ever *not* worn one with me.

"I used a condom," Blane said. "I don't know—I guess maybe it broke or something. I wasn't paying a whole lot of attention." He hesitated. "I'd been drinking that night. You and I had talked the night before and it was still . . . on my mind. I don't think I was as considerate with her as I should have been." His face was stark with grief.

"Are you saying you were using her that night to get back at me?" I asked. "Because you thought Kade and I were sleeping together?" The very idea that my actions had caused Blane to take his frustration out on Kandi made me ill. If I hadn't slept with Kade, Blane might not have gone over there or had sex with Kandi that night. He might not now be the focus of a murder investigation sure to ruin his career, if not his life.

Blane's smile was bitter. "Not such a hero now, am I." The self-loathing in that statement was something I'd never heard from Blane before.

"This is all my fault," I said with dawning horror. "All of it."

"What? No! Don't be ridiculous," Blane said, walking over to me. "I'm not blaming you for my actions, Kat. I just wanted to explain—"

"That everything you did that night had nothing to do with Kandi and everything to do with me!" I interrupted, my voice shrill. "Tell me that's not true."

"Listen to me—" he began.

I jumped to my feet and headed for the door. I couldn't breathe. My chest felt as though it was wrapped in tight bands that squeezed the air out of me. It was my fault. Kandi was dead, Blane's life was ruined, all because of me.

Blane made a grab for me, but I tore my arm away and threw open the door. "Kat, wait!" he called.

Kade was standing in the hallway near the front door, sorting through a stack of mail. He looked up when I hurried toward him.

"Keys," I gasped. I just needed to hold it together for a few more moments, just until I was alone. "Please."

His blue eyes were intent on mine, seeing way too much as he handed me his car keys without a word.

I felt Blane's hands settle on my waist.

"Don't leave," he said.

"Let me go." I tried to twist away, but he held me even tighter, pulling me in to him.

"You can't leave like this," he said, and I could hear desperation in his voice.

I fought now, self-preservation kicking in. "I said, *let me go!*"

I was suddenly free and I stumbled forward a couple of steps.

"She wants to go, so let her go," Kade said, his voice like steel.

"Don't get in my way, Kade," Blane threatened, trying to push past him.

"What the fuck did you do now?" Kade retorted, blocking Blane's path to me. "For you supposedly being the responsible one, I seem to be cleaning up a lot of your messes, big brother."

"Out of my way!" Blane shoved Kade, who didn't budge.

"You want her, you're gonna have to go through me."

I jerked open the front door and glanced back, but Blane and Kade were locked in their own battle of wills as they stood nose to nose. My vision blurred and I turned away. Moments later, I was in Kade's Mercedes, speeding away from Blane's home.

~

For a while, I just drove and didn't pay a lot of attention as to where. I kept replaying the conversation between Blane and me over and over inside my head.

Now that I'd had some time, I realized Blane hadn't been blaming me, but that didn't make me feel any better. I was angry at Blane for how he'd treated Kandi, when I thought I'd never have any reason to sympathize with her. Was it a relationship she'd gone into with her eyes wide open? Yes, but that didn't lessen the fact that Blane had taken advantage of her affection, using her to salve his own emotional wounds.

I drove until there was nothing but countryside around me and the road was a narrow path winding through trees, their branches overhanging and shading it. On a whim, I pulled onto a dirt path and turned off the car.

I untied the scarf from my neck, got out and started walking, realizing before long that the pumps I wore were ill-suited to hiking. Reaching down, I took them off, leaving them where they lay.

The grass was cool under my feet, the feel of the earth against my soles taking me back to when I was young and my mom never could get me to wear shoes outside in the summer. Even after the time I'd stepped on a bee, I still regularly ditched my shoes to feel the warmth of the sun-kissed ground between my toes.

I stumbled upon a clear glade among the trees, spots of sunshine breaking through the clouds to dapple the ground. The grass hadn't grown very high, so I sat down. I had a passing thought that I was getting the nice dress I wore dirty but couldn't bring myself to care enough to get up.

It wasn't as hot as it should have been for July, and it was even nicer in the shade. I was glad for the brief respite from the Indiana summer sauna.

I closed my eyes, deliberately bringing to mind happier times when my parents were alive. I knew back then that my dad had wanted a son, but I never felt he was disappointed that he had a daughter instead. One time when I was still small, I'd asked him if he wished I was a boy.

"Turns out, I'm more of a girl daddy than a boy daddy," he'd said with a smile as he hoisted me in his arms. *"God knows best, sweetheart, even if we don't always see it right away."*

The sounds of the country calmed me. The breeze rustled the leaves on the trees, birds chirped nearby, and I could hear the distant buzz of a bee or two.

I lay down on the grass and stared up at the sky. The clouds were breaking up, their white, cottony shapes drifting by as the sun moved slowly overhead.

I must have dozed off, because the next thing I knew, I opened my eyes to see Kade standing above me.

"A princess asleep in the forest?" He held up my shoes, dangling from his fingers. "Shall I call you Cinderella or Sleeping Beauty?"

I smiled, my heart leaping in my chest to see him, but I wasn't surprised that he was there. I'd known he'd find me, as he always did.

I sat up, running my fingers through my hair in case there were any leaves or grass in it. "I don't feel much like either at the moment," I said.

"That's all right," he said, sitting down next to me. "After all, I'm hardly Prince Charming." I noticed he hadn't even bothered to change his clothes before coming after me.

"How'd you find me?" I asked.

He cocked an eyebrow. "You seriously think I wouldn't have a way of tracking my brand-new car?"

I laughed lightly. Of course. Should've known. He was close enough that I could lean my head against his arm, strong and solid beneath my cheek.

"How'd it get to this point?" I asked after a while.

Kade's sigh said he knew exactly what I was talking about. "Who the hell knows?" he said quietly. "It just . . . did.

"I gave Blane the DVD Tish brought," he continued. "Thought we'd use it as blackmail rather than you going to the cops."

"Will that work?"

"James values his reputation more than he wants to put Blane away. I think it will."

"Can't we get more evidence for what he did to Kandi?" I asked.

He shrugged. "I added the phone records, that will help, but I don't know if we can do any more without dragging Blane into it again. If James will drop the charges, that may have to be enough."

That made me sad. Kandi wouldn't see justice for what had been done to her.

"Blane's not going to go see James himself, is he?"

Kade shook his head. "Nah. I'll go see Junior later." He turned and looked down at me. "I wanted to check on you first."

"I'm fine," I said.

His smile was without humor. "Of course you are."

Just then, I spied a basket sitting on his other side. "What's that?"

"I thought you'd be hungry, so Mona packed some food. She insisted on putting it in an honest-to-God basket."

"A picnic?" I said, delighted. I crawled to the basket and opened it. "It's been ages since I went on a picnic."

"You like eating in the dirt, bugs getting on your food, and grass sticking to your ass?"

I laughed, pulling out the containers Mona had packed. "Now who's the princess?" I teased.

Kade grinned at my joke, the genuine smile wiping away the hard edge in his eyes. I quickly glanced away, my heart hurting because he looked like that so rarely.

"So let's see," I said, removing lids. "Fried chicken, grapes, cheese, strawberries, and brownies. Yum." I reached farther into the basket and pulled out a cold bottle of white wine. "It seems she remembered everything," I said, my eyebrows climbing. Surely, Mona wasn't playing matchmaker?

"Except silverware," Kade said, peering into the basket.

"You don't need silverware with fried chicken," I said, rolling my eyes.

I handed Kade a corkscrew from the basket and he opened the wine. We ate, passing the wine back and forth like teenagers sneaking a bottle of booze. I teased him about his reluctance to get his fingers greasy with the chicken.

"You are such a baby," I said, grinning. I clambered over to him and held up a chicken leg. "Some things are meant to be a little messy."

His grin turned wicked. "I don't mind messy. In fact, I have a whole list of activities that are meant to be messy. Coincidentally, they all involve you. Clothing optional."

My pulse quickened and my smile faded.

I was really going to miss him.

Kade's grin melted away, too, as we stared into each other's eyes. I dropped the chicken leg, leaned forward, and kissed him.

I could taste the wine on his tongue and I buried my fingers in his silky hair. My body pressed against his and his arms crept around my waist to pull me closer.

When he lifted his head, we were both breathing hard. My hands moved to cup his face. The soft shadow on his jaw was a gentle abrasion against my lips as I pressed my mouth to his cheek. I brushed kisses along his jaw and down his neck, my fingers moving to the buttons of his shirt.

"What are you doing?"

"You have to ask?" I murmured against his skin, freeing more buttons.

His hands grabbed mine, stilling them.

"I heard you and Blane arguing," he said. "Is this about getting back at him?"

I couldn't blame him for asking. The way the three of us were tied so closely together, it was an obvious question.

"This has nothing to do with him," I said, looking into his eyes. "It's about us. You and me."

I reached behind me and slid down the zipper of my dress. Standing, I dragged it over my head and tossed it aside. The look on Kade's face made me glad I'd worn a lace bra and panty set that was the palest ivory, nearly matching my skin.

I straddled his legs and settled myself on his lap. His hands automatically moved to my back. I pressed my mouth to his once, twice, then looked into the ocean-blue of his eyes.

"Are you going to make me ask?"

My question seemed to break through Kade's stunned immobility, his mouth taking mine with a fevered desperation.

It was an easy decision, wanting Kade to make love to me. I loved him, though I couldn't tell him that. Blane and I were over, and there was no future for Kade and me. I had a brief moment of regret. That day I'd first seen him in the courthouse . . . Maybe if I'd said something then—

But what was past was past and I couldn't change it. What I could do was make a memory.

Sunlight filtered through the trees as the last of the clouds drifted away, bathing us in a warm glow. Kade's hair shone like a raven's wing in the light. His hand brushed my hair as he kissed me. I pushed his shirt off his shoulders and down his arms. His hands left me briefly while he shrugged off the garment, then were back and sliding up my back to unhook my bra.

I broke off our kiss, smiling softly at him as I tossed aside the scrap of lace. Our bodies pressed together and my breath caught at the feel of his skin against mine. Hearing Kade's groan, I guessed he felt the same.

He touched me so carefully, so reverently, as if I weren't real, that I might disappear at any moment. His head bent to my breast, the heat of his mouth closing over my nipple. The gentle suction of his mouth sent a direct current along the nerve tracing between my legs and I moaned.

Kade licked and stroked and caressed me as though we had an eternity together, until I felt as though my skin was on fire from the inside out. My panties were long gone, removed at some point by Kade, and now I lay on my back, his hand between my legs.

I clutched at his shoulders as he kissed me, the strokes of his fingers making my thighs tremble. His mouth moved to my breast again, his tongue doing things that made me whimper. His hand moved faster between my parted thighs, my knees bent and open shamelessly wide.

Kade's head lifted and I felt his eyes on me, but I couldn't stop the wave of intense pleasure that crashed over me and I cried out with the force of it.

When I opened my eyes, Kade was watching. Embarrassment struck and heat flooded my cheeks.

"You look like a goddess," he said roughly. "The sunlight on your skin, your breasts. Your hair like a river of gold against the grass. This"—his hand moved, a long finger still inside me—"hot and wet for me, like liquid silk."

I found his belt and loosened it, undoing the button and sliding the zipper down. Kade helped me get rid of his pants and my mouth ran dry at the sight of him, fully naked in the warm sunshine.

The breeze rustled the trees, cooling my overheated skin. I went willingly into Kade's arms, our mouths melding in mutual need.

He lay down on his back, pulling me astride him. "It's only fair my skin take the brunt of this, princess," he said. "My hide's thicker than yours."

He was hard and heavy in my hand, his eyes drifting closed at my touch, his brow creasing as though he struggled for control. I lifted myself up and sank down onto him, going slowly when I felt a twinge inside, letting my body relax to accommodate his length.

I memorized how Kade looked lying on the summer grass. His chest was carved muscle, the faint scars that marked his past nearly invisible in the sunshine. His eyes were so blue, they seemed to reflect the sky overhead, the look in them as he watched me something I knew I'd never forget.

Kade's hands settled on my hips, keeping me steady and I rose and fell on him. Sweat broke out on his forehead as I rose until he was nearly outside my body, then slowly sank back down. A groan left his lips and I smiled.

"I take that back," he said. "You're not a princess but an evil witch, bent on torturing me."

I repeated the move, my body molded to his size now so it wasn't uncomfortable. His fingers dug into my hips so hard, I knew I'd have marks later, not that I cared.

"I wouldn't want you to, you know"—I bent down to whisper in his ear—"forget." I was teasing but the look on Kade's face was serious when he replied.

"As if I could ever forget you."

I sat back up, pushing him in deeper. My hands splayed across his chest as I moved faster on him.

"That's right," he encouraged. "Don't stop, baby." His grip tightened, his hips thrusting up hard into me.

Something close to a scream ripped from my throat as my body convulsed around his. Kade thrust again, and again, then he shouted his climax even as mine kept going, spurred on by the spasms of his cock inside me.

Afterward, I was boneless, falling forward to rest on his chest, my head tucked into his neck. Both our bodies were slick with sweat and I was glad of the breeze. Kade's hand brushed my hair back from my face, his fingers trailing through the long strands to draw lazy patterns on my back.

"I told you I don't mind certain messes," Kade said.

I smiled. "So you did."

We lay like that for a while, our bodies still joined, our hearts beating in unison. If I could have, I'd have taken the moment and pressed it between the pages of my mind, to keep it with me, this fresh and pure, always. I committed to memory the smell of the balmy breeze as it drifted across us, the feel of Kade's body, warm and strong underneath mine, the sound of his heartbeat, the rise and fall of his chest as he breathed.

Finally, I rose, pressing a kiss to Kade's lips before I got to my feet. I dragged my dress over my head while Kade pulled on his pants. I held my hair out of the way while he slid the zipper up the back of my dress. He kissed my neck, his arms crossing over my stomach as he held me.

"I need to get to work," I said.

"Which reminds me, I have something for you."

I turned around and he handed me a key.

"What's this for?" I asked.

"Your apartment is done. That's a key to the new lock."

My stomach seemed to drop. I hadn't been prepared for this, though I should have been. Of course it was time to go home now. Time to remove myself from Blane's and Kade's lives. My hand fisted around the key, its edges biting into my palm.

"Thank you," I said, avoiding his eyes and hurriedly blinking back the tears in mine.

"You okay?" Kade asked.

"Fine," I said, grabbing my bra and shoes. I didn't see my panties anywhere. "Just need to get going. Tell Mona thanks for the picnic."

Kade grabbed me around the waist and kissed me until I was breathless. "I'll come by later," he murmured against my lips. "After I take care of James."

"Don't kill him," I said. "Promise me."

"I don't like making promises," he said.

"Promise me this," I persisted, looking into his eyes.

Kade's lips pressed in a thin line and he didn't look happy about it, but he nodded. I smiled softly and gave him one last tight squeeze.

"Did you bring my car?" I asked.

"That piece of shit you drive now?"

"That piece of shit is cheap and gets me where I'm going," I teased. We exchanged keys and Kade picked up the basket, walking me back to the car.

He opened the door for me, then pressed another kiss to my lips, as though now that he knew he could kiss me, he didn't want to stop.

"The fact that you're wearing nothing under that prim and proper dress is all kinds of hot," he whispered in my ear.

A shiver went through me and I laughed, reluctantly pushing him away. "I'll see you later, okay? Be careful."

Kade watched me get in the car and drive away—and if tears poured down my face as I glanced in the rearview mirror, there was no one to see.

≈

My apartment was as good as new—better, actually. New carpet, paint, and furniture. I assumed I had Kade to thank for the furniture.

I'd just gotten dressed in my work uniform when there was a knock at the door. I glanced through the peephole and recognized my landlord, Mike. About my height, he was stocky, but from too much beer rather than working out.

"Hi," I said when I opened the door. "The place looks great. Thanks for taking care of it."

"Yeah, well, fixing the damage from the accident wasn't cheap," he said, the belligerence in his tone taking me aback. He handed me an envelope.

"What's this?" I said as I opened it.

"The bill."

My jaw dropped. "But . . . this is for over three thousand dollars!"

"Like I said, the repairs weren't cheap."

"I don't have this kind of money," I protested.

He shrugged. "You've got two weeks to pay it or I sue you. Your choice." He turned away and jogged down the stairs.

Shit.

No time to think about that right now, though. I hurried into the bathroom to smear makeup over the *J* still visible on my chest. The deep V-neck shirt didn't cover it at all. Makeup at least made it less obvious.

I took a deep breath before going into The Drop. I really hoped no one besides Tish knew about what had happened with James, but I didn't hold out a lot of hope for that.

Scott was working as well, and he did a double take when he saw me. I gave him a tentative smile as I stowed my purse under the bar.

"Hey," he said, coming up next to me, "I heard about what happened, and I have to tell you how sorry I am for leaving you alone that night." He was so upset, so sincere, I had to give him a hug.

"It's okay," I said. "It wasn't your fault."

His hug was tighter than I expected. "I never should have left you alone," he said.

"Stop beating yourself up," I said. "I'm fine."

Scott pulled back, a wry smile on his lips. "I heard you kicked his ass. I had no idea you were such a badass."

"I'm full of surprises," I teased, glad that apparently Romeo hadn't shown the video to anyone.

"Kathleen!"

I turned around in time to see Tish right before she flung her arms around me.

"Oh my God, I'm so glad you're okay!" she said, choking up.

She was practically strangling me, but I held on to her, thankful for my friends.

"I'm fine," I assured her when she finally let go. Her eyes were wet with tears. "Don't cry or you'll ruin your makeup," I admonished her with a smile.

Tish sniffed and smiled a little back. "I hope it was okay to give the DVD to that guy," she said quietly so only I could hear. "Since he had your phone and you were staying with him, I figured you trusted him."

With my life, I wanted to say but didn't.

"Romeo was so upset," she continued. "I've never seen him like that before. I thought he was going to start crying right in front of me."

My eyes practically bugged out of my head. Romeo was an Italian throwback to 1985 who'd seen too many mafia movies. He thought gold necklaces were the ultimate badass accessory and always wore leather wristbands for the same reason. I didn't think he'd ever been in a fight, though, and he always reminded me of a dog that was all bark and no bite.

"Seriously?" I squeaked.

"Oh yeah, and he turned fire-engine red when he told me about it. He practically begged me to talk to you so he wouldn't have to."

Huh. Romeo cared. Who knew? But that begged another question.

"Tish," I said, "did anyone else watch the video?"

She shook her head. "Just Romeo. I, uh, wanted to . . . but didn't." She smiled ruefully. "Not to be morbidly curious or anything, but I was worried you wouldn't go to the cops."

"I'm not going to the cops," I said.

"What? Please tell me you're not serious." She looked stunned.

"Did Romeo tell you who that guy was?" I asked, lowering my voice.

Tish shook her head.

"It was the district attorney."

Her eyes widened in shock. "Are you fucking kidding me?"

"I wish I was," I replied. "Listen, we're still going to use it, I just won't be going to the cops." I gave her a meaningful look and she seemed to catch on.

"So long as the bastard pays for what he did," she said firmly.

"Does everybody know?" I asked.

"No, just Scott, me, and Jeff."

I supposed that was something. I really didn't want everyone looking at me with pity in their eyes.

Business was steady for the evening and I was glad because being busy kept my mind off of Blane and Kade. I didn't know what I was going to say to Kade when he arrived, I just knew it was going to hurt. I worried about what was going on with James, and prayed Kade would be safe and not do anything stupid.

So I was relieved when I saw him walk in the door a few minutes before closing. He'd changed into jeans, boots, and a black button-down shirt that he wore untucked. I knew that meant he had a gun wedged in his jeans at the small of his back.

Kade sat down at the bar and I drank him in. The top few buttons of his shirt had been left undone, the black fabric not quite as dark as his hair. His jaw was shadowed because he hadn't shaved since early this morning. His gaze caught mine and his lips curved into the smirk I knew so well.

I grabbed two beers and popped the lids, setting one in front of Kade.

"Well?" I asked, anxious to hear what had happened with James.

"He folded like the spineless piece of shit that he is," Kade said, lifting his bottle to clink against mine.

I let out a pent-up breath, relieved beyond words that it was over, then took a healthy swallow of beer. "So Blane's in the clear?"

Kade nodded. "Charges should be dropped by morning."

I was glad that something good had come out of that horrible encounter with James. Reporting him to the cops would have resulted in a messy, public battle that I may not have won. Now, at least Blane had benefited from James's stupidity.

Scott and I finished cleaning up and stocking the bar. Kade followed us out the door and Scott locked up. He gave me another hug before he left, despite Kade's glare when he did so.

"You good?" Scott asked me, eyeing Kade suspiciously.

"Yep. See you later."

Scott nodded and headed for his car. I was parked around back. Kade slotted our fingers together as we walked.

"I have a great idea," Kade said when we got to my car. He pulled me to him, wrapping his arms around me as he nuzzled my neck. "It might get messy, though."

The dark seduction in his voice made a shiver run through me and I squeezed my eyes shut. I had to be strong, no matter how much I wanted to go back on the decision I'd made.

"We can't," I said.

"Sure we can," Kade said, brushing his lips over my ear. "I have a maid."

"That's not what I mean," I said, flattening my hands on his chest and giving him a push. "I mean us, you and me."

He raised his head and our eyes locked. His brows were drawn in confusion.

"What are you talking about? Why not?"

"We can't be together, Kade," I said softly, my voice sad. "You know that."

Kade's Adam's apple bobbed up and down as he swallowed. "I'll keep working that other job, the business I started," he said. "I'll keep you safe. I swear it. You don't have to do this."

Each word was like a shaft of iron through my chest. A sob welled and tears stung my eyes, but I clung to my composure. I had to get through this.

I had to lie.

"It doesn't matter," I said. "I just don't feel the same way about you as you do for me." I paused and said the hardest sentence I'd ever uttered in my life. "I don't love you."

Kade looked stricken and I immediately wished I could take back the words I'd just said, the words that had hurt him.

"But today," he said. "You were happy. *We* were happy. We made love—"

"Sex, Kade," I interrupted. "We had sex, that's all."

"You're telling me it was just fucking for you?"

"You're beautiful," I said. "And you've saved me so many times—"

"So you were *thanking* me?"

"No, that's not—"

"Fuck you."

My throat closed at the cold fury on Kade's face and I pressed my lips tightly together, biting the inside of my cheek so I wouldn't cry. I'd known he'd hate me for this, but I still wasn't prepared for how much it tore me apart.

Kade moved closer and I instinctively stumbled back, the menace in his eyes making me afraid of him for the first time in a long time.

"So now you expect to go back to Blane?" he hissed.

"He's going to be governor," I forced out, "and his wife will be the First Lady of Indiana. Why wouldn't I go back to him?"

"Oh, I don't know—how about because you fucked his brother?" Kade spat. "Twice."

"Blane loves me," I said through lips gone numb. "He'll do whatever it takes to get me back."

My eyes were dry now. Forever leaving Kade with the idea that I was the type of person who'd do those things was an agonizing ache in my gut that made me want to double over.

Kade didn't speak for a moment, his blue eyes studying me. Then he snorted in contempt. "You fucking bitch."

And those were the last words Kade Dennon said to me before he got in his Mercedes and tore off down the empty street.

CHAPTER SEVENTEEN

I didn't sleep. I couldn't. Kade's face as I said those things to him kept replaying inside my head. I stared at the ceiling and tried to breathe. Every time I thought of what I'd done—realized that I'd never see Kade look at me the way he had just hours earlier when we'd made love—I felt as though I couldn't get enough air in my lungs.

I had yet to see if the play I'd made had worked.

I was up early, seeing no sense in lying in bed any longer when I wasn't sleeping, and was trying to get a cup of coffee down when the news came on. I watched, hoping Kade had been right last night about James.

Blane's face flashed on the screen and I grabbed the remote to turn up the volume.

"Charges have been dropped by the district attorney's office against gubernatorial candidate Blane Kirk in the murder of Kandi Miller. Though the DA's office denies any political motivations, Charlotte Page, attorney and spokesperson for Blane Kirk, says otherwise."

A video clip showed Charlotte speaking to a bevy of reporters. "It's obvious this was nothing but a smear campaign against my client as we're heading into the heavy campaign season," she said. "It's reprehensible that the death of

Miss Miller has been twisted and used for political backstabbing."

A knock sounded on my door and I muted the television as I got up to answer it, wondering who could be here this early and hoping it wasn't Mike.

When I saw who was outside my door, I thought maybe Mike would have been the lesser of two evils.

"Hey," I greeted Blane warily after I'd opened the door. "I just saw they dropped the charges against you. Congratulations."

"Kade was able to convince James that it was in his best interest to do so." He paused, then seemed to force out the next words. "Thank you, for letting us use that video rather than you bringing charges."

I shrugged. "Nothing would have happened to him if I'd charged him, I'm sure, and I would have been dragged through the mud."

"Speaking of Kade," Blane said, "he told me what you said last night, about us." He paused. "But I don't buy it, the whole First Lady of Indiana thing. Why would you say that to him? The Kathleen I know doesn't give a shit about my money or title."

I panicked, thinking fast. "Did you think none of this would change me?" I asked. "I'm not the same naive, stupid girl I used to be, Blane."

"I don't want to marry you if you don't love me," Blane said. "And I think you feel more for Kade than you're letting on."

"Maybe *you're* the one who's naive."

"You'd never hurt Kade like that. You'd never hurt *me* like that. This isn't you—"

416

"It is now," I interrupted. I was desperate to get him to leave before I broke. "Why does it have to be about love? Don't you think you owe me, Blane? Or should I go to the press and do a tell-all? Or maybe to the cops and tell them how William Gage *really* died."

Blane's lips thinned, his face like granite. "I don't respond well to threats, to me or my brother."

I was counting on that.

"Then go," I said, stepping back inside my apartment. "I never want to see either of you again." I jerked the ring off my finger and threw it at him. Blane caught it, clenching it tightly in his fist

"Kade means everything to me," he said. "You hurt him in a place he's never allowed anyone to touch."

I swallowed, the knife twisting hard inside my belly, and shut the door in his face.

My chest felt tight enough to strangle me. My knees gave out. I sank to the floor, sobs I couldn't control ripping me apart from the inside out. Destroying my own character in the eyes of the two men I loved most was the hardest thing I'd ever done, and it had taken a massive amount of will not to say anything to defend myself, not to explain.

But I'd done it. I'd managed to put Blane and Kade back together at the expense of losing both of them forever. They wouldn't even remember me fondly, but only with loathing and disgust.

Now I just had to learn to live without them. Again.

≈

I went by the bank later that day to deposit my paycheck and tips, which was when I got another shock. I'd completely forgotten that Kade had "paid" me for the job in Vegas, and despite my telling him not to pay me much, he'd deposited over two hundred thousand dollars in my bank account.

I sat in the drive-thru, staring in shock at the ATM receipt. Of course Kade would do that, though now he might regret it.

A car honked behind me and I hurriedly pulled forward. At least I had the money to pay Mike, which I did later, sticking the check in an envelope addressed to him.

Guilt ate at me, not only about the money but also for what I'd said. Telling Kade the truth hadn't been an option. He and Blane had been at each other's throats because of me, and choosing one over the other would do nothing but drive the wedge even deeper. They were both amazing men, and I kept telling myself how lucky I'd been to be a part of their lives, even if it had been temporary.

Which didn't help a whole lot when I lay alone in my bed at night.

~

The day of Clarice's wedding dawned sunny and beautiful. She was having an outdoor wedding at an old, historic mansion on the outskirts of Indy. The wedding wasn't until close to sunset, to beat the heat, but that didn't stop me from having a severe case of anxiety all day long.

I knew Blane would be there, he was Clarice's boss. And I didn't doubt that Kade might show up, too. He'd known

Clarice as Blane's secretary for a long time. She was one of the few who knew of their relation.

I studied myself in the mirror. The bridesmaid dress looked perfect. I'd decided to wear my hair half up and half down, the sides pulled up and back in a cascade of waves. The cut from James had healed, only a few marks remained on my neck from the collar, and I'd used makeup to disguise those. I wore four-inch sandals the same pale pink as the dress, and even my short legs looked long with the combination of the shoes and the short skirt.

I had a drink to calm my nerves, then headed to the wedding, both hoping I'd see them and terrified that I would.

The mansion was beautiful in the late afternoon light, dapples of sunshine breaking through the shade provided by the large oaks that grew by the house. I parked the car and took a deep breath before getting out.

The members of the wedding party were on the second floor, which is where the wedding planner sent me. When I stepped into the dressing room provided for the bride, my breath caught.

"Clarice! You look beautiful," I said, moving forward to give her a careful hug. I didn't want to mess her up. Her dress was a simple white gown with lace adorning the bodice. The same pale pink as the bridesmaids' dresses accented hers. Her face was wreathed with smiles.

"It turned out great, didn't it?" she asked.

"Absolutely!"

Clarice's sister was there as her maid of honor and we got to know each other while Clarice finished her makeup. The florist came by to give us each a bouquet.

"Have some champagne," Clarice said, handing me a flute filled with the bubbly golden liquid.

"Where are the kids?" I asked.

"My mom has them corralled downstairs, to keep them from messing up their clothes," Clarice said, taking a sip from her own flute. "So who'd you bring to the wedding?"

"No one," I said, draining my glass.

Clarice frowned and started to say something, but I gave her a tiny shake of my head. I really didn't want to talk about it, especially in front of her sister, who I didn't know. Clarice seemed to get the message, because she changed the subject.

The three of us laughed and chatted while we waited, finishing the champagne. I tried hard to just be happy for Clarice and not think about how, if Blane and I had not broken up, I'd have been getting married soon, too.

The wedding planner came up to get us when it was time for the processional, and I checked my makeup in the mirror before following Clarice out into the hallway and down the stairs. I was really glad of the champagne. My head was a little fuzzy and I could smile, both of which would make it much easier to walk down that aisle as a bridesmaid instead of a bride.

The sun was setting and the garden where the pristine white chairs were set up was aglow with strings of lamps. The air was thick with the scent of hydrangeas and roses. Music started playing—they'd hired a string quartet—and the soft strains of a violin meant it was time to begin.

The groomsman who was to escort me was a nice guy named Neal who taught with Jack. He said he had a girlfriend, which was a relief because I certainly didn't want to have to deal with anyone hitting on me tonight. A head taller than me, he was a nice-looking guy who coached the high school baseball team. I took his arm and he grinned at me, oblivious to my jangling nerves.

I pasted a smile on my face and walked down the aisle, trying not to look on the left side. Unfortunately, there were only about a hundred people in all and my eyes were drawn unerringly to Blane and Kade.

Both were dressed immaculately in suits and neither of them gave even a flicker of recognition when they saw me, their expressions blank. My smile turned brittle and I glanced away, but not before I noticed Charlotte sitting between them.

The surge of anger and jealousy I felt didn't surprise me in the slightest.

My hand resting on Neal's arm started to tremble. He caught my eye and gently laid his hand over mine, giving it a reassuring squeeze. He probably thought I was nervous. I clutched his sleeve and concentrated hard on putting one foot in front of the other. When Neal deposited me at the end of the aisle, I breathed a sigh of relief.

The rest of the processional and ceremony was a blur, as I tried not to feel the weight of their stares on me. Maybe they weren't staring, who knows, but it felt like they were. My entire body was as stiff as a wooden statue and I prayed for it to be over. Someone got up and began to sing a song after Clarice and Jack exchanged vows, and I squeezed my eyes shut in dismay.

My skin was warm, then cold, and I couldn't seem to feel my feet any longer. I stared at the candles directly in front of me, their flames gently flickering in the warm twilight breeze, and didn't even notice when everything went dark.

~

I opened my eyes and immediately realized what had happened. I'd passed out *in a wedding*, for crying out loud. This was a new low. Thank God that girl was still singing the song. Hopefully, I hadn't been out long.

"Are you all right?" Blane asked softly, crouching down next to me.

I nodded, mortified. "Help me up, please."

He helped me to my feet and I saw Clarice watching me with worry in her eyes. I smiled to let her know I was okay.

"Sit down for a moment," Blane said. He didn't wait for an answer, but led me to the front row where there were several empty chairs.

I sank into one and was surprised to see Blane take the seat next to me. He had my bouquet in his hand and set it on the chair beside him.

Blane looked at me, leaning close to whisper in my ear, "You're as white as a sheet, Kat." He took my hand, squeezing it in his much larger grip. "You haven't eaten today, have you."

I avoided answering the non-question, though why he cared, I had no idea. He should hate me now. "Shhh," I hushed him, keeping my eyes on the bride and groom. They looked so in love, gazing into each other's eyes. My own eyes stung and I refused to blink as the figures of Jack and Clarice gradually grew more and more blurry. The man holding my hand had *almost* been the one to stand at my side and pledge his life and love to me.

Finally, I had to blink, two tears spilling from my eyes to trace down my cheeks. I hurriedly brushed them away as Blane handed me a snowy-white handkerchief. I dabbed my wet eyes as he leaned toward me again.

"I know everything you told me and Kade was bullshit."

I jerked back, my panicked gaze flying to his, but there was no telling what he was thinking.

I looked away, handing his handkerchief back to him as the song ended. "Flowers, please," I requested, avoiding his eyes.

Blane wordlessly handed me the bouquet and I resumed my place next to Clarice's sister.

A few minutes later, I was again taking Neal's arm to walk back down the aisle. I didn't look at Blane, but Kade caught my eye. His face was empty of all expression as he looked at me, and I didn't know whether to be glad that he wasn't still angry or upset that apparently he felt nothing at all.

Everything inside me hurt and I gladly accepted the drink Neal got for me as we sat down at the head table.

"You okay?" he asked.

"Just embarrassed," I said with a shrug.

"Who was the guy?"

I hesitated. "My ex."

Neal's brows lifted. "For an ex, he sure flew up there fast enough," he said. "You'd barely hit the floor before he was there."

I finished my drink. "Mind if I have another?" I asked.

Neal grinned. "I'd be drinking if my ex was here, too," he said conspiratorially.

I didn't even mention that the man I was in love with was also there, and that he happened to be my ex's brother. Maybe if I had, Neal would have just brought me back the whole damn bottle. As it was, he kindly kept refilling my glass as we ate dinner, making me laugh with stories about the kids he taught. Afraid that Blane was watching, I managed to get a few bites down.

As the waiters cleared the dessert dishes away, Neal leaned over to me. "So who's the guy I wouldn't want to meet in a dark alley that's staring at us?" he teased. "He looks ready to kill me."

I glanced over to see Kade standing by the wall, drink in hand, watching me. The look on his face was one I knew well, and it sent a familiar shiver of foreboding through me. If Neal knew just how capable Kade was of killing him, he wouldn't joke about it.

"Another ex?" Neal asked.

I grimaced. "Sort of."

"No worries," he said. "I kind of like the idea of playing knight in shining armor." He grinned, a dimple appearing in his cheek.

I smiled my thanks. Neal was a nice guy and I thought his girlfriend was a lucky woman.

Clarice and Jack danced their first wedding song and I sipped champagne as I watched. She looked so happy. Halfway through, Clarice's youngest child, a five-year-old named Mary, ran out onto the dance floor with them. Jack hoisted her into his arms with a laugh, holding her with one arm while wrapping the other around Clarice. I was so glad for them. Jack was a good man who loved Clarice and her children.

When it was time for the members of the wedding party to dance, Neal took my hand and led me onto the floor. Clarice and Jack looked sweet and I watched them over Neal's shoulder.

The song ended, melding into another tune. I recognized the opening strains of "Someone to Watch Over Me" when I heard him.

"Mind if I cut in?"

Neal's face lost its friendliness as he looked at Blane. "That's up to the lady," he said stiffly.

"It's okay," I said with more confidence than I felt.

Neal reluctantly released me and I turned to face Blane. He took me in his arms and spun me away from Neal.

I'd imagined Blane and me dancing at our wedding, but it hadn't been quite like this. I felt as though I were made of glass, moments away from shattering completely.

"This is unnecessarily cruel, don't you think?" I asked stiffly.

"What are you talking about?"

I looked up at him, into his gray eyes, and the look on my face must have clued him in, because his hold on me gentled and his face softened.

"You don't think this is killing me, too?" he asked, pulling me closer.

"Then why?"

"Because I've been thinking," he said. "Replaying everything in my head, because it just doesn't make any sense."

I said nothing.

"What you said doesn't line up with what I know about you," he continued. "You never gave a damn about being a governor's wife. You'd never sell me out to the press, and you'd sooner take the fall for Kade than turn him in to the cops. The only thing you've ever really cared about . . . is the relationship between Kade and me."

My gaze dropped from his and I stared at his tie. Perfectly knotted, as always.

"Look at me, Kat," he ordered, and I had to obey. "You played us. Both of us. Because you knew how I'd react to Kade being hurt, threatened. Those things you said, they were all lies. You lied to both of us."

My heart sank. I should have known Blane would see through it. His job made him an expert at reading people, divining their motivations, and finding the facts underneath their lies. I knew I wouldn't be able to fool Blane any longer. I was surprised I ever had.

"That's not true—" I said weakly, but Blane jerked me closer, squeezing the air from my chest.

"Isn't it?" he snapped. "Tell me the truth, goddammit."

I couldn't take any more. "I told you once that I wasn't going to come between you two," I blurted. "So I did what I had to do. Now you and Kade can put the pieces back together and move on. I was only making things worse. You know that."

"Who the hell do you think you are to just decide to walk away?" he retorted. "Do we mean nothing to you?"

"You and Kade mean everything to me!" I protested. "I made the only choice I could. Please, Blane, just let it go. Let *me* go."

"You love me . . . but you're in love with Kade, too." It wasn't a question.

A wave of pure sadness enveloped me. "Does it matter?"

"Yes, it fucking matters!"

The stubborn set of Blane's jaw made my stomach clench in knots. He couldn't tell Kade. It would just hurt him and leave the two of them in a worse situation than before. Kade had never cared what happened between him and Blane if it meant he and I could be together. But I did. And even if Kade didn't realize it sometimes, he needed Blane more than he needed me.

"You can't tell Kade," I implored. "Promise me—"

"Can't tell me what?"

My eyes slipped closed in dismay at the sound of Kade's voice behind me.

Whatever communication they had must have been silent, because the next thing I knew, Blane let me go, spinning me around into Kade's arms.

Kade's piercing blue eyes seemed to devour me as we turned slowly on the dance floor. He was heartbreakingly lovely and I drank him in, my fingers itching to push back the lock of inky black hair that had fallen over his brow.

I wondered if Blane had shared his suspicions with Kade about the things I'd said, but that question was answered by the next words out of his mouth.

"So what is Blane not supposed to tell me? That you were just fucking him, too?" He put his lips by my ear and hissed, "So tell me, which brother's better in bed?"

Kade always knew just where to aim his barbs and I sucked in a breath as they hit their mark with painful accuracy. I had to keep going, no matter what Kade said to me.

"So it seems your sights tonight are set on the guy who's trying to get you drunk," Kade continued, his lips twisting in a sneer. "You should know he's a teacher. I hear they make shitty salaries."

"No one wants to go home alone from a wedding," I said, forcing a sweet smile.

A nerve pulsed in his cheek at that. "I can put in a good word for you, if you want." He leaned forward to hiss in my ear. "Mention that you're a damn good lay."

The ice that had consumed me when Blane and I broke up now threatened to encase me again, only this time it was to protect myself from Kade.

I looked up at him. "Why, thank you," I said with forced politeness. "And that wasn't even my best work."

Kade suddenly pulled me through the doorway into an empty hallway. He pushed me against the wall, imprisoning me there with his hold on my arms. "Tell me you didn't mean what you said the other night," he rasped. "Tell me we have something between us, that you feel something for me, something besides fucking gratitude."

The fury and agony in his eyes was nearly my undoing. But I couldn't let him have hope—there was no future for us. So I said the only thing I could think of that would guarantee his hatred.

"You're nothing but a criminal," I said. "A murderer and thief. Did you think I could forget that?"

Kade looked as though I'd hit him, his face etched with pain.

I pulled away, knowing I wouldn't be able to hold on to my composure for much longer, nor could I bring myself to hurt Kade any more than I already had. He reached for me, but I evaded his grasp, hurrying down the hall and up the stairs.

The ladies' room was on the third floor and I nearly collapsed with relief when I got there, tears already pouring down my face. The lounge area was blessedly empty. I sat in a chair and stared at the floor, not bothering to wipe my face.

I couldn't believe what I'd said to Kade, my conscience screaming at me to go find him, apologize, tell him I didn't mean a word of it. But then where would we be? Right back where we'd started, with me driving a wedge between Blane and Kade.

After a few minutes, I calmed down. I heard the hub-bub of people and realized Clarice and Jack had left for their honeymoon. I'd missed their departure, but I doubted she'd noticed, not with all the people there.

I got up with a sigh, went to the sink, and washed the streaked makeup off my face. No sense worrying about it. I could go home now.

The door opened as I was touching up my hair and Charlotte walked in. I stiffened, immediately on my guard.

"Nice wedding," she said.

"Yes," I agreed. I didn't offer anything else. I had nothing to say to her.

"Too bad yours was canceled," she said, coming up beside me and setting her purse on the counter. "It must have been hard to see Blane here."

Now she was just being a bitch. I smiled at her in the mirror. "Sweet of you to care."

"Oh, I don't," she said. "I was just making an observation." She smiled back and disappeared into a stall.

I spun around, determined to vent some of my frustration on her. My arm brushed her bag and sent it toppling to the floor, the contents spilling out.

"Shit," I muttered, crouching down to pick up her things. I righted her bag and dropped a lipstick in when something caught my eye. It was a stun gun, like the one I'd used on James a few months ago in that hotel room. I couldn't blame Charlotte for keeping something for protection handy on her. I should do the same.

Grabbing a few more things, I stuffed them into the bag, and something clicked inside my head. I froze, reaching in the bag to turn the stun gun so I could look at the prongs.

Kandi had been immobilized with a stun gun. The prongs on Charlotte's weapon appeared to be the same length and width apart as the red marks on Kandi's neck. We'd assumed a man had killed Kandi because of the rape, but a stun gun that stopped Kandi's struggles would have made it easy for another woman to smother her.

"What are you doing?"

I jumped up, startled, to see Charlotte staring at me, her eyes narrowing.

"N-nothing," I stammered, setting her purse back on the counter. "I accidentally spilled your purse—that's all. Sorry about that." I forced another fake-friendly smile, my heart racing inside my chest.

Charlotte said nothing, just studied me, and I held my breath. Then she smiled, too.

"Not a problem. Thanks for picking everything up."

"Sure." I turned away, relieved, and headed toward the door. I had to get out of there, find Blane, and tell him what I suspected. I glanced in the mirror at Charlotte. Our eyes caught. And that's when I realized . . . she knew.

I flung myself out the door just as Charlotte reached me. The restroom led into a wider seating area that led onto a terrace open to the warm summer evening. No one was there and I could hear the music drifting up from below.

Charlotte tackled me and we went down with a thud. I flipped over and backhanded her across the face, sending her sprawling. I clambered to my feet as she grabbed for her purse.

"Don't try it," she warned, blocking my path. She held the stun gun.

I swallowed hard. I was sure that if she touched me with the weapon, I wouldn't wake up.

"What are you doing, Charlotte?" I asked, backing away as she slowly advanced.

"You know what I did," she said. "I can't let you tell Blane."

"Why would you kill Kandi?"

"I didn't mean to kill her," Charlotte protested. "It just . . . happened."

"How do you just happen to kill somebody?" I retorted.

"I went over there that night because I knew she was sleeping with James," she said. "I also knew she'd been talking with Blane. The last thing he needed was to hook up with a woman who was already cheating on him. How do you think that would look in the press?"

"So, what, you decided to try and get her to stop? But ran into James there instead." I can imagine how that had gone over.

"James was never there," she scoffed. "I thought he was, that it was his semen I smeared on her. Turns out it was Blane's. I didn't know he'd already been screwing her.

"You know, this is all your fault," Charlotte continued, her eyes flashing with anger as she advanced. I continued my retreat, slowly backing away from her while eyeing the stun gun.

"How is that?" I asked.

"All I had to do was get you to go to Xtreme," Charlotte said. "Summers was supposed to take care of the rest."

My gaze flew to hers in shock. "Oh my God," I breathed. "You were the one who had me go there from the very beginning." When Charlotte had started at the firm, the first assignment she'd given me had been to check into the case of Julie Vale, a young woman who'd been attacked while working at Xtreme.

"If it hadn't been for Blane's obsession with you, you'd no doubt be dead by now and with no one the wiser."

"Who told you to do that?" I asked. "Who wanted me gone?"

"Unfortunately for Kandi," Charlotte continued, ignoring my question, "she knew a lot of people in Washington, and she never forgot a face. She recognized me, realized I interned with her father, and figured out I'd been sent to . . . help Blane."

"And did helping Blane include getting me out of the picture?"

Charlotte smiled. "Bingo."

My back pressed up against the terrace railing. I could go no farther.

"She threatened to out you to Blane," I guessed. "So you killed her, thinking James would take the fall—only Blane nearly did."

"Luckily, James is an idiot who can't see past besting Blane," she said. "And you turned out to be useful after all. Though I would have thought Blane would kick you to the curb himself after you slept with his brother. You are such a white-trash slut. I have no idea what he sees in you." She motioned behind me. "Get up on the railing."

"I don't think so," I said.

"You can either take a swan dive off here yourself, or I'll stun you and throw you over. Either way, you're so distraught over Blane dumping you—again—that you're going to end it all right here, right now, at Clarice's wedding."

"No one's dying tonight."

Charlotte whirled around to see Blane and Kade standing just inside the doorway. Kade had his gun in his hand. I breathed a sigh of relief.

"Put down the stun gun, Charlotte," Blane continued, taking a couple of steps toward her.

"How long have you been there?" Charlotte asked.

"Long enough," he said.

I'd spotted them but had kept Charlotte talking, needing her to confess everything so Blane could hear it.

Charlotte smiled. "You may have me, but you're not having her."

Before I could react, she spun around and shoved me backward over the railing. I heard Kade shout as my hands scrabbled for a hold on anything as I toppled over, catching hold of the bottom edge of the terrace.

A gunshot rang out and the stun gun Charlotte held fell to the ground with a clatter. A moment later, her body hit the floor.

I grunted from the effort of holding on, terror pounding through my veins. The muscles in my arms screamed in protest and I knew I couldn't hold on much longer.

Blane and Kade appeared over the railing. My eyes locked with Kade's.

"Help me. Please." My voice felt strangled inside my throat.

"As if you have to ask," he muttered, already climbing over the railing to stand on the ledge. Blane held tight to his belt as Kade reached down to me. His hands closed over my arms and he pulled me up, handing me to Blane before swinging his own leg back over the railing.

I was a heartbeat from hysteria, my close call one too many in the past few days. Blane enveloped my trembling body in his arms.

"It's okay now," he soothed me. "You're okay."

I sniffed. "Is she dead?" I asked, my voice muffled against his chest.

"No," Blane replied. "We just used her stun gun on her." He gave me another squeeze, then gently turned me around.

Kade stood a few feet away, his gaze hungrily taking me in. His lips were pressed tightly closed, his hands clenched in fists.

"I'll go call the police," Blane said. I didn't turn but heard him leave, his footsteps echoing as he crossed the hardwood floor.

Kade and I stood there in uncomfortable silence. Tears stung my eyes, but I determinedly held them back. Finally, I spoke.

"Thank you," I managed to get past my clogged throat. "For saving—"

"Shut up," he interrupted, but the words had no heat. Kade took two steps and I was suddenly in his arms, his mouth on mine.

We kissed as though it might be our last, the world disappearing around us. I could taste the salt of my tears on his tongue, feel the warm brush of his thumbs on my cheeks as he cradled my face in his hands. The strong beat of his heart reverberated inside my chest as I pressed against him, my arms slipping underneath his jacket and around his back. The warmth of his body soaked through the crisp linen of his shirt to my palms.

When we finally parted, he rested his forehead against mine, our breaths intermingling.

"I'm so, so sorry," I whispered through my tears. "Those things I said—I didn't mean them, didn't mean any of it."

Kade's thumbs caught my tears and wiped them away. "Shhh . . . I know. Don't cry, princess."

The sound of sirens in the distance made me step back and Kade shrugged out of his jacket, swinging it over my shoulders. His scent rose from the fabric and I clutched it to me.

Blane was with the cops when they entered the room, just as Charlotte started coming around. He glanced at us, his expression unfathomable, before turning to answer a question from a cop.

Kade curved an arm over my shoulders, holding me close as we gave our statements to the police. I watched as Charlotte was led away in handcuffs, her malevolent gaze piercing me as she passed.

We followed Blane outside. "We'll meet you at the house," Kade said to him, guiding me to his Mercedes.

"What about my car?" I asked.

"I don't give a shit about your car," Kade said, opening the passenger door. "You're coming with me. Get in."

I shut up and did as I was told, recognizing Kade's instinctual need to keep me close after what had happened. I felt the same.

The inside of the car was warm and I folded Kade's jacket, laying it on the backseat as he slid behind the wheel. He pulled off his tie and tossed it in the back along with his gun, undoing a few buttons on his shirt before starting the car.

The glow from the dash softly illuminated the carved features of his face as he drove. I kicked off my shoes before turning toward him and drawing my knees to my chest.

Kade's hand reached for mine, bringing it to his lips to brush a kiss across my knuckles before settling our hands on his thigh.

We had a lot to talk about, but it could wait. It was enough to just be together.

We pulled into Blane's driveway right behind his car. I got out with Kade, my eye catching something as Blane joined us.

"Who's here?" I asked, pointing to a man standing in the shadows of Blane's front door.

Blane frowned. "I have no idea."

We followed Blane up the walk until he paused, about ten feet from the man. I could see him more clearly now and recognized him.

"Geoff," Blane said. "What are you doing here at this hour?"

Kandi's father took a step closer into the light cast from the lamppost.

"Did you think you could just get away with it?" he asked, and only now did I see the gun in his hand. "You killed my daughter, Kirk."

Kade stiffened next to me and I remembered with a sinking sensation that his gun was still in the car.

"I didn't kill Kandi," Blane said, his voice calm and clear. "We found the person who killed her. She confessed just hours ago."

"I don't believe you," Geoff said. "I know the evidence. I know what they found, the DNA match." The bitter anger in his voice made me wince. "You strung Kandi along for years, treated her like she wasn't good enough for you. Then you killed her, defiled her, and are blackmailing James so he won't prosecute."

"I don't know what you're—"

"Don't lie to me!" Geoff shouted. I was terrified he was going to shoot right then and there, but he seemed to get a hold of himself. "James told me what you did. How there'd be no justice for my little girl unless I took matters into my own hands."

Kade slowly dropped his arm from my waist, his palm settling on my stomach and giving me a push backward until I was forced to take a step away from him.

"James put you up to this?" Blane asked.

"He didn't put me up to anything," Geoff said. "Sometimes it's just what a man has to do. What a *father* has to do. I won't let you kill my daughter and get away with it."

437

"You don't want to do this," Blane said, sounding a lot calmer than I was feeling. "Put down the gun. Let's go inside and talk. I'll explain—"

"Always the smooth talker, aren't you, Kirk?" Geoff cut in. "That won't save you this time."

I knew what Geoff was going to do a split second before he did.

Kade did, too.

He shoved me hard to the side, then stepped in front of Blane just as Geoff pulled the trigger.

CHAPTER EIGHTEEN

A scream tore from my throat as the impact of the bullet sent Kade falling into Blane. Geoff shot again and Kade's body jerked. Blane pulled out his gun even as he supported Kade, firing back at Geoff in a rapid hail of bullets. Geoff fell and didn't move. Blane gently lowered Kade to the ground.

I dropped to my knees next to Kade. Blane ripped Kade's shirt open and the air froze in my lungs.

There were two holes in Kade's chest, both oozing blood.

"Fuck, that hurts," Kade gasped.

"Why the hell would you do that?" Blane cried, furious.

"Seemed like a good idea at the time," Kade groaned, his eyes squeezing shut.

"Don't talk," Blane said. "I think your lung got hit."

"Then stop asking me questions."

"Blane! Kade!"

I turned to see Mona and Gerard running toward us. Mona skidded to a stop, her hand covering her mouth at the sight of Kade.

"Call nine-one-one," Blane ordered. Gerard turned and ran to do his bidding.

"Help me," Blane said, grabbing my hand. "Cover this wound here."

My hands shook, but I did as he said. Kade's warm blood seeped between my fingers. I couldn't see properly, tears spilling from my eyes, but I didn't move. Blane shrugged out of his jacket and tore a sleeve off, pressing it against the other wound in the middle of Kade's chest that was bleeding even more profusely.

"Kade, can you hear me?" he said loudly. "Stay with me, brother."

Kade's eyes flickered open. "This is why I'm not the hero," he managed. "Getting shot hurts like a sonofabitch."

"If I'd known you wanted to play target practice, I could've shot you myself," Blane said, his voice thick.

"You've got shitty aim."

Kade's hand lifted slightly, as though searching, and Blane grasped it, holding him fast.

Sirens screamed in the distance. Thank God. They were on their way. My hands were slick with Kade's blood as I struggled to keep any semblance of composure and not fall into hysterics. I didn't want to break down, not yet, though tears poured down my face. I swallowed down a sob.

"Don't cry, princess," Kade murmured, his gaze swinging to me. He blinked, his eyes slow to reopen. Blood had begun to seep from his nose and mouth as he breathed, a bubbly red-tinted foam. The sight of it sent my panic ratcheting even higher.

"If you die, I'll never forgive you," I managed to say through my tears.

The barest hint of a smile curved his lips. His breathing was becoming more labored now and I prayed for the ambulance to hurry.

"And you still have to take me to see Britney," I said quickly. "I can't go by myself."

Kade tried to speak, but the words were too faint for me to hear. He pulled at Blane's hand until he leaned over, placing his ear next to Kade's mouth. I couldn't hear what Kade said, but Blane pulled back and looked Kade in the eye.

"I promise."

The solemn sincerity in Blane's voice terrified me more than all the blood. It had the finality of a vow made to a dying man.

"No, Kade, please!" I cried as his eyes slipped closed. His grip on Blane's hand went lax just as the ambulance screeched to a halt in the driveway.

I was vaguely aware of men around me, crouching down next to me.

"You can move aside, ma'am. We'll take it from here."

I shook my head. I couldn't move my hands. Kade would die if I did. Blane had said to keep them on the wound.

"It's okay, Kat. Let them do their job." Blane wrapped his arms around me, lifting me up bodily. I struggled in his grip.

"No! He'll die!" I sobbed.

The men were moving fast, doing something to Kade that I couldn't see. A stretcher sat next to him, but they hadn't yet moved to put him on it. Kade was motionless on the ground.

Blane turned me toward him, away from the scene.

"Don't watch," he said in my ear. He held me tight, one hand pressed against my head, keeping me from turning.

I clung to him, sobs racking me. I tried to breathe, tried to pull it together, but all I could think about was that Kade might die and I hadn't told him the truth. I hadn't told him I loved him.

"Let's go," Blane said, loosening his grip on me. "They're taking him." He took my hand and we hurried to his car, speeding down the road in the wake of the ambulance. The sirens cleared the path and the Jaguar kept pace, so we pulled into the hospital nearly right behind them.

Blane filled out paperwork for Kade while I paced the hallway. Dried blood still stained my hands, smears marring the pink of my dress, but I didn't care. Somewhere close by, Kade was fighting for his life.

Mona and Gerard came hurrying into the waiting room, both of them wrapping me in a tight hug. We didn't talk. We didn't have to.

Blane finished the forms and sat, knees spread with his head in his hands. I continued to pace, watching the clock as the minutes crawled by. No one spoke.

"Mr. Kirk?"

Blane looked up, then jumped to his feet as the doctor approached.

"Mr. Dennon's being moved to the OR for surgery," he said. "One of the bullets punctured his lung, the other is lodged in his chest, possibly nicked an organ or two. There's been significant internal bleeding."

"Is he going to be okay?" Blane asked.

"Mr. Dennon's wounds are serious, I'm not going to sugarcoat it. But we won't know more until after surgery.

I'll do my best and we'll keep you posted." He disappeared down the hall.

Blane's eyes filled and he let out a choked gasp, as though he'd been holding his breath. I went to him, sliding my arms around his waist and laying my head on his chest. He buried his face in my hair and crushed me to him.

We held on to each other, and I wasn't sure who was holding up who. My tears dampened his shirt while my neck grew wet with his.

When we finally parted, my hand stayed in Blane's as he walked us to the bathrooms. I went into the ladies' room and washed the blood from my hands, also splashing water on my face. There was nothing I could do about the dress. Every time I caught sight of the bloodstains—Kade's blood—I felt like I was going to lose it all over again.

A cop came by, taking statements from both Blane and me about the shooting. I couldn't concentrate, my mind preoccupied with worry for Kade.

Blane and I sat side by side in the waiting room with Mona and Gerard. Gerard had gotten coffee for us, but I couldn't drink it.

More people entered the waiting room and I glanced up.

"Chance!" I leapt to my feet just as he reached me, throwing my arms around his neck. His presence triggered a fresh round of tears.

He hugged me, brushing his lips across my forehead. When I eventually pulled away from him, I saw that Lucy had come, too.

"Thank you so much for coming," I said, giving her a tight hug. "Where's Billy?"

"A friend of mine is watching him," she said.

"How'd you know?" I asked Chance.

"I'm part of the IMPD now," he said. "I heard about the shooting and came as quick as I could." He paused before adding, "You know I'm not a fan of Dennon's, but I know how you feel about him, so I came for you."

"Thank you," I said. "I appreciate it."

Lucy and Chance took up the vigil along with the rest of us. He wore a button-down shirt over a T-shirt and shrugged off the former, giving it to me to wear over my bloodstained dress.

Time crawled by and I wanted to scream with frustration. I couldn't sit and began pacing again. What if Kade didn't pull through? What if he died, right there on that operating table? Tears occasionally slipped down my cheeks, but I was too numb to notice.

When the doctor finally stepped back into the room, I was both relieved and terrified of what he might say.

"Mr. Dennon came through the surgery all right," he said. "We had a little trouble getting the bullet out of his lung, but barring any further difficulties, he should recover. The second bullet fragmented, but we were able to get it all. He's a lucky man."

My knees shook and I would have collapsed if Chance had not jumped up and put his arm around me.

"Can we see him?" Blane asked.

The surgeon nodded. "He's in the Surgical ICU and he's sedated, but you should be able to peek in on him shortly."

Chance led me to a chair and I sank into it. He sat next to me, supporting me with an arm around my back.

Blane hugged Mona and Gerard before returning to the seat next to me. His hand found mine as we shared a look of deep relief.

Someone else caught my eye and I glanced up, my breath catching in my throat.

Senator Keaston walked into the waiting room, his gaze scanning the occupants before landing on Blane and me. Blane got to his feet.

I remembered what Kade had said, that Keaston had been the one behind the attempt to get Blane to throw a trial—and that he had hired men to kill us. Kandi's father had been a close friend of Keaston's. Was he the one who had Charlotte send me to Xtreme? Would he have done that if Keaston had asked him to?

"I heard about Kade," Keaston said gravely to Blane. "How is he?"

"He's going to make it," Blane answered.

Keaston gave a sigh of relief that I didn't buy for a second.

"And I heard the charges against you were dropped," he said quietly.

Blane nodded. "The real killer confessed earlier tonight." Blane's gaze was shrewd as he spoke, eyeing Keaston.

"Well, that's convenient," Keaston said with some surprise.

"Yes, it is. And I have Kathleen to thank for both those events."

Keaston locked eyes with me for the first time. His expression was a polite one of bare recognition. He gave me a curt nod before turning back to Blane.

"Call me with news of Kade," he said, reaching out to give Blane a firm handshake.

"Will do."

And then he was gone as quickly as he had come.

We all sat in silence for a moment, then Lucy spoke.

"I can't believe you would still speak to that man after what he did," she hissed, standing and confronting Blane.

"What?" Blane asked in confusion.

"I know politics is a dirty business and the men in it have notoriously short memories," she spat, "but Kathleen was your *fiancée*, for God's sake!"

I rose and got in between them. "Lucy, what are you talking about?"

Lucy tore her gaze from Blane and turned to me, then blanched. "Of course," she breathed, "you don't remember, do you?"

"Remember what?" I said, a sense of foreboding creeping over me.

Lucy took a deep breath. "On the boat," she said, "Matt told us who paid him to take you, that it wasn't just an accident, that he was supposed to make you disappear. For good." She looked up at Blane. "It was Keaston."

Blane didn't speak, didn't move, didn't even blink. "What did you say?" he said at last in a hoarse whisper.

"Keaston used Summers to get Kathleen," Lucy repeated.

Chance was standing now, too. "Are you kidding me?" he asked Lucy, then turned to Blane. "Your own uncle tried to have Kathleen killed?"

"That's not all," I said quietly.

Blane's head whipped around. "What do you mean?"

I looked up at him. "The photos," I said. "The photos he gave you. Kade saw them the other day, after you were arrested. He realized something I'd overlooked. No one knew where we were going to be when those pictures were taken. The only guy who knew was the same one who betrayed us." I paused. "Keaston was the man who tried to have Kade killed in Denver."

Blane went pale. He turned away without a word, bracing his hands on his hips. I knew he was trying to get control, trying to come to grips with the reality of who and what his uncle truly was.

Chance turned to me. "We'll go now," he said. "I'm glad Dennon's going to be okay." He hugged me.

"Thanks for coming," I said, embracing Lucy, too.

"I'm sorry," she said in an undertone. "This probably wasn't the best time to tell him that. I just saw that guy . . ."

"It's okay," I assured her. "He needs to know."

Mona and Gerard soon left as well. "Call me if anything changes," she told Blane. "I'll come back in the morning so you can go rest."

The waiting room was empty except for Blane and me, and I watched the clock, anxious to see for myself that Kade was all right. Blane sat down next to me.

"I had no idea," he said, pushing a hand through his hair. "I can't—" He broke off, bending to rest his elbows on his knees and pressing his fingers hard against his eyes. After a moment, he took a deep breath and sat up again. "He was like a father to me," he said. "I just don't understand why he'd go to such lengths to hurt the people I love." His eyes were vividly green and too bright.

I reached to take his hand. "I'm sorry," I said. Blane had such little faith in people as it was, but to have this kind of revelation about his uncle had to be devastating.

We sat in silence until a nurse stepped into the room.

"You can come see him now," she said to Blane.

We both stood and she looked at me. "I'm sorry, immediate family members only. Are you immediate family?"

"She is." Blane's statement was unequivocal.

The nurse looked skeptical, but she didn't pursue it and instead led us down the hall to the ICU. "He's still sedated," she explained. "But you can go in for a short while."

I held tight to Blane as we walked into the partitioned space, the nurse pulling the curtain closed behind us for a little privacy. Tears sprang to my eyes instantly when I saw him.

Kade was hooked up to several machines, one of which I recognized as a ventilator. An IV dripped fluid into his arm and there was a chest tube attached to him. Dried blood still flecked the skin around the gauze covering his wounds.

I leaned into Blane and he supported my weight as we stood next to the bed. Kade was sickly pale, and the sound of the ventilator pushing air into his lungs was something I knew I'd hear in my nightmares. It shook me, seeing him so vulnerable. He always seemed larger than life, as if nothing could touch him.

"Why did he do that?" Blane said, his voice thick. "Why did he have to jump in front of me? I'm supposed to protect him, not the other way around."

"He loves you," I answered. "It's no more complicated than that."

"I'd do anything for him," Blane said. "Even lose you."

I looked up at him and he seemed to read the confusion on my face.

"If you love him, want to be with him, I won't stand in the way."

I didn't know what to say. I looked back at Kade lying so very still. I couldn't think about it now. Getting through the next five minutes, the next hour, seemed insurmountable—much less anything longer than that.

Blane and I stayed in that spot for a long time, keeping our silent vigil at Kade's bedside.

ABOUT THE AUTHOR

Tiffany Snow has been reading romance novels since she was too young to read romance novels. After fifteen years working in the Information Technology field, Tiffany now works her dream job of writing full time.

Tiffany makes her home in the Midwest with her husband and two daughters. She can be reached at tiffany@tiffanyasnow. com. Visit her on her website, www.Tiffany-Snow.com, to keep up with the latest in *The Kathleen Turner Series*.

Turn the page for a sneak peek at *Point of No Return*.

Point of No Return

I hated hospitals.

Sickness and death. Grief and worry. The endless antiseptic corridors of a hospital were filled with them.

Which was why I was standing in the maternity ward, gazing at the newborn babies through the window.

It was the middle of the night or really early in the morning, depending on your point of view. Since I hadn't gone to sleep yet, I guessed it felt more like the former than the latter.

It had been only a bit over twenty-four hours since my world had nearly ended.

Since Kade had almost died.

Kade Dennon. Ex-FBI agent, assassin-for-hire, cyber hacker with no fear of ever getting caught. He'd seemed larger than life. Unstoppable. Then he'd stepped into the path of a bullet to save his brother.

A few inches higher and it would have been the last thing he did.

The babies swam in my vision and I gasped for air, just then realizing I'd been holding my breath. My nails cut into my palms as I clenched my hands into fists. Holding myself together was getting harder and harder the longer Kade was unconscious.

I'd left the hospital earlier today for a few short hours. Mona had made me. A surrogate mother to Kade, she'd taken me under her wing as well, making me go home to change and eat something.

I hadn't wanted to take off the bloodstained bridesmaid's dress I'd worn. It was stained with Kade's blood, and I felt an irrational fear that taking it off would make it seem as though I'd forgotten about him.

But I forced myself to put the dress carefully aside, shower, and pull on fresh clothes. I wasn't sure what—I just grabbed the first thing I touched when I opened my closet. Eating was out of the question. If I'd had any food in my fridge, which I didn't, there was no way I could've eaten it. My stomach was cramped in knots, and the thought of trying to get something down made me nauseous. All that mattered was getting back to the hospital. Back to Kade.

It was surreal, the people I passed as I drove back to the hospital. Everyone acted as though life were normal. My world had fallen apart, but the sun still shone like it was any other day.

Mona frowned when she saw me return so quickly. I gave her a wan smile and she sighed.

"He's going to be okay," she tried to reassure me. "The doctor said he'll recover. Trust them, Kathleen."

That's me. Kathleen Turner. It had nearly been Kathleen Kirk until my fiancé, Blane Kirk, had broken our engagement. He'd accused me of having an affair with his brother. His brother being Kade.

Blane Kirk was a Navy SEAL turned attorney and politician. He was an expert at reading people, and it was nearly impossible to lie to him. Blane's accusation and our subsequent breakup had broken my heart. He'd been wrong about Kade and me. We hadn't been having an affair . . . then.

Now, I wasn't so sure.

Kade had swept back into my life months after Blane and I broke up. He'd taken me to Las Vegas, shown me the town, partied with me Vegas-style. Then he'd made love to me. Told me he loved me. I hadn't realized until later that I was in love with him, too.

Now he lay unconscious in a hospital bed with two gunshot wounds, and he had no idea how I felt. Because I hadn't told him. Afraid it would only drive Blane and Kade further apart, I'd pretended to feel nothing, to want Blane only for his money and Kade for sex, practically daring them to hate me.

I'd prayed it would be enough to repair their relationship, broken because of me, and I had nearly succeeded. If Blane had been less intuitive, if both of them hadn't known me as well as they had, it might've worked. But they'd seen through my lies, my desperate gamble to remove myself from their lives.

I didn't know where things stood now, not really. A grief-stricken father had precluded any discussion, and Kade had stepped in front of a bullet intended for Blane, sacrificing himself for his brother without a second's hesitation.

Yes, they said Kade would recover, that he had made it through surgery okay, but that didn't relieve the guilt gnawing at me for how I'd treated him. And until he opened his eyes—until I could see for myself that he was still the Kade I knew—I could think of nothing else, *do* nothing else.

Blane and I sat through the day at Kade's bedside. We watched as they removed the ventilator, our hands tightly connected as we saw Kade's chest rise and fall on its own. We took turns running home, at Mona's behest, to change. Occasionally, one of us would take a break, leaving the other to keep vigil for a short time.

Which was how I found myself standing in the maternity ward staring at the babies.

One of them, a little boy by the pale blue cap on his head, was fussing. Somehow he'd gotten his arms free from the blanket swaddling him, and his tiny hands were curled into fists as he cried.

A nurse walked over to him, scooping him up in her arms and settling him on her shoulder. She wandered closer to the glass as she shushed him. When she turned her back, I could see he'd quieted. He was wide awake, his blue eyes open and taking in the world around him. He was beautiful, perfect, and it seemed as though our gazes met through the glass as he began sucking on his fist.

Pulling myself from my reverie, I glanced at my watch, surprised to see I'd been gone from Kade's room longer than I'd intended. Blane was probably wondering where I was.

Hurrying back, I was both relieved and disappointed to see that Kade was still unconscious They wanted him to wake up on his own and I prayed that would be soon. The pain medication they had him on was heavy-duty.

Blane had fallen asleep in the corner armchair while I'd been gone, but even in sleep, his face was creased with lines of worry.

I sank into the plastic chair drawn up next to Kade's bed. His lax hand rested on top of the sheet covering him. I curled my palm into his, carefully scrutinizing his face for any reaction.

His hair was inky-black against the stark white pillow, the silky strands mussed. Reaching forward, I pushed back a lock that had fallen across his forehead. My fingers brushed his cheek, the stubble from two days' growth softly abrading my skin. I ached for his eyes to open, to hear his voice, for his lips to curve into that knowing smirk I knew so well—the kind that said he knew exactly what you were thinking. And it seemed he had always known what I was thinking, had always been looking out for me, from the moment we'd first met.

Carefully, I rested my head on Kade's arm, savoring the feel of his warm skin against my cheek. I closed my eyes and breathed in. Kade's scent was faint, the smell of medicine and antiseptic masking him. I let out a long sigh. I wished I could sleep—I was so tired—but I knew I wouldn't.

Kade's fingers twitched slightly in mine and I sat up with a start, my gaze flying to his face. His eyes were open, his gaze steady.

Emotion clogged my throat and I couldn't speak, my face crumpling into tears.

Kade's hand slowly lifted to my face. I covered his hand with mine, tipping my head into his palm cradling my cheek.

"Don't cry," he whispered. The ventilator had been rough on his throat and his voice was a low rasp.

Kade had always hated to see me cry, so I tried valiantly to stop. Turning my head, I pressed my lips to his palm, then forced a watery smile.

He opened his mouth again, but I pressed a finger to his lips. "Shhh. Don't try to talk."

He ignored me. Big surprise.

"C'mere," he said, the word barely audible. He tugged on my hand.

"I can't," I said, wondering if the pain medicine was making him a little loopy. "I'll hurt you."

"Bullshit. Need you."

Kade tugged again and this time tried to sit up, too. A grimace crossed his face. Alarmed, I put my hand on his shoulder to still him.

"Okay, okay," I said quietly. "Just lay down, all right?"

He lay back down on the bed with a sigh. I kicked off my flip-flops and climbed into the bed, carefully arranging myself on my side and trying not to disturb any of the equipment still hooked up to him. Kade wrapped one arm over my shoulders and pulled me closer.

It was him. He was alive, and judging by how he was already bossing me around, he was the same Kade. And despite everything I'd said—all those things that had hurt him—he still wanted me. Everything was going to be okay. Somehow.

Kade's lips pressed against my forehead. I looked up at him. His blue eyes were clear as he studied me.

"I love you," I whispered. "I'm sorry that I didn't tell you before. But I do. I love you."

Kade didn't react for a moment, and I was suddenly afraid that he hadn't understood—that the pain medication and being unconscious for so long had made him too groggy. But then he spoke, his words a low rasp in my ear.

"You would have to tell me that when I'm laid up in the fucking hospital," he said.

I huffed an unexpected laugh, and his soft smile made my heart feel lighter than it had in weeks. My whole body relaxed into him and my eyelids drooped. God, I was so tired . . .

～

Blane Kirk watched the scene from the shadows in the corner. He'd woken when Kat had settled into the chair by Kade, but had remained quiet. His heart had leapt when he saw Kade's eyes open, relief flooding him. Kade was okay, was going to recover.

Blane couldn't have lived with himself if his kid brother had died while saving his life.

The whispered words that Kat and Kade spoke had traveled across the room to Blane. Hearing Kat tell Kade she loved him had been like a hot knife sliding between Blane's ribs, even though he'd known for far longer than she had.

Where did the three of them go from here? Blane couldn't say. All he knew was that he loved Kade and Kathleen beyond anyone and anything else—and he'd do whatever he had to in order to see them both happy. If that cost him Kat forever, so be it, but he wasn't going to give up until he heard it from her own mouth that they were over. She loved Kade, but she loved him, too, which meant he still had a chance.

Blane could tell that Kat had fallen asleep, her body relaxed as she lay tucked next to Kade. Fiddling with the bed controls, Kade eased the bed up slightly so they weren't lying flat, but Kat didn't stir. Blane was glad she was asleep.

She'd been awake for nearly forty-eight hours straight, almost dead on her feet from sheer exhaustion. Dark circles marred the delicate skin underneath her eyes, and her face was drawn and pale. The only thing Blane had seen her consume was coffee.

Not once had she blamed him, or had even hinted that she knew the whole reason Kade had nearly died was because of him. But then again, it wasn't in her character to think that way. If only Blane had realized that months ago. So many what-ifs . . .

What if Blane hadn't been so jealous of what he'd so clearly seen between Kade and Kathleen . . . If he hadn't listened to his uncle . . . If he had believed Kat instead of Robert . . . If he hadn't given in to old habits, using Kandi in a way that left him feeling ashamed now . . . If he hadn't been so angry that night, the night after he'd realized Kade and Kat were in Vegas together, sleeping together . . .

The *what-if*s could paralyze him with regret.

Kade was stroking Kat's hair now, his fingers combing slowly through the long, strawberry-blonde locks. His expression was rapt as he gazed down at her, and if Blane had had any doubts as to the depth of Kade's feelings for Kat, they would have been washed away in that single, unguarded moment.

Suddenly, Blane felt like an intruder. The naked adoration on his brother's face was something private. Kade wouldn't appreciate that Blane was spying on them, even if it was unintentional.

Blane closed his eyes, then gave a big sigh and yawn. He stretched before opening his eyes again. As he'd expected,

Kade's expression had shuttered, his gaze now on Blane rather than Kat.

Rising from the chair, Blane rubbed an imaginary crick in his neck as he walked toward the bed. It didn't escape his notice that Kade seemed to instinctively draw Kat closer, as if to claim her as his.

"You're awake," he said softly, so as to not disturb Kat. "How're you feeling?"

"Like I got shot," Kade deadpanned.

"That tends to happens when you get in the way of bullets."

Kade's lips twitched.

"Thought I was going to have to wake your ass up myself," Blane said. "She wasn't going to make it much longer if you didn't." He nodded toward Kat, who slept on, oblivious to the conversation taking place.

Kade glanced back down at her, his face softening.

"She's one tough chick," he softly said, brushing his knuckles gently down her cheek.

"In some ways," Blane agreed "In some ways not."

Kade looked back to Blane, who met his gaze.

"Are we going to do this now, brother?" Kade asked, his voice deceptively smooth, though Blane could see a flicker of fear in his eyes. Kade's hold tightened on Kathleen, as though he was afraid that Blane would take her from him.

"You mean talk about the elephant in the room?" Blane said dryly, cocking an eyebrow.

"She'd get pretty pissed off if she heard you call her an elephant."

Blane grinned. Kade never failed to amuse him, even when they were talking about something so serious. For a moment he just reveled in the knowledge that Kade was alive, was going to be fine. Thank God.

Blane couldn't help reaching out, his fingers lightly grasping Kat's lax hand. She didn't stir. Kade's eyes narrowed, but he didn't protest Blane's touch. It seemed as though each of them wanted to mark her as his.

"She told me she loves you," Blane admitted, "*and* me. What that means, I have no idea. But we can talk about that later. For now I just want you to get better."

Kade's grip on Kathleen loosened, just a fraction.

Blane pretended not to notice, though his gut twisted. Too many mistakes and, eventually, you couldn't go back. He vowed not to make any more.

Blane glanced at his watch. "It's late, and I'm beat," he said with forced nonchalance. "Since you've reasserted your presence among the living and coherent, I'm going home to get some shut-eye. I'll be back in the morning."

"Sounds good," Kade said, resting his head against the pillow. His eyes slipped closed.

Blane turned away and headed for the door. Pulling it open, he glanced back one more time.

The dim lights cast a faded, golden glow over Kade and Kat. He'd resumed stroking her hair and she still hadn't moved.

"Kade," Blane said.

He glanced up.

"Thank you. For saving my life."

The ghost of a smile flitted across Kade's lips. "The least I could do," he said. "You saved mine first, remember?"

Blane shook his head sadly. "No, I didn't. Not really." He paused. "But *she* may have." His gaze fell on Kat as Kade's brow furrowed, then he turned and left, quietly closing the door behind him.

～

Sunlight streaming in through the window woke me in the morning. I squinted, and it took a moment for my sleep-fogged brain to realize where I was and who I was with.

Kade.

He'd finally regained consciousness last night, and now I lay curled into him, his arm slung over my shoulders and mine draped low across his abdomen. The heart monitor beat a quiet, reassuring rhythm while the IV hooked to Kade's left arm steadily dripped its fluid down the plastic tubing.

His eyes were closed, the evenness of his breathing signaling that he was sound asleep. I dearly wanted to wake him, see his eyes and hear his voice again, but I resisted the temptation. I knew he needed to rest.

Being careful not to disturb him, I eased out of the bed and slipped on my shoes. After using the bathroom and splashing water on my face, I felt more awake. The few hours of sleep I'd gotten by Kade's side was more than I'd had in days, though I was still tired. I felt like I could lie down and sleep for a week.

As I came out of the bathroom I suddenly realized . . . Blane wasn't there.

Maybe he'd gone downstairs for coffee or something? I prayed I was right, but knew it was more likely that he'd woken, seen me in bed with Kade, and left.

I hadn't meant to fall asleep. I'd just been so tired and so relieved to speak to Kade, but now I regretted climbing into bed with him. I didn't want to dwell on what Blane must be thinking.

The thought of Blane and Kade still being at odds, even after everything that had happened, had my stomach churning with nausea. Grabbing my purse, I decided to go get some coffee. Everything would look better once I had some caffeine in my system. Even hospital coffee was better than nothing.

Unfortunately, I didn't spot Blane in the cafeteria as I'd hoped I would. My heart sank. I must have been right in guessing that he'd left. Was he angry with me? He couldn't be angry at Kade, not after what he'd done to save Blane. I'd much rather have him mad at me, though I didn't want to hurt either Blane or Kade—I loved them both too much for that.

I sipped my coffee, loaded up with cream and sugar, as I headed back to Kade's room. The sound of voices greeted me as I drew closer to his partially open door. I recognized Mona's voice as she spoke, and her husband Gerard's. Kade must have woken. They would be overjoyed to see him conscious again.

I paused outside the door, glancing in just long enough to see Kade sitting upright in the bed while Mona, Gerard, and Blane surrounded him. Mona laughed, likely at something Kade had said. I could hear his voice, a low rasp when he spoke, but it was too quiet for me to understand what he was saying. They were all smiling, even Blane.

I thought about going in—I wanted to go in—but my feet wouldn't obey.

They were all there together, happy. A family. If I went in, there'd be tension, putting a strain on everyone. Blane's smile would become forced. Kade would be stressed, the last thing he needed as his body tried to recover. Mona and Gerard wouldn't know what to say, since no one would want to talk about the elephant in the room.

Me.

I didn't want that, for any of them. So I did the only thing I could think of doing.

I turned around . . . and I left.

Here ends the first chapter of *Point of No Return*.

Check Tiffany's website, www.Tiffany-Snow.com, for more information on *The Kathleen Turner Series*.

ACKNOWLEDGMENTS

Thank you to my husband and daughters, for understanding that even though Mommy is home now, she still has to work.

Thank you to my wonderful editor, Maria Gomez. I greatly appreciate your support and enthusiasm for this series.

Thank you to Leslie for your encouragement and willingness to read and reread and reread. And read again. I apologize for the many book hangovers I caused you.

Thank you to my wonderful gang of girlfriends who are always wanting to read more about Blane, Kade, and Kathleen—Paige, Stephanie, and Lisa. I can't tell you how much I value your friendship.

Thank you to Catherine Bybee and Dr. Dennis Block for their invaluable assistance on all things gunshot wound and ER related.

Last but certainly not least, thank you to Montlake and the team of people there dedicated to their work and the authors they represent. I couldn't have wished for a better place to be.